Reconciliation

Reconciliation

DOROTHY SPEAK

Stories

Library and Archives Canada Cataloguing in Publication

Speak, Dorothy

    Reconciliation : stories / Dorothy Speak.

Issued also in electronic format.

ISBN 978-0-9880455-0-7

    I. Title.

PS8587.P24R42 2012   C813'.54   C2012-904025-8

Cover photo: Jordan Craig
Author photo: Ruth Steinberg
Design: Miriam Bloom, Zsuzsanna Liko

Printed and bound in the United States of America.

To Emily

Also by Dorothy Speak:

The Counsel of the Moon
Object of Your Love
The Wife Tree

Some of these stories were originally published as follows:

"Reconciliation" in *The Antigonish Review*
"The Opposite of the Truth" in *Descant*
"Windfall" and "The Sins of the Father" in *Ottawa Magazine*
"Authenticity" in *Dalhousie Review*
"A Penny to Save" in *Wascana Review*
"Clemency" in *Grain*
"Altered States" in *Dalhousie Review*
"Group Lessons" in *The New Quarterly*

The author would like to thank the Ontario Arts Council and the City of Ottawa for financial support.

Contents

The Opposite of the Truth

BENTA OFTEN PICTURES THE DAY she closed up the matrimonial house after the divorce from Dwight. Carrying a dustpan, broom, rag mop, she pursued the movers from room to room. Empty of their furniture, the spaces turned unfamiliar, fickle, full of ambivalence and accusation. Benta felt betrayed by the stunning clarity in the house, by the luminosity of the bare, alien walls. A breezy, treasonous June day blew through the rooms, sweeping away her recollection of what had happened here, like milkweed scattered by the wind. She did not know if she should be trying to hold onto these ruinous memories or if it was wiser to let them go. She bent and swept, bent and swept, passed a mop in wet circles over the hardwood floors. To leave the corners of the house dust-free, the floors shining, to remove every last footprint, every trace of life, was what she wanted. Sweeping up the past and throwing it in the trash can, leaving no evidence of the marriage. Expurgation. Closure. The process was palliative, fortifying, acutely painful.

Between that house and the one in which Benta now lives, she moved into a high rise apartment building down by the water. She might have done this to irk Dwight, to throw in his face the elusive ocean view they had coveted during their marriage.

The rooms of this apartment were like prison cells, so small that if she stood in the middle of any of them, she could reach out and touch all four walls. Such a quantity of pure light poured in through the windows that Benta had to put on sunglasses to keep from developing a migraine. There, she lasted only three months. The altitude made her head swim and the heat in the cloistered rooms sapped her desire to live and, also, she had to admit to herself that she couldn't afford the rent.

"Oh, for heaven's sake, talk to me," says Benta.

"Why should I?" asks Lourdes.

"You're my friend."

"I told you I didn't want to meet him."

"Well, it was an accident." Benta says.

"Sure it was. You knew I'd be here. You knew it was my journal time."

They're sitting outdoors at a coffee shop on a pleasant village-like street. Along here there are health food stores, bookstores, art galleries, fusion restaurants, some with decks out back giving a glimpse of the ocean.

"You didn't act very friendly with him," says Benta. "You might have hurt his feelings."

"His teeth are very yellow."

"Well, I'm glad you noticed the important things."

Lourdes is so thin that the bones in her face are painful to look at. Over her smooth scalp, she's wearing a small velvet cap, of which she seems to have a whole array, in gem-like colours, the plush fabric gathered at the side with rhinestone brooches. These fez-like hats expose her vulnerable looking ears and raw temples, pale and smooth as soap, the ropy tendons at the nape of her neck, the hard, naked, bluish lobes of her skull.

Where does Lourdes get these hats? Benta wonders, but is careful not to mention them. She remembers the day when Lourdes' hair started to come out in handfuls. Benta suggested they go wig shopping. The very idea enraged Lourdes. She got out of Benta's car and slammed the door. Then Benta got out too and slammed hers and they stood in a parking lot hurling insults at each other. *Shallow, anti-feminist, a fossil* was what Lourdes called Benta. Lourdes wasn't interested, she told Benta, in camouflage, just to make other people feel comfortable. She was facing her condition head-on. Benta countered that this was just a bunch of masochistic crap. She said Lourdes didn't have the imagination to reinvent herself. That was when Lourdes took her purse and smashed it down on the hood of Benta's car. Its chunky clasp left a deep imprint.

"Who's going to pay for *that*?" Benta shouted.

"Maybe it will make you listen!" screamed Lourdes.

For a month afterward, they didn't see each other. Then one day they met for lunch and set their friendship going again, with no reference to the fight. Had they been wary of each other since then, now that they knew they'd been harbouring harsh judgements about each other? Not really. It was too late in their relationship for caution. They were both in too deep.

One good thing about cancer, Lourdes reads to Benta from a list in her journal, is that worrying about whether men find you attractive is over. You know for sure they don't. One good thing about cancer is you finally realize men aren't important.

"You can't get laid without men," Benta points out.

"That makes them useful," says Lourdes, "not important."

"Why only men?" Benta asked. "Men aren't important when you have cancer or people in general?"

"People. When you get cancer, no matter how people think they're helping you, essentially, you're on your own."

"Even best friends?"

"Even best friends."

"Even me?"

"Especially you."

The reason their friendship has endured is that they've always felt free to tell each other the opposite of the truth.

This is in a city on the west coast. This is on the quiet side of the inlet, a narrow, mile-long table wedged between the water and the mountains. Separated as it is from the city proper by a high span bridge, it has a hamlet-like feel. Beatniks, artists, musicians, dope-heads. That's who camped here at one time, way back, after the city had stopped being a dull, sleepy seaside town and had started to burgeon, and this district was for a while an alternative neighbourhood. But now it's smugly middle class. Here in the cafe, Benta and Lourdes are surrounded by professionals with job security, leisure time, disposable incomes, holiday tans.

It's a neighbourhood that has more to do with what Benta once had and threw away than with what her life is now. But she's still over here every day. Early in the morning, she leaves her blue-collar suburb and follows a busy freeway to this borough, where she jogs on the sea wall, among the fleet, high-breasted, stone-buttocked, pony-tailed women who are the age of her daughter. Later in the day, Benta returns, sits in these cafes drinking coffee, reading, making notes for her column in the city section of the local newspaper: articles about dog bites, sewer backups, potholes, petty vandalism.

There was a time when Benta lived just up the hill from here, a calf-straining, heart-thumping climb from the ocean, in a house with perennial gardens, a musical brook, a picturesque bamboo bridge. She and her husband, Dwight, were comfortable but not wealthy, though they might have been on their way to wealth. Yes, that is pretty certain. They had many friends in high places. They entertained often and got asked to go out. Benta knew a lot of people back then. Now, they're all gone from her life. Now, she supposes, The Young Wife knows them.

Benta lives over with the plumbers, the electricians, stonemasons, carpenters. A district of pickup trucks and rusted out cars and cracked, bellowing mufflers. Sometimes, Benta dreams of moving back to this picturesque neighbourhood, in which she meets Lourdes for coffee. Well, *always* she dreams of living back here, but at one time she actually took measures. In moments of despair, she'd call a young real estate agent she knew, a thirty-year-old. He'd take her through tiny old houses or new condos with square footage so small that she was sure she should be able to afford them. She kept hoping the numbers would add up differently. Falling interest rates were bound to help, she thought. She showed the agent a list of her income and expenses. They sat in his black Volkswagen while he patiently worked out the figures. She wanted some mathematical miracle from him. After awhile, after a few years, he gently refused to meet with her.

"Are you sure you understand how mortgages work?" he kidded her over the phone. "If you haven't won the lottery recently, maybe we're wasting your time and mine." Or, near the end, "Are you having another little crisis, Benta? Another panic attack? Just take a deep breath and it'll pass."

Lourdes, on the other hand, lives in a low-rise apartment on this very street, a trendy, exclusive, chic building smoothly stuccoed in taupe and cream. Her apartment has deep balconies on three sides, terraces really, the size of rooms, furnished with live orange trees quivering in the salty breeze and boxwood shrubs pruned to look like swans and hip-high pots of flowers maintained by a gardener. Lourdes knows how to throw Horst's money around. Well, it's not his money anymore, is it? It's hers.

Horst was a widower. When he died of cancer, he was eighty and Lourdes was fifty. She took care of him toward the end, two years of pushing him around in a wheelchair. They never married, never even cohabited, though he begged her to be his wife. Benta doesn't know how much money Horst left Lourdes. Millions, she suspects. Well, at least one million, or two, but that's enough, isn't it? Benta wonders if Lourdes has left her something in her will. She hopes so. She hopes their friendship is up to at least that. She's not Lourdes' friend because of this prospect, but it's an inducement not to cross her. Benta could not have admitted this even to herself.

"Clayton isn't bound by external measures of happiness or success," Benta tells Lourdes at the coffee shop. "He's rejected career and materialism and all that claptrap, just like I have."

"Technically, you may have rejected it," says Lourdes, "but ideologically, you haven't. You wish you were still rich."

"No, I don't."

"Yes, you do."

"Clayton is drawing out my true self. I feel reborn."

"Clayton is a drop-out and drop-outs turn into losers."

"I didn't know you were so black-and-white."

Benta's tenant, Nile, says he has something to show her downstairs. He has knocked on the cheap, hollow, scuffed wooden door at the top of the basement steps and waited there for her to come and open it. She's been reading the newspaper at the tiny kitchen table, where the sunlight floods in through the corner window. She gets up and goes into the hallway that leads also to her bedroom and to the spare bedroom where she watches television and to the narrow bathroom. She opens the door and sees Nile standing there, his expression grave.

"There's a problem downstairs," says Nile. "Come and look at it."

"Why don't you just tell me what it is," Benta says.

"You need to see it for yourself." Nile is always looking for excuses to get her down into his apartment. He wants to show her the crack in the kitchen floor, the caulking lifting around the bathtub, the ant traps he's had to set.

"No, I don't. Just describe it for me," Benta tells him.

One day in the spring, Benta had bought a bike at a garage sale. Wheeling it home, she came upon a man working on his driveway, surrounded by bicycles in varying stages of repair. This was out in front of a small wooden two-storey house in need of a coat of paint and new roof shingles. Benta stopped and spoke to the man, who did not look up, but continued to work. She asked if he could patch the bike tire for her or replace it, whichever was necessary.

He said he supposed he could, in a grudging, disinterested tone.

"How much would that cost?" she asked. "I only paid ten dollars for the bike. I haven't ridden a bike in twenty years. I hope I can remember how. I don't know what made me buy it. Maybe I'm just ready for a change in my life. Yes. That must be it."

Now, he stopped and straightened up and observed her as though she were insane.

She asked if he could have it ready the following Saturday. He might and he might not. He never made promises, he said. She would have to come by in a week's time and see how things were going. He was thin but strong looking, like a stray dog. He had a sandy-coloured ponytail. He wore an undershirt and over that a plaid flannel shirt unbuttoned and hanging out over a pair of greasy jeans. Benta could smell the sweat on him.

The next Saturday, Benta went back. Though he didn't seem surprised to see her, he told her, without apology, that the bike wasn't ready. In fact, he hadn't even taken a look at it. Overheated from the walk, Benta asked if he minded if she rested in the shade on the driveway for a moment. He didn't care, he said. She wondered at his indifference. She could have taken the bike and left but she needed the repair and didn't want the trouble of going somewhere else.

For a few minutes, she walked around, fanning her face and looking at the bikes on the driveway. That morning, she'd dressed up in a flowered skirt and a crisp white linen blouse, though the latter was quickly wilting, it clung to her back as the day's heat pressed down on them like a stone. She sat down on a wooden crate and watched the man work. He made her think of her father, a car mechanic with a genius for mending things, for salvaging materials, a patience with finicky adjustments. After awhile he went into the house — he walked in a slow, jaded, somewhat arrogant way — and brought out two beers and handed her one. He squatted down easily, loose-jointed, on the driveway to smoke, his arms resting on his thighs.

He seemed to be amused by everyone. He said the world was full of lost souls chasing after dreams — wealth, fame, material possessions — that would never satisfy them because, once they got these trophies, they'd always be able to think of something else they needed to go after, something they thought would make them even happier. His own credo was to take it easy, enjoy life while he could, never do anything he didn't really want to do. Benta saw the truth, she saw the truth in what he said. She felt strangely altered by his simple words, lightened, freed, absurdly happy, giddy with an obscure relief.

Later, after the beer drinking — it turned out to be more than one beer, they'd drunk several by the time four-thirty rolled around and the shadows on the street were protracted and the pavements were cooling and the contours of the houses and the trees had softened in the oblique and hazy light, and Benta herself felt weightless, unmoored, surreal — it was only natural for him to take Benta inside and show her the flat he rented from the woman upstairs. And then, around seven, to order a pizza, for which Benta paid because he said he had a little cash flow problem at the moment. Already, Benta was attracted to his surly and wryly mocking ways, to his veneer of apathy. In bed, Clayton told her that she needed to lie back and relax. She needed to let herself go. He said he could tell she'd never had real sex. He would show her how it was done.

Benta is driving Lourdes out to see the healer. They leave the city and head up the coast about twenty miles, then turn inland and go a little way further. It's raw, fruitless, alien country here, rocky, with thin, fragile woods. Lourdes sleeps part of the way, with her seat tilted back, swaying slightly with the motion of the car. From time to time, Benta glances over at her with guilty curiosity, cataloguing the changes that have occurred since Lourdes became sick. Lourdes used to be beautiful but now her features are sharp and her cheeks hollowed out and this makes her look bitter, though she insists she's not, she has accepted her possible death. Embraced it, in fact, because cancer has transformed her. As the body is subverted, so the spirit grows more robust. She's like a refined metal, she says, released from the slag of the body.

"So, you're an ingot now," says Benta, still angry that Lourdes has refused a second round of chemotherapy.

"That's right."

The healer has told Lourdes to stick close to home, read, sleep, conserve her energies, eat fresh fruits and vegetables. She is not to resist what's happening to her body. So many people try to battle cancer through force of will. That's the wrong idea altogether, says the healer. Leave the body free to work its native therapies. He is opposed to chemotherapy. All chemotherapy does, he says, is chase the cancer away to hide in other parts of the body. That's why it surfaces later, in the lungs, the bones, the pancreas, havens to which it has fled.

"That's a neat theory," Benta has told Lourdes, "but what if he's wrong? By the time you find out, you could be dead."

"I think he's helping me," said Lourdes. "I feel better already and I've seen him only three times."

"It's all in your head."

"Maybe that's the key place," said Lourdes.

Lourdes had slept with Dwight for a while following the breakup of Benta's marriage. Lourdes and Dwight went to concerts together, to lectures, to the opera.

"We connect on an intellectual level," Lourdes told Benta. They came from similar backgrounds. They'd had parents who taught university. As children, they'd been given music lessons, tennis lessons, nannies, staggering spending allowances, personal libraries, trips to Europe, summers by bodies of water. Benta had not known there were people of her generation whose parents had gone to university. She'd thought they all, like her own father, had only grade eight.

"Oh, yes," said Benta with light sarcasm. "I forgot. You're both from the upper class."

"There's no need to be bitter," Lourdes told her.

At the time, Benta wasn't sure how she felt about Lourdes and Dwight dating. Yes, she was. She felt anger, betrayal, hurt. Even a bizarre and irrational jealousy, though she didn't want Dwight back. No, not at all. But after she left him, Dwight didn't come running after Benta. This surprised and disappointed her. Everyone who runs away wants, in some part of them, to be pursued. Even if they intend never to go back, being pursued confirms that what they had before they cast it off was worth something. But Dwight said that as far as he was concerned,

Benta was dead. When she heard this, she lay on her bed for a whole afternoon without moving, as though she were lying in a coffin.

Benta hadn't asked for anything when she left Dwight. No furniture, dishes, alimony.

"That was dumb," Lourdes tells her now.

"I know. I was young."

"Forty?"

"Well, *younger*. I had ideals. His values made me puke. I wanted to wash my hands of him forever."

"So that you could cleanse yourself in the river of poverty."

"Now I'm more sensible."

The reason she finds Benta so endearing, Lourdes has said, is that she can always be counted on to make the wrong decision.

"That's me!" Benta agrees cheerfully. "Every day is an opportunity to screw up! That's why I get out of bed in the morning!"

It was from Lourdes that Benta learned of Dwight's marriage. Benta hadn't really felt old until she heard it was a younger woman. Dwight and The Young Wife now live high up on the mountainside where builders are clear-cutting the forests to make way for new neighbourhoods. They own a modern house cantilevered out over the fall of the hills. Far below, the harbour shines like a blue sapphire. Dwight has his ocean view now. As far as Benta can remember, the single force that united her and Dwight through fifteen years of marriage was a desire for a house looking out on the water. It was the only thing they could fix on in common. Would an ocean view, Benta sometimes wonders, have kept them together? If they'd had the water to look at, they wouldn't have had to look at themselves: a horizon that pure, that definitive, might have relieved the claustrophobia of their marriage.

Once, Benta ventured up to Dwight's new neighbourhood to take a look. She ascended the twisting roads cut, wherever a foothold could be found, into the rocky side of the mountain. The gears of her rusty coupe ground around the tight switchbacks. She passed houses in cedar and stone or glass and steel or stucco painted the colours of sherbet. There were sheer drops and massive retaining walls. High privacy fences, electronic gates, ornamental shrubs, professional gardens, their soil dark and oily with mulch. Under her tires, the fresh asphalt hissed, black as liquorice, the curbs high and beautifully sculpted as works of art.

At one time, the views from these slopes were the domain of eagles, bears, intrepid hikers who toiled up into the high forests. But soon there would be nothing left here, there would be nothing left of the inky trees. The developers would continue their logging until they'd chopped them all down, the Douglas Fir, the Ponderosa Pine, the Golden Spruce. Despite this destruction, it was beautiful. Truly, it was beautiful — the vertiginous elevation, the thin, dizzying air, the cathartic winds, the cleansing silence. Driving up there, Benta developed a constriction in her chest having to do with longing and grief and bewilderment and the way in general that life had turned out.

Nile got Benta into bed after her mother died. Her mother's death seems to have been the point at which all her desperation about finding a man started. She came home from the funeral, got out of the cab and walked up her cracked sidewalk. She put her suitcase down in the front hall and listened, listened to the silence in her life. Then there was a timely knock on the basement door.

She went and opened it and it was Nile. Living with him downstairs now was a girl named Briar. It was Briar whom Benta had asked to retrieve the mail while she was gone, but here was Nile with the wad of envelopes in his hand. Though he was the original tenant, Briar was the one Benta had gotten to know a little. Sitting at the sunny kitchen table, Briar had held Benta's hand in hers and traced its tracks with the tip of her finger, interpreting Benta's health line, her marriage line, her sex line, her fate line. In the intelligence of Briar's finger, Benta sensed wonder, youth, vulnerability. For a living, Briar gave palm readings down at the local vegetarian restaurant, to anyone who would pay her.

Reaching to take the mail from Nile, that day after her mother's funeral, Benta began to cry. Nile stepped swiftly, opportunistically, up out of the stairway into the dark passage. He put his arms around her, pressed her head to his shoulder. Don't cry, he said softly. Don't cry. Everything is going to be all right. Deftly, he manoeuvred her along the hall to her bedroom, gently pressed her, still wearing her trench coat, down on the mattress, began to work at her buttons. She clung to him.

Benta believes that Nile deliberately exploited her that day. He was lying in wait, she wagers, when she got out of the cab in front of the house, home from burying her mother. A person did not have to be a psychologist to anticipate her weakened state, her receptiveness to a sympathetic embrace.

She never told Lourdes about sleeping with Nile. She was too proud. This surprised Benta. She'd begun to think she had no pride left.

The healer's house is built into a knoll. The house has a veneer of phony white brick nailed over the ten-test, an effect that is jarringly suburban in this deserted setting.

"You could come in, you know," Lourdes tells her. "There's a place to wait. Downstairs there's a little vestibule kind of thing. Or you could sit upstairs in the living room. I've seen people doing that."

"I'm fine here."

"I could introduce you to him after my session."

"What for?"

"You know, he doesn't deal only with terminal illness. He treats people for all kinds of things, physical *and* emotional."

"My emotions are fine. I'm happy. Clayton makes me happy. Maybe that bothers you."

She watches Lourdes pick her fragile way toward the house and disappear through the door beside the garage. It's a mixed day, with frothy clouds scudding across the sky. From this rise in the land, Benta has a view of a stone barn in a nearby field, of an A-frame up on a cliff. In her rear view mirror, she sees a yellow school bus roar past on the road below, churning up dust. She sits and listens to the crows calling and looks at the thin woods and at strings of broken post-and-wire fencing snaking over the stony hills. She did not know there was a place in the mountains so bereft of beauty.

"No distractions here," Lourdes had explained. "No frills or comforts. Everything pared down to the bone. That's how you discover yourself."

The sun breaks through the clouds. The sky begins to go pink. The car has grown cold. Finally, Benta looks at her watch impatiently, gets out of the car and goes into the house. It's unfinished inside, in a state of evolution. The floors are sheets of plywood nailed down, the walls are rough drywall crudely taped and plastered. Downstairs, she passes a stack of firewood, a pair of antique cross-country skis, a table with pamphlets advertising acupuncture, meditation, spiritual awareness. She climbs a narrow stair to the kitchen. On the stove is a pot of congealed soup.

Benta stands on the rudimentary floor and listens. All is silent. In a room beyond the kitchen, a lamp burns. She tiptoes toward it and stops in the doorway. It's a kind of sunroom with roughly framed windows around three sides, looking out at the rocky land, the spindly trees, the dying afternoon, a tinted sky. In the middle of the room, a tall man stands over a high bed on which Lourdes lies with her eyes closed. He has one hand up her sweater, the other on her thigh. His long black hair trails down his neck, his beard bushes out at the sides. He is thin, almost emaciated. John the Baptist, she thinks. A lumberjack-prophet in a plaid shirt. From where she stands, Benta can see his whole body quivering. Then, though she keeps perfectly still, he suddenly tenses and his head swings around. He meets her gaze, his eyes penetrating, fiery and transparent as those of an animal in a dark wood. Benta shivers and backs away.

Benta had never seen herself as a landlord. She had not thought she would ever be so short of cash as to resort to having a complete stranger living in her basement. As far as she can see, she has not traveled much distance from her origins, from the poverty of her parents' home. In fact, she may be worse off. She doesn't like to think about this. But maybe she's in denial. Maybe this is where she truly belongs. Beside her house is a laneway where teenagers collect for skateboard competitions and to smoke weed. She's built a high wooden fence to shut them out but she can still hear the small thunder of the skateboard wheels and smell the marijuana smoke. The boys have sprayed dirty words on the other side of the fence, the side she can't see, but they still shake her. *FUCK PUSSY BITCH*. Sometimes at night when she's trying to fall asleep, this is what glimmers across the inside of her eyelids, these obscenities, as though spelled out with neon tubes.

Clayton plans to move in with Benta.

"You really are desperate, aren't you?" Lourdes says.

"I'm content when I'm around him. It's hard to explain. He calms me. He makes me feel less panicky about life, less anxious when I look at the future. Not so worried that I'm an utter failure." Clayton has told Benta that she's changed since he met her. She is less uptight now, he says. She doesn't look so angry all the time.

"I never expected this," Benta says.

"Yes, you did," says Lourdes. "The first time you slept with him, you thought: *marriage*."

"Oh, I don't think," says Benta girlishly, "I don't think we'd ever get married."

"What about your dream of moving over here?"

"I've changed my mind about that. I've rearranged my values. I see that's all wrong, now. I'm embracing my roots."

Nile confessed to Briar that he'd slept with Benta. Just out of the blue he told her, for no apparent reason, other than mischief, perhaps. When Benta came home from work, she found Briar sitting on the bottom step out back, waiting to talk to her, her suitcase at her side. She was a shy, naive girl with thick red hair reaching down over her behind. An old fashioned, substantial girl from a small fishing village up the coast. She walked around the city in ankle-length cotton dresses. People noticed her, she turned heads, she got honked at a lot, not for her attractiveness, but because of her oddity. Copper coloured freckles covered her from head to toe. Not a pretty girl at all but a sweet one.

"It wasn't my idea," Benta told her. "It was only the one time."

Briar had told Benta about the séances she'd performed. The exorcisms. About her ESP. But if she was truly psychic, Benta wondered, perhaps unkindly, why didn't she know about what had happened between Benta and Nile?

"I thought you were a better person," Briar told Benta in her soft voice. "I looked up to you. Like a big sister or a mother, even. All the time I've been here I was full of admiration and — and love. I just wanted you to know that." She picked up her suitcase and walked across the lawn and through the carport and down the laneway where the swearwords were written three feet high.

Benta thought Briar must be heading for the bus stop. She considered jumping into her car and following her, offering her a ride into the city, to wherever she wanted to go.

One day, Benta goes to the coffee shop for her customary rendezvous with Lourdes. For years, they have met twice a week, with the exception of the brief periods when they weren't speaking to each other. The time, for instance, after Lourdes found out she had cancer, when she said she didn't ever want to see Benta again. She said that, in her weakened condition, she couldn't afford to be around negative people. Being around pessimistic, tactless people like Benta, who said she'd rather be dead than live without a man for the rest of her life — being around people like that was, according to Lourdes, like chemo itself, that is, like pouring poison into her own veins.

Lourdes doesn't show up at the coffee shop. Benta goes home and calls her. No answer. She's worried about Lourdes. Maybe she's gone up to see the healer on her own. There's little else she does now. Then Benta remembers that she has a key to Lourdes' apartment somewhere. After a long search, she finds it in the front hall table drawer. Very early the next morning, she drives over to Lourdes' apartment, enters her building, takes the elevator to the penthouse, lets herself quietly into the apartment, in case Lourdes is still sleeping. The rooms shimmer with light. Through the open balcony doors, the wind, the smell of the ocean sweep in. On the terrace beyond, where there is a big square canvas umbrella fluttering in the breeze, are Lourdes and Clayton in white housecoats, which shine supernaturally, like vestments. Between them is a table laid out with heavy silver, thick linen napkins, coffee cups, a plate of croissants, glasses of orange juice dazzling as jewels.

Benta has journeyed a long way from the flat farmland and the claustrophobic industrial towns of her beginnings. She migrated four thousand miles with Dwight, from the narrow means of her childhood to this mountainous city. To journey any further would entail walking into the ocean. She does, however, dream of escaping somehow. On crystal clear days, walking beside the ocean, she sees the gulf islands floating far away on the horizon like stepping stones. She hopes that this will not prove to be her only option for metamorphosis. She prays that she will never be so eccentric as to move to one of those islands to live among the garlic growers and jam makers and duck raisers, the glass blowers and quilt-sewers in their sad, incestuous little communities. The crazies and the hermits and mavericks and freaks. She hopes she'll never become that peculiar or mad.

"You were the one who introduced us," is the feeble justification Lourdes offers later. "You insisted on bringing him to the cafe. If you hadn't, he wouldn't have known I existed."

Lourdes says, "It was just the one time. It was only once. One night. Is it such a big deal? Why is that such a big deal? It's not as if he never slept with other women. Dozens of them. Hundreds, probably. Indians. Mexicans. Not women of my calibre. You should be glad his taste seems to be improving. You've had a good effect on him." This is a joke, she hastens to explain when Benta doesn't laugh. She said it only to inject a little levity into the situation.

Lourdes has come over to Benta's house. She arrived by cab and struggled up the corrupt flagstone sidewalk. She begged to be let in. Benta is busy purging the house of all signs of Clayton's presence. She takes his Johnny Cash and Loretta Lynn CDs into the kitchen, lays them out on the counter, smashes them with a wooden meat mallet, sweeps the shards into the garbage. In the living room, she pulls out the classical music she'd put away. She turns on Rachmaninoff's *The Isle of the Dead* full blast, while Lourdes, leaning on her cane, tries to follow her around, tries to shout above the volume, though her voice has grown thin, dry, reed-like. She can't keep up with Benta. By the time Lourdes enters a room, Benta has turned and gone elsewhere. The house buzzes with Benta's energy.

Benta tells herself she feels exhilarated, set free. She will reclaim her life, in all its fallibility and neuroses. For the shallow pleasure of having the weight of a man's body on the mattress beside her, she relinquished a lot, she now admits to herself. *Lowering your standards* was what Lourdes had called it, now a somewhat ironic judgement. From her cupboards, her drawers, Benta recovers all the items Clayton found pretentious. Her fake Ming vases. The little Persian carpet at the front door. The collection of glass paperweights. The baroque flower arrangement on the pedestal in the picture window. The still-lifes she painted when she was married, which he'd mocked for their earnestness.

"And anyway," Lourdes adds, her face glassy with paradox, "I'm not exactly a threat. I'm a dead woman, aren't I?" Under other circumstances, Benta would have argued that Lourdes had as much chance as anyone to live a long life. She would have said life was precarious for everyone. But today she has no interest in shoring Lourdes up.

What she says is, "I hope so."

"You said he'd cured you of so many things," Lourdes explains. "You said he'd led you down a new path. I needed to find out if he could do the same for me."

"I don't know," Lourdes says, "I don't know what happens to women when they get cancer. Their whole value system changes, their perceptions of others. Their perspective on life becomes a little skewed. They grasp at straws. That must be it."

"You're saying that because you have cancer, you don't have to have morals?"

"We just see life in a way no one else sees it. It's like we have x-ray eyes."

"Bullshit," says Benta.

"Maybe it was a foregone conclusion that he'd come to me once he'd met me. Isn't that the precept of modern relationships? To fracture and wound and betray and humiliate? Maybe it was preordained."

"Maybe I'll go up to the country and sleep with your fucking healer!" Benta shouts. "How preordained would that be?"

Sometimes, Benta drives by the cafe, on the lookout for Lourdes. She herself has never again set foot in the place but she goes by to take a look. If the weather is chilly or if there's a cold winter rain falling, she doesn't, of course, expect to see Lourdes outside at a table, writing in her journal. During these weathers, Benta slides slowly past in her car, searching for Lourdes' brittle figure in the window, perhaps in the corner beside the yellow brick wall where Benta herself used to occupy a stool at the counter, facing out. Years ago, friends advised Benta that if she sat there long enough, chances were a man would walk past, would double back and come through the door and sit down beside her. In fact, they said, there would be so many men lined up to talk to her that she'd have to give out numbers.

The day after she stepped into Lourdes' apartment and saw Clayton out on the terrace picking an orange from a tree and handing it to Lourdes, like a pantomime of Adam and Eve, Benta went to a hardware store and bought a gallon of red paint. She drove over to Clayton's place and got out of the car. With her keys, she pried the lid off the can and began to paint words in two-foot letters on the garage door with a wide brush. While Benta was engaged in this act, Clayton's landlady came onto her flimsy balcony, in a housecoat, her hair in bristle rollers, and shouted down, "Hey! What do you think you're doing? You stop that! I know who you are! I've seen you around here! Another one of his sluts! Don't think you're the first one!"

FUCKING MY FRIEND. That was what Benta wrote.

"I'll get the police after you!" warned the woman, and she hurried back inside.

The police never came to arrest Benta or fine her or even speak to her about her vandalism. Maybe Clayton interceded. Was he capable of such chivalry? When she passed by in her car the next day, the message was gone. Painted over. For a moment, Benta felt dizzy with confusion. She wondered if her destructive act had been only a dream. She thought maybe it had never occurred, her revenge. But of course it had. At the sight of the freshly painted garage door, Benta felt erased.

But Lourdes might be dead. For at least a year, Benta watches the obituaries, hoping to see Lourdes' name there. Finally, she stops this, realizing it's a twisted and ultimately self-destructive thing to do. Now she doesn't know how she feels. Some days she hopes Lourdes is six feet under and other days she thinks she'd like to try to patch things up with her, put their history behind them, start fresh, as, in the past, they've managed, out of resilience, forgiveness, destitution. Resuscitation. Compromise. Hypocrisy. She wonders if all female friendships are so warped and deadly.

Benta does not think about what she and Clayton did together, the manner and the places in which they made love. His bold appetite, his crude and shameless performance. The acrobatics they engaged in have come to seem to her preposterous, mortifying, corrupt. To recall these scenes has become too devastating. Soon, they are a hazy memory, something that happened to another woman. She believes she will never have sex again. She will not have the opportunity or she will not credit a man again or she will not trust herself, her own judgement. She will fold inward upon herself like a dried leaf. She will raise herself above lust, pleasure, like a high priestess.

"Do you spend a lot of time analyzing?" the healer asks Benta. "All your energy is in the top portion of your body, from the chest up. All resistance is in the right breast and right solar plexus and right ovary. Do you isolate yourself? Do you tend to be an island? It shows, when I push here," he says, indicating her chest. "When I push here, you push back. I need to get you to talk. Then your defences are down. Otherwise, you won't let me in. I need to find a way in, if I'm going to help you."

He's standing beside the bed. He puts a thin hand over her heart and one on her stomach. He tells her he's trying to channel the energy from the top of her body to the bottom of it, using his own limbs as a conduit. The force is supposed to travel from Benta through him and back to Benta, amplified. "The key area is your gut. That's where the core of the emotion is. I'm just a medium between the self and the divine energy."

He closes his eyes, frowns and wags his head as though to focus, shoots air through his nostrils, shudders and twitches from time to time, like a stallion, or like someone who's received an electric shock.

"Can you feel anything?" he asks. "Can you feel anything?"

"What am I supposed to feel?"

"Heat. A tingling sensation like a charge traveling along a conductor."

"No," she says. "No, I don't feel anything."

"I have the energy turned up quite high. About twenty-four out of sixty. I wouldn't want to keep that up for very long. Some people can feel it at a level of one."

It's October.

The healer's hands are on Benta, inquisitive, brazen. She trembles. She wants to weep with gratitude, revulsion, fury. A comfort and a devastation are what his words are. Turning her head, she gazes out the window, observes the stripped trees in the soft, silvery woods, the garden of dead sunflowers, rusty and dried up and burnt by the fall wind but still tall and erect, like an army of blasted soldiers. She hears the grievous cry of migrating geese overhead. It is a bright day, with filmy clouds draped like scarves across the sky. Benta doesn't know if she should have come here. She's never sure anymore what's a mistake and what isn't. There don't seem to be any purely right choices.

Windfall

AN EVENING IN MAY. Orm and I are in our bedroom, where he is pulling on his jogging clothes. In the room, there is a fragile glow, a golden reflection flung off the shadeless street, the bleached sidewalks, the bald dusty pavements, the houses opposite, throwing back the evening sun.

"Do you think we should try again?" I ask him.

"No, I don't."

"Why not?"

"Because I know it will hurt."

"How do you know? We haven't tried in a long time. It's been months. We haven't had sex in months."

He can still jog. He doesn't feel the groin pain when he jogs. It's different muscles, he says. He can jog and he can ski. He's been all over town, to specialists, had every test known to man. Nobody can find the cause of the pain, no lump, no cancer. I feel sorry for him. It can't be good for his manhood.

"Do you think the pain has anything to do with your father?" I ask him.

"What do you mean?"

"Well, it started just after — *you* know."

Last October, Orm's father killed himself. He and Orm's mother were alcoholics. They'd had one of their drunken rows and Orm's father went into their bedroom and got out a revolver he kept in a bureau drawer. He stuck the barrel in his mouth and pulled the trigger. Hearing the discharge of the gun, Orm's mother did not even go into the bedroom to investigate. It was easier to pick up the phone and call Orm. He had to go over there and calm her down, call the police, brew a pot of black coffee to sober her up, try to clear away the empty beer bottles and wash up some of the dirty dishes and pick up around the house for the sake of respectability before they arrived, then clean up the mess once the ambulance took the body away. The blood on the bedclothes, soaked through, of course, to the mattress. Blood on the walls.

We have all read about the children of alcoholics, their over-developed sense of responsibility. How they spend their childhoods concealing their parents' dirty secret, trying to manifest to the world a picture of normalcy, making excuses at school for why their parents didn't turn up for meetings with the teacher, swallowing their dismay and their shame. From the time he was ten, it was Orm, a mini-adult, who did the grocery shopping, cleaned and cooked, paid the utility bills, dealt with the outside world. At school, there were breakfasts provided for children who hadn't eaten. Orm was too proud to go. He preferred to starve, rather than let on.

Now, he's writing monthly cheques to his mother.

"How much?" I've asked him.

"Enough for her not to suffer."

"That'll come in handy at the liquor store," I pointed out.

In January, he sent her on a holiday to Florida.

"I'd like to get a look at Florida myself, some day," I told Orm, my face skinned with bitterness and hurt. "I've never seen Florida. Did you know that?"

"Of course I knew that!"

"Do you think she was sober enough to remember it?"

"Look," he said impatiently, "she's grieving. Are you going to begrudge her a little vacation?"

"When was the last time you and I went anywhere? I haven't been on a plane in ten years."

Tonight in the bedroom, I say to Orm, "Maybe it's psychosomatic. The groin pain. Maybe it's some parent-child-grief thing."

"Stop playing shrink."

"A male-virility-loss reaction."

"What crap!"

"Maybe it's a delayed response to your father's inadequacies."

"He did his best."

"Your body saying, in effect, that you never actually had a parent at all."

He sits on a corner of the bed to tie his running shoes. I step behind him and wrap my arms around his shoulders. He is not handsome by conventional standards. He has a long brick-shaped head, a crooked nose, broken in a high school football game, a broad, loose, gangsterish mouth, eyes pale as water. All his looks lie in his height and his pectorals, his broad back, his air of willingness to shoulder a burden. I think of our love-making, the look of Orm when he's on top of me, wearing the flinty jaw of a coal miner, going in deep, into the darkness, his chin thrust out, dogged, unfaltering, workmanlike.

"Don't," he says, shaking me off. "I've got to get going." Lately, he's seemed restless and I put it down to the perfumed spring air, the suddenly luminous evenings, the heat breaking open the soft earth, the twisting winds driving a blinding grit down the street. He stands up and looks at me. "Your hair is grey," he says critically.

"It has been," I say, confused, reaching up to touch it, "it has been since high school. It was grey when you kissed me in grade nine."

From the bedroom window, I watch Orm's figure disappear down the street, see the youthful discharge of his long legs, his body powerful, explosive as a buck, the soles of his new running shoes flashing in the slanting light.

We live in a suburb, on a street of identical, small-windowed, pale-bricked bungalows built in the sixties — yellow and pink and grey. In twenty years, there's been little turnover here. People move into this neighbourhood and stay until they die. There is a VON nurse who comes around to the elderly, a tired, plump woman climbing out of her white coupe carrying a medical bag. Today, an ambulance crept down the street.

"Someone got sick today," I told Orm at supper. "Someone may have died."

"Who was it?" he asked, but I couldn't tell him. "Why is it that you aren't acquainted with anybody around here?" he said.

"I don't know. I forgot. I forgot to find out who they were." How could this happen? Now it's too late. Too late to intercept our neighbours in the street and tell them my name, or even to wave at them as we pass each other in our cars. It would be hypocritical.

It matters not. I am happy here. I never want to leave. This landscape is everything I desire for my children — unshakeable security, continuity, the utterly predictable. They will abide here in this same house, the place of their birth, amongst their familiar, threadbare possessions, until they leave for college. For the rest of their lives they'll carry with them, in the back of their heads, like a precious piece of archival film, the memory of walking home from school along these pure, unembellished streets, to our simple, horizontal house, climbing the porch to the peeling door, finding me waiting for them.

In the hallway, I pause outside Zoe's door, knock respectfully.

"What?" she calls with hostility. She is always in her room, with the door closed. I stand there, tormented, exiled, uncertain. Taking a deep breath, I open the door a crack, find her sitting cross-legged on her bed, tapping at her laptop keys. Even at this age, she carries home on her the smell of school — grimy desks, pencil lead, erasers, over-heated classrooms. She turns and glowers at me. I step forward, stand there fidgeting, a shy, foolish smile on my face, awkward, unwelcome, a stranger in my own home.

"You'll break my nose some day," I say with weak humour, "closing this door in my face."

"Why do you follow me, then?"

"I don't follow you."

"*Mom*," she says flatly, "I can feel your breath rushing in under my *door*."

I ask in one breath, "How are things going with your friends? How is life? Are you happy?"

"If I say, *yes*," she asks, "will you go away?"

So much like a woman is she now that it takes my breath away. The low-cut tops, the soft cleavage, the radiant white breasts, the long sensuous hands. She has my mother's sleekness and her slender hips, her magnificent raven hair, which falls forward like a curtain around her face, mysterious, seductive. She doesn't eat enough. I could fit my hands around her waist. Like her father and her brother, she is unusually tall. (I have heard the three of them refer to me as the *pygmy*. I am short, soft-bodied, white of skin, shapeless of leg, matronly in spite of being petite.)

"Your father thinks I should go out and get a job," I tell her.

She looks at me blankly. "What could you *do*?" she asks with brutal logic.

Behind me, our son, Cyrus, slips into his room with a bag of cookies and a litre of milk. He's six-foot-six, three inches taller than his father, with a pair of size fifteen feet planted firmly on the ground. Obliviously handsome, blonde, with a girl's creamy skin, he is loose-jointed and graceful as a giraffe. Like Orm, he's a whiz in maths and sciences, he seems to absorb them by osmosis, effortlessly achieves high marks. He is captain of the basketball team, the football team. He's so cooperative, so amiable that it's hard to believe he's Zoe's sibling. They aren't close. They shun each other, share nothing in common. "Girls think too much about stuff," I heard him tell Zoe once. "They make everything so complicated."

Life will, I know, always be easier for Cyrus than for Zoe. It will slide over him like a nourishing river. I am constantly in awe of the clarity of his world, transparent as a piece of glass, his unfaltering trajectory, the smooth orbit of his life. He will be successful without trying because he surrenders to the flow of events. He is instinctively organized, fearless by nature, can think of no reason to doubt himself.

My mother and I are eating sandwiches over in a part of the city where there is a vast hilly park with old, old trees and spectacular boulders rearing like whales out of the ground, their rough hides lacy with patches of lichen. I picked her up in my rusted Chevy and brought her here to sit with me at the granite tables of an old stone gazebo and look out over the glittering river and the purple hills. This is a May afternoon in a northern city of rivers and canals and manmade lakes and, in winter, profound cold and deep snows.

When we crossed the park from the car, I noticed that my mother now carries herself differently, as though she's shed a heavy brace confining and burdening her body all these years. Nothing tangible about her has changed. She hasn't lost weight or become more fit. But she walks these days with the tread of a younger woman, a woman of forty rather than sixty-eight. Her step is buoyant, her limbs seem weightless, her body made of oxygen. Her skin glows, her face is firm and youthful.

"Have you had a facelift?" I ask her enviously. We're eating salmon sandwiches, holding onto the brittle waxed paper wrapping to keep it from fluttering away. In the distance, a car slides silently past on the scenic drive ringing the park. A woman crosses the rolling lawns with a big black dog on a leash, disappears into one of the dips and valleys scored with the asphalt path that twists and climbs through this grassy sanctuary. We hear only the wind sighing high above us in the soft, bottle-green pines, the twittering of birds.

"What?"

"A facelift. You look different."

Her head tilts back playfully and she laughs. Even her laughter is new, I think. It's like a wind chime fashioned from fine silver rods, its music pure, clear, pitch-perfect. She has a dignified bearing, classic looks, the broad, dark beauty of the movie actresses of her youth — not the flashy, brittle type, but the deep, sound, enigmatic ones: Patricia Neal, Anne Bancroft. A wide mouth, big black eyes, thick hair pulled away from a high curved forehead and held behind her ears with tortoise shell combs. People notice her, she still turns heads in public. Today, she smells of some light perfume, the faintest sweet fragrance, a girl's scent.

Far below us, at the foot of the friable shale cliff, pleasure boats skim like white gulls across the water. My mother points down, indicating a spot on the road below us, where you can pull your car in and stand under a roof of Spanish tiles and look at brass plaques with arrows pointing to the shabby, haphazard towns on the opposite shore.

"Remember," she says, "when the logs used to float down from the hills all summer, how they spilled out here? Once, I was standing with your father at that lookout just below and we saw a tiny tugboat pulling a huge log boom. And he said to me, 'That's what I would have liked to have done with my life. Piloted one of those tugboats. Lived on the river, slept below deck on a cot, eaten out of tin cans, a bachelor. Plied up and down the shore with the wind in my face and the sun in my eyes and the roar of the engine in my ears. No attachments. Not a care in the world."

"Dreamer," I remark.

"That's what he wanted," explains my mother without rancour. "A life that had nothing to do with us."

"I don't understand," I tell her. "How could you have let all that happen? Our life back then? How could you have been so helpless? Why didn't you straighten Dad out?"

"I don't remember," she answers without guilt. "No, it's true. I don't remember any of it. It's all a blur."

Seeing her lightened now, so freed, I burn inside. Why, I wonder, staring down at the sparkling water, do I invest in these picnics with her, always searching for some payoff, some acknowledgement I don't even understand? My mother has trouble listing the names of her children in order of birth. She has lost track of how old we are. She forgets our birthdays. What I want her to say is that I'm special, that in some small way I stood out from the rest of her dozen children.

"I loved you all," she smiles at me, sliding skilfully away from turbulence, like a leaf on rippled water. It's not that she's callous, only that she is happy, so happy, now that my father has Alzheimer's and has been confined to a nursing home.

My father was once a rug salesman. All day long he peddled Chinese carpets, Persian carpets, carpets from Pakistan, some as thick as the heel of your hand, some in wool, others woven in pure silk, shining like lakes. To display to customers their lustre, their nap, their weave and knotted fringe, he spun them out like a magician into the middle of the showroom floor. I used to relish the feel of a carpet on my bare feet. On Saturday mornings I sometimes went in to the store with my father and I'd lie down on a stack of rugs piled two feet high.

"The princess and the pea," my father would say, passing by. He was a short fat man with pink hands and wavy hair stiff with Brylcreem. "That's who you are, Shirley. The princess and the pea."

I'd never heard of the story, never been read to. But I liked the sound of it.

Then one day when I was twelve, I noticed how my father rocked comically on his pudgy legs and how he bowed and scraped to the customers as though they were kings and queens instead of ordinary people with cash, and how when he bent over in deference to them, his fat behind thrust out through the shallow, torn pleat of his madras jacket. Rideau Street was where he bought all his sports coats because it was what he could afford and because he thought they made him look dapper and possibly because he fancied himself working some day in a carnival or a circus, attired like this. I saw the customers talking behind their hands and laughing at him when he waddled away. The following Saturday, when he asked, "Are you coming into the store with me, Shirley?" I answered, "No," and I could tell from the pain in his face that he knew I'd seen through him.

My father worked for his brother, my Uncle Leon. Leon paid him a living wage but my father was fond of betting on the horses. He told my mother to think of it not as a risk but as an investment. Some day, he said, he'd get lucky and his windfall would purchase our way into a new life. There began a pattern wherein my mother would shake us out of our dreams in the middle of the night. Surely there were a dozen of these incidents between the time that I was six and sixteen?

"Wake up," she'd whisper. "Don't talk. Don't make any noise. We're leaving. We're moving to a new place." At these moments, I didn't recognize her. Leaning over my bed, her face shadowy, tired, dragged down by gravity, she looked like an ugly old woman.

"Why? Why are we going?"

"*Shhhh.*"

We grew into an army of little soldiers trained to rise and dress in the dark, dedicated to our mission, dutiful, unquestioning, silently pulling on our clothes, throwing our meagre possessions into paper grocery bags, tiptoeing, shoes in hand, along the apartment hallways, past the doors of our neighbours, past the superintendent's apartment, and down the back stairs. After awhile we understood the importance of stealth, silence, speed. We knew the drill. It had become second nature.

From neighbourhood to neighbourhood, flat to flat, we drifted, outwitting the rent collector. I remember Uncle Leon showing up unexpectedly late one evening with a pot of curried chicken left over from a banquet he'd just attended. It was more food than we'd seen in a week. He noted us sleeping four to a bed and the living room couch made up with a pillow and blanket for my mother.

I heard Leon say to my father, "You damned fool! Haven't you ever heard of the condom?"

My father blushed, hung his head, cowed by my uncle's scorn. Leon was a small, handsome man with a neat grey wig. Like my father, he was short but he towered over him by virtue of the energy and intelligence in his face, his entrepreneurial mind, his expensive suit in nubby grey wool, finely cut to show off his trim midriff.

I have no memory of a home, no place in which to frame my childhood. All I recollect is a jumble of dark rooms, narrow hallways, apartments furnished with the belongings of land-lords I'd never met. Why — you may ask — why be upset about all this now? It's finished. You may say: Look. Look at this. This photograph in *Life* magazine showing a genuinely poor child sleeping on a mattress behind a fridge. That wasn't you. You were never this poor. At least you had a proper bed.

Once, like refugees, we lived for a whole summer in a camp (there is a museum now standing in this field) on the edge of the city, in a couple of tents my father begged from an army surplus store. From there, we could look down a slope to the river. Every afternoon, my mother took us along a path, its fine dust velvety on the soles of our bare feet. On either side, sumac rose higher than our heads. We reached the river. It was a rain-less summer following a dry spring, and the water dropped very low. In our underwear, we waded far out into the river and splashed and swam, while my mother stretched out on the flat exposed rocks lining the shore and lit a cigarette. As usual, she was pregnant. She had twelve pregnancies in as many years. She was never without the weight of a child in her belly or in her arms. That summer, she would have been the age I am now, a striking woman with thin, tanned hands, lying beside the river in the middle of the afternoon, wearing a faded maternity dress.

At the end of August, when the sumac on the river bank were turning crimson, Leon showed up, spoke to my father, handed him an envelope full of money, said he could come back to the store. It seemed my father had dipped into the till to fatten his horse-betting kitty. "Let this be a lesson to you," I heard Leon tell him, and my father smiled and hugged Leon and wept with remorse and gratitude.

These days, my mother plays bridge, goes to movies, takes yoga classes, rides a bicycle, has joined a book club, attends pot luck dinners with women who seem to have materialized out of thin air. Before this, she never had any friends. She waited until we were all gone to become a whole person, to break free of my father, to have a life we could imitate. Several times a week, she visits my father and they sit at the window of his room, which looks out on a small fenced yard, by seasons snowy or sleek with rain or fragrant with mown grass or carpeted with orange leaves. My father, once again a child, talks about the boats he thinks he sees sliding by in his make-believe life.

"How is Orm?" asks my mother. We are packing up our picnic things, making our way across the park to my car. Twenty years ago, when I followed Orm to university in southern Ontario, she said, "Don't chase after that boy, Shirley. Don't crowd him. Give him some breathing space. Let him become what he needs to become. Learn to stand on your own two feet." Which of course was rich coming from her, a woman who never stood up for anything, let alone for herself. My mother and Orm like and respect each other. Orm has said to me, "See the changes in your mother since your father went into the home? She's remade herself. She's got interests and pursuits. She's constructed a new life out of nothing. She's become a modern woman," and I know this is a dig at me.

A letter comes from Orm's office. It's three o'clock in the afternoon and I'm sitting in the back yard reading Jane Austen. I've read all of Austen a dozen times. I'm in love with that era. Orm says all the women in those books were man-crazy twits. He says I've been buried in the nineteenth century all my life.

I hear heavy footsteps in the grass and I look up to see a big, clumsy, flatfooted boy in a brown uniform approaching me across the grass.

"Excuse me, Ma'am," he says. "I have a delivery for you. I tried knocking out front but there was no answer. I thought maybe I should look back here. Your door is open, all the windows. I figured someone was at home." He thrusts an envelope in front of me.

"But this is from my husband's office," I say, reading the letterhead.

"I wouldn't know about that."

"Why would someone there be sending me a letter?"

"I couldn't say, Ma'am. I just need you to print your name here on this line and sign beside it." He presents me with a clipboard.

"But what could this mean?"

"Ma'am, what's in the deliveries has nothing to do with me. My job is to get the signatures." He shuffles restlessly in the grass. He has a plain, dogged, unexcitable face.

"There must be a mistake," I say, noticing within myself a feeling of alarm, my body gone hollow.

"How could it be a mistake?" He is growing impatient.

"I don't know."

"Are you Shirley Roach or not?"

"Yes, I'm Shirley Roach."

"And this is Cardigan Street? 490 Cardigan Street South? Are you going to accept the letter? It says urgent. I can take it back but what if it's something you need to know?" I look up at him and see swimming in his young face an enviable practicality, a peculiar depth of understanding about life that I may never obtain. Is this the currency of a professional bearer of messages, both good and bad?

He goes away whistling.

Dear Shirley

I thought for a long time what would be the best way to tell you I am leaving you and that our marriage is finished. I concluded that a letter would be the appropriate thing and less impersonal than papers served to you by my lawyer. There wasn't any point in telling you face to face, because no amount of discussion or arguing will change my mind.

At first, I think this is a prank. A practical joke. Some sick person up to mischief. But no, here is Orm's familiar signature at the bottom of the page, scrawled with the very fountain pen I gave him for Christmas.

I know you're going to be thinking that what you're reading here isn't true or else that things will blow over and go back to the way they were, because you are a person who gets stuck on an idea and won't look around to see reality. So I'm urging you now to take what I'm saying seriously. I won't be seeing you again, Shirley. I don't want to talk to you about any of this. My mind is made up. My decision is final. There's no turning back from here. From this point on, we can handle everything through our lawyers. It will mean less conflict and that's best for the kids. We have to think of them first.

Over our years together, I've grown, both professionally and personally, but you seem to me just the same as you were when I kissed you for the first time in the tuck shop at Glebe Collegiate. After awhile, a person who doesn't change ceases to be interesting, and if a person doesn't interest you, you can't bear to stay with them anymore except out of pity. I did that for a long time, but eventually you realize you aren't being true to yourself or fair to your partner. You were never the right one for me, Shirley, even back in school. We fell into a relationship when we were nothing more than kids. We were young when we married, with the pressure of an unwanted pregnancy making up our minds for us. I don't know what I was thinking back then. I don't expect I was thinking at all. I certainly didn't know myself.

I don't love you anymore. It's that simple. I've met someone more suited to me. Being with her makes me feel alive again. She's exciting. She's physically active. She's passionate about life. She's all the things you've never been.

I have everything with me that I need for the moment. I'll come over some day in the future when things have settled down to collect the rest of my stuff. My skis and books and other miscellaneous things. I don't want anything else from the house, the furniture and so forth. You can keep it all.

Don't contact me, Shirley. Don't try to see me. It will only bring you grief...

There is a crash, the gate flies open, and Cyrus sails into the yard on his bicycle. He springs off, throws it down in the grass, the back tire spinning, its spokes flashing in the sun. He launches himself toward the back door.

"I got a letter from your father," I tell him.

In mid-flight, he stops, his body not fully arrested, arcing toward the house, brimming with energy and intent, half-twisted around to look at me, one foot hanging in mid-air.

"From Dad?" he says, confused, distracted, anxious to get inside. After school he is ravenous.

"He says here that he's leaving me. He's moving out."

"Where's he going?"

"To live with another woman."

"That Heidi person?"

"Will you wait for me?" I used to beg Orm on the mountain. I was never a skier but I made an effort, just to be with him. "You're not going to just tear all the way down, are you?"

"Don't worry, I'll wait for you," he promised. And at the beginning of each season, he did pause at the turns in the hills and at the crests preceding the sheer plunges. He watched me coming down. "You'll be fine," he'd say. "This one is a piece of cake."

To alleviate his boredom, he skied into the forests lining the slopes, sliding smoothly as a jackrabbit over the hillocks, weaving between the birches, his hips swaying, his knees like coil springs, his shoulders so broad and solid and square to the hill. But then, gradually, as the season wore on, I'd find myself alone on a precipitous, icy grade, wondering where Orm had disappeared to and if he was trying to kill me with the vertical drop. There I stood in the falling snow, my heart pounding, skiers whizzing by me as though they had wings, and, with sharp and nervous turns and twitches, I'd make my way slowly down the hill.

Orm would say at the end of the day, "I waited for you at the lifts all morning, like I said I would, but when I didn't see you, I thought maybe you'd passed me."

"Fat chance of that," I told him.

"And then, in the afternoon," he claimed, "I searched for you on the slopes. I don't know why you can't pick this sport up. It's so simple. Why do you have to be so full of fears?"

This past winter was the worst. He didn't even join us in the lodge for lunch.

"Where's Dad?" the kids would ask as we sat in the cafeteria amongst hundreds of noisy children. "I thought he was eating with us."

"Oh, he probably got the time wrong," I'd say, unpacking our sandwiches. "Or maybe he got stuck on a lift somewhere."

At the end of the day, we'd meet up with Orm in the parking lot, and his face would be wind-burned and he'd look happy and exhilarated, and I could see he hadn't thought about me the whole day.

"Will I still get my allowance?" is what Zoe asks when I tell her about Orm's desertion. I've pursued her to her room after school.

"It's important," I call through the door. "Let me in." She's sitting on her bed, painting her toenails black.

"Here, let me read you the letter," I say, but she claps her hands over her ears. "I don't want to hear it!" she shouts, her face contorted. "You're not supposed to make me take sides. Why are you and Dad such a fuck-up?"

I go down to the cellar and find Orm's skis, his poles and boots, carry them up to the living room. From the garage, I haul in cordwood, kindling, build a roaring blaze in the fireplace. I set the tips of the skis in the flames, watch with satisfaction as they begin to glow. I kneel there, feeding them into the fire as they burn away. The room grows hot, suffocating. It is spring, after all, too warm for a fire even with the windows thrown open. I'm sweating heavily, but I welcome the sense of purification, catharsis. There are sparks and small explosions, powerful fumes, black smoke from the paint and veneer and layers of glue, the ski wax, but the fireplace has a good draft and sucks it up the chimney. Soon, I sense Zoe standing in the living room doorway.

"What's that smell? What are you doing, Mom?" she says, her voice alarmed, quavering. "Aren't those Dad's skis?" She disappears and a moment later she's at the front door, a satchel slung over her shoulder. "I'm going over to Erin's," she tells me and I think: there is no betrayal like that of another woman.

An hour later, the phone rings. It's Zoe. "I'm staying over here for a few days," she tells me. "Erin and I are working on a history project together."

"Don't you need to come home and get some clothes?" I say. "A toothbrush?"

"I'll just use her stuff."

"But you're not even the same size."

"Mom," she says firmly, "I'm seventeen. I think I know how to clothe myself."

I say, "I could use some company, Zoe. I'm all alone here. Cyrus had to go back to school for a basketball practice."

"You'll be alright, Mom," says Zoe. "People get jilted all the time by their partners. I see it every day at school."

"But those are just children," I say.

I pick up the phone again and dial my mother. I read the letter to her.

She says, "I'm sure Orm gave this a lot of thought before he acted. I'm sure he didn't do it lightly. He's not a frivolous man. I expect he's feeling very conflicted." She sounds unsurprised by the turn of events. I know she wants to tell me she saw it coming. When she was young, when she was my age, she had no clue what was going on in her own life, but now she thinks she can see right through mine.

"Does that sound conflicted to you?" I demand. "What's conflicted about it? I never read anything so cut and dried in my life."

"There's more to it than that," she says. "There's more than what's in that letter. There always is." The television is going in the background, in her living room. Her voice fades away for a moment, and I know that she's turning her head, trying to see the screen. Then I hear the volume turned up.

"It will all work out for the better, Dear," she says.

"Mom! This is not *Coronation Street!*"

"Don't worry about Zoe and Cyrus. They'll adjust. You'll see. They'll get over it in no time. Unless they're like you. You were the least adaptable of all my children."

Well, at least I stood out in some way, I think, strangely pleased. I tell her, "I'm going to go down and see him."

"Don't do that."

"I'm going to confront him in his office. Cow him."

"The poor man."

"Embarrass him into coming home."

"Leave him be, Shirley. You had a good life with him. He worked hard to give you that. It's something to be grateful for."

"All that stuff about the pain in his groin?" I say. "That was just bullshit. There were no doctors. There were no tests. He fabricated the whole thing. An elaborate excuse not to have sex with me while he was screwing that skier."

"Oh, I don't think Orm would make a thing like that up. I don't think he'd lie to you."

At four-thirty the next afternoon, I drive downtown and park in front of Orm's building. It's a beautiful afternoon, sunny, with a soft, sweet wind blowing down the canyons. The glass towers, turning red in the late-afternoon light, are like a blazing forest. It is many years since I've come down here and I'm astonished by the expansiveness of the streets, the sleekness of the architecture, the leafy parade of young oak trees growing out of iron cages. I sit in my car with the windows rolled down and watch the workers leaving the building, streams of them, a great rush at five o'clock, moving swiftly, spinning out of the revolving doors, an optimistic holiday spirit in their step. Already, the traffic on the streets is light, people having left early because of the Victoria Day weekend ahead.

Five-thirty passes, five-forty-five. I begin to fear I've missed Orm, that he's slipped by among all the crowds, but then he emerges from the great rotating door, accompanied by a woman, who must be Heidi. She is just the way I imagined her: tall, with the meaty limbs of an alpine girl, her face golden from the sunny slopes, her hair thick and blond. Lifting my hand, I'm ready to lean on my horn, but it's not necessary because Orm looks over and notices my car. He and the woman stop, speak for a moment, consult their watches. I see that they are at ease with each other, committed, intimate. And in this moment, I understand that overnight the world has tilted, that all the forces of nature are now rushing in a new direction and that if I don't want to be swept off the edge of the earth, I'm going to have to travel with them. The woman turns, leaves Orm, sets off down the street, dignified, unhurried, guiltless, her backside solid in a smart periwinkle business suit, not a heavy woman but a sturdy one. She will not be a fragile flower on Orm's arm.

Orm walks over to my car, impressive in his height, his grace, his confidence, so in his realm down here among these business towers that it occurs to me that I've never given much thought to his job or what's important in his life. What I wanted to say, the things I'd been thinking all night, turning over and over in my head until it ached, don't seem important or even plausible anymore. They are just folly. Looking down, I see with some embarrassment that I'm wearing flip-flops, a loose old faded housedress I don't even remember putting on.

Orm stands beside the car, achingly handsome in a navy blue suit, a crisp white shirt. I half expect him to yell at me. I sit there feeling shame, humiliation. I cannot blame him. I cannot blame him for his repudiation of me. Already, I see in him the transformation. He looks rested, refreshed, disburdened, happy, at peace with himself in a way I've never seen him before. In a fashion he could not manage while he lived with his parents or — clearly, I now see — with me. He removes his sunglasses, and I notice for the first time the soft puckers around his eyes, the skin loosened there with age, and also the surprising dusting of white hair at his temples.

"It's a beautiful weekend," he says easily, as though I've come down here to discuss the weather or exchange pleasantries.

"I know."

"You should be home, thinking of ways to enjoy it."

In his voice is none of the sternness of his letter, which I have torn up, pieced back together with Scotch Tape, torn up again. He speaks with such benevolence that my hands stop trembling and all the anger eases out of me. And I think: why not follow his lead? For the moment, at least? Why not just let him guide me into this new arrangement?

"I can't imagine how I will." My voice falters.

He reaches through the window, sets a comforting hand on my shoulder. I feel the strength of his long fingers. "You'll think of something. You're going to be alright."

"Am I?" I say, dabbing at the corners of my eyes with the hem of my dress.

"You're well rid of me," he tells me.

"That's an unfeeling thing to say."

"Now you can become the real you."

For an hour, I drive around the city, not even noticing where I'm going or what I see. At last, I find myself out on the western parkway. I pick a place to leave the car, get out and follow a path beside the river, find a bench to sit on and look out at the copper water. It is after seven on a long, fragrant spring night. The rush hour traffic that flows along this boulevard has, of course, died down by now. There are only a few cars carrying people out here to see the sunset along the water, walking or jogging or rollerblading. Some have bicycles strapped onto the backs of their cars. They swing into parking lots, lift the bikes down, spin along the rolling pathways.

I notice the flat rocks on the shore and realize I am near the museum and remember that this is the place where we camped that summer while my father tramped around town looking for a new job, a silly, terrified smile printed across his benign face. We ate brown-sugar-and-cinnamon sandwiches for supper and occasionally wieners, which my mother cooked on a fire made of twigs we collected along the river after our swim. We wrapped the hot dogs up in Wonder Bread. With the other children in the camp, we played hide-and-seek, flitting like phantoms in and out among the trees until well after dark. Sometimes my father woke us at midnight, called us out of the tents, which smelled so richly of oil and dust and, we imagined, of soldiers, to look sleepily at the full moon and its reflection floating like a milk glass lamp in the river. What, I now wonder, was the harm in all that? Some children would have given their eye teeth for a summer like it.

One day I meet my mother unexpectedly on a street far from where she lives. She is coming out of a store, laughing, on the arm of Uncle Leon. She's wearing saddle shoes, a polo shirt, a short madras golf skirt that could have been made out of the material from one of my father's old jackets. She is taller than Uncle Leon, who draws himself up, trying to match her height.

"Mom, what is this?" I say.

"I just bought your mother her own clubs," Uncle Leon interjects happily, pointing to a long leather bag slung over his shoulder. "She's showing an aptitude for the game."

My mother looks happy, radiantly selfish. The grey in her hair is gone. She's dyed it, I see, an expert rinse, nothing harsh, and she's bleached the nicotine stains off her straight, strong teeth and applied a gash of crimson lipstick to her mouth so that now she looks once more like the woman who guided us down to the river to swim, that shiftless summer. Her face is tanned and healthy-looking. Her legs are burnished. And I think: all my life, all my life, I've been angry with this woman who was essentially harmless, except in her insistence on having babies. Why?

Leon tells me that in the summer, he'll be taking my mother up to his cottage in the Laurentians. He intends to teach her how to paddle a canoe. "She's going to learn to relax and take life easy," he tells me. She's going to learn to identify the whooping swan and how to tell a white pine from a red. In the winter, he says, they'll be in Barbados, where he owns a house on the west coast. My mother will be away a lot, he tells me firmly. He has been widowed for three months. He looks as though he's forgotten he ever had a wife.

"But what about Dad?" I ask my mother.

"I thought *you* could visit him," she says. "I thought you could take your turn."

In the nursing home, my father sits at his window with a blanket over his knees, basking in the summer sun falling on his polished head. He is always glad to see me. He knows I am a familiar face but he does not recall why. Sometimes he reaches out and touches my cheek as though he hopes this will help him to remember who I am. If I mention his years as a carpet salesman, he looks at me with confusion and denial. Gone are his checked jackets, his polyester trousers. Here they dress him in pyjamas, tracksuits, running shoes. He does not talk much, but he can still sit up in a chair and he can still smile. Some days, he is docile, cooperative, gentle, happy. Others, he is anxious or distracted. Beside us stands a rehab walker. Later, I will guide him on his shuffling journey to the bathroom, help him undo his clothing, flush the toilet for him.

In a local pharmacy, I came across a pamphlet describing the progression of Alzheimer's disease, the various changes the victim goes through. I can see that my father is rapidly approaching the advanced stage. He has been imprisoned in this secure unit in the nursing home for over a year, but I have visited him only in the past two months. I never wanted to come here and see him. I thought I could lock away with him all memory, all injury of the past. But now, seeing him every week, I am able to embrace it, to take it into myself. Life has its own ebb and flow, I've learned, and it's wise to swim with the tides, keeping your chin above the crest of the waves as best you can. And wasn't my mother doing just this, stretched out on the rocks beside the river all that homeless summer, soaking up the sunshine, savouring the taste of a cigarette, listening to the happy screams of her children splashing far out in the shrunken river?

The Sins of the Father

WITH THANKS TO SIMON TOOKOOME

Men in kayaks,
come hither to me
And be my husbands;
this stone here
has clung fast to me,
and lo, my feet
are now turning to stone.

THE NURSE STARTED TO COME IN the mornings soon after Louise moved home. Louise was finishing her thesis in her father's study and from there she could hear the nurse getting her mother into the shower and then back to bed, all the while talking cheerfully. The nurse was no bigger than a twelve-year-old girl. The first day Louise opened the door to her, she was tempted to go straight to the phone and call the agency and ask, "Why have you sent us this child?"

Instead, she said to the nurse, "My mother is a sack of bones but she weighs a ton. I can't budge her and I'm twice your size. I don't see how you're going to be able to move her." The nurse smiled and touched Louise's arm. "That's my worry, now," she said softly.

The nurse had worked for years with cancer patients at the hospital, she told Louise, out on the deck, where they sometimes drank iced tea in the afternoon, while her mother slept. She hooked these patients up to chemotherapy and when they went home they had her phone number to call with their questions and their fears and their despair. She'd loved this work, but sometimes she'd cried all the way home from the hospital because of the things she'd seen. The weight of it became too much. Too many stories to keep in her head. Then, she'd turned to private nursing. One story at a time. Louise's mother was to be her last patient. After Louise's mother, she planned to retire. She needed to rest and enjoy life, she'd decided. She was only fifty but she was worn out. Louise thought she looked sixty.

After the nurse arrived, the house seemed liveable, as though she'd thrown all the windows open and let out whatever had been choking them. She asked how Louise was bearing up. She had a way of holding you with her eyes so that you couldn't get out of answering her questions. Her tiny face was lined with the sorrows of others, her body held in tight, as though her joints were locked in sympathy, her skin dark and leathery looking like someone who'd spent a lifetime too close to a tremendous heat.

The mother's bedroom was on the front of the house, overlooking a strip of park and a narrow canal and then a handsome old red primary school. The children poured out of it to play tag or bounce balls in the paved yard. Their bright clothes flashed through a screen of poplars. In July, her mother had said, "If I can just hold on until the children come back to school." On September fifth, Louise went into her room and said, "There you are, Mom. You got your wish."

It was a hot, gusty autumn. The luminous clouds of August continued to scud across the sky. It did not seem possible that anyone could be dying in such robust weather. Her mother's skin grew translucent, it acquired a bluish tinge, her eyes were bright and fiery, like dying embers, the flesh around them melted away so that the sockets looked hard as stone. Months before, she'd let her stomach swell up until she looked pregnant before she consulted a doctor. The surgeons opened her up and found the cancer had spread from her ovaries to her liver and kidneys. She'd refused chemotherapy, which might have bought her a few months. "Oh, why bother with all that destruction?" she'd said.

"You waited so long to go to the doctor," said Louise. "Why?"

"I don't know. I don't know. Something happened in my head." She looked at Louise, hoping she'd understand. Louise couldn't. She was twenty-six and her mother was fifty-nine.

Her mother asked Louise to open the window. "Won't you be chilled?" Louise said, because now she was skin and bones. "I want to hear the children playing," her mother said. It was only little boys banging sticks on metal tins and little girls running and screaming their high-pitched, hysterical screams as they played tag, storm the mountain. "It's like music to me," her mother said. "They're so happy. Their naivete makes me feel alive." Louise wondered if this was some kind of reproach to her for growing up, for going so far away to study.

Louise's father had called her in England and said that her mother was dying and that it was important she get on the first plane home. But as soon as she arrived, he told her he was leaving for the Arctic. He was to participate in a collaborative dig with colleagues from Greenland and Siberia. Louise followed him around the basement, while he gathered together his sealskin parka and mukluks and his trowel and brushes and measuring instruments and sifting screens and field books. Tentatively, she said, "Dad, I don't know if you should be going." He was not a man to be opposed. He'd never been questioned at work and Louise's mother had never challenged him and, since she herself did not think she even knew him and also because she feared him a little, Louise could not confront him either. He answered impatiently, "This dig has been in the planning for five years. It's the biggest circumpolar effort ever held. It was my brainchild and I'm the chair and I can't not be there."

"But what about Mom?"

"That's why *you're* here. I need to be able to depend on you."

"But what if she doesn't last? What if she dies while you're gone?"

"She won't die while I'm gone. She'll wait for me. She always has." He was over six feet tall, with his same youthful wiriness and explosive energy. As a child, Louise had seen his picture in the archaeology journals stacked on their coffee table, almost more than she saw *him*. She remembered studying the long vain face, the biting eyes, the high forehead obdurate as a stone tablet, the nineteenth-century goatee.

The nurse knocked lightly, entered Louise's room and put a sandwich on the corner of her desk. What was Louise working on, she asked. Louise flipped through her thesis, showing the nurse the drawings of tattooed women, the lines and ellipses fanning out from the nose and mouth, the deep V shooting down between the eyebrows, the decorative patterns of dots and spurs. A thread was coated with soot from the stone lamp, she explained, and drawn under the skin with a needle. Tattoos were a sign of beauty and power, she told the nurse.

"So, through your studies, you are following in your father's footsteps," the nurse observed.

"I truly hope not," answered Louise.

Louise remembered being young enough to forget she had a father, he being absent for such long stretches. When he reappeared, she ran, frightened, to her mother, burying her face in her skirt. He followed, knelt before them, tanned, radiant, vigorous from months of camping on a landscape that had changed little in four thousand years. He smelled powerfully of wild game and animal clothing and seal oil smoke. From his pocket, he'd pull something protected by a soft cloth, unwrap it. It spilled out into his hands, which were scarred from digging, with lost fingernails and knuckles scraped and bruised. The object would be so small it swam in his palm: the tiny figure of a man, perhaps, no more than an inch and a half long, with a bulbous head, stiff arms, legs curved as though he suffered from rickets, sockets for eyes, a flattened nose, coarse parted lips. Louise remembered thinking these findings ugly, and wondering how the pursuit of something so insignificant, so crude had distracted him from them for so long. It was for this that they'd been abandoned?

"You can't look at your mother's death as a rejection of you," said the nurse.

"I don't."

"That's good."

"But I'll be the one left behind, won't I?"

"What about your father?"

"He'll have his ego to keep him company. He'll have his propaganda."

Early on, the nurse had asked Louise, "Is there a husband? I haven't seen him around."

Louise laughed bitterly. "Oh, yes, but he chooses not to be here."

The nurse searched Louise's face. "You're angry about this."

"I wish *she* were."

"If she were angry, maybe she couldn't die in peace."

"He's never been here for anything important. Why would he be here for this? This is only a *death*."

One afternoon when her mother was sleeping, Louise sat down in the living room and picked up an anthropology journal. There she read an article her father had written, describing his thirty-year friendship with an Inuk named Josephee. He was a rebellious camp leader who still clung to the land, refusing to take a Christian name or to live in the white man's prefab houses, which he found hot, noisy and hard to maintain, with doors on which one was expected to knock before entering. This Inuk maintained a large dog team, could build a snow house in half an hour, was so skilled with the use of a forty-foot whip that he could snap the head off a ptarmigan from that distance. He recounted to Louise's father a bygone time when the migrant caribou herds were so vast that you could hear their approach for two days, when the passing herd was thick enough that a hunter was able to walk among it at leisure, looking for the fattest one, kill it with a knife strike behind the ear without frightening the rest. He'd taught Louise's father not to travel across the snow in a straight line, but to walk the way the surface moves, always searching the horizon for animals. He instructed him in the practice of placing a down feather over the ice hole in order to detect the breath of the rising seal and thus know the precise moment at which to thrust with the spear. He showed him how, when a hunter killed a caribou, it was important to offer the dead animal a drink of water to ease its suffering, shake its hooves as a sign of gratitude, remove the sinews from its legs gently so as not to cause it pain.

Looking down from her desk, Louise saw that the trees in the park were turning now, muted tones because of the persistent balminess, no drama to their colour, just a quiet, golden dying. The leaves rained steadily from the trees, drifting down in the now windless afternoons. Each day the sun dropped lower in the sky. Inch by inch, it crept across her mother's bed, over the shallow hills and valleys of her figure. So brittle had her skin grown that it split open at will as though perforated. The nurse dressed these lesions. She drew blood samples from her mother's ear lobe because the veins in her arms had collapsed.

The nurse told Louise, "You should go out. Isn't that the reason I'm here?" One afternoon at a coffee shop on Bank Street, Louise ran into a man named Vito, a colleague of her father's and a family friend. As a child, she'd called him "uncle" because he came to the house at Thanksgiving, when her father was up North, and at Easter or Christmas when her father was lecturing in Europe or Russia or Australia, or when her mother needed advice about a leaky basement or an icy roof. He had none of her father's physical presence. He was short and homely, bald, with wire rimmed glasses and a soft gut. Not handsome, but attractive because of his warmth, his shy, modest, friendly manner. A nice man in nice blue shirts. Now, at the coffee shop, he leapt up and pulled out a chair for Louise to sit down.

"Well, I can't stay long," Louise said.

He bit his lip and looked out the window at the passing traffic. "It's a goddamned shame, about your mother," he said, and when Louise didn't answer, he became nonplussed and said, "I know you're wondering why I haven't dropped in."

"No, not really," said Louise coolly. A lie. His emotion seemed a sham to her. She did not need him. She did not even know if she liked him anymore, to be truthful. She didn't like her father, either, and possibly she no longer loved her mother. If her mother had had any sense, she could have had this cancer nipped in the bud. Now she'd trapped them all in her demise. She was stupid, stupid.

Louise had come home full of ego, believing her thesis solid, infallible. But when she read it over, it seemed facile, shaky in logic. Her confidence in it crumbled. She'd begun to write round and round the chapters, adding and deleting. It was being lured back here, to this goddamned intellectual wasteland, that had undermined her. She was afraid of being trapped here, of somehow not getting back to London. These people were pathetic. She hated them. When she was young, she'd loved Vito like a father. She remembered sitting on his lap when she was very little. The thought of this repelled her now. She knew this was probably unfair but she didn't care.

"I just feel so worn out by it all," said Vito.

"What do you mean?" asked Louise impassively.

"I just can't step in for your father anymore. It's too much."

"Well, I don't think we expect you to." She was bending over now, angry, gathering up her sweater and bag, preparing to leave.

"No, wait," Vito said, holding up his hand. "I'm sorry. But at this point you must know."

"Know what?"

"You must have guessed by now."

"Look — ," said Louise, irritated, her nerves frayed, "I really have no idea — "

Apparently, her father did not sleep with the members of his excavation teams, the passionate archaeology students on their summer field assignments, the young and adoring novices. Their faces bronzed like his, their ponytails streaked blonde by pure Arctic sunlight, earth embedded beneath their fingernails, wearing thick wool socks, hiking boots, down-filled vests. Sensitively removing half an inch of soil at a time, delicately investigating with their probes and brushes, learning from her father the techniques of stratification, hoping to pick up from him the sixth sense of the archaeologist — an intuitive feel for the subtle distinctions between layers of earth, the textures of the soil. He evidently was professional enough to resist creeping into their tents at night, though they no doubt excited him with their discoveries of broken harpoon heads, ivory knife handles, sealskin buckets, all so pristinely preserved by the cold dry climate, the deep permafrost of the North.

No, instead, he bedded the Inuit women, the throat-singers, the snow geese-hunters, the kelp-gatherers, the collectors of eider duck eggs, the keepers of the stone cooking lamp. Some of them still wore their hair wrapped decoratively around sticks, tattooed their faces and arms and breasts, had abandoned newborns in the snow because the previous year's child was too young to pull from the *amautik* hood and strap to the sled during migration.

When Louise told her, her mother just smiled in a sad, deep way, her skin luminous, shining with its own ineffable light. She said, "I think Vito always had feelings for me. Didn't you ever wonder why he never married? He was in love with me. And I think he imagines things about your father. He's always coveted your father's job. He wanted his fine office. He wanted to be out in the field, not behind a desk. Now it's too late for him. He's turned bitter. And besides, what if your father did sleep around? I still love him and I know he loves me. We've had happy times. Compared to your father, Vito is a very small man."

Her mother had met Louise's father forty years before at the museum. He'd plucked her out of the secretarial pool, the daughter of Polish immigrants, pig farmers who spoke a halting English. Their greatest pride was that she'd married well. "If I hadn't met your father," she'd told Louise more than once, "I'd still be a typist. People sit up and take notice of me when I tell them I'm Attila Kaplan's wife."

Louise, standing beside her mother's bed, exploded. "Why do you have to be so passive? Why have you never wanted anything? Why did you decide to die?" Then she burst into tears, out of shame at ever telling her mother what Vito had said in the first place. But her mother's refusal to discuss it further was, for Louise, a betrayal. Her mother's solidarity with her father — she could not accept it. She felt like an outsider, a door slammed in her face.

Later that evening, her mother told her, "What Vito said — that's just mythology. Your father is famous. Larger than life. Legends spring up around a man like that."

Now every tree in the park was bare, but the maple beside her mother's window stood dense and yellow. Every afternoon, Louise went out and gathered its falling leaves from the driveway, the quivering tines of the fan rake scraping the asphalt. The exercise made her feel alive. She filled up bag after bag. Still the leaves fell. She looked up at the branches. The bounty of the tree never ceased. The bags stood like soldiers at the kerb. At night there were flashes of white lightning, apocalyptic, but no rain.

Louise sat in the kitchen and wrote the obituary for the newspaper. The nurse left. Her mother rang her little bell. Louise went upstairs, feeling disloyal, treacherous, the piece of writing folded in her pocket. At first there had been morphine patches, but now there was a small box that administered a continuous drip into a port in her mother's arm. She was no longer reading on her own. Even the weight of a pocket novel in her hands taxed her strength.

Louise dreamed of her father eating *muktuk* and raw seal meat and sleeping with a woman beneath the luminous blue curve of the snow house roof. By the flickering light of the seal oil lamp, he traced her tattoos with his finger, touched her teeth, ground down to stubs from chewing his water-stiffened boots until they were soft and supple enough for him to wear the next day.

One afternoon, she left the house and walked to the post office, carrying her completed thesis, its pages heavy as a child in her arms. The streets were strangely quiet, deserted, the bleached sidewalks blinding in the sunlight, the pavements shimmering with an unnatural, prolonged heat. Heading home, lightened and cleansed by the dispatching of her thesis, she came to the small picturesque bridge spanning the canal, and paused at its crest to lean on the stone balustrade and look down at the water and the long, narrow lawn stretching away from its banks. The shadows of the naked lindens and acacias and butternuts fell sharp and black across the emerald grass. Not a branch stirred. The schoolyard was empty. Suddenly Louise felt the air rush out of her lungs. She hurried home. At the front door, the nurse met her.

She'd driven to the airport to get her father. She'd considered letting him get a cab and ride alone into town along the wooded parkway, friendless, daughterless, wifeless. It was what he deserved. They stood beside the conveyor belt waiting for the luggage to slide out of the chute. His shoulders shook with weeping. "I don't know what I'll do without her," he said. Louise did not tell him he was a fool. All around them, people waiting for their bags were unmoved by his grief. This was the norm today, everything laid so bare and shameless on television, in films and grocery store magazines. Emotions had come to seem nothing, a cheap display.

"Hello?" her father had shouted over the crackling line, when she'd reached him by two-way radio. "Hello?"

Louise heard him well enough. She could have called back across the geography. She preferred to let him hang out there for a moment in the Arctic wind. The North Pole would melt before she'd comfort him.

At the airport, he turned to her, his eyes rimmed with red. His face said: You left her, just as I did. You know that, don't you? You're no better than I am. You deserted her for a foreign country.

The weather had turned sharply the day after her mother died. In the park, the air hung with mist. Early in the morning, Louise noticed a commotion on the inlet. She went outside to investigate, saw a small crowd gathered on the bridge. Three kilometers south, a young deer had entered the canal where there was a boat launch. He'd swum before dawn across the manmade lake and into the narrow canal, dreaming possibly of thick forests ahead, soft riverbanks, succulent vegetation, asylum. Instead, he found concrete walls, stagnant water rank with algae. In the morning darkness he became confused. Panicked, he plunged this way and that, his thin legs, his fine hooves cutting the water. Deeper and deeper into the city he headed. The morning traffic was building and, in the distance, sirens wailed.

It was seven o'clock before a jogger with a cell phone called 911. The animal rescue people arrived. In a motorboat, they pursued the deer into the inlet before Louise's house. The animal came to an impasse beyond the little bridge. The rangers shot him with a tranquillizing dart, hauled him into the boat, taped his hooves together, fastened a canvas blind over his eyes. He lay there, trembling, dignified, beautiful. Nearby a young child holding her mother's hand began to cry. People crossed the road from the bus stop. They stood transfixed, in their business suits, in their high heels, briefcases in hand, grateful for a glimpse of the magnificent creature. The rich colour of his coat, the water dripping from his flanks, the rebellious heaving of his chest. In a moment they would have to tear themselves away and ride downtown to the glass towers, to their ordinary lives.

My mother, Louise wanted to tell them all, *my mother has just died.*

> *I speak with the mouth of Qeqertaunaq,*
> *I will walk with leg muscles strong as the sinews*
> *On the shin of a little caribou calf.*
> *I will walk with leg muscles strong as the sinews*
> *On the shin of a little hare.*
> *I will take care not to walk toward the dark.*
> *I will walk toward the day.*

What You Never Had

I AM STANDING IN THE UPPER hallway of Hap Monument's house, listening to him downstairs in the kitchen getting out the cold supper his housekeeper left him. I pass along the hallway, wearing Hap's gold and burgundy striped dressing gown. My hand, sliding along the smooth, fat banister, makes me feel good about the house and my place in it. Into the high-ceilinged bedrooms I wander, over the wide smooth mahogany floorboards. The three-foot-thick walls of the house keep the rooms cool as a root cellar. I pick up a dish, a heavy silver candlestick, a fine porcelain figurine. Once, Hap saw me do this. "I wouldn't steal it," I said defensively, and he answered, "Why would I think you would?" though he knows I come from a family of felons. My crooked relatives are a curiosity for him, they make me interesting, he says. If he sees me opening his wife's drawers, fingering her jewellery, he just laughs. He tells me he finds my audacity, my inappropriateness refreshing. He is the most recent in a dynasty of mayors, all elected fair and square, though nobody ever ran against them.

Hap's family founded Monument. It fled New York State during the American Revolution and, for its loyalty to the British Crown, was granted two hundred acres here along the river. Soon it was operating a dozen water-powered industries and today tourists can go and look at the abandoned creamery, the ironworks, the gristmill. Most of the real estate in town is still part of the Monument estate. Hap lives in the ancestral home, its facade like a temple, its matching side porches facing east and west, like the decks of an ocean liner, so that the house resembles a great ship sailing solidly on an emerald ocean. In the middle of Main Street it stands, much photographed, the centrepiece of the town.

At the back of the house is a den where, stealing along the dark footpath at nightfall, I find Hap watching television in his slippers. I slide through the handsome colonnade of poplars at the back of his property, approach the mansion, which shimmers like a wedding cake in the half-light, the roof blushed pink in the sunset. I hear the television going, canned laughter. Its blue light flickers across a row of flowering crabs on the dusky lawn. Through the screen window drifts the sweet smell of tobacco. Hap smokes the same pipe his great grandfather did. It is part of the trappings of his office. When he kisses me at the back door, I taste pipe smoke in his mouth, smell it on his skin.

Hap is a big, soft, round man too spoiled and lazy to exercise. He suffers from kidney stones. His feet swell and burn. At night, he soaks them in Epsom salts. Sometimes, the miniature carrot-topped housekeeper, Mrs. Churcher, who is eighty, old enough to remember Hap in diapers but still able to whip around the house like a little red fox, prepares the footbath for him. When her night off coincides with the business trips of Hap's wife, Delia, I steal over to the house at sunset. In the high, downy, four-poster bed, I imagine I smell on Delia's pillow the poisonous oxides she uses in her glassblowing. I picture the silicon dust sifting into her lungs, I will it to tear at the vulnerable air sacs.

I have visited Delia's gallery, a red brick Victorian house at the end of Main Street. It is filled with her perfume bottles, lamp shades, glass orbs turning on satin ribbons in the windows, shooting their tints like coloured stars across the walls. I've stood at the big window overlooking the workshop where she moves about in her tough overalls, her mannish work boots. I've watched her gather molten glass from the orange mouth of the furnace, inflate it on a blowpipe, pinch and shear and score it with her long instruments, flatten it with wooden paddles. In contrast to Hap's fine, pale, girlish complexion, hers is drawn, leathery and coffee-coloured from a lifetime of exposure to ovens burning at two thousand degrees. While his hands are white and pudgy, hers are hard, lean and blistered and scarred from flying sparks.

I can scarcely believe my eyes when I see my mother walking along Main Street one April afternoon. There are tour buses that come out here from the city. She's got on one of those. As she approaches me the hem of her dress ripples around her knees, the sun shoots through the cloth, defining her thighs. I am stunned by her looks: young, refreshed, her face having shed ten years on the journey.

"I should have kept going," I say when she reaches me, open-mouthed on the sidewalk. "I shouldn't have stopped until I got to China."

"They won't follow us," she says of my brothers. "They don't have a car and I didn't leave a note."

"They're too drunk to find the city limits anyway."

"They're good boys, deep down."

"*Good!*" I spit out.

"They're human beings, is what I meant. And I do sometimes enjoy them. You have to admit, they're great raconteurs."

"They're professional liars, is what they are. And they're a lot less trouble when they're in jail."

"I'm sorry," she says with a smile of helplessness, bewilderment, "I'm sorry for all the mistakes I made."

My brothers had been drunk too frequently in the hallways of her apartment building, they'd thrown up once too often in the stairwell. No longer could my mother withstand the approbation of her neighbours. When she'd tried locking her door, my brothers just kicked it in. I restrain myself from saying, *I told you so. I told you not to give them your new address.* Now, finally, she tells me, she has crossed the Rubicon. In her hand hangs an old suitcase from her youth, made of plaid cardboard with brass clips on the corners and a handle carved from polished whalebone. She has become a strangely elegant woman, the mother I've desired all my life, willowy and hair gone gray. Her clothes, worn out but clean, have a surprising dignity to them. Her dress, printed in a delicate pattern of grey, pink, raspberry, is one I remember from my adolescence. Time and again, she wore it to sit in court and listen to the testimony of victims of my brothers' crimes. Like an old wedding dress, it has gently yellowed.

Now, who should come ambling along, content, puffed up, as though Monument was the whole world, but Hap? I introduce my mother and Hap says it's a good thing she came, she could probably teach me something about life in a small town.

My mother blushes. "Oh, my goodness," she says, one hand, in a crocheted glove, fluttering at her face. "I don't know about that."

I raise my eyebrows at Hap. In the shadow of his deep-brimmed hat, his face is unreadable. He and my mother smile at each other with a strange recognition. They are, after all, contemporaries. With only half a decade on him, she could be his older sister. I stand beside them, feeling excluded. I tell Hap that my mother has no place to stay. He says he has something for her and that he won't charge her a dime. She begins to protest.

"Let him if he wants to, Mom," I tell her.

I would not canonize him for giving her the house it turns out he's speaking of, possibly the ugliest in the town, clad in phoney brick pulled off a shingle roll. But my mother has never lived in a house. She reveres it like a temple. She loves every ceiling crack and paint bubble. Sitting at the kitchen table in the mornings, she writes letters to her jailbird sons. At the post office, she pushes thick envelopes across the counter to me, addressed to the prison in her stenographer's handwriting, lovely loops and spheres. I take a felt marker and black out her return address. I pick the envelopes up experimentally, trying to weigh the words in my hand. What could they contain, I wonder? What does she tell her sons about her life here, which, though simple, seems to be rich in ways that I cannot grasp? Looking over my shoulder, she spots the kettle on the corner of my desk. I read the question in her mind. Would I go so far as to steam her letters open and read them? I remind her that it is a criminal offence to tamper with the mail and that I am not cut from the same cloth as her sons.

Sometimes, if she reaches the post office around noon, I lock up for an hour and walk with her to the grocery store. I drop avocados, date squares, cream puffs into her cart, hoping to fatten her up. She looks at me, quizzical and patient, her eyes saying: I've always been thin. Why do you wish I were different? Who is it you want me to be?

One of her sons went to prison for beating up his best friend, breaking his jaw in eight places. The doctor said he'd never seen such severe damage except from a car accident. My mother used to go to the prison weekly. With the other women waiting for visiting hours to begin, she stood outside the massive green copper penitentiary door with the great decorative rosettes in its recesses. The other women had brittle bleached hair and wore tight revealing clothes. My mother was convinced they were all hookers. After some years of these pilgrimages, she began to find that the big security door crashing down behind her gave her bones a cancerous ache. One day something snapped. She walked out of the prison, slid her sunglasses on, caught the intercity bus home and never returned. Such are the small wonders, the petty salvations of life. One day you discover that you can no longer carry on with something you've told yourself all along didn't trouble you in the least.

About the same time, she stopped going weekly to put flowers on my father's grave. The ritual was paralyzing her, she said. My father, Birdis Taylor, died at the asphalt works three days from retirement. He fell into a hopper, a twelve-metre-deep funnel used to store gravel, and got wedged in the spout at the bottom. Paramedics were lowered by rope and harness to begin resuscitation efforts. He'd suffered a severe head injury and was pronounced dead on the scene. It took an hour to pry him loose from the narrow passage. It was thought that he was knocked into the hopper by a piece of moving machinery swinging around, oh so slowly, to strike him in the head. Who could this surprise, my father being by nature distracted, an escapist, a dreamer? His demise seems to have released my mother. She will not spend the rest of her life with a small, sad, interior man who seemed powerless to direct his life.

"All he ever wanted," she told me after the funeral, "was to sit in a boat with a fishing rod."

Now my mother has become a reader, so distracted by literature that she seems to have forgotten about me. I will go along to her house after work, thinking that we could enjoy a meal together, but she will not be home. Retracing my steps, I notice her over at the river, seated on the bank, her fine head bent to a book, her shoulders tense with concentration. There were rivers galore back in the city but she claims she never noticed them. Humbler by comparison, a mere creek, this one, she says, is life-giving. Crossing the lumpy grass, passing a local artist at his easel painting the water, the locks, a scene you see over and over in the shops here, I say to my mother, "How about supper?" For a moment I am filled with hope. It is on the tip of my tongue to spill the beans about Hap and me. She pats the canvas bag at her knee and says, "I've got a cheese sandwich here. I suppose we could share it. But do you have a book to read?"

"Never mind," I say. "It's alright. I'm tired. I should go home."

"Yes, go home. Go home and rest."

At the back of the narrow post office space, my desk is pushed against a window. When business is slow, I sit there and browse through magazines subscribed to by people in Monument. I can look out across a shimmering strip of park, at the white pleasure boats rising into view or dropping magically from sight in the lock. The lockmaster is there, in his baggy khaki shorts, his green shirt with its patch pockets, his thick wool socks and heavy boots. Sometimes he looks over at me and waves but I don't acknowledge him. He bends and straightens, bends and straightens, cranking the rusty iron wheel that operates the locks. The sound of the heavy chain clanking over the pulley wheel carries across the grass to me. One day, absorbed in a magazine, I am startled by a light tapping on my window. I look up and see him, gesturing for me to raise the sash. I get up reluctantly and do so.

"If you ever want a tour of the museum, I'd be happy to oblige," he says. He would be forty, forty-five years old. Not an attractive man: a big misshapen nose, a broad slack mouth, pockmarked cheeks, a chiselled chin. His bare, boney knees are like chips of flint.

"I'll keep that in mind," I say unenthusiastically. I can read his name, stitched in gaudy red letters on his chest: *Sherwood*. He says, "Is that your mother I see you with sometimes? She's beautiful, isn't she? You look a bit like her." I scowl and push the window down. Wait until I am Mrs. Hap Monument, I think. Then the likes of him will have to scrape and bow, won't they?

I say to Hap, "I haven't seen you much. Why don't I see you?"

"Delia's around. The trade fairs aren't until the fall. You know that," he answers.

"Why don't we come out here anymore?"

"We're here, aren't we?"

"Not that often. Not as often as last summer."

"It's too hot out here for your shenanigans."

"Some day I'm going to walk in that front door," I tell him.

"Yes, you are," he agrees.

"Instead of sneaking round the back at night like a prostitute."

"You're no prostitute," he says. He lifts my hand, kisses the palm, smells the materials of the post office on it.

"Brown wrapping paper," he says, just to exasperate me. "Mucilage. Stamp pad ink." He touches my fingers where they are raw from the friction of binder twine.

"Some day I'm going to be the mayor's wife," I declare. I picture myself decorating his Packard for the annual town parade with streamers, balloons, flowers fashioned from Kleenex. I dream of being able to boss Mrs. Churcher around. "Then all of this will be mine," I gesture at the thin wood in which we are sheltered, at the fields shimmering magically beyond it. To the north and south of town, Hap owns acreage, fields and woods, hills and valleys, lakes even, I don't know what-all. Out into this territory he's spun us, one finger commanding the steering wheel, north, across the river. Soon, the land climbing up into wilder country, forests and twisting roads. Finally we entered a dusty opening, some tractor path, bouncing through ruts until we slid into this fragile stand of birch.

Turning in the car, I take his fat face in my hands. He has removed his brown fedora and parked it on the dashboard. He eases loose the knot of his pink polka dot tie.

"You never take anything seriously," I tell him, turning his head in my hands so that he is forced to look at me.

"No, I don't."

"You just agree with everything I say."

"Yes, I do." His eyes are a transparent blue, lucid as the sky.

"When was it you said you were going to tell her?"

"As soon as her business gets over this slump." I wonder if he is worried about the family money being torn away from him through divorce, ripped right out of this town.

"What if it never does?"

"Now, that is the question of a pessimist."

"I'm tired of waiting."

"Patience is a virtue."

"Don't lecture me," I say playfully. "I'm not your daughter."

"You could be," he grins. I am thirty-five, he is sixty.

Hap presses a button and the windows slide down. The dry heat, the powdery smell of tinder woods in July, pour into the car. The sun flashes off the long hood of the Cadillac. Overhead, leaves lift and turn and rustle in the soft wind. A dappled light floats and shifts over us as though we are under water. The leather seats grow hot, the backs of my thighs run with sweat. Hap opens his door and climbs out, the airy blanket of last autumn's brittle leaves sighing beneath his feet like an oracle. He slips out of his jacket, folds it, drapes it across the driver's seat with a self-parodying flourish. He opens the back door. I clamber easily between the seats to join him there, reach out my arms. One after the other, he removes my garments, flings them over his shoulder in mockery of something, maybe of himself. Sunlight, falling through the trees, through the car's rear window, flickers over our skin, as though we are scattered with gold coins. Hap applies himself to me in a cordial, efficacious way, as if sex is not too important, but not to be lived without, either. We hear the hiss of a car flying past on the nearby road, we are serenaded by the chorus of birds. All around, birch glimmer in the motley light, black seams and wounds velvety on the bone-white bark.

Later, in the front seat, Hap blots his face and neck with a fine handkerchief starched and ironed by Mrs. Churcher. The smell of his Old Spice blooms powerfully in the car. Slipping the noose of his tie over his head, he slides the knot up against his fleshy throat. Over his shoulder I can make out the soft outlines of the town, the silver church spire, the flag fluttering from the gatehouse museum, the four massive chimneys of the Monument ancestral home.

"Why don't we build a place right here on this spot?" I ask him. "Let her have that old heap of stone."

He reaches out and messes my hair. "You're a funny one," he says.

"I can give you a houseful of kids."

"I'm too selfish and happy to want them."

"You need children to carry on your name and run this town. Who's going to be the next mayor? Aren't you worried about that?"

"I'll think of something." He turns the key in the ignition. "I need to get back to town."

"What for?" I ask but he only looks at me with fake injury. He took on the mantle of mayor when he was just twenty-two. He can do the job in his sleep.

A hot night in August. To escape the stifling rooms of my house, I slip out into the evening where the cooler air lifts the hairs on my arms, fans the nape of my neck. It is nearly September. By eight o'clock it is getting dark. Passing Delia's shop, I see a sign posted on the door. I go up the porch steps to read it. *Closed due to family emergency.* Just then, her assistant emerges from the dusk, pushing his bicycle round the corner of the building. He explains, "Her mother died. She had to go to the Maritimes. She'll be back next week." A chill goes through me. If Delia is away, why has Hap not invited me to come over to the house? I head back toward his place, asking myself what it is

I might have done to cause his feelings for me to cool. Because they have, haven't they? I am forced to admit this for the first time. Whatever it is, I think, I will reform. I will make amends. I will twine him once more round my little finger.

When I reach his house, I see the entire first floor ablaze with lights. Throwing caution to the wind, I cross the front lawn and slip round the back, where I find the door, as usual, unlocked. Inside, the smell of cooking. On the kitchen counter, a roast of beef gleaming on its platter. A woman's laughter, light and musical as a wind chime. In the dining room, I find my mother seated at the table in a dressing gown I recognize to be Delia's, pale blue satin with a lime-green trim. Behind her stands Hap, bending over to kiss the top of her head. He is wearing a pair of beautiful twill trousers and a brilliant white shirt unbuttoned to the waist, revealing his fleshy chest and stomach.

The room is brilliant with flickering candlelight. On the table, a bottle of champagne glistens with condensation. From the stereo comes old-time dance music. Jimmy Dorsey. The two of them turn simultaneously to look at me, Hap's hands still pressed to my mother's face, his fat fingers splayed across her cheeks. My mother's expression is one of confusion. What am I doing there, she is wondering? She is impossibly radiant, a woman I never knew existed. Perhaps I noticed this change in her before, but thought it was the effects of the river air, of the novels of Hemingway and Steinbeck. But no. I note that she is not so bony now, she has filled out in a sensual way, her collar bones, her neck and jaw softened. Her skin glows, her cheeks are pink, her hair shines. Behind her, Hap has straightened up, erect and dignified. In the candlelight, his lips are soft and red, his face both remorseless and relieved, as though, a coward at heart, a man who never speaks the truth until he has to, he knew it was only a matter of time before I found them there.

I want to say to him: it was *you* who came looking for *me*, not the other way around and I picture the first time he dropped in at the post office, tipping his fedora at me and bowing like a nineteenth-century gentleman, saying, "Welcome to Monument. I hope you stay. Most people do. There's no place like it." And then in the following weeks, coming in every single day, a man who'd grown up having his nose wiped and his shoes polished by servants and who had probably never mailed a letter in his life, now suddenly finding a need to deliver the town hall's outgoing correspondence to the post office in person.

Out on the sidewalk, I sink down on my knees, my face buried in my hands, my forehead pressed to the ground. Who should find me in such a compromised posture but Sherwood, suddenly beside me, firmly drawing me up by the shoulders, saying, "What's going on? What's happened to you?" Back to my house he guides me. He says, "Will you be alright alone? Would you like me to stay? I mean, I could just sit here in this chair and make sure you get through the night. I'm not a person who requires much sleep."

Me, he had to hide from Delia, but my mother Hap wastes no time bringing to his wife's attention. The very next week, the glass shop closes. Delia's showcases and tools are loaded into a truck. A sign reading: *MOVED: Come and see me in Nova Scotia* goes up on the door. From my window, I see a white panel truck lumbering along the street, weighed down with her kilns,

Delia gripping the wheel, her sharp brown profile floating in the driver's window. Hap had once said to me: she is a woman who knows how to cut her losses.

Word soon travels round that Hap and my mother are to be married. The ceremony will take place at the Baldachin Hotel. All of Monument is invited. "Are you going?" I ask Sherwood. The newspaper write-up mentions the original fir wood floors of the hotel banquet room, the five-foot-thick stone walls, the Venetian crystal chandelier weighing three tons. For a honeymoon, they fly off to some place called Anguilla. When they return, Hap seems to me to have more dignity. He is not so self-mocking, not such a caricature. He appears more at peace with himself. Evidently, his contentment as mayor of Monument was all a facade, a duty thing. He plans to make this his last term in office. He and my mother intend to travel. They will spend the winters in Mexico, Argentina, New Zealand. As for all Hap's sleeping around, the populace of Monument doesn't bat an eye. He could commit homicide one day and, the next, they'd call him a saint.

Sherwood follows me out into the country, where I go in the evenings to walk on the dirt roads. He must be watching for me, because he is not far behind.

I say to him, "I don't believe she didn't know I was with him."

"How could she?"

"You knew. Everybody in town knew, it now turns out. Why wouldn't *she*?"

"She's not given to gossip. She kept to herself." In the dying light Sherwood's face is pitted like the crust of the moon.

"She could see I was happy about something," I say. "It would have to be a man."

"Maybe she thought you wanted to keep your secrets."

"He made a laughingstock out of us."

"Your mother's holding her head high. Why can't you?"

"She's got that house, that's why she's has her nose up in the air."

But I'm ashamed of what I've said. My mother wouldn't know how to be a snob even if she took a course in it.

"I thought I was going to be somebody in this town," I tell Sherwood.

"You're the best postmistress we've ever had. Isn't that somebody?"

My mouth trembles. Sherwood pulls me to him. His hands have a metallic smell from turning the lock crank. He presses his scarred face to mine. In his apartment above the stone lock house, he makes love to me. I think of his wife who, I've heard, developed a lump on her tongue. The doctors cut it out but the cancer had spread. Her head swelled up, the size of a watermelon, she became so freakish she could not go out in public. Sherwood kept her at home until she died.

It is no palace Sherwood lives in. The bare stone walls sweat in the heat. The birch floors are rough and warped. In a corner stands a cot, behind a flowered curtain. On the open kitchen shelves, the crudest of ironstone dishes form towers. The evening light falls blue on his long lean body, his narrow hips. He asks me to move in, to be his wife. I tell him that I'll give him an answer when I get over Hap.

My mother still sometimes reads beneath the willows on the riverbank. I see her there, bent over her book, but I cannot yet go and speak to her.

"What is it you thought you were going to have and miss the most?" Sherwood asks me. "The big house? Being the mayor's wife? I can't give you those."

"Hap could make me laugh," I say. "He didn't take life seriously." Which is the worst thing I could say because Sherwood doesn't have a funny bone in his body.

I tell Sherwood that I lost my mother twice: once to my brothers and now to Hap.

"Maybe that's not true," he tells me. "It's all in the way you think about things."

In a dream I say to my mother, "Proceed with caution. Hap's a serial adulterer. He's a predator of young women."

"But I'm not young," she answers.

Sherwood asks me, "Why be jealous of others if you have what you want?" Of course, his simplistic questions exasperate me. The smell of the river hangs in his hair, behind his big ears. Under his fingernails collects the red powdery rust from the chains that snake and rattle over the lock wheels. He pulls the roast chicken on his plate apart with his ochre-coloured hands.

In time, I am almost able to walk past the great white house without being aware of it. But, one afternoon late in the fall, I think I hear the voices of my brothers coming from behind it. I see figures resembling them turning cartwheels in the yellowing grass. Mentally stunted adults. Oversleeping now in the high downy beds of the Monument Mansion. Care? Why should I? But naturally I do.

Winter comes and Sherwood goes out in the morning to plough the city parking lots, string Christmas lights across Main Street, shovel the town hall steps. He takes pride and pleasure in these humble tasks. For Christmas, he buys us skates. We climb down a crude wooden ladder he fashioned, a twenty-foot drop to the surface of the frozen river, and glide away over the ice.

Seizing my mitten-clad hand, he searches my face to see if I am happy. "You can't miss what you never had," he says and I try not to wonder if this is true.

Reconciliation

AT THE START OF A BRILLIANT OCTOBER, when it seemed that autumn was a lie and that the trees would stand forever full and green against a summer sky, Joyce Boivin disappeared. Gilles Boivin did not call the police, for his wife had left him a note, which he tore up and then forgot what it had said. Their daughter, Imogene, finding herself unexpectedly alone after school that Monday night, turned on every light in the house at five o'clock. At six, she sat on a stool in the kitchen, found her father's law firm in the yellow pages, and called him. He was so astonished to hear her voice, that she expected him to ask, "Imogene who?" She explained that she had finished her homework, practised her recorder, what should she do next? Mommy wasn't home.

Her father, always rational, asked, "What do you usually do?" It was a question that, in view of the circumstances, seemed irrelevant to Imogene, and shook her confidence in him.

"Well," she answered, her voice, suddenly high and thin, like a soprano reaching for an impossible note, "we usually eat dinner."

"Not to worry," he said, confident. "She's probably stuck in traffic somewhere. Maybe she had car trouble." He was in the middle of a multi-million-dollar deal, he said. He couldn't come home right now, even if he had wanted to. She was to remain calm and to call him back if her mother wasn't home by seven.

Imogene hung up and went upstairs. She sat down at her desk and sorted through her collection of bus transfers, organizing them by colour, putting a rubber band around each bundle. Tiring of this, she observed the second hand labouring jerkily around the face of her wristwatch, and thought of the tiny machinery going round and round inside the watch, of the earth spinning magnificently and imperceptibly beneath her feet, of the stars and planets doing the same, each in its own necessary, dizzying, unstoppable orbit, until she felt motion sickness and had to bend forward and rest her brow on her math scribbler.

That night, on her way to bed, Imogene found her father with a roll of Scotch Tape at the kitchen table, trying to piece her mother's message back together. Having been taught that the voice on the other end of the line, the contents of letters were none of a child's business, she did not ask what it said.

"She says she's searching for something," her father tossed the reconstructed note on the table, disgusted. "I'm not even convinced it's from her. She didn't sign her name. 'Don't worry,' she says." When he looked up at Imogene, as if expecting an explanation, she burst into tears.

"Don't be a goose," he said, jovially, tucking the bed covers up around her chin. "I bet she's home tomorrow." For a month, when he wasn't aware she was looking at him, Imogene's father wore an expression like he was biting down on iron.

The first week of her mother's disappearance, life for Imogene and her father was optimistic, even festive. It was all a dream, from which they would soon awake. Mommy had taken a surprise holiday, wasn't that clever of her? She might have been in the next room: this is Mommy's favourite tie. Mommy likes this television program. Imogene's father made a game out of everything: the last one out of bed in the morning was a dirty rotten egg; the first one dressed got a nickel. They lived in style: for a week, they didn't open the fridge. Each evening, her father arrived home at eight carrying a briefcase full of work and take-out food that sweated through the paper bag. They ate pizza, fried chicken and coleslaw, fish and chips, egg rolls and chop suey, submarine sandwiches.

While Imogene pried the lids off paper containers, setting the food out on two plates, her father tore open her mother's mail.

"She must be on every mailing list in the country," he cried, amazed. He read it all: poring over magazine offers, pro-choice, anti-war, Marxist propaganda. He searched for clues to his wife's motives, while Imogene read a book propped against the milk jug.

Their house was close to downtown on a narrow street parked solidly with cars and lined with trees two centuries old. Every year of Imogene's life, her parents had told themselves they would move; it was not a family neighbourhood. Now, Imogene and her father, stepping out into cool, damp mornings, breathed deeply, in unison, euphoric. At nine years, Imogene, like her father, believed in the surface of things: didn't the sun continue to rise in the east? Weren't the brick houses on their street still standing in their habitual sequence? Didn't the cable cars persist in clattering into the subway station, which they passed on their way to a delicatessen?

For breakfast, Imogene, reading from a plasticized menu, ordered a donut and a coke float. Her father did not notice what she ate, but stared out the window at the pedestrian traffic and drank bitter tea. The aproned man behind the glass counter made a sandwich for Imogene's lunch. On the side of her head, Imogene wore a tam she had found at a garage sale. Waiting on a corner with her for the Number 18, which would take her to a transfer point, her father stared at her. "You look grown up in that hat," he said. The first morning, Imogene's lower lip began to quiver.

"Hey!" her father coaxed, gripping her shoulders. "You're not going to turn to mush on me, are you? Look, if you feel like crying, I want you to say to yourself, 'I'm no cry-baby.'" He nudged her. "Come on, say it now, say it." Imogene shook her head and would not repeat the ridiculous sentence, but she did begin to laugh, nervously, and bit her lip, remembering something her mother had told her: "When you were very little, I used to have to take you into your room and close the door. Your father hated the sound of crying. Imagine having to protect a man from his own child."

One evening, Imogene found her father in her mother's closet, a scotch and soda in one hand, digging into the pockets of her clothes.

"What are you looking for?"

"Evidence."

From her bed, she heard him night after night, talking in low tones on the phone, his voice woolly, incoherent, penetrating her bedroom door, sliding off the curved acoustic walls of her dreams long after he had hung up. He called people who knew him as half of Joyce and Gilles Boivin. Once, either awake or asleep, Imogene thought she made out, "She'll come back on my terms!" her father's voice rising to a shout. On her way to the bathroom at two a.m., she bumped into him groping his way down the dark hallway and watched him fall, fully clothed, into bed.

Imogene woke her father at six-thirty the first Saturday morning. Stumbling to the window, he looked east and saw the trees black and motionless against a pink sunrise. When he turned to Imogene, who stood barefoot in a flannelette nightgown, it dawned on him that he had her on his hands for forty-eight hours. For the first time since Joyce left, he panicked, picked up the phone and called in the reserves. His mother, a woman with a powerful, square body, marched off a plane on Saturday afternoon, wearing the expression of an army sergeant.

"Don't worry," she waved her hand on the drive in from the airport. "I'll get things under control." It was a relief to again have a woman in the house. She headed instinctively for the kitchen and was struck by a front of cold, rancid air when she opened the refrigerator: vegetables and fruit oozed from plastic bags. She shovelled it all into the garbage. She attacked the vacuuming with such fury that Imogene hid in her room; her father escaped downtown to catch up on his work. Before going, he advised his mother in a voice that carried up the stairs, "It's important that everything seem normal." On Sunday afternoon, rain fell against Imogene's window. She sat on her bed, a blanket wrapped around her bare feet. Her grandmother set cookies and a glass of milk on her night table.

"My, aren't you lucky to have such a nice room!"

Imogene looked up from her book and saw, bending to pick up clothes thrown in a corner, a woman who believed she'd never made a mistake. She asked her grandmother when she would be going home.

"I can stay as long as you need me," her grandmother reassured her. Pausing to look down at Imogene, she sighed, "Thank God I'm not young anymore."

When Gilles came home that night, the house was running more smoothly than it ever had when Joyce was in charge. "Mother, you're a wonder," he shook his head, smiling.

"I don't think she ever bleached Imogene's socks," his mother reported. On past visits, Gilles and his mother had always conversed in French, despite the fact that Joyce couldn't understand a word. Now they spoke English, for Imogene's sake. Joyce wasn't mentioned by name all week. Imogene heard only "she this" and "she that," and always in the past tense.

"The last time I was here," Imogene's grandmother reminded her son at dinner, "you said something she objected to. Some inconsequential thing. She ran out in the street and began to beat her head with her fists. You had to drag her back inside. Such a display."

Gilles looked dumbly at his mother, as if he suffered from amnesia. Imogene quietly placed her knife and fork side-by-side on her plate and went to her room. Her father said, "I didn't realize until she left that I loved her fiercely."

"Imogene needs new clothes," his mother, seemingly deaf, said. "Her sleeves are riding up to her elbows, her trousers don't reach her ankles. You'd think a mother would have noticed that."

"If there's another man, that will simplify things," Gilles said.

"I'll cook a roast for dinner tomorrow night," his mother told him.

In the mornings, Imogene's father made an early getaway. Her grandmother asked her daily, "Did you have a good sleep?"

as if this mattered to a child, as if a child could remember. She stood at the stove, in a housecoat, ready to thrust a hot breakfast in front of Imogene. They shopped for clothes after school. Imogene had only to look sideways at something before it was bought for her.

"Why do you walk around with your arms crossed over your chest? Do you think it's time you got a training bra?" her grandmother demanded in the middle of a department store. In recent months, Imogene's breasts had grown from hard nodules, the size of marbles, to something more fleshy and disturbing.

"No," Imogene, wanting nothing more than a brassiere, answered quickly. Now, she was allowed to wear good dresses and leather shoes to school. She came home with them deliberately scuffed, torn, streaked with grass stain and chalk dust. Her grandmother polished, mended, soaked. Her father didn't notice what she wore.

Gilles' mother went home the following weekend. There was no arguing that life had improved since her arrival: the glass tables in the living room shone. Dinner was served sharply at six. Imogene had gained five pounds in a week. But somehow it was all wrong. They were used to the house the way Joyce had kept it; she had been the first to admit she was a slob. Gilles' mother couldn't sit down, her energy exhausted them. Gilles discovered he was almost as frightened of his mother as he had become of Joyce since she had left.

"We have to cope on our own sooner or later," Gilles said to his mother at the airport, an explanation for why she was being sent home early. To Imogene, he confided wryly when he tucked her into bed, "You're the only woman I seem to get along with," making her glow with pride.

Once Imogene's grandmother had gone, the house seemed empty. Between them, Imogene and her father could not occupy more than two rooms. Now, they did not know if it was the grandmother or Joyce whom they missed. But, together, they made progress: they dined at home now, heating up things out of cans, listening to the evening news on the radio while they ate. Gilles, recognizing Joyce in Imogene's habit of heaving massive sighs, snapped, "Where did you learn that?" and Imogene found herself holding her breath.

Each night, Gilles turned on the brass lamp on his desk, unpacked his briefcase, prepared for an evening of work, then sank back in his chair and stared at the black windowpane. The rage that had made his hands shake was replaced now by a weight in the chest that accompanies a belated grief. Lighting the first cigarette he had smoked in years, he walked through every scene of his life with Joyce that he could remember, which were surprisingly few. The ones that came to mind involved transactions: three house purchases evenly spaced over twelve years; buying the cottage up in Halliburton; acquiring an income property. He listened for dialogue, but heard only shouting.

Next door, cross-legged on the floor beside a metal trunk in which she kept souvenirs, Imogene sorted out old photographs, artwork, school notebooks. She read through every story she had written since kindergarten. Laughing, she brought Gilles a bouquet of tulips she had once made for Joyce out of Styrofoam egg cartons and pipe cleaners. That morning, Gilles had received a phone call from Imogene's teacher, who was alarmed at the persistence of Joyce in Imogene's compositions.

"It will be easier if we don't mention your mother anymore," Gilles told Imogene. When she blinked at him, uncomprehending, he explained, "Once we left you and went on a holiday to France. You were a little over one. When we came back, you knew me but you didn't recognize your mother. You screamed when she tried to pick you up. You see, it's possible to forget a person." Then, looking at the wall, he said with surprise, "We fought the whole time we were in France. One day in Paris, your mother got mad and walked away. She spent the whole afternoon sitting on the steps of Sacre Coeur with those — those black peddlers." When Imogene had gone to bed, Gilles picked up the phone. He had begun to look up old male friends; people who hadn't heard from him in years heard from him now.

"I'm a bachelor again," he joked, sick. "Well, a bachelor and a father."

On the third Sunday, Gilles turned the thermostat on the living room wall up to seventy. The smell of dusty metal pipes filled the house. They put on heavy sweaters, and went out, their fingers turning numb in the morning air. Imogene exhaled clouds of white vapour. Now, the puddles in the gutter gleamed with a brittle skin of ice and, yes, the trees would turn red and orange and yellow after all. Imogene associated the crackling of dry leaves underfoot with a period when she and her father began to settle into a comfortable sadness. They cut across an empty schoolyard, walking on grass brittle with frost. At a small hardware store on Bloor Street, Gilles purchased a new lock for the front door. That afternoon, he carted Joyce's clothes across the hall to the spare bedroom. "Some of these dresses I never saw on her," he told Imogene, then heard Joyce's voice, "You never looked." Moving her clothes out left him strangely shaken, as if, in handling the tweeds and silks, the very texture of her skin had rubbed off on his hands. He crushed the collar of a blouse against his face. The smell of her perfume, mingled with perspiration, was more familiar than ever. Breathing it in, he continued to believe that Joyce did not have another man.

They celebrated Imogene's tenth birthday on October twenty-fifth. She did not want a party this year; she said she was too old. Solemn, her hands clasped, in a small restaurant where pink napkins blossomed from stemmed glassware, she had no idea what she had ordered, but knew only that it sounded adult and foreign. When dessert arrived, Gilles handed her a small velvet box containing a pearl on a gold chain. She forced a smile.

"You thought your mother would call today, didn't you?" Gilles guessed.

"No," Imogene stared sternly out the window, blinking. "No."

So, for a month, Imogene had not known if she had a mother or not. Finally, when her father bought her an orange cat, she understood that Joyce wasn't coming back. Imogene picked up the cat and weighed it in her hand, thoughtful, watching her father's face.

The sound of Joyce's voice on the phone that night was as familiar as the sound of Gilles' own blood rushing past his ears. He realized that she had been speaking inside his head for weeks, in disconnected fragments of salvaged dialogue. A month had not prepared him for what she had to say. Imogene, pressing her thumbs into the springy grey pads of her cat's paws, saw her father's jaw lock, his chest begin to heave, his hand grip the kitchen counter.

Gilles shouted into the phone, "You never said you weren't happy!" Then, hearing the dial tone, he slammed the receiver down, smashing his fingers.

At school, Imogene's friend, Martha, whose mother had remarried and whose father was "working on his third wife," explained to Imogene, "She'll ask for custody."

"What's that?"

"The mother always wants the kid."

In the middle of November, Imogene was told she would spend the weekend with her mother and her mother's lover. At least, that was what she and Martha, snickering, called him. Lover-boy. Imogene went to her mother by temporary court order; that much she was told. Her father drove her across town on Friday after school to a neighbourhood neither of them had ever been in, where the streets were narrow, steep and slippery from a sudden, freak snowfall.

"It was my turn to bring you breakfast in bed tomorrow," Imogene said. Clinging suddenly to the makeshift life she and her father had fashioned for themselves, she bit her nails.

"I'll take good care of the cat," her father promised. He parked the car, and took her hand. "I want you to ask your mother to come back home." When Imogene's face fell, he said, "No, listen to me. Sure we're getting along fine, you and me. But three is still a better number, isn't it? We could be a family again." Imogene, confused, betrayed, was not sure what she wanted.

Lover-boy knocked Imogene's father down in the snow that afternoon. Her mother, seeing the car pull up, had come out of the house and down the porch steps. Gilles followed Imogene, carrying her suitcase up the snowy walk. Then they saw a stranger, a man with an insolent face, step out on the porch. Joyce, sensing his appearance, did not look behind her, but froze on the bottom step, her hand half way to her mouth. Gilles sized the stranger up briefly. Turning to Joyce, he said, "You whore," and was satisfied by her unhappy smile that he still had the power to hurt, if not to surprise, his wife. A moment later, he lay stunned in the snow, blood trickling from his nose onto his white shirt. Imogene stood gaping.

"Go into the house," her mother ordered her, but they both knew she had relinquished her authority over Imogene. That night, in a dream, Imogene saw her father's blood — quarts of it spilled in the snow bank, making a trail leading back to his car.

In Imogene's mind, the fistfight, the blood and words like *whore* went together with her mother's new life. Later, she would realize that Joyce was not, of course, a whore, but had moved in with a younger man who had lived with a series of women. Together, they rented a white house the size of a cottage. A screened porch ran across the front of the house and this was where Joyce had dumped the few belongings she had brought with her. That weekend, Imogene saw her mother's familiar things — a pair of purple suede boots, a portable typewriter, a suitcase with the initials J.B. disappear under snow drifting in through the screens.

In the kitchen, Joyce rebuked her lover. "I told you to stay inside." He looked away, scowling. His name was Luke. Imogene immediately saw that he was no man: he was a decade younger than Joyce. Observing his transparent skin, his soft sullen mouth, she did not see how he added up to her and her father.

Joyce laughed bitterly, her head in her hands. "Oh, we never argued about anything important. Only sex and money. You know," she said to Luke, throwing her head back, "when I saw him get out of the car, I couldn't believe he'd once been my husband." Seeing her mother's glazed smile, her bright watery eyes, Imogene wondered why it had ever come as such a surprise to either her or her father when Joyce disappeared. For years, it seemed, Joyce had hung, like a cliff-dweller, between sanity and madness. Finally, she had chosen the course of sanity, but this was something that, at ten, Imogene could not forgive.

"You're wearing a man's sweater," Imogene told her. Her mother was big-limbed, awkward, flat-footed. Gilles had always heaped scorn on these traits. Now, Imogene saw grudgingly that her mother could be herself.

"So I am," Joyce looked down at herself. "I could never wear your father's clothes. His shoulders were too narrow." The shapeless grey pullover, the corduroy pants, a pair of soiled sneakers made Imogene's mother more graceless than ever. She was a meaty woman; she could have knocked down most men. Meeting Imogene's critical gaze, she smiled, shrugged, self-consciously pushed her unkempt hair back, nervous as a girl on a first date. "You've got plump. You've ruined your good shoes," she said, as though in retaliation, then bit her lip.

"I'm allowed to wear whatever I want now," Imogene said.

Joyce took her into a small, dark room at the back of the house, barely large enough to hold a single bed and a kitchen chair. A table lamp stood on the floor, throwing a strange cone of light on the ceiling and casting unexpected shadows around Joyce's eyes.

"I want you to feel at home here," Joyce said, setting the suit-case on the chair. "I'll put curtains on the window as soon as I can afford to. This reminds me of my room when I was a girl." Imogene noticed a gift-wrapped box on the bed. "I didn't call on your birthday because I thought it would upset you," Joyce explained. "I didn't want to spoil your day." Imogene looked straight at her mother as if to say: Don't lie to me. I don't believe your stories anymore.

Joyce went into the kitchen while Imogene unpacked her suitcase, hanging her clothes on wire hangers in a narrow closet.

"Poor Imogene," she heard her mother say to Luke. "She's too young to understand and too old to ask why."

For dinner, they ate soup and toast. "I always was a rotten cook," Joyce said in a celebratory tone. As if Imogene could forget. Luke seemed satisfied with the meal, or perhaps he did not notice what he ate. He read a book at the table. He was writing a doctoral thesis on a Canadian poet. Imogene glared at him. "It's rude to read at dinner," she said. Luke looked up, carefully marked his place in his book and put it down beside his bowl, folding his arms.

"Alright," he challenged her. "Say something interesting." Imogene looked down, confused. "These plates are plastic," she said.

Joyce laughed. "Now, I'm not tempted to break dishes anymore when I get mad."

After dinner, Joyce introduced Imogene to Luke's plants, which occupied half of the narrow living room. They were called Donna, Alice, Joanne, Katherine and Phoebe, after his assorted former roommates who had made presents of them. Luke crept about with a pitcher of water, talking softly to their leaves, then returned to the kitchen, which had the only light bright enough by which to read. Joyce sank to the bare living room floor holding a coffee mug, though there was serviceable furniture in the room. Imogene sat stiffly on the coach.

"How are you and Daddy doing?" Joyce asked.

Longing suddenly for her imperfect life with her father, Imogene's first instinct was to close ranks. She met her mother's gaze, unblinking. "Daddy doesn't yell at me," she said.

Joyce's face reddened, as though slapped. Then she recovered. "I'm glad. Daddy knows how to cope. He has a gift for bouncing back. But — you mustn't let him become bitter."

"If you cared about how he felt, you wouldn't have left," said Imogene. Then she repeated something she had heard so many times the words seemed hollow. "He wants me to be happy."

Joyce said, "You have to understand that there's nothing wrong with Daddy. It's just that Luke is more right for me."

"You never said anything nice about him when you lived at home," Imogene rebuked her mother.

Joyce sighed. "Be fair," she said.

"I have some homework I have to do," Imogene said, and retreated to her little room. At eight o'clock, Joyce brought Imogene a cup of hot chocolate. Propped in bed against her pillows, Imogene glanced up warily, looking, Joyce thought, like an innocent prisoner in a Spartan cell. Joyce picked up a scribbler from the bed.

"Is this your handwriting?" she asked.

"Of course it's mine," Imogene snapped. "Whose did you think it would be?"

"It just looks so mature," Joyce said, defensive, then began to read the page.

"That's private." Imogene snatched it.

When Joyce and Luke got up at nine on Saturday, they found Imogene fully dressed, sitting on the edge of her made-up bed, washed in the pale winter light.

"You've developed some good habits lately." Joyce peered at Imogene. "What are these scratches?" she asked, touching her arm.

"I have a cat now."

They would go to the zoo, the first of many outings planned for these weekends, for Joyce wanted the word mother to equal "fun." Luke came along under duress.

"You have to get to know her. Be tolerant."

They tramped through snow to Luke's old Buick. Indicating their tracks, Imogene said, "Daddy says people who don't shovel their walks are good-for-nothing."

Joyce sighed. "Daddy has a lot of middle-class values." She and Imogene stood in snow while Luke tried to start the car. Finally, when it roared into life, steam pouring from the hood, he rolled down the window. "She won't last all winter," he warned Joyce.

"Well, maybe we'll get lucky," she said. Imogene had overheard them talking about the possibility of Joyce taking the Volvo while Gilles kept the house. Joyce wasn't ready to fight for her share. She didn't want that materialistic clap-trap. Also, she could not pay a lawyer.

"Don't let him rip you off," advised Luke.

Joyce laughed, opening the car door. "You sound like my family. Except for the French Canadian part, they thought I married well."

Imogene got in the back seat.

"You could sit up here with us," Joyce told her.

"No, it's too crowded."

Luke raised an eyebrow at Joyce, then pulled away from the curb. They sped across the city on the freeway. When they passed the exit that would have taken her home to Albany Street, Imogene, looking out her window, said, "You're not really my mother anymore. You're more like an aunt."

Luke reached and turned up the volume on the radio.

The zoo was deserted. They watched blue-winged ducks walk, as if by some seasonal magic, on the surface of a frozen pond.

"I'm cold," Imogene complained.

"Why didn't you wear your hat, like your mother told you to?" Luke demanded. Joyce frowned at him. In the mammal pavilion, Luke sat on a bench and pulled a book from his pocket. Joyce and Imogene stood at a window and watched the polar bears swimming. Diving into the water from above, the bears swam toward the window, their noses grazing the glass. Then they rose to the surface. From below, Imogene and her mother saw the bears' magnificent paws treading effortlessly in a dream-like slow motion.

"It's amazing, really. Isn't it amazing?" Joyce asked and Imogene shrugged. Joyce was trying to photograph the bears underwater, waiting for one to come close to the window. Luke had given her a camera. When Imogene saw it hanging around her neck, her mind said *ridiculous*. Her mother had always been hopeless with anything mechanical. The photographs she had shown Imogene the night before all looked like they had been taken at dusk or at high noon with the aperture pointed at the sun.

"Take a look," Joyce offered the camera. Imogene shook her head, though she was tempted to peer through the viewfinder at a world that, to her mother, was suddenly fresh and original. They walked out of the building into the wan light and thin silent air that Imogene associated with Sundays at the zoo. Joyce said that maybe this was the last place she should have brought Imogene. It reminded them too much of their visits here when Imogene was a child. Imogene said nothing.

They were the only people in the cafeteria. Joyce bought them hamburgers, counting the money out carefully for the cashier. Imogene insisted on French fries as well. They sat at a small arborite table at a window. Outside, flamingos walked on stick legs over frozen ground.

"Why did you buy her those fries?" Luke, sitting across from Joyce, demanded.

"She wanted them," Joyce shrugged.

"But what about her weight?"

"She hasn't had a good day."

"It looks to me like she never has a good day."

"How would you know?" said Imogene, her mouth full. "You're not my father. You're not anybody."

Luke's lips tightened. "Little bitch," he said. Joyce reached across the table and slapped his face, then stared at him, dismayed. Imogene looked from her mother to Luke. Blinking for a moment in confusion, Luke shot up from his chair, knocking it over. He threw down his napkin.

"Good riddance," said Imogene when Luke had stamped outside. After they'd eaten, Joyce gathered up the empty cups and papers. "Come on, let's go home," she said, tired.

"To Albany Street?"

"You know what I meant."

Luke got out of the car at the university to do some research. Joyce took the wheel.

"When will you come home?" she asked him.

"Maybe I'll sleep here," he threatened. Imogene climbed over the seat to join her mother in front.

"What's your play about?" she said. Joyce seemed pleased with the question.

"It's about a girl. Yes, a girl your age."

"You could write a play just as well living with Daddy and me."

"Well, no I couldn't. Daddy never saw the importance of what I was doing. He's a right brain person and I'm a left brain. You'll understand some day."

"You know, you shouldn't feel you have to take sides," Joyce told her now. But Imogene had never really cared why Joyce had left Gilles. What she wanted, without knowing it, was to understand why her mother had left her behind as well. Now, she felt not bewilderment, but an anger that choked her. She turned to Joyce.

"You only think of yourself. You never cared about me. Everything has always been for you, you, you!" Her face was thrust in her mother's. Joyce, one eye on the traffic, grabbed Imogene by the hair, shaking her. Imogene's forehead struck the dashboard.

"Child abuse, child abuse!" Imogene shrieked. "I'll call the children's aid! I know the number!" Joyce pulled the car onto the shoulder, still holding Imogene. They glared at each other, seething, their faces inches apart, each recognizing both themselves and each other, both enemy and stranger, a mother and a daughter they had been looking for since Friday night.

"Calm down, breathe deeply," Joyce told Imogene, her own hands shaking. Finally she released her. "I don't expect you to understand." Hearing this, Imogene felt a huge relief and cried in her hands.

"Winter is retreating," Joyce announced, looking out the window at rain on Sunday. All afternoon, Luke and Imogene had sat in a wash of light at the kitchen table. For Joyce's sake, Luke was trying harder. He was teaching Imogene to play chess.

"She's no dummy," he told Joyce, and Imogene grinned. Gilles was to fetch her at four. Joyce watched her pack her bag.

"Aren't you taking this?" she asked, picking up the gift, still wrapped.

"No," Imogene looked at her evenly.

"You've toughened up, haven't you? Well, I guess this was really bought for another girl." Joyce pushed it to the back of the closet shelf. For the first time Imogene felt curiosity about the package, wondering what it might reveal about her past self. However, she resisted the urge to open it.

When Gilles pulled up in front of the house, Joyce told Luke, "Don't show your face." Imogene looked out the front door at her father, the cat on his lap, and said, confused, "I want to live here with you."

"Well, that's something we can talk about," Joyce told her.

But Imogene, carried away in the car, saw through the rain-streaked window a large awkward woman on the porch, waving, resolutely solitary.

A Penny to Save

MY EARLIEST MEMORY OF MY FATHER takes place on a spring evening. We are sitting, the five of us, in the kitchen and we have just finished eating supper. There is a queer feeling in the room: a natural disappointment, perhaps, in the ordinary events of the day, an inertia, a listlessness as we face the evening hours. We may always feel this way but tonight it seems all the more acute because it is spring and we are amazed by the softness of the evening, the sky's prolonged luminosity, the daylight so plentiful after months of winter dark. The bright hours ahead seem an astonishing, an undeserved gift, a dream too fragile to enter.

This is the moment at which my father chooses to reach and lift me from behind the kitchen table, placing me on his knee. He begins a familiar ritual devised to bridge the gap between afternoon and evening, an entertainment to carry us into the night. I am very young, five years old. I feel the strength of my father's arms drawing me effortlessly off the bench, the stability of his thighs rising to meet me, solid as the earth. He grasps the band of my trousers and pulls it down, exposing my soft belly. Taking his knife, he scoops up a gob of butter and brings it toward me, threatening to smear it over my naked stomach. To buck and squirm and endeavour to escape would simply thrust my belly into the glistening fat. I can only retreat, my back driven against my father's chest, my stomach contracting each time the knife makes a pass. And yet, I am content to do this, to be locked within my father's powerful embrace, to experience the heat of his body, his skin next to mine, to feel his adult heart beating against my back, to smell the beer on his breath. Wheezing, snickering, squealing with excitement, dismay, I look down at the comedy of my stomach going in and out, like a bellows. Appalled by the sight of my own pale, soft flesh, I am also pleased to be the centre of attention, as the knife approaches, halting always within an inch of my belly.

My father had never played the buttering game in front of company, but one April evening, there at the supper table sat his friend, E.P. Sloane, roaring at the sight of it, tears of enjoyment leaking from his eyes. E.P. Sloane and my father had grown up together in Saskatchewan, lost track of each other during the war, somehow hooked up, now that they had families, here in Ontario, two thousand miles from their birthplace.

E.P. Sloane and my father had come in that afternoon around four o'clock, smelling once more of the country, of foreign roads and rural environments. They stood in the kitchen, bulky in the narrow space between table and fridge, looking like hobos in their dark clothes. E.P. stood six feet tall, but there was something spoiled, self-indulgent, soft about his body, something unclean, though it was clear that he bathed, was vain about his long fingernails and his strawberry blonde hair glistening with cream. My father said expectantly to my mother, "We've brought home supper."

My mother, who'd been rolling out pastry with a powerful thrust of her arms, laid down her rolling pin and wiped her hands on her apron. The table was dusted with flour, the floor beneath her feet slippery with it. Peel, pared from each apple in one unbroken spiral, lay like a nest of ribbons before her. So did the lid of a pie, a near-perfect circle, ready to be placed upon the fruit-filled shell, sealed using water applied with a fingertip, pinched around the perimeter between thumb and finger to produce a decoration like a rope. These were her materials: dough, flour, fruit, water.

E. P. Sloane and my father held out, for my mother to see, two buckets glistening with small fish, their bodies, beautifully draped one upon the other, dense and silvery as a pail of mercury.

"Ugh!" my mother grunted impatiently.

E. P. and my father lingered restlessly in the kitchen, their faces burnished, fresh air still filling their lungs, the stink of fish on their hands, the cuffs of their pants still wet and smelling of river, surely not the local stream, shallow and muddy, where we often swam, but some shining channel, some distant and mythical waterway silver with schools of flashing fish.

"Smelts!" said my mother with disgust.

My father was crestfallen, perhaps because of the radiance of the fish, their firm resilient bodies, their plenitude, the satisfying burden of them in the pail. Already he could imagine the weight of a bellyful of them, the contentment after dinner.

"These are good fish," he protested. "Tender and tasty."

"They'll be the devil to clean. If you expect me to do it, you've got another think coming," said my mother.

"What the hell! We bring home the grub and we have to prepare it too?"

"I've got my hands full with my own work."

"Alright, then. Alright, we'll clean 'em," said my father defiantly.

My father and E.P. carried the fish to the cellar, their boots loud on the wooden stairs. I followed.

E.P. and my father pulled out long sharp knives, dipped into the pails, brought forth victims, slit their bellies. The flesh fell open, clean, tender wounds. E.P. Sloane waggled a fish in my direction, laughed when I jumped back. He squeezed it, so that it shot out of his hand, struck my face. I felt the cold, the slime. E.P. guffawed.

"What's the matter? You squeamish? You scared of a little dead fish?"

My father carried the gutted fish up to the kitchen. "There you go. Clean as a whistle," he told my mother, his voice conciliatory, proud, but nothing they did could please her. She refused to smile. She brought out two cast-iron frying pans, cracked them onto the stove, turned the fish in the spitting fat, though she seemed to take no pleasure in it. She flipped the bodies. They were fleshy. They were meaty. They grew firmer, they stiffened up. Their skins darkened, turned crisp. They sang like a choir in the bubbling, sizzling butter.

Though not invited, E.P. sat down at our table every night for supper, "as though it was his God-given right," my mother complained under her breath. I welcomed his presence because it unsettled her: the danger of impropriety, a skilful belch, perhaps, an off-colour joke, references to *Jews, Bohunks, niggers,* threats to the rules of etiquette, propelling of food onto the fork with the ball of the thumb, licking of knives, all put her on her guard.

"Have you looked for work at all?" my mother asked E.P. and my father.

"Oh, we been looking."

"Where? Where have you been looking? Where do you go every day? What do you do?" she asked, exasperated, though she could see from the dust on the car that they'd been out in the country again, they'd crossed county lines. All the reforms she believed she'd wrought in my father were in danger of sliding backward, all she thought she'd achieved by getting him off the prairie, transplanting him to Ontario, where there were to be found a kinder terrain, forests to buffer the elements, windless hollows, a nature less bent on destruction, proper towns, civilized populations, table manners.

"Oh, we got plenty of irons in the fire," said my father and E.P., smirking at each other. It seemed they couldn't take their lives in the East seriously anymore. They did not expect their exile from the prairie to last. The camaraderie between them, united as they were in their longing for the West, in memories of their youthful crimes, shut my mother out.

"You were drinking down there again, weren't you?" she demanded, and indeed, during the fish cleaning, E.P. had slipped a case of beer in to my father through the cellar window.

"Oh, we only had one or two."

"I'd love to know where you get the money for it."

On a platter that night at supper lay a slew of leftover fish, more than we could eat in one meal, the only abundance I ever remember in that house. My own belly, when my father pulled down my trousers, was white as the slit guts of the tiny fish growing cold in congealed butter. E.P. Sloane's face turned red as a pomegranate when he saw my tummy going in and out, eluding the buttery knife.

"Lookit her!" he roared. "Lookit her playing hard to get. Oh, she's playin' hard to get, ain't she? But she wants it, don't she? She wants it, alright. Don't let her get away with that, Trip. Butter her up good. Let'er have it!"

"Trip, she's too old for that," said my mother, though she'd never objected before this, perhaps because I had my father's eyes, pale as water, his look of rebellion, and therefore was not worthy of rescue.

"Oh, just look at her stomach! Oh, she's disgusting!" said my older sister, Lydia, the mirror of my mother, with her thick black hair, her broad features, her distaste for crude displays.

My brother, Esper, slid off his chair, drew a yoyo from his pocket, slipped the loop onto his finger, began to spin the yoyo through the air. He performed Walking the Dog. He knew eleven tricks, some of them advanced, performed them all with deep gravity and devotion, as though he believed his whole future lay within that spinning disk. Perhaps it did. He had ambitions. He talked about starting yoyo fairs, running competitions, inventing his own yoyo tricks and illustrating them in a saleable booklet. My father supported this idea. He told Esper he could make a million with it. When it came to the making of fortunes, my father always spoke in terms of millions. Anything less wasn't worth the trouble.

"Gimme that knife, Trip," said E.P. Sloane. "I'll smear her if you ain't got the nerve."

My mother pushed her chair away from the table and began to clang pots in the sink. E.P. Sloane reached for the knife. On the dinner platter, the fish scales shone mother-of-pearl-silver-blue-green, as though they swam still in the fabled river, alive. My father held onto the knife, brought it closer than ever before, the curve of my belly acquiescing now, no point in struggling, no escape any longer, rising obligingly like bread dough to meet the knife. The butter went on, thin and glistening, not even real butter but margarine bright as marigolds, melting against the heat of my skin.

I heard Lydia gasp, gulp air. Esper looked up, forgot his yoyo. It descended, bobbed drowsily, came to rest in the Sleeping position. I understood suddenly that I had been an object not only of entertainment, but of ridicule. My mother turned away from the sink, her hands dripping with dishwater.

"Now you've gone too far, Trip — "

"You distracted me, clattering those pots."

Gone was the sense of safety in my father's encircling arms, the spirit of collusion. I drove my buttocks against his thighs, my heels skidding down his shins, my strength greater than his now, until I'd slithered off his knees and my shoes met the floor. I ran down the back hall.

"I hope you're happy now," said my mother.

"Oh, we were just having fun," my father answered.

The driveway had begun to heave with the spring thaw. I stepped barefoot into the soft mud, reached a midpoint before I was stopped short by the rope, with which my mother had tied me to the porch so that I would not, like my father, run away.

At the curb sat Esper, running a candle up and down his yoyo string. The coat of wax would keep the disc riding smoothly. He drew a piece of sandpaper from his pocket, folded it over, slipped it into the crevice between the spools, ran it along the wood with a light pressure. A fine powder came off onto his fingers. The rasp of the paper carried across the still afternoon.

Out on the street, Lydia was skipping with her friends. The double-dutch ropes turned and turned with a steady hypnotic rhythm, dreamlike, looping and looping, falling over and over like the arcs of a lawn sprinkler, striking the pavement with a dry, hissing beat. The chorus floated across the yard, a steady incantation.

> *Adolph Hitler sat on a pin*
> *How many inches did it go in?*
> *One — two — three — four — five*

E.P. Sloane's green Dodge came up the street and slid into the driveway. My father went into the house and E.P. sat on the porch step.

"You're quite the tomboy, ain't you?" he said, smiling at me. I looked down at myself, saw sunlight, falling through pinprick holes in my straw hat, throw a constellation of stars across my bare chest.

"Why can't you be like your sister?" E.P. asked. "Pretty skirt. Nice fresh blouse. Maybe you're not a girl at all."

"Yes, I am."

"You're a boy under them pants, ain't you? Been fooling everybody, eh?"

"No."

"Maybe I should check. How much you wanna bet? A nickel? You got a nickel to bet with?"

"No."

"I didn't think so. But that don't matter to me. Tell you what. I'll put up a nickel and if you're right, you can have it. If you're wrong, I'll think of some other way you can pay me back."

His hand went into his pocket. He brought out a nickel and showed it to me. I saw the thick-bodied Canadian beaver atop his lodge, the coarse pelt, the industrious forepaws, the long talons. E.P. flipped the coin and up came the head of the young Elizabeth, freshly crowned, our new queen, her neck, shoulders naked. Already, I imagined the nickel's weight in my own palm. I reached for it. By now I understood the scarcity and importance of money. Here was the coin my mother had wondered about, the lucre that bought beer for my father and E.P. Sloane. But with the deft movement of a magician, E.P. withdrew the nickel from my reach.

"Wait a minute, now," he warned. "Not so fast. Let's not rush things. Let's not jump the gun."

I'd never been so close to him before. I saw the deep cleft in his chin, his long hooked nose, his scalp sunburned and scattered with grey freckles of large and irregular shape, like flat river stones. He was seated awkwardly on the lower step, all his flesh thrust together, pressed in upon itself. Again the skipping chorus reached us:

> My father is the butcher
> My mother cuts the meat
> And I'm a little meatball
> That runs up and down the street

Now E.P.'s finger was travelling down the ridge of my spine. I felt the dexterity, the cunning of it. Suddenly it seemed like the whole of his body was concentrated in that fingertip — his hairy arms, his fleshy shoulders, his soft chest — all this was funnelled into that one broad finger, powerful as a magic wand, sliding down my backbone, rising over the vertebra, enjoying every one, exerting a slight pressure on each, as though counting pebbles in a line. The nickel glinted in the sun.

> *I won't go to Macy's anymore, more, more*
> *There's a big fat policeman at the door, door, door*
> *He grabs me by the collar*
> *And makes me pay a dollar*
> *I won't go to Macy's any more, more, more*

At the curb, Esper's yoyo whirred. His body tensed with the concentration of a magician, his chest a narrow washboard, his legs bronzed, the tips of his big ears sunburned. He threw a *Figure Eight*, a *Texas Cowboy*, a *Dog Bite*. He watched the yoyo's flight, sent it away, brought it home, all with deep ardour. He enjoyed the responsiveness, the simple intelligence, the trustworthiness of the yoyo, its round sensuousness, its weight, the feel of it sliding smoothly back into his palm, like a lover.

> *Two in the middle and two at the end*
> *Each is a sister and each is a friend*
> *A penny to save and a penny to spend*
> *Two in the middle and two at the end*

E.P. Sloane's hand slipped inside the cord of my jute pants, his thick wrist pressing hard as a stone into the small of my back, his whole hand spreading out now, hungrily. I heard a soft moan, sad and tired. Now his palm slid down over one buttock, fit perfectly there. My cheek fell into his hand like a grapefruit, ripe for the picking. At that moment, the whole of the perfumed afternoon seemed to fit within the curve of E.P.'s fingers: the fragrant yellow rind of the sky, the cracked cement slab beneath E.P.'s feet, the missing porch spindles, the heaving, breathing earth, the elm branches overhead, splitting open like soft lips, buds releasing overhead, unfolding like tongues, the arid *tap tap tap* of the rope on the street, the drone of the skipping psalms, the *whirr* of Esper's yoyo, a watery sound floating out the window — my mother washing linens in the kitchen sink.

E.P. Sloane's breath came shallowly. His fingertips moved back and forth on my behind, seeking texture. His touch was infinitely pleasurable to me. The skin on my buttocks grew prickly in response, goose bumps rose. I felt panicky, thrilled, though I knew from the tight look on his face, his perspiring forehead, his bright eyes, that something was wrong. Good or bad, I wanted that something to happen. I sensed the tension in his fingers, the excitement, the fear. I understood that this was only preparation, foreplay. What lay ahead was business, a fair exchange, a financial transaction. I was anxious for him to explore further, to complete his investigation. What I had to offer equalled the nickel. Measure for measure. The coin would be mine.

> *Apple on a stick*
> *Makes me sick*
> *Makes my heart go 2-4-6*
> *Not because it's dirty*
> *Not because it's clean*
> *Not because you kissed a girl*
> *Behind a magazine*
> *So, come on, girl*
> *Let's have some fun*
> *You can wiggle*
> *You can waggle*
> *You can do the twist*

But I betcha five dollars
You can't do this
Close your eyes and count to ten
If you miss you're a big fat hen

At that moment, my mother called down the cellar stairs. "Trip? Trip, when are you going to clean up those fish bones? I can smell them all the way up here. Where's E.P.? Get him to help you."

I heard E.P. gasp softly. Intake, swallow of breath, like a swimmer coming up. Once more I reached out for the nickel but again E.P.'s fingers closed on it. I had not earned it. It was only that which was still to be discovered that equalled the nickel. We both knew nothing had been proved. Proof would have to wait for another afternoon. I heard E.P.'s knees cracking as he rose quickly from the porch. The nickel dropped back into his pocket, clinked against its companions there. He stepped lightly up the stairs, money jingling merrily. The screen door slammed.

Esper came up the driveway toward me.

"I've learned a new trick, Mame," he said excitedly. "Want to see it? Watch this. *Spanking The Baby and Burping Her.* That's what it's called. Isn't that great? Some day I'm going to be a yoyo champion, Mame. I'm going to compete all over the world. Maybe you could be my assistant. How would you like to see China?"

All in together, girls
How d'you like the weather, girls?
January — February — March — April — May

Made-Up Stories

ON THE THIRD DAY, Pilar is once again out on the deck at sunrise waiting for her mother to appear. She drums her long fingers on the railing. Her family believes this is a beautiful spot, her sisters and her mother and her father do, but they've never been anywhere, like she has, they don't know. She sees the ordinariness of it, the claustrophobic evergreens, ravaged by Canadian winters, crowding its perimeter. It saps her energy. It drives her wild.

Over her right shoulder, a distance away in the shelter of black pines, where the ground is dusty and root-bound and bald, leans the old cottage where they came all those summers when they were little, a shabby clapboard three-bedroom bungalow painted white. Her sisters, Betty and Cath, are over there right now, sleeping. The lumpy mildewed mattresses and the raw slivery floors and the chipped bathroom tub fill them with nostalgia, and this family is big on nostalgia. The night of her arrival, Pilar started out over there, but Cath cried all night, not about Billie but about Storey Toogood, her boyfriend, who's just dumped her to go back to his wife. Cath's whimpers penetrated the walls.

"Oh, for God's sake," Pilar muttered, checking the clock at midnight, one, two, tossing and turning, punching her pillow, bedclothes twisted around her body like rope. Finally, she shoved all her stuff in her duffle bag and crossed in the dark to the new cottage and went down the hallway to one of the ridiculously small rooms and threw herself down on a bed.

Now, she hears her mother's heavy footsteps coming down the hall and then cupboards opening and closing in the kitchen. Pilar crosses the deck and slides the door open, walking with a dancer's agility and grace. It's a big cottage with many odd angles and doors and balconies, the proportions all out of whack, none of it making any sense, a hodgepodge of ideas. All the rooms are the wrong size and the wrong shape and there are myriad styles and materials mixed together. Her father had meddled with the plans, he'd bullied the contractor. He didn't know a damned thing about architecture, he was a caterer, for god's sake. It was all very ugly. Pilar had told her parents this.

"Why would you say such a thing?" Cath had asked her.

"Well, I can't *lie*."

Already, the kitchen is filled with the smell of fresh coffee. Pilar watches her mother cracking eggs into a bowl.

"Do you want me to do that?" she asks. "What are you making? Is this for scrambled eggs?"

"Pancakes. No, it's all right. Your father likes me to do them." Her mother is wearing a man's flannel checked housecoat. She is a big-boned, solid, square woman, in no way feminine, but nevertheless striking. Her face has a strength and her sturdy body a resilience, an absorptiveness that invites confidences. Pilar knows that her mother knows that she's up early to talk to her about things she might not want to hear, but, never one to shirk her responsibilities, her mother has come out here anyway.

"Why do you cater to his whims?" asks Pilar. Towering over her mother, she's built like an adolescent boy, hipless, with breasts the size of hockey pucks. She has long hands and long feet. Everything about her is long, her teeth, her torso, her legs, her face, which is like a horse's. No one knows where she got this body. Like her mother, the rest of the family is short, dense, slow-moving. Pilar used to say to her mother, "Is Dad really my father? I don't look like the rest of you. I mean, you can tell me. I'd prefer it if he wasn't. I'm hoping you slept with another man."

"How are you doing?" she asks now, "I mean, about Billie?" because her mother has shown no sign of emotion. "You don't have to be a rock. Dad doesn't have a monopoly on grief." She's confiscated the bowl from her mother and is whipping the eggs with a whisk she's found in a drawer. Once Pilar decides to take something over, they all know there's no arguing with her.

"I'm fine."

"Did you ever think Dad would live this long?" she asks her mother. She's opening up cupboards and getting out flour, salt, nutmeg. "What are the doctors saying now?" Weren't they told he was going to die in a year? That was ten years ago. But it appears he isn't going to die any day, like they said he was. He doesn't actually have one foot in the grave. Who was the idiot who said that? Who said only one year? What they'd been through: *Don't anger your father. Give your father his way. Walk softly around him. He doesn't have long to live. Any emotional upset might knock him out of remission, send his cancer cells multiplying like crazy.* Bullshit, thought Pilar.

Pilar escaped from this family at the earliest opportunity. She ran off at eighteen to get a degree, though her father said university was for losers. Then she began to write in order to further set herself apart from them. Her sisters went straight from high school to the family business. Pilar does not respect them much. She does not think they are very smart. They've never stretched themselves and, worse, they've let their father take care of them. Princesses.

Pilar is a fiction writer. At first, she had to explain to her family what the word *fiction* meant. "You know," she said, exasperated, "made-up stories." When she came home with her first published story collection, Cath asked when she was going to write "a real book," by which she meant a novel. Her father read the book jacket and Pilar heard him say to her mother, "Now why would anyone want to write about things like that?" He came to Pilar and said, "If you want story ideas, I can give you some good ones. My life has been full of interesting things." No one in the family has read any of Pilar's books. They do not read here. They flip through magazines and watch television. Anyway, because of a few sex scenes in her stories, her father has decided that her writing is filthy.

"Listen," says Pilar to her mother, "we have to dispose of the ashes today."

"Do we?"

"My plane leaves tomorrow."

"I thought it was Thursday."

"I moved it up. I have to get back to my work. I know Dad's going to be mad I'm leaving early."

"He'll get used to the idea."

"That's not the same as not being mad." Onto the stove, she slaps a skillet. "What he said last night," she shakes her head angrily. When Pilar had refused to play charades with them, he'd called her "a selfish bitch." She doesn't know anyone else whose father would say such a thing to his daughter.

"He didn't mean it. Don't leave because of that. Find a better reason," her mother tells her.

"I'm not going until we scatter those ashes."

She'd flown out here as soon as they called her, roaring up to the cottage in a red sports car she'd rented at the airport to show them that no matter what had happened, she knew how to hold onto life, to shake her fist at it. Though it was only three in the afternoon, her father disappeared down the side stairs and they heard his feet in the heavy gravel under the deck and the door of the booze fridge open, the clink of bottles. Every day, he went down there and counted the number of *Pinot Grigio* and *Pino Noir* and *Sauvignon Blanc*, the varieties of beer and how much gin, vodka and rum he had frosting in the freezer compartment. He'd been a big name in catering and nothing was worth having unless in quantity. He carried a tall glass pitcher of martinis out to them. By four o'clock, they'd finished it off. Why not, especially today, with the body waiting in the nearby town to be dealt with? He mixed another one, and then another. After darkness fell, he had to take a flashlight down under the deck. They heard him stumble.

"We've had enough," they called down, but he made them keep drinking, until they all felt like their heads were full of broken glass.

The third time he disappeared to get the vodka, Pilar said to her mother ironically, "Alcohol's a toxin, right? I hear it's really good for cancer."

"He knows," her mother said lightly, resignedly. "He knows he shouldn't drink. He doesn't always. Usually just when there's company."

"Yeah, I'll bet. He's got enough booze down there for a nation."

"He has to *live*, you know," said Cath. She was the youngest sister, Pilar the eldest, Betty in between.

Their father came back out onto the deck. A motorboat roared by. The lake is fifty miles long and nearly as wide and it's full of coves and peninsulas and islands. These days, people fight to buy a place here. Their father never stops reminding them what a genius he was to have invested here. Every summer, he tells them how much he could get for the property if he put it on the market, how much it's appreciated. He likes to have a price tag on things. It's the only way he knows what anything's worth.

"What is the plan for the body?" Pilar asked after their father had sat down again.

"The remains," Cath corrected her.

"We've got that family plot in the city," said their father. "I paid good money for it. We're going to put him there."

"I don't think that's a good idea," said Pilar. "I don't think Billie would want that."

"Dead people don't have feelings," said Cath.

"You know what I mean," Pilar told her.

"I think we should do what Dad wants," said Cath.

"What about Billie? What about what Billie would have wanted?"

"We don't know *what* he wanted," said Cath.

"He didn't run away to Brazil for nothing," said Pilar. It had been Brazil and Mexico, as far as they could tell, and Cuba and maybe California and Haiti, they didn't know where all he'd been, in ten years. He'd never phoned for a bailout, a disappointment to their father, who was dying to say, "That sponge, that freeloader."

"I think he would have wanted to be cremated and have his ashes scattered someplace where he would have felt free," Pilar said. "I think we need to honour the spirit in which he lived."

"You don't know that unless you have some telepathic connection to him," said Cath. "Maybe we should get out the Ouija board."

"I don't think the way he gets buried changes anything," said Betty quietly.

"His ashes should be scattered on a mountaintop or thrown out of an airplane or into the lake here," declared Pilar.

"Over my dead body," said their father.

Breakfast is delayed on this third day because no one is up yet. Pilar leaves the kitchen and goes down the back hall to the bedroom where she's been sleeping and closes the door behind her. She dials the phone. It rings eight times before Walker picks up.

"Jesus Christ," he says tiredly.

"I'm going crazy here," she says. Walker did not want to come out for the funeral. Like Betty's husband and Cath's, before she got divorced, he knows that Pilar is a boat-rocker. All the men, the in-laws, have grasped that it's safer to stay away when Pilar visits, best to keep out of the line of fire. When Walker doesn't accompany her, Pilar's family is always disappointed. "Walker didn't come? Where's Walker?" they ask. "When are we going to see Walker again?" It makes Pilar sick. "Walker is so intelligent," they say. "Isn't he intelligent?" All except Cath, who thinks he's full of himself. "Too bad brains aren't everything," she says scornfully.

Through the small window, here, on the back of the cottage, Pilar looks at the dusty gravel lane leading out to the four-lane highway. She can see the traffic flying by, hear the hiss of the cars, and every minute or so, the thunder of a ten-wheeler. It's hot and airless in this little room, with its cheap panelling and shag carpet and fake quilt.

"Tell me I'm not part of this family," Pilar says to Walker.

"You're not part of that family," Walker says.

"Tell me I'm not like them."

"You're not like them."

"I don't belong here," she says. A pause.

"Where *do* you belong?"

"I might have to kill Dad."

"Why don't you just accept him for what he is? Why don't you let sleeping dogs lie?"

But, Pilar thinks, if she were a person who let sleeping dogs lie, he never would have married her, would he?

"He's driving me crazy," she says.

"You take him too seriously. You take *yourself* too seriously. Say hello to your mother for me." He hangs up.

She can't win an argument with Walker. He has his PhD in mathematics. She fears his brain, his quotients, his equations. He's working out of home now, as a consultant. No longer does he bathe daily, or change his clothes. He's begun to smell sour, like an old man. He shaves less and has let his greying hair grow. She thinks, with his long nose and small mouth, that he's beginning to look like a badger. When she left to come out here, when she was throwing her suitcase in the car, he said to her spontaneously, on their driveway, "Give me a kiss," and she, caught off guard, asked, "What for?"

They had met on a summer job. They were traffic counters for the city, stationed on the same street corner. At the end of the first day together, they'd both gone to their supervisor and asked to be assigned to a new partner. He said no dice. All summer, they had nothing but scorn for each other. She told him he was arrogant. He said she was a rebel without a cause. He said she should have been a man. At the end of August, they went back to university without even saying goodbye. In October, he phoned her and asked for a date. She had been waiting for his call.

In bed, all these years in bed, it had been a fight to see who could get on top and stay there, who could dominate and punish and call the shots. Their sex was full of indifference and despair, anger and pride, coldness and heat, narcissism and nihilism.

Before dessert the first night she was here, Pilar cornered her mother in the kitchen. "What the hell happened?" she asked. "With Billie? What did Dad say to him? Did they have a fight?"

"I didn't hear one."

"Tell me what happened. Start at the beginning."

Pilar's parents had got up the morning after Billie arrived and found his bedroom empty. "What the hell?" their father said at breakfast. "What the hell? He's home for less than a day, he doesn't even tell us he's coming or where he's been for the last ten years, and then he disappears without saying goodbye?" At lunchtime, he went out to the garage to get charcoal for the barbeque. He found Billie's body turning slowly on the end of a rope. Sunlight, angling through a window, struck Billie's bare blue feet. He smelled of sweat and marijuana. The cuffs of his jeans were still wet from when he'd gone out in the boat the night before.

On finding him, their father ran out of the garage and pressed his forehead and arms against it and their mother, seeing this, dropped a pot lid, which turned and turned on the kitchen floor. She rushed out the side door, asking, "What? What?" but she already knew. She ran back into the cottage and called 911. Then she and their father entered the garage and pulled a heavy wooden worktable over and he got up onto it and then she did too, and he put his arms around Billie's hips and hoisted him up so that she could slip the rope off his neck. They eased the body down onto the table. Outside again, their father doubled over, weeping and shaking. "Breathe. Breathe," their mother instructed him, her hand on his neck. The paramedics arrived but there was nothing they could do but take Billie away to the undertaker in the village.

That first night, at dinner, their father had said to them, to the four women, "He never thought about other people, that boy. He always did what he bloody well pleased. He never amounted to a damned thing. If he'd worked for me, I would have made something of him." He'd felt broken, earlier, when he found the body, but now he was fighting back.

"He didn't want to be your galley slave," Pilar told him.

"If he'd stuck with me, he wouldn't have got involved with drugs. Drugs are why he's dead." Her father's nose, after so many drinks, was like a damson plum, purple and swollen.

"That's just stupid," said Pilar. "All he ever smoked was weed."

"It rotted his mind. It pushed him over the edge."

Following her call to Walker, Pilar comes out again into the kitchen. She hears a scrape and turns to see Cath, shameless in a string bikini, pulling a long chair across the deck, into the sunshine. She settles into it. Her body glistens with oil. Already, sweat is pooling in the hollow of her throat and in her navel and running in a river between her breasts and in the deep folds of her stomach. Her arms wobble and her ankles are fat and even her feet are pudgy, like a baby's. She's brown as a nut. Vain and pretty, soft and tactile. There is an ease to her body, a somewhat slutty surrender. Pilar, who in contrast is all angles and edges and steel, might be a little jealous of her. She turns to her mother and says, "She can tan herself black and he won't come back to her."

The previous morning, Pilar, up early and out on the deck, heard the sound of an outboard motor approaching. A flashy boat pulled up to their dock. It was Storey Toogood. He owned a cottage five doors down. That was the problem with this province, this lake: you couldn't get away from the people you hated. Pilar went down to speak to him.

"You've got some nerve showing your face here," she told him.

"I just want to speak to Cath."

"She's not here."

He smirked. "We both know that's not true." He was stunningly good-looking, a pretty boy, like Tom Cruise. "I just came to give her my condolences."

"She doesn't want comfort from you."

"You can't stop me from getting out of this boat and looking for her."

"Oh, no? There's a gun up in the shed. I know how to use it. You set one foot on this property and I'll blow your head off."

"Sure you will."

"Cath's not interested in your hypocrisy. Why don't you go home and fuck your wife?"

Moments after he'd left, Cath came running out of the old cabin in baby dolls, barefoot. By this time, Pilar and her mother were up on the deck with cups of coffee.

"Who was that I heard talking down on the dock?" she asked.

"Just someone looking for directions," said Pilar.

"I thought it was Storey. I thought I heard Storey's voice."

"Must have been a bad dream," Pilar told her.

"Mom?" said Cath. "Was it Storey? Was he here?"

Her mother took a deep breath. "I was still waking up," she said. When they were growing up, she'd taught them, "You can always find a way not to tell a lie." The oblique sun shone on her face. Her skin was dry, papery, fragile-looking.

Cath glared at Pilar and stormed back to the little cottage. Pilar called after her, "You said you hated his guts! You said you wished he'd drop dead!" She turned to her mother for support, for justification.

"Why does she want to be his doormat?" she asked.

Her mother looked out at the lake. "Love is confusing," she answered quietly.

At nine o'clock on the morning of this third day, the kitchen is filled with the *glop glop* of the spoon lifting the pancake batter. Butter sizzles on the griddle. Its sweet smell floats through the house. On the hot steel, four circles of batter bubble and spit. There is a movement in the hallway and Pilar and her mother turn their heads and see her father emerge from the bedroom in his pyjamas and shuffle across the hall to the bathroom. His eyes are red from crying. Pilar thinks his grief more than a little hypocritical. Yesterday, her father was out on the driveway with a rake, smoothing over the gravel Pilar had thrown up when she skidded to a halt in the sports car, making him turn purple. He called Pilar over. "I think," he said, pausing with the rake planted in the gravel, "your brother might have been gay. I think he might have been a faggot."

Over at the smaller cottage, the door opens and Betty appears. She comes toward them, her feet silent on the bed of red pine needles. She has an attractiveness that is hard to put your finger on. It has to do with contentment. She is a little overweight, though she is not as big as her mother, who has thickened with menopause. Her body is solid, practical. In the kitchen, she opens the cutlery drawer and carries utensils over to the breakfast nook.

"Will you take over here?" Pilar asks her mother, handing her the spatula. She goes to the side door just entered by Betty, steps outside and gulps air, like a drowning person. She crosses the gravel drive and steps inside the garage. She breathes in the smell of axel grease, dry timbers. Standing very still, she tries to feel Billie's presence. They had both got away from their father, she thought, but he'd had more imagination, he'd taken greater risks. Why had he come home? Why had he come out here and found a heavy rope and set a piece of firewood up on the floor and stepped onto it and kicked it away?

From the deck, she hears Cath call in to her mother and to Betty, "I wish she'd stop going in there. It's morbid. That garage should be off-limits."

A loud *shhhh* comes from Betty. Like her mother, Betty neither understands nor sees the point in conflict. She is always trying to bridge the gap between Pilar and her father, between Pilar and Cath. She will be the peacemaker of the family after their mother is gone.

But Cath won't stop. "Does she think we're stupid or maybe blind? What's she looking for? A suicide note? If there was a suicide note, we'd have found it long before she showed up."

The morning after the day she arrived, when everyone was still sleeping off the martinis, Pilar had driven into town. She found the undertaker's, and went in and told a young man that the family had given her the authority to sign the cremation papers. She instructed him to get a move on. They needed the ashes *now.* Then she went to a coffee shop for a couple of hours and read a newspaper and watched the tourists and cottage owners coming into town. Her hands were shaking. Why? They had always scorned this little backwater, and now here she was having her brother's body incinerated by people they'd privately mocked. She went back to the funeral parlour and picked up the ashes. They were still warm. The slight young man who handed them to her said, "Are you the famous Hatchers from the city? The caterers?"

"I'm not involved with that," Pilar said.

"What do you do, then?"

"I write books," she said. "I'm published." His face lit up.

"Should I have heard of them?" He took a pad from his breast pocket and held a pen to it with his slender fingers and asked for the names.

It was late morning by the time Pilar got back to the cottage. The family had eaten breakfast and cleaned up the dishes and now the women were back in the kitchen making lunch. Her father stood by a table in the living room, cracking open pistachio nuts and tossing them into his mouth. A thick, dense man. Wearing shorts and a flowered shirt that shot way out over his big gut. Robust and bronzed. Some cancer victim. When Pilar walked in with the ashes, her father demanded, "Where the hell have you been? What the hell is that?" He was a commanding figure, handsome, like Ernest Hemingway. The thick white hair, the tanned, square face. All he needed was the beard and the peaked captain's cap.

Pilar answered, "Now you won't have to go into town and have a funeral and get involved in all that claptrap you've always hated. You and Mom are tired."

Her father shouted, "I'm not so feeble that I can't go to a goddamned funeral!"

Her mother said, "You don't have a suit to wear to a funeral. You gave them all away when you retired."

Pilar said, "What the hell's he going to wear in his own coffin if he doesn't have one goddamned suit left?"

Then her father went out onto the deck and roared at the lake. Soon, they heard his voice coming from the master bedroom, talking to the funeral home, shouting as if he didn't know how phones worked. Their mother got up and went inside and took the receiver from him. He had to have an extra long nap that afternoon. He always napped after lunch. The medications he was on made him tired. The cancer sapped him. It was only prostate cancer, though, and what was that? Apparently most men died of other things before prostate cancer managed to kill them. Why hadn't they been told this at the beginning?

She called Walker and told him about going to the undertaker, about the ashes. He asked her why she hadn't just set fire
to the cottage.

"I have to follow my own conscience," she said. There was a
silence on the line. She wondered if he was thinking about the
man she'd slept with.

She'd met another man a few years ago. She'd carried on an
affair with him for eighteen months. Then he was transferred
overseas, to a law office in London. He asked her to come with
him. Overjoyed, she packed one small suitcase, she waited on a
designated corner at three on a summer afternoon for him to
pick her up and take her to the airport. He said he would have
her plane ticket with him. All the while she stood there, she felt
crazy, terrified, maniacally happy. But he never appeared. She
waited there several hours, pacing, biting her nails, until long
after she knew the plane had left. She had to take a bus home.
Walker was there when she entered the house with her suitcase.
"He changed his mind, did he?" he said. So. Somehow, he'd
known all along. He told her he didn't care if she stayed or if she
left him now. It was all the same to him.

She went to bed that night determined to leave the next
morning. But her resolve weakened. She rose and went to her
study and began to write and gradually, over the morning,
she convinced herself she could not leave the forest surround-
ing their log house, she could not relinquish the familiarity
and the beauty and the safety of it. At eleven, she broke from
her work and went to the kitchen and made a hearty stew. She
called Walker to the table. They ate in silence. They carried on.
It didn't matter to him that she'd slept with another man. This

indifference did not surprise but it did wound her. Rather than guilt or victory, she felt humiliation. *I'm worth more than that,* she wanted to shout at him. *I'm worth your jealousy, at least. Why was she a woman a man could not even feel jealousy about?* She went to the mirror and looked at the gaps between her teeth, at her small, lash-less eyes.

After her father got up from his nap, he said to Pilar, "Couldn't they find something better than a shoebox to put him in? It shows a lack of respect." He was hunched now. The shock of the cremation seemed to have stooped him.

Pilar said, "Just because it's white and rectangular doesn't mean it's a shoebox."

Then he went down under the deck again to do his inventory of the booze fridge before getting them all drunk once more. Pilar went and called Walker.

"For god's sake," he said. She'd taken the phone down the hall to her parents' room and was standing at the sliding door looking out at the lake. Behind her, on the bed, the quilt still held the imprint of her father's body, where he'd curled up like a foetus for his nap. Every call to Walker she'd made from a different room of the cottage, hoping that the changing view out the windows, of the highway, the woods, the water, would transform, redeem the conversation.

"Did anything come in the mail?" she said to Walker.

"Not since you asked six hours ago."

"Did anyone call? My editor, maybe? If this book doesn't get accepted, I'll die. I haven't published anything in ten years. I don't know what's wrong with me." She has two books out there.

They received moderately good reviews but now they're out of print and forgotten. Yes, she'd had a brief burst of success but now she is failing.

"I don't know if I'll ever write another book."

"You don't have to. You could go out and find a job."

"Writing's all I've ever done. Where do you think I could get a job now? Who would hire me?"

"I wouldn't. You're too much of a trouble-maker."

"That's not what I wanted you to say."

"What did you want me to say?"

"I wanted you to say, 'You're immensely talented. You can't stop writing. You owe it to the world to write another book.'"

"It's not up to me to say that. It's up to you to say it to yourself."

"Thanks for nothing," she said, and slammed the phone down.

Before breakfast on this third day, Pilar goes out onto the deck and stands over Cath. "We said this was the day we were going to sprinkle the ashes." Cath's nakedness, her flesh disgust Pilar, truly they do.

"I heard *you* say that," says Cath. "But I didn't hear anyone *else* say it." Her magazine, fluttering in the lake breeze, is stained with tanning oil and sweat.

"Are you going to put on some clothes?" Pilar asks.

"Is there some rule that says you can't scatters someone's ashes in a bathing suit?"

Their father had financed a small business for Cath's husband, a bike shop. Pilar thought her father had practically purchased this husband for Cath. Cath had slept around a lot in high school, she had developed a reputation. She gave herself freely. One day, Cath went into the bike shop and found her husband in the back room on the floor among the gears and derailers and tires, with a student he'd hired for the summer. He said later that he'd been teaching her bike maintenance.

Cath had once said to Pilar, "You ran away, only to marry your father." Cath had almost failed to graduate high school. She was the stupidest person in the family. And yet she could come out with something like this. Cath had two children, now ten and eight, two nice, not very smart boys. Pilar and Walker had not had children. They did not like children. They did not see the point in them. They justified their decision by telling themselves they would have made lousy parents. They were probably right. They did not want to have to entertain the emotions of children. They did not hold much truck with feelings.

In the alcove, they eat breakfast, the parents in the chairs facing the bay window, the three daughters on the built-in bench with their backs to the glass. Pilar says, "Are we going to scatter those goddamned ashes or not?" She looks older than she did when she arrived three days ago, she looks older than fifty. Cath rolls her eyes for the hundredth time. Their father slams his mug down on the table. Coffee leaps out of it.

After breakfast, Pilar pulls the rowboat down the grassy slope to the shore. She may be thin but she's strong. She doesn't want any help. They are all too fat-bound to be of any use anyway, she thinks. She brings the boat alongside the dock and ties it up. She climbs back up to the shed and gets the life vests down from the wooden dowels and throws them in the boat. She returns and finds the oars and carries them down and slips them into the locks. The sun is high, big and blinding in the sky.

"Let's go, everyone!" she calls up to the cottage. Her father comes out onto the deck and looks down mutinously. He descends the stairs and stands on the dock. The others follow. Her mother, who's been doing the breakfast dishes, approaches, drying her hands on a tea towel.

"We can't all fit in there," says Cath. "We'll drown."

"There's room," Pilar tells her. She is in the boat, balanced on her haunches.

"I'm sure as hell not going," barks their father, his eyes popping with anger. "I'm not getting in a boat with someone who tells me I killed my own son." His belt rides very low beneath his big gut. He has legs like a sailor, strong, keeping an easy balance, his feet spread wide, on the floating dock, which rises and falls gently with the wave motion. His legs are brown, the hairs on his bulging calves golden, and his feet, in Birkenstocks, are deeply tanned, the skin on his toes thickened at the tips, his heels white and cracked from the summer's exposure to water.

"I'll stay here with Dad," says Cath.

"Mom? Betty?" says Pilar neutrally. She is prepared to go by herself. To hell with all of them. Betty and her mother get in and the boat sinks deeper. Then Pilar can't resist taunting her father, "Maybe it's best you don't come, anyway. Maybe the last thing Billie would have wanted is for you to touch his ashes." She is looking up at him, at his thick nose hairs.

"Pilar," chides Betty softly. Water laps at the pilings. The boat rocks gently. Their father turns red. Wind is blowing up under his stretched shirt, revealing his pink stomach. His loose khaki shorts snap around his knees. Pilar releases the rope from the dock hook. "This is your last chance," she tells her father. "Are you going to get in this fucking boat, or not?"

He takes a step. The deck is wet and slick from a night of rain. He falters, slips on the greasy wood, catches his balance, drops one foot into the boat. It keels deeply. Betty and their mother grab at the sides but Pilar keeps her balance, grasping the oars. Cath climbs in too and sits as far away from Pilar as she can.

Their mother has the box of ashes in her lap. She wears baggy capris to cover the lumpy veins snaking like purple ropes up her legs. Her hair is iron-grey and cut much shorter than their father's. It always has been. She has never been feminine. Womanly but not feminine. On her feet are sandals with heavy straps. Her mother, thinks Pilar, is like the lake: calm, constant, life-giving, reflecting a reliable picture of yourself back at you. Her floppy hat flips up in the breeze.

Pilar seizes the oars, pushes down, pulls back and feels the water resist, her biceps straining. Betty has a piece of paper in her hand. It flaps and crackles in the breeze. She'd said that morning, "Should we be taking something we can read?"

"Like what?" asked Pilar.

"Something from the Bible or a prayer book? I don't know." Betty's husband is a mild, happy, anger-less man. He is a high school music teacher. He loves people. He loves Betty. They never quarrel. A very boring couple, Pilar had always thought. Now, for the first time, she envies Betty.

They move out silently over the lake, with only the sound of the oars dropping into the water and the water running off them as they arc into the air, drop and arc. Cottages appear along the shore, among the trees. Their own grows smaller and smaller. Canada geese float nearby, bathing themselves, scooping their slender, dark heads again and again into the water. Their white throats. Their hard black eyes. It is a lake rich with pickerel.

Their fat, opal bodies shine below the surface, in their flashing, silver schools. A seagull rises on the wind, floats, sinks, circles, dives to catch a small fish. The sun has climbed high in the sky. The water glitters and flashes.

The wind blows Pilar's brittle hair straight back. It borders on orange. She coloured it herself. When Walker saw it, he'd said, "Halloween isn't for five months." Pilar has no trouble moving the great weight of the boat. When they were growing up, she was always the best at everything here. The best diver, the best swimmer, the best water skier. Everything physical has been effortless for her. Cath's body, in the skimpy bikini, gleams like a seal's, fleshy and smooth. She has her eyes on Pilar, glaring from behind dark glasses. Pilar pretends not to notice. She sees that Cath is once again displaying on her ankle the fine gold bracelet that Storey gave her. Pilar is tempted to reach out and tear it off. Her mother's face is calm and accepting. Betty looks at the trees on the shore, at the geese, the clouds, enjoying everything she sees.

Pilar glances at her father. He is turned sideways in the boat, one knee bent, watching the far shore. He does not look cancerous at all, thinks Pilar. He looks healthy and strong. His sturdy legs, his bronzed arms with their mat of bleached hair. At first, in the boat, he had looked angry and captive. Now his face has settled into an expression of pain. The wind rifles his magnificent hair, which stands up on his head, thick as wheat. He looks — something. He looks noble and handsome. Valiant as a ship's admiral. His neck is very red, his thick lips are working, trembling one moment, pressed together then next. Pilar feels an unexpected pang of pity for him. She can see that, despite his instincts, he is trying to rally to the moment, to rise to this occasion. He looks confused, proud, stubborn, alone.

Suddenly, she feels a welling up of self-doubt, possibly of self-loathing. She is like an executioner rowing her prisoners to their deaths. None of them wants to be here. She suspects they fear her. This realization shocks her on some deep level. The oars grow heavier, the load of the boat a greater burden. She feels both detached from these people and deeply connected to them, as though by an umbilical cord. She has forced her will upon them. Perhaps she does not really know what Billie would have desired. Perhaps she is mistaken. She does not know him, she does not know herself. She has called her family *philistines*. She became a writer because she wanted to be more important than they were. But she hasn't achieved this, has she? She has lost her voice. She feels empty. Like she has nothing left to say. But how could that be? She's older now. She has more life experience, more wisdom.

"Wisdom?" Walker had said dubiously, when she tried to talk to him about this.

Now, she sees the innocence of her family. There is nothing wrong with them. They are merely naïve. They are harmless. As they reach the middle of the lake, she raises one oar and digs into the water with the other. The boat swings in circles, the shore slides round and round, dizzying.

"What's going on?" says Betty with a puzzled smile.

"She's being an idiot," says Cath. "Mom, tell her," but their mother says nothing.

Pilar lets go of the oars and gets up and dives beautifully into the water, her body arcing like an arrow.

"What the hell are you doing?" her father roars.

"I've changed my mind," she calls, treading water three yards from the boat. "I don't care about the ashes. Do what you want with them. Go back. Go back without me. I'll swim from here."

"Can you do that with your clothes on?" her mother asks, concerned.

"God damn it!" their father shouts.

"Lucky duck!" Betty calls to Pilar, waving cheerfully. "You get to cool off! I'm melting in this sun!"

"Oh, for god's sake!" says Cath, and she gets up and squeezes past the others and takes the oars and turns the boat around. "Drama queen!" she calls to Pilar.

It takes Pilar fifteen minutes to swim back to shore. She takes her time, her thin brown arms arcing confidently, rhythmically through the air, her hands cutting into the water like blades. She does the breaststroke, then the back stroke, gazing up at the puffy clouds. When she arrives, her mother is waiting on the dock with a towel, her figure like a solid piece of timber, straight up and down, dense and rooted. Pilar grips the wooden ladder and climbs up, her clothes stuck to her body. The others are already up on the deck, playing three-handed euchre. Their laughter spills down on Pilar and her mother. Her mother gives her the towel and places a thick hand on her shoulder. Pilar remembers, when she was young, how warm her mother's body always was when she hugged her. She'd like to do that now, but she is too proud.

"I hate this family," Pilar, towelling her hair, tells her.

"I know you do."

"Is that wrong?"

"You have to be yourself." Her mother has never tried to interfere with anything in this family. She has never tried to head off events or persuade people to do or not to do things.

"You could have made him a better person," says Pilar.

"He can't be any other way. He's tried."

For a long time, Pilar has believed that there isn't a thing she can learn from her mother, there is nothing her mother has to teach her. This arrogance appals her now. Tomorrow, she will fly back home but suddenly she's afraid to go. She cannot leave without knowing that her mother loves, accepts, understands, forgives her. But how can she find out? She is too haughty to ask.

Once, some years ago, Pilar said to her mother, "You have to stop being Dad's puppet." It seemed that her mother could stand to hear almost anything from Pilar without flinching, but Pilar could see that this one comment had wounded her. "I'm sorry," Pilar said.

"I feel so on the outside here," she tells her mother now, on the dock. "Why is that? Why do I feel so on the outside?" What does she want? After all? Does she want to be inside this family, or outside it? How can she be fifty and not know what she believes in, what is important?

"I don't know why I'm calling you," she confesses to Walker on the phone.

"Just to interrupt my concentration," he answers.

It is seven o'clock now. Everyone else is outside. They've finished dinner and they've drunk a great deal and they are boisterous, as though they've forgotten all about Billie. Pilar tries to resist the thought that they are simple. That they readily forget tragedy in favour of inebriation. She's taken the phone into her parents' bathroom. She looks at herself in the mirror. She does not wear makeup. Walker has said he hates her with makeup on. And yet she does not believe he ever looks at her. Now, she sees the hard lines around her mouth. How has she become so bitter? She longs for tenderness. Last night, she'd dreamed about the young man at the undertaker's. She does not know why, but she feels badly that she will never see him again. This is ridiculous, of course. She remembers his blonde hair, his soft-looking skin, his slender hips. In the dream they were in bed together. She closes her eyes for a moment and recaptures the sensation of his body lying on top of hers, the lightness of it, the youth and innocence.

She looks out the bathroom window at the cruel, stupendous lake. Surely there is something important she had wanted to say to Walker, but now she cannot think what that might have been.

"Did you eat that stew I left you?" she asks.

"I don't remember."

"Well, have a nice life."

"You too."

When she hangs up, she acknowledges that she does not want to go back to him. She does not want to go back to him but knows of course that she will. Does she love Walker? She is almost certain she doesn't. But she can't leave him. She cannot support herself financially and, anyway, it's too late, at fifty, to leave. She does not want to be alone. These days, their marriage is all about negotiation, fallback positions, treaties and arsenals, lies and half-truths, threats and bluffs and counter-bluffs and double-crosses.

From her pocket Pilar now draws the piece of paper Betty had in the boat but never got to read. Pilar found it in the old cottage before dinner, when she'd gone over there to look for a hairbrush she'd lost. Pilar unfolds the paper and reads Betty's handwriting.

> *I am the way, the truth and the life.*
> *But what is the way?*
> *What is the truth?*
> *What is the life?*

She steps to the bathroom window. She looks out at the brilliant lake, the sun jangling on its surface. Into her view move her parents. They stand together leaning against the railing, also looking out. They put their arms across each other's thick shoulders.

What is this love they feel for each other?

Pilar does not understand it.

What is this love?

Group Lessons

OVER THE THIRD BOTTLE OF WINE Cleo declared, "I've just had an inspiration. I'm going to take guitar lessons." They all turned to regard her warily, especially Lincoln, because Cleo's ideas, usually brazen and impossible, always had repercussions. From the living room stereo, the gentle strains of Gordon Lightfoot's "Affair on 8th Avenue" drifted to where the flickering light of a dozen candles set the glass dining room table ablaze with dancing reflections.

These evenings always began ambitiously with Prokofiev or Britten, but by the time the men were pouring the liqueurs and the women were nestled in the deep white leather chairs, they had succumbed to the bittersweet nostalgia of Lightfoot or Feliciano, or were feeling a brief middle-class guilt after listening to one of Joni Mitchell's songs stirring their dormant social consciousness.

Cleo's plan was so brilliant and somehow obvious that the others, perhaps a little jealous of her originality, wondered why they hadn't thought of it themselves.

"Well!" cried Keith, throwing up his hands like a conductor ready to plunge an orchestra into music. He was a demonstrative, mischievous man whom Lincoln instinctively distrusted.

"We should *all* take lessons together." He rose from the table and moved with the liquid, predatory hips of a panther across the carpet to raise the volume on the stereo. For an instant, his athletic figure, in black slacks and black turtleneck, was reflected in the vast living room window that Jane refused to curtain because their backyard was enclosed by a crescent of beautiful old conifers, with an oblique family of white birch leaning in the centre of the lawn. Beyond the black window, the January night was luminous as an enchanted stage design. The trees sagged with the winter's heaviest snowfall, and the snow itself was fluorescent. The birdbath, bearing a foot-high crown of whipped cream, offered itself as a huge parfait. It seemed to them all that the whole world had been put to sleep, as in some drugged fairy tale. But, by unspoken rule, no one complained of feeling buried in this dull little town in which they'd all found themselves, approaching their forties, Keith practising obstetrics (and getting pretty sick of it) and Lincoln carrying on a thrifty law practice.

"Well, I don't know..." Lincoln, private-school-ish in a tie and tweed jacket, a perfectionist who didn't like to be made a fool of, seemed worried. "I've never played an instrument." He was a slender, dark man with horn-rimmed glasses and a clean, rigid jaw.

"I haven't either," Jane shrugged softly, smiling at them all with deep dimples. As she rose from the table to clear the plates, her smooth, golden face shone like a moon, and her gleaming Joan of Arc haircut threw back the candlelight. "But I'll give it a try." No one expected her to be any good at it. She didn't need to shine at anything because she was an excellent mother, long before women began making a competitive career of motherhood, as well as being a good cook and tennis player.

Tranquility seemed to emanate from Jane like heat as she floated through the calm open spaces of this house, through broad archways, past long expanses of glass, her shadow falling mellowly on vanilla walls. It had been her idea to carpet their house in mushroom broadloom so that she could move silently from room to room, light-footed and self-effacing as a gentle, sleek house cat. She gave off the impression that she could steal up on people and read their minds when they weren't looking. Not only Keith, but Lincoln and Cleo sensed this too.

The following morning, hangovers notwithstanding, they were all surprised to find that they remembered what they'd said about taking guitar lessons. On Monday, Jane was able to arrange for group lessons through Domenic's Music, at which they were all relieved and pleased because it had occurred to them that, in a town of so little imagination, there might not be a single soul who knew how to play the guitar. On the same trip, she cleaned out Domenic's complete stock of recordings by Lightfoot, Feliciano, Joni Mitchell, and Ian and Sylvia. That Saturday, they converged on Domenic's to buy themselves six-string guitars, carrying cases, picks, music stands and four copies of Jack Albert's *New Guitar Course Book I: the modern guitar course that's easy to learn and fun to play!*

Late that afternoon, Hilda, a sturdy blonde Dutch girl in a faded denim shift, arrived at the Hewitts' house to give the first of a series of weekly lessons. The Hewitts' children, Zoe (age 8) and Jude (age 6) were sent around the corner to the Oxleys' house, where a babysitter and the two Oxley children awaited them. With her back to the fireplace, into which Lincoln, moments before the Oxleys' arrival, had angrily pitched the week's newspapers left habitually by Cleo to collect on the sofa and chairs,

Hilda beamed at them with a red face and big round cheeks. The four students sat forward on stools in a semi-circle before her, the men flanked by the women, though Cleo would have liked to sit front and centre, since the lessons had been her idea in the first place. Hilda rested her guitar on her left thigh, placing it at a forty-five degree slant against her heavy breasts and curling the other thick leg beneath her. The others imitated her pose. Some time was spent tuning the guitars to Hilda's pitch pipe, but soon she had them playing the notes E, F and G on the first string.

They advanced through three untitled exercises of fifteen measures each, Cleo in the lead, striking her strings a little too vigorously and impatient with the whole notes, the men struggling heroically to keep up, Lincoln holding his guitar rather clinically, Keith gripping his like an adversary. Hilda drew their attention to how naturally Jane held the guitar.

Lincoln said Jane reminded him of Sylvia Tyson.

"It's easy for Jane," Keith said with mock jealousy. "She's been cradling babies for years."

Hilda laughed with a high giddy bubbling as though she were a carbonated drink being squeezed. At everything that was said, especially by the men, she laughed. Jane noticed that sometimes Hilda's fizzy laughter was followed by an almost imperceptible flickering of her eyelashes, as though a button had been pushed somewhere in her head to open a secret journal wherein she stored away private observations.

If Cleo, Hilda suggested, would just bend her right arm a little and pinch her left thumb and forefinger closer together in holding the neck of the guitar, pointing her thumb at the head-piece, she'd achieve better sound. Also, she should at all times, as illustrated in the book, rest the small finger of her right hand against the sounding board when striking the strings.

"That's a lot to remember all at once," Cleo snapped, looking every inch the ready-made folk artist in corduroy skirt, fringed scarf and tan cowboy boots rising to mid-calf. "My hands are too small," she demonstrated, and even Lincoln was surprised to notice her dainty porcelain fingers. "Anyway, it feels much better my way," Cleo insisted.

"Nevertheless," said Hilda, smiling neutrally but evidently prepared to throw her weight around if necessary, "developing good technique is absolutely essential."

How long would it be, Keith wanted to know, before they'd be able to play the accompaniment to Lightfoot's "Canadian Railroad Trilogy?" He already knew all the words, he said. Hilda laughed, dazzling him with her square white teeth and said, "That depends on how hard you work. In the meantime, you'll have to be satisfied with "Two-String Rock," and "Jingle Bells," which I want you to practise over the next week. You'll need to learn the notes B, C and D on the second string for that. The book will show you how. Get all six notes down cold."

"Isn't that rushing things a bit?" Lincoln, scowling as he fingered the first and third frets one last time, asked. "I don't know when I'll find the time to practise."

"I hope you won't begin holding us all back," Cleo warned him, flipping eagerly through the music book. "If you do, you'll have to drop out. We'll get you to cook the dinner while we take our lesson."

Whereas the Oxleys' house was a lengthy bungalow suited to the couple's taste for empty white spaces, the cool lines of modern furniture and ornamental topiary flanking the flagstone walk, the Hewitts lived in a two-storey grey brick with a red door, rose gardens, and a low picket fence all around. Cleo had painted the living room and halls a deep rust and furnished the house with antique benches, a thick, round dining room table with row-backed chairs, a blonde sideboard, a Quebec armoire with diamond design, wooden decoys, ladles and bowls, coal-oil lanterns, butter churns, clay jugs and iron pots, stencilled blanket chests — all of this long before Canadiana became trendy.

Where she ever found time to collect these things nobody knew, for she was the director of the town's Little Theatre, and she was always in a frenzy, clattering up and down the uncarpeted stairs of the house in high-heeled boots and long flowered skirts pursued by her two complaining children, and tying up the phone looking for babysitters. Lincoln complained that he could never reach her. The freezer was packed to the door with TV dinners and that night, after Hilda had left, Cleo was serving a dinner of packaged rice, a roast, which she drew, black and smoking, from the oven, frozen broccoli, an apple strudel bought at the bakery downtown, because *Helen Keller* was in final rehearsal and Cleo was going to slash her wrists if the play didn't come together.

"The table isn't even set, for Chris' sake," exploded Lincoln, red in the face. He and Cleo, looking remarkably alike — for Cleo too was tall, thin and taut as an over-tuned string, with the same black eyes and dark curls — were jostling one another impatiently in the tiny kitchen, setting each other off like a string of firecrackers. The late afternoon sunset streamed in on wicker baskets of all shapes arranged on the kitchen wall, and turned the expensive hanging cookware Cleo had never used into a row of copper suns. With a well-manicured thumb, Lincoln crushed an ant on the counter, producing an audible crunch.

"I see those bloody ants are back again," he growled at Cleo. "If you'd get the bloody house cleaned — "

Cleo, draining the broccoli in the sink, steam enveloping her head, shouted back, "I can't get a bloody cleaning lady to come because the bloody place is too dirty!"

Keith and Jane, drinking wine on the sidelines, exchanged glances. While Jane retreated to look at a grouping of sepia photographs, Keith, despite her signals from the living room, continued to hang in the doorway just for the entertainment, feeling, as he said to Jane later, that a dose of healthy bickering was good for any marriage. It was hard to tell why the high-strung Hewitts and the easygoing Oxleys got together at all, except that the company of professionals was hard to come by in this town. But, to be fair, the Hewitts liked the Oxleys because they never fought and Keith could make any cocktail with his eyes closed and Jane was a fabulous cook — not gourmet, but good home cooking with, like Jane herself, the simple, nutri-tive qualities of plain white bread. Keith, on the other hand, was fascinated by the electricity and drama of the Hewitts' relation-ship, which made marriage look dangerous, unpredictable and ironic, like it was on television.

"Hilda certainly laughs a lot," Cleo later said at the scarred dinner table, above which an antique fixture with six milk-glass tulip shades picked out a frost of grey hairs among her curls.

"I guess she's just self-conscious," Jane reasoned.

"Well, it could get on your nerves."

Why, Hilda was robust and healthy and optimistic, a breath of fresh air, was what Keith then said in her defense.

The wine and the guitar music, to which they now had their ears involuntarily tuned for the sound of the notes E, F and G on the first string, had evidently given Cleo romantic ideas, for she reached past the pitcher of dried cornflowers to squeeze Lincoln's fingers. But Lincoln frowned and cleared his throat, withdrawing his hand uncomfortably. On their way home that night, Keith, slightly drunk again, took advantage of the balmy evening to push Jane in behind the flowering dogwood on the northwest corner of their property, where he tore at her buttons and made love to her in the deep snow, grateful that she'd worn her loose, plaid jumper that night.

During the next week, while snow fell thick and steady, creating a free-form drift against the Oxleys' living room window and rising like a sea to the carpentered knobs of the Hewitts' picket fence, Jane and Lincoln bent tirelessly to "Three-String Rock" night after night. Their down-strokes answered each other across the lamp-strung, snow-wrapped block, long after Keith, laden with the creeping suspicion that he might be tone-deaf, turned in, and after Cleo, storming in from rehearsals, cursing and tearing her hair out, climbed the stairs vowing somehow to fit in her practicing the following day.

At the next lesson, the Oxleys' house steeped with the sweet bouquet of lamb curry, Jane and Lincoln proudly compared callouses on their fingers. It quickly became clear to Hilda, who had turned up looking tenacious, younger than ever and possibly slimmer in sneakers, jeans, a white turtle-neck and a yellow sweatshirt, which lit up her sunny hair, that Keith and Cleo were going to present problems.

"I'd be playing a lot better if I had all day to practise, like Jane," Cleo noted.

"Maybe Jane's simply talented, " suggested Lincoln, fixing Cleo with a stern look, and shifting his chair slightly closer to Jane's to escape the threat of Keith's size-twelve shoe, which dropped like a sledgehammer, keeping time. They ploughed through a cheerless interpretation of "Jingle Bells," in which a thorough Lincoln, his violet lips pressed together, showed the early marks of a flawless technician, and Jane played with poetic feeling. Cleo, who'd squeezed in less than an hour's practice, managed to keep up by playing roughly every third note. Keith, many of his notes flat, produced a disconcerting echo, finishing each line a full measure behind the others, though he seemed happy to do so. Hilda got up to lift Keith's instrument from his hands and swing it with her powerful arms against her chest, as though it were lightweight as a feather. She plucked the strings investigatively with her square, white thumbnail, but the guitar proved to be in tune. Keith, frowning earnestly, his large, balding Charlie Brownish head tilted to appreciate the vertical landscape of Hilda's womanly form, was impressed by the tensile strength of her fingers, by her height and by the fine curve of her long nostrils.

Hilda tested their understanding of time signatures, the treble or G clef, the relative value of notes, tied notes, rests and repeats. She introduced notes G and A on the third string, and together they plodded through a mournful version of *Au Clair de la Lune*." Cleo had to be reminded to keep her left wrist away from the fingerboard so that her fingers would have greater flexibility and extension.

"I *am* keeping it clear," Cleo snapped back.

"I don't think so," said Hilda, unshakeable, her eyes falling on the black beauty mark Cleo had penciled just below the downward curve of her obstinate mouth. Hilda reminded them all that the hand and wrist should be held in a curved manner, with the fingers separated from each other and ready to fall like little hammers on any of the strings desired.

"Ready to fall like little hammers on any of the strings desired," Keith recalled after the Hewitts had bundled up late that night to meet the deep freeze of a record low for February, and departed down the Oxleys' pathway, guitar cases in hand, their footsteps creaking on dry snow. "Isn't that lovely?" he asked Jane, who agreed it was lyrical. "Like little silver hammers," repeated Keith, carrying the liqueur glasses into the kitchen.

"Aren't you embellishing it a little?" Jane, filling the sink with soapy water, raised her eyebrows.

Over the following weeks, in the twilight of his study, on the safe side of the locked door, Lincoln scarcely heard Zoe and Jude, in Cleo's evening absences, running wild, hounding up and down the stairs, shouting and slamming doors until they fell, exhausted and fully clothed, into bed. Practising relentlessly until his aching fingers could perform a rapid, crisp, impeccable chromatic scale, he began to acquire the drawn, high-strung look of the dedicated musician. Down the street at the Oxleys', Jane, her dark head inclined to her speed drills, pretended not to count the number of times Keith's reflection was thrown up in the living room window as he passed between the TV room and the liquor cabinet. Once he stopped to ask her why life wasn't fun anymore.

"Isn't it?" she said, surprised. "Maybe if you got your guitar out?"

"How about a skiing holiday?" he suggested, but Jane said she didn't want to fall behind in her practicing. The Oxley boys (Lloyd, 14, and Raymond, 11) joined Keith sadly before the television, their serious gourd-like foreheads and pale eyelashes blue in the glare of Hockey Night in Canada.

"Why is Mom always playing that guitar?" they wanted to know.

"Boys," Keith said to them, "what would you say if your old man gave up medicine and opened a bar?"

It seemed that every lesson brought on a bright, sunless gale, with snow swirling in many little independent twisters, and one Saturday at four o'clock, the air was so thick with it that Keith started to pull on his boots, determined to go out and rescue Hilda, thinking she might have taken a wrong turn on her trek from the bus stop. But then she appeared, her blonde crown and pink angora headband the only part of her visible above the snow banks, which by the end of March were high and straight as walls. She blew in through the front door in her down vest, with all the rosiness and durability of a champion skier.

Hanging Hilda's vest up in the hall closet, opening her guitar case for her as she flexed her frost-nipped fingers and held them out to the roaring fire, Keith learned, over the weeks, the vital statistics: her age (23), her circumstances (fourth-year university), where she lived (with her parents in a nearby suburb) and other useful trivia. As she stood, solid as a tree, beside him,

Keith sensed from the density of her limbs, from her erect, forthright carriage and the way she planted her feet side-by-side, that Hilda was a girl of substance.

In a corner of the room, Lincoln and Jane engaged in a pre-lesson warm-up, ambitiously picking out the notes of a duet, or Lincoln, who always kept a page or two ahead of Jane, helped her with her sharps and flats. For the first time in years, Jane was letting her straight hair grow down past her jawline and now that she'd bought some short skirts, roomy sweaters and African beads, Lincoln said that she looked like a university student.

"Who, Jane?" Keith, overhearing, said.

Even Cleo, who by the time they'd reached chord study knew she was sunk, was grudgingly impressed by Lincoln's virtuosity on the plectrum exercises, but she accused him of showing off and by the end of March she was also complaining that she was running out of recipes.

"I didn't know you *had* any recipes," quipped Lincoln.

In fact they were all beginning to feel a little claustro-phobic together, and Cleo wondered out loud if the lessons were somehow to blame for the protracted winter: it seemed that, as long as they sat there playing their guitars, the snow in the Oxleys' backyard — sculpted by wind and freezing rain into a brittle, moon-like surface of craters and crusty knobs — would deepen and deepen. Hilda, sensing their restlessness, suggested that Jane and Lincoln might wish to use part of the hour to prepare a group of duets for the music festival. Thereafter, half-way through the lesson, Hilda turned her exclusive attention to Jane and Lincoln, who had gone to Domenic's together one afternoon to choose a songbook from which they selected three duet arrangements for guitar: "Greensleeves," "How Should I Your True Love Know?" and "*Plaisir d'Amour.*" While Jane produced a good, clear, felt tapestry, against which Lincoln's deep, rapidly ascending and descending arpeggios resonated like streaks of purple and gold, Cleo went off to make phone calls and Keith, grumbling, mixed drinks, giving special attention to a banana daiquiri for Hilda who, by this time, was routinely lingering after the lesson for refreshments.

One evening, when Jane was settling Zoe and Jude into bed over at the Hewitts', before her weekly practice with Lincoln, Keith found Hilda's phone number in Jane's address book.

"Do you think I have a future as a guitarist?" he asked Hilda, half in jest, when she came to the phone.

"I can't offer a lot of hope," she admitted sympathetically. "Maybe the guitar isn't your instrument." She'd broken off studying for her midterms to come to the phone, and Keith pictured her barefoot with her golden hair hanging in her eyes.

"I never really wanted to play the guitar," Keith confessed. "I just wanted to be able to sing like Gordon Lightfoot. But I don't want to stop coming on Saturdays," he said. "I like seeing you. I like hearing your sparkling laughter."

"Whatever you say, Mr. Oxley," she effervesced. "You're paying for the lessons."

Early in April, all the snow melted miraculously between one Saturday and the next, and the Oxleys arrived at the Hewitts' feeling naked and newborn without the burden of boots and coats. Keith, nifty in khaki pants and deck shoes, distracted by the golden down on Hilda's forearms and by her thick, swinging ponytail, which brushed her bare, brown shoulders like a silk tassel, reminded them all that there was no such thing as spring in this part of the world, only deep winter followed immediately by summer heat. With warm, sweet air from the open windows swelling in his nostrils, Keith was afraid that with the change in seasons, Hilda might fly away like a strong bright bird to a new nest. Jane, glancing up from the score of *"Plaisir d'Amour"* to appreciate the straight, bone-white part in Lincoln's spray-stiff hair, felt herself and Lincoln hurtling together on a headlong downhill course, advancing fast as a mad spring runoff toward a calm, open sea, toward something larger and more enduring than a musical duet.

After the lesson, Jane, without knowing why, moved swiftly up the stairs to meet Hilda returning from the washroom. There on the landing, where dust particles were held in silver suspension in the astonishing, unlimited light of the late afternoon, she told the unflinching Hilda, "You know, of course, that Keith is an alcoholic." It was the first time she'd ever admitted it to herself, let alone to anyone else, and while the revelation shook Jane so that she had to grab the walnut railing for equilibrium, it also absolved and liberated her because now she saw a way out.

Half an hour later, just as Hilda was finishing her daiquiri, Keith's private prayers were answered by a flash downpour, which obligated him to drive the umbrella-less Hilda home rather than have her get drenched at the bus stop. He returned in time to hear Cleo answer a distress call from the babysitter, who was threatening to abandon ship because Zoe and Jude would not stop throwing their dinner at the Oxley children. Neither Cleo nor Lincoln wanted to go over to settle the children down.

"Why is it always *our* children who get the blame?" Cleo demanded of Lincoln after hanging up the phone. Jane and Keith were keeping each other cold company in the living room.

"Well, I'd rather have children who live life with passion than those passive, anaemic Oxley boys!"

"Shut up, Cleo!" Lincoln warned. Then he accused Cleo of producing two monsters. Zoe and Jude, he said, were just like Cleo: stubborn and flighty and selfish. When he was left alone with them, which was practically every night, they wouldn't do what he told them. *Flout* was the word he used, which Keith thought a touch medieval. "They flout my authority," Lincoln said, pounding his fist on the kitchen counter.

"It's funny," Jane observed to Keith as they followed the greasy, rain-wet sidewalks home that night. She pointed out that Lincoln and Cleo looked so much alike, and yet the children didn't resemble Lincoln at all. They were both spitting images of Cleo. "I don't know how Lincoln has put up with Cleo all these years," Jane said smugly.

"Well, Lincoln's a bit of a prick, himself," said Keith, irritated by the suggestion that Lincoln had shared confidences with Jane.

"Do you think so?" Jane looked up at him, surprised.

"Don't you?"

The night reeked with the smell of earthworms. They'd left the Hewitts' early, under a soft lavender sky. At the edge of the property, Keith put his guitar case down in a puddle and bent to retrieve something he noticed beneath the dogwood bushes, whose vein-red branches were now pregnant with new buds. Jane took from his hand her lost overcoat button, each of them privately recalling with bitterness and disbelief that January night they'd lain in the snow.

Masses of yellow tulips quivering beneath the Oxleys' sculp-tured Japanese yews trumpeted their congratulations on a transparent May morning when Jane returned from the music festival bearing a first-prize certificate in the guitar duet, novice category. She entered the living room, whose palisade of black conifers kept it forest-cool in spring and summer. There, with his back to her, was Keith, clumsily picking out the notes of "Does Your Mother Know" from a Lightfoot songbook lying open on the coffee table, his voice a confident and tuneless bass. So pathetic and vulnerable was he with his guitar crushed to his chest, that Jane felt great tenderness for him at that moment and was about to step forward and touch his shoulder when the boys burst in from a baseball game, demanding lunch. Following an ambivalent afternoon of nauseating doubts and cold fears, Jane stood between Keith and the television and told him, "I want a divorce. I've gone to Lincoln for legal advice."

At first everyone was surprised to learn that Keith and Hilda had been carrying on, because Hilda had seemed like such a wholesome, conservative girl. Now, in retrospect, her tactics were obvious and subversive. How easily Jane and Lincoln had played into her hands, letting her manoeuver them into a liaison that left Keith in an emotional void!

Within months, Hilda, cumbersome with twins, was occupying the long, grey bungalow with Keith. She pulled up Jane's claustrophobic broadloom, put down straw mats from an oriental import boutique, and suspended hanging bamboo chairs from the living room ceiling. Whereas the house, in Jane's care, had been perfect and sterile, like a museum preserved under glass, Keith and Hilda lived like transients amid huge paisley throw cushions, the smell of burning incense and the loud playing of rock music, which filtered through the match-stick blinds in the living room and penetrated the sombre ring of pine trees. Keith stopped drinking and went to work with fresh appetite, discovering his examination rooms to be full of glorious sunshine and the veiny, translucent bellies of his pregnant patients sound and beautiful as a fortune-teller's radiant globe.

Jane and Lincoln, taking with them the four children and three guitars (Cleo's instrument having been discovered in its case in the basement when the house was packed up) eventually moved to the provincial capital. Gradually, as Lincoln settled into his new appointment as a district court judge, and as much of Jane's energy was spent policing the wars between the children, playing the guitar seemed to have become redundant. The instruments were shoved to the back of a closet, many of their strings popped from the children trying to tune them. From time to time, Keith and Hilda read in the newspaper about Lincoln's unprecedented decisions in divorce cases, wherein he granted custody of the children to the father.

Cleo crossed the ocean to study under a prominent British theatre director. Jude and Zoe, returning from summer visits with her, reported that she now spoke with a genuine British stage accent and was deliriously happy in her tiny west-end flat, which she shared with a colony of mice. Theatre people in London, she told the children, always lived in infested flats.

Do No Harm

"MAYBE IT'S THE END OF THE WORLD," my receptionist, Teneka, suggests when I come out at noon to find the waiting room empty. "All of a sudden, the phone started ringing and everyone cancelled their afternoon appointments. I got out the waiting list. There are two hundred names on it. I must have called twenty of them. Nobody could make it in." She looks at the disbelief in my face. "I know. It's unheard of." She shrugs and laughs softly. "Maybe it's the apocalypse," she says. For a moment, I can't decide what to do. I am not good at spontaneity. When I turn away she calls after me, "Why don't you take the afternoon off? When was the last time you did that? You deserve it. You're tired."

Back in my office, at the front of this narrow little house that serves as my clinic, I sit down at the roll-top desk. A Tiffany lamp throws an amber glow across the Persian rug, the oak armoire, the Martha Washington chair. It is my wife Vera, a fervent reader of *Architectural Digest*, who put this room together. She says I need this welcoming atmosphere to break the ice, as I have no bedside manner. Of course she is quite right. People, I know, take me for some kind of tight-ass, because I am ramrod-straight, formal in demeanor. There is nothing I can do about this. I do not find it easy to smile at people. I've never thought I had a pleasant face and smiling just twists it into something comical.

I am a pain specialist and for forty years people have been coming to me with their migraines and spinal injuries and botched back surgeries, their physical or emotional trauma, their pain in the face, arm, shoulder, hip. Often their malady is not a physical one but the powerful action of the mind on the body. When I ask them to describe what they feel, I see pictures in their eyes: a sharp poker, a circle of heat, two rough stones grinding together. Some never get better. They deny the effectiveness of treatments because they don't want to go off workers' compensation or because only here in my examination room are they ever physically touched or because their sickness has become their friend. I send them for MRIs and CT Scans and Myelograms. I authorize opiates and anti-inflammatories, administer steroid injections, cortisone, nerve blocks. Sometimes, I will resort to prescribing placebos because I know a patient will do just as well or better on a phony pill as on a potent one. This is not deceit but compassion.

At first, I think I'll spend the afternoon working on my book on facial neuralgia, but I find myself shuffling restlessly through my notes. Beyond the window, sunshine exploding in the street is a temptation. I picture Vera and me sailing down the parkway, the top of her red convertible turned down, the river a blue ribbon flashing below the cliffs. We could stop at that little cafe at the bottom of a steep road, have a glass of crisp white wine on the floating dock.

I tidy my desk, pull my jacket on, say good day to Teneka and leave. Outside, I walk south a few doors to a small grocer and search among the buckets of flowers set out on the sidewalk. I choose three bouquets of gerbera, take them inside and wait for them to be wrapped. Retracing my steps, I pass the clinic. Through the glass door, I see Teneka at her desk, the flickering light from her computer turning her face blue. Behind her rises a cold wall of filing cabinets. For a moment I feel a twinge of guilt that I've never thought of touching up her area with — oh, I don't know — silk flowers, a few pictures, perhaps an aquarium, a carpet on the linoleum floor.

I know nothing about Teneka, really, other than that she is a spinster. Thirty years she's worked for me and I've never even asked her where she lives or if she has family, siblings and such. How she spends Christmas or in which month her birthday falls. She's never asked for holidays or an increase. For all I know, I'm still paying her what I did a decade ago. She doesn't seem to have any needs. I don't take much notice of her and I believe she doesn't want to be noticed.

A few more yards and I make a left turn and climb a short steep curving hill into our small neighbourhood, a pocket of parallel streets running to the river. I need merely follow along a few blocks, perhaps a mile, to our house. The streets here are narrow and the houses hug each other cozily. Old stone cottages stand alongside clapboard row dwellings where mill workers used to live, or tall, thin merchants' houses in red brick. It is a pleasant place to walk, with little traffic. Nothing gives me more pleasure than heading home on a Friday evening bearing a bouquet of flowers for Vera. Though she often greets them with irritation, saying, "Why do you always have to come in with them when I'm busiest?" I know she likes to set them about her tables.

But it is not Friday, it is Wednesday close to high noon and at first I wonder if this accounts for my feelings of disorientation. But to be truthful, the absence of patients for the afternoon has unsettled me. Although I like my work, it has occurred to me recently that it doesn't seem to mean much. I have not accomplished anything lasting in my life. I have not taken any risks or done anything remarkable. I know I am a grey sort of person. Sometimes, I think I haven't understood anything at all that's happened to me. Often, recently, I am feeling this way and turning over these thoughts as I walk up the hill from work. But as soon as I see Vera, I am reassured. Her never-look-back attitude, her utter command of life, fortify me. I do respect her. Possibly, I even fear her. But I also worship her and long for the moment when we lie in bed and I can hold her hand, which is the one intimacy she still abides.

It is a day of stunning heat, and soon my shirt is stuck to my skin, but I do not remove my jacket. Vera says I have a washboard chest and a sports coat lends me physical substance. Passing along the dappled sidewalk, under a line of ash, elm, maple, through patches of amethyst shade refreshing as a dip in a pool, I imagine taking Vera by surprise, perhaps finding her in a bikini on the back deck, where she tans herself to a nut brown, her belly glistening with oil. If I go up and kiss her, she will turn her temple to me. She says that to kiss at this age is ridiculous. I do not contradict her. I have found she is usually right about things. She can spot falseness long before I can. She is the one true and reliable thing I know in life. When I met her, I was twenty-six and a resident at the hospital. Vera was receptionist in day-surgery. At the time, I thought she was magnificent, and I still do. I walked past her station every day just to get a look at her. It soon became clear that part of what she wanted in life was me. I have never understood why.

This is my world, this daily trek from home to office and back. Vera says that if it weren't for my occasional detours to visit our daughter, Lane, who lives only a stone's throw away, my life would be nothing but a corridor. She says that I have never developed the skills to make friends and in her harsher moments she says that I do not even know what friendship is. If this is true, I believe it is too late for me to change. There are few men in my life. In fact, I can think of none. My father has been dead so long that I have to take a photograph out to remember what he looked like. So my mainstays, basically, are two women — Vera and Lane, unless of course you count Teneka, whom I've certainly never thought of as a woman. And also our friend, Ursula, who drops in several nights a week on her way home from work, often staying for dinner, blending seamlessly into our life. I cannot in all truth say she's *our* friend. If Vera heard that, she'd waste no time reminding me that it is she and Ursula who are friends and that I am just a lucky bystander. She's not motivated to say this out of unkindness but a desire for truth. I admire Vera's dedication to clarity. Really, she is a model of integrity to us all.

I breathe in the perfume of wisteria. A block ahead of me on this very street stands Ursula's house. I am still some distance from it when I see Vera's red BMW pull up in front. It occurs to me that she might have come there to retrieve something she's left behind, a sweater or a book, perhaps. When she gets out of her car, I almost call out to her, but something in her bearing and her attire stop me. She wears a black lace skirt I've never seen before, very short, exposing her bare, brown thighs. Also, a sleeveless satin blouse that flashes like fire in the sun, a pair of those suicidally-high heels I've seen on young women. There is a brazen sway to her backside, a ripe anticipation in her body. Pressing her key into the lock, she disappears inside. An instant later, a low sleek Jaguar whizzes past me, creating a small wind that throws my tie up over my shoulder. The car skids to a halt behind Vera's. A man leaps out, shoots across the sidewalk, bounds up the porch, his feet ringing on the wooden boards. The door swings open, I see Vera's hand float out, tanned, her wedding diamond catching the sun. One foot on the threshold, the man seizes her hand, pulls her playfully toward him. I see the curve of Vera's bronzed shoulder, her face tilted toward his.

Confusion is rampant in me. I slip behind a telephone pole. The door slams shut. Still, I linger there, pressed against the dry, burned wood, the powerful smell of creosote in my nostrils. I feel the heat of the post against my jacket, hear the rough, splintered wood tearing at its fine threads. I do not know what to do. I think of going up, pounding on the door, shouting through the open window beside the porch, demanding an explanation. Unthinkable. The street shimmers with heat. Cars pass and I duck my head, hoping it is no one I know. I am sweating heavily and my tie feels like a tightening noose. What a fool I must look. A girl of twelve or so comes along the sidewalk in a t-shirt and jeans. On her feet are bedroom slippers. She carries a baby's soother in her hand. She smiles a conspiratorial smile at me, as though to hide behind a telephone post is normal behavior for a grown man. I wonder if the whole world is mad.

Turning, I retrace my steps, hurtling back down the hill, wondering what kind of figure I cut, rigid, erect, the flowers trembling in my hand as I bound down the slope with long strides. Reaching the clinic, I burst inside. Teneka looks up. "You're back?" she says. "Did you forget something? What's happened? You're white as a ghost." I rush past her and into my study, where I tear off my tie, throw my jacket in a chair. In a moment, there's a soft knock at the door. Teneka enters and sets a glass of water on my desk. "Have you had some shock? Are you not going home?" she asks.

"I'd like to be left alone," I snap.

"What shall I do with these?" she asks, holding the gerbera out, and I realize I dropped the flowers on a chair in the waiting room.

"Throw them out, for all I care," I say impatiently.

"Something's happened. I wish you'd tell me." Out of the corner of my eye, I see her at my elbow, short and graceless, wearing a shapeless turtleneck sweater, baggy trousers, flat, laced shoes. The contrast with Vera's provocative attire makes me hate the very sight of her.

"I'm alright, I tell you. I can't work with you pestering me."

"I'm sorry." She creeps out of the room.

"Could you close the door?" I call after her.

"Of course."

I hear her flat-footed steps retreat down the hall. In a moment comes the sound of water running in the little bathroom off the waiting area, the clink of glass against the faucet. I don't know what to do next. I notice that my hands are shaking with — what? Shame? Bewilderment? Shock? I can't work. My thoughts race. I stare at the tall walnut carvings we brought back from Africa and which Vera said would look good here. Their long, pointed breasts seem to mock me. The hours slip past and soon it is after five o'clock. Through the window comes the thickening sound of rush hour traffic. Finally, I emerge from my office and there are the gerbera, still in their paper wrapping, propped in a jug of water, ready for me to take home. Teneka stands behind her desk, a filing drawer open, her arms lifted.

"Are you sure there isn't something I could do — ?" Her white hair has no shape. It is fine and messy. She never seems to get it cut. The long bangs hang over her owlish glasses. I leave without saying goodbye.

Arriving home, I catch the voices of Vera and Ursula out on the back deck, the sound of ice clinking in glasses. I pause for a moment in the kitchen and listen. I used to like the idea of them out there, these two attractive women. It flooded me with — what? A sense of safety? This is nonsense. I am not a child. What, then? Luck? Until today, I thought a man could not have a better life than mine. I take a deep breath and step out into the fluid light of the late afternoon. Ursula rises gracefully, crossing the deck to greet me.

"Lyon, how *are* you? she asks, with an emphasis that makes me feel she truly wants to know. She has a deep, throaty voice, like a thirties movie star. Her eyes are large and watery, their blue fading in recent years. Her full lips, a loose strand of her iron-grey hair, brush my cheek. I feel the fleeting touch of her cool fingers on my neck, smell her light perfume. This intimacy still surprises and moves me. A part of me understands that it is just her friendly way, but another senses there is a special connection between us, despite what Vera says.

"Oh, Lyon is always the same," says Vera in a tone of boredom.

"You always look so wonderful in your jackets," Ursula tells me. I watch her curvaceous figure as she returns to her chair.

At a time when other women are going about barelegged, her slender legs are sheathed in a kind of fine stocking that reminds me of the ones my mother wore in the forties. There is nothing of struggle in Ursula. I have always thought of her as a lovely tree, with life gently flowing through her graceful branches. She has said she has no expectations of life. This is surprising in a woman who came from some money (though she seems to have squandered it all). She was raised in a wealthy Toronto neighbourhood, attended private schools. While Vera has to strive for class, Ursula is the real McCoy.

"We've just been catching up on our friends' colourful lives," Ursula tells me.

"Lyon wouldn't understand," jokes Vera. "Don't you know he's colour-blind?" What others have sometimes taken for harshness in Vera I always understood to be a game we played and while it's true that she made up the rules, I believed that without her, I'd have no game at all.

"We're empty," Vera tells me, holding out her glass. "Be an angel, will you? Get us a refill?"

"Let me do it, Lyon," says Ursula, half-rising in her chair. "You had a tiring day."

"He's a drug-pusher," says Vera, waving her back down. "How tiring can that be?"

"Poor Lyon," says Ursula. She wears her hair pulled back from her forehead and held with combs. This and her Chanel suits are a throwback to a more elegant age. I'd always thought that Ursula's body flows outward, whereas Vera holds hers in, playing her cards close to her chest.

I step back into the kitchen, drop more ice in the tumblers, splash bourbon in, open the fridge to look for mint. Wind blows through the house. Out on the deck, the women's voices carry on. Why, I ask myself, have I always been happy to sit back and listen? Why am I am no good at repartee? The sun blazes off the doors of the old garages, in various stages of collapse, lining the narrow laneway running behind these houses. A neighbour's car creeps along, its tires crunching on the stony pavement.

"I've decided we're going to Italy," Vera announces when I rejoin them. "And I've asked Ursula to come with us."

"Maybe Lyon needs time to think about it," says Ursula, flashing me her dazzling smile. She is, in a word, stunning. Life seems to flow over Ursula, whereas Vera bends it to her will, like a dry branch.

"Oh, Lyon's fine with the idea."

"That sounds splendid," I say.

"What did I tell you?" Vera asks Ursula. "Good doggie," she says, patting my wrist.

"Lyon, dear," says Ursula with concern. "Are you not well? You look a little blue this evening."

"Oh, Lyon doesn't have emotions," says Vera with a wave of her hand.

I go upstairs and look about the bedroom. Nothing out of the way. Noticing the laundry basket, I raise the lid. There, thrown carelessly on top, is a set of lacy red underwear I've never seen on Vera. I pick it up, press it to my face, breathe in. Then I go to Vera's closet and begin to push her clothing aside, one piece at a time, so many of them. I wonder for the first time what she needs so many clothes for? I've never questioned the size of her wardrobe. I've always been proud to be seen with her, of how she can create herself in one image, then another. Now, I know all this was not for me, but for this lover, or maybe many of them. I come upon the lace skirt, the red satin blouse I saw on her this afternoon. I stroke the slippery fabric with my fingertips, like a blind man trying to get his bearings.

In the kitchen after Ursula leaves, I say, "What did you do today?"

"Oh, I was here, puttering around."

"I called you at noon. I wanted to take you to lunch. I had no patients after twelve. You didn't answer the phone."

"Maybe you dialed wrong."

"I think I know our own phone number."

For the remainder of the evening, we barely speak. Vera seems to detect no difference to our norm. I am in turmoil, scarcely able to control my emotions. Stealing glances at her, I notice the crude bulb on the end of her nose, her small, knobby chin, her coarse complexion. The thinness she has worked to maintain over the years I'm afraid makes her look hard as stone. I am reminded of something she said to me when I first met her: "I'm going to get what I want out of life, or I'll tear the world down."

Despite my humiliation, I am inexplicably aroused in bed. Vera's back is turned to me, her profile so like a reliable landscape, with its ridges and valleys. I sidle over to her, full of supplication, and when I get close, she says, "I'm exhausted. Don't breathe on my neck. You know I hate that. You're suffocating me." And so, I have to retreat. On the soft mattress, there is no dignified way to accomplish this. Across it I creep, moving first my butt, then my knees, like some kind of insect or crab, awkward, scalded, ugly to behold.

I stare at the darkness, listening to Vera's deep breathing. People pass on the sidewalk below. Muted laughter. I get up and go downstairs and turn on a few lamps and wander through the rooms of the house, which is by no means grand, but which Vera's talent with antiques and carpets and collectibles has made look rather posh. At the beginning of our marriage I was bewildered and surprised. I felt — well, shy, I suppose — as these trappings took shape around us and more than a little in awe of her taste and her fierce pursuit of beauty. I felt unworthy, not sure I fit in. I learned in a way to be defined by the statement Vera made in our home, knowing she always had better ideas than I. Now, glancing about at the deep burgundy and indigo and evergreen paint, which so darkens the rooms, and the carefully chosen vases and perfectly placed bowls, I suddenly see how little this has ever had to do with me.

On Monday evening, when Vera is at her book club, I go for a walk. It is an evening of meaty cumulous clouds, dense as mountains. Finding myself on Ursula's street, I notice her lights on and a moment later I am ringing the doorbell. I had always thought my feelings for Ursula were complicated but when she opens the door, I realize they are in fact quite simple: I have always had a bit of a crush on her. We sit down and exchange small talk and I can see that she is wondering what I'm doing here. She is in a shapeless track suit and her hair is tousled and she wears no makeup. I haven't seen her this way before. In a corner, the television continues to flicker, a hint perhaps that she'd like to get back to her program. She is a watcher of soap operas and late-night talk shows.

I ask to use her bathroom and she says, "Yes, of course," and I climb up the narrow stairs with their soiled carpet and rickety, chipped railing. This is an old house, rundown and in need of a facelift, and cluttered with dusty knickknacks, photographs and memorabilia. There is a stale smell of unopened windows and an air conditioner set too low. Instead of entering the bathroom, I turn at the top of the stairs and make for her bedroom. I stand in the doorway, feeling foolish, not knowing why I'm here: curiosity? masochism? grief? I stare at the lumpy bed, with its worn chenille cover, at the stained, crooked, fringed lampshades and the pile of books and mess of newspapers on the floor and the jars of creams on the night table. I try to picture a scene of passion here. I think: what is this hovel, compared to our bedroom? Everything I've given Vera? I look out the window at the street. A city bus roars past, blowing up eddies of dust on the bleached sidewalk. A man passes, walking an old, crippled Airedale.

"I saw Vera come in here the other day with a man," I tell Ursula, downstairs.

"Oh, dear," she says softly, her face neutral. Her eyes look small and tired and her cheeks are papery and full of fine lines. Her hands are dry looking, the skin transparent and hanging loose. At this moment, she seems to me old and ordinary and maybe not very smart. She dropped out of university at twenty. She said she was having too much fun to study. She married, bore two children, got divorced. I wonder what kind of love life she's had. Vera has hinted that Ursula has slept with many men, some of them the age of her son. She does not know what guilt is, or regret. Once, I said to Vera, "Ursula is very easy with life," and she snapped, "She lacks ambition."

"Who is this man of Vera's? How long has it been going on?" I ask Ursula.

"I really couldn't say."

"You can't, or you won't?"

"It's none of my business."

"You made it your business when you provided a boudoir for her."

"If I hadn't, someone else would have."

"I was hoping you'd help me," I say. "I thought you were my friend."

"Dearest, I am," she says earnestly. "And if you had a secret, I'd keep that too."

I get up and pace the room, feeling angry, duped by — someone. Ursula? Vera? Perhaps mostly by myself. There is a lot of furniture here, different seating arrangements, too many chairs and pictures and cushions and throws. I had thought Ursula's life had a pleasant chaos about it, whereas for Vera there are always structures and goals and rules. But now Ursula's world seems only shoddy. She has always been a great raconteur, a spinner of racy tales about the unorthodox people she's known. At this moment, it seems like she is two people: the fictional, entertaining one, and the real one, living in this deteriorating house.

"You could talk to Vera about it," she tells me.

"I won't beg," I say adamantly.

She looks at me for a moment. "You've always been a pleaser, Lyon."

"I don't see what's wrong with that."

"Maybe it bores Vera." She gazes out the window, musing. "This is just a frivolous fling. I doubt if she loves him. Maybe Vera can't love *anyone*." She looks back at me. "Have you never looked at another woman?"

"Never."

"Maybe you should have."

"I've never been unfaithful to her," I say passionately.

"Of course you haven't."

Out on the porch, I turn to Ursula with some envy. "How are you always so happy?" I ask.

"Why, dear one, I'm just grateful for every day I'm alive. It's that simple."

Late on Saturday afternoon, Vera and I are driving along the commercial street on which my clinic stands, and when we pass it we notice the lights on. Through the glass front door we can see Teneka's figure hunched over her desk, a not-unfamiliar sight. "There's your girlfriend in there, doing your bidding," says Vera. It is not the first time she's made such a remark, and it has always bewildered me. Once when she said it, I reached across in the car and squeezed her hand as if to say, "Don't be silly," but she pulled hers away, telling me, "Keep both hands on the wheel. It makes me nervous when you don't." I glance over at her now and see her profile looking very bitter. Her chest is deeply tanned and freckled and leathery looking from sun exposure. She is wearing those pedal-pusher things, exposing the varicose veins creeping up her ankles.

Once, when I expressed the mildest objection to something she'd done, she said, "If you don't like it you can go and live with Teneka," and I answered, deeply wounded by the suggestion that, if I didn't have Vera, all I'd be able to get is someone like Teneka, "What do you mean, go and live with Teneka? What are you talking about?"

In the kitchen we unpack the groceries in silence. Vera gives me a sideways look. "I hope you're not sulking again," she says.

"What are you sulking about?"

"I'm not sulking about anything," I answer with irritation. She pauses, looking out at the alley, the sun reflected off a white garage door. Her hair is short and spiky, brown with blonde streaks, which I've always thought looked like a raccoon's coat. She hasn't worked since we married. She's filled her life with yoga, bridge, art courses, antique hunting. I had always admired her for fashioning happiness out of nothing, but now I see that what she's come up with is not happiness but some sort of deception of me and perhaps more so of herself.

I say to her, "Who is this man you're sleeping with?" I hadn't intended to ask, hadn't believed I had the courage.

She is silent for a moment, and then she turns, her face hard and closed, and says, "It has nothing to do with you."

"Well, that's a little absurd."

She says, "You're very dull, Lyon. I've put up with it all my life and I think that's a lot. I don't expect this dalliance will last. It's just my little hobby at the moment. I don't take it seriously and I don't think you should either. Now there's no reason for us talk about this anymore." Turning back to look out the window, she says matter-of-factly, "If I don't have something new in my life, I'll go insane."

I slip out into the fragile light of the evening. Closing the red lacquered door behind me, I feel a sudden and inexplicable relief, a tremendous weight lifted off my shoulders, as though I've shed a heavy armature. It feels good to be out and not knowing where I'm going. At first, I walk aimlessly up and down the neighbourhood streets but soon I am crossing a field of long swaying grasses and turning onto a narrow dirt path that follows the river. It's a soft, humid night. There are trees along the path and I pass in and out of their shade. I stop at an open area and look across the water. The river is narrow here and muddy, meandering and slow, funky-smelling, the shore choked with reeds and wildflowers and musical with the croaking of frogs. The sky turns pink. There are many people out at this time of day in this narrow park, walking their Afghans and their golden retrievers, or ambling alone, lost in thought. It is a place of solitude and contemplation, the wind off the river a healing force. I see a neighbour who has grown thin from cancer and another who recently lost his wife to heart disease. We wave enigmatically at each other and move on. Facing the water are old houses, some of them renovated, with decks added to take advantage of the river view, others tenement houses with rickety fire escapes. Now, into view comes the apartment Lane rents on the back of a little stone cottage. I cross the grass and call out to her and she appears at the screen door and says with soft surprise, "Dad, what are you doing here?" and lets me in.

We have, as I said, only the one child. I had thought we'd have more but Vera said she was not going to spend her life wiping children's noses. At the time, I did not allow myself to be disappointed, though it seems to me it would have been nice to have more noise and commotion in the house and also for Lane to have a playmate.

I step across the threshold. There is a pot of soup simmering on the stove. The place is filled with the smell of lentils and Indian spices. In her late teens and early twenties, Lane drank a lot and I suspect she did her fair share of drugs. But now that she is nearly thirty and anxious about never finding her Path in Life, she's adopted a substance-free lifestyle. She lives on tofu, kale, carrot juice. She is small-boned, fair-skinned, copper-haired. I never knew where she got that red hair. On her narrow shoulders hangs a thin, shapeless cotton dress. She shops at what they call 'vintage' stores, but really, it's just other people's old clothes. There used to be a stigma to this, but for her and her friends, it's a badge of honour. She crosses the room in clumsy rope sandals. I remember her being pretty and delicate when she was a little girl. She is still attractive but not in a particularly feminine way. She doesn't fuss with her looks. I sometimes wonder if she's gay. I hope she isn't but if she is, I guess that's alright.

Like most young actresses, she's out of work a great deal of the time and must supplement her income with waitressing and the occasional retail job. I don't see how she could be happy about this but she never complains and she won't let us give her money. Looking about her little apartment, I cannot tell what is poverty and what is purity. I envy her lack of possessions and wonder if it is a necessity or a deliberate rebellion against the materialism of her parents.

It is on the tip of my tongue to say, I've left your mother. I've nowhere to go. I wondered if you'd let me stay here. I know now that this is why I've come here. But in the adjoining room of this small place a mattress lies on the floor. There is not even a couch here to offer, only loose cushions lining a wall. And I wonder with some disgust — have I gone through life not noticing anything? The idea that Lane could take me in is ludicrous. I had even hoped that she might have some fresh, naïve wisdom to offer me, her life being unclouded by disappointment, betrayal, error, despair. I'd intended to say: I don't know what to do. Tell me what I should do next. Now, I feel embarrassed at how little I am in command of my life.

Lane makes a pot of tea and we go out and sit on the cracked and crumbling flagstones of a little patio and look at the Canada geese floating by and the distant skyscrapers, hazy in the downtown heat. I have always thought she was closer to me than to Vera. We are both quiet people, Lane and I. We know the wisdom of standing back and letting Vera get what she wants. Tonight, we sit on broken webbed chairs. Without looking at me, Lane reaches across and finds my hand and holds it generously in hers. With some wonder, I look down on it, soft and white and small, and I remember being amazed at how well she played the piano as a child, given the shortness of her fingers. Even then, she was a clear-headed girl, so wise for her years that it shook me.

Now, she says to me, as though, earlier, she'd read my mind, "I don't like to own anything. I need to be able to move anywhere in the country — the world — with just a rucksack." Then she adds suddenly, her voice pained and passionate, "But I have to keep *wanting* things. If you don't *want* anything in life, you don't *get* anything," and I turn and look at her profile and see that her face is full of youthful fear.

It is dusk now and I pass the lane that runs behind the houses on our street, its pavement dusty and uneven and lined with electrical poles and sagging wooden garages and garbage pails. The sight of it makes me stop in my tracks, because suddenly it strikes me, like a blow in the chest, how shabby and sad and banal it looks, this back alley of our lives, where deception and anguish and betrayal and capitulation have quite likely found their home. Someone committed suicide here in their garage six months ago, their lungs filling, mercifully perhaps, with carbon monoxide. Who can blame them? Perhaps I knew all along that there were secrets in my marriage but simply turned a blind eye, as it was simpler and more diplomatic and less troubling to do so. The evening is bittersweet, the loneliness that fills me, I now realize, is nothing different, really, from what I've felt all my life, and so I know that it can be borne.

I must consult a phonebook in a glass booth on a corner to find out Teneka's address. I drive along a parkway and turn into a blue-collar neighbourhood of subsidized townhouses and tiny bungalows clad in fake brick, some of them with religious shrines on their small lawns, some still decorated, now in May, with Christmas lights and inflatable snowmen and Santa Clauses. It appears that I do not pay Teneka enough for her to live in a better district. When she opens her door, I am momentarily tongue-tied but the look on my face tells her my story.

"Trouble at home?" she says. She is wearing a flannel nightgown, it being, after all, nearly ten o'clock.

"I realize this is very irregular," I say.

"It's fine."

"But I couldn't think of anywhere else to go."

She steps back, inviting me in. In the living room are many shelves bearing the crystal vases I've given her over three decades as Christmas presents. Vera may have picked some of them out. I see them all lined up there and feel both touched by Teneka's loyalty in putting them on display and embarrassed at what little care and imagination I've shown in my gift-giving. Suddenly, I feel very tired.

"I must lie down," I say.

"Of course." She leads me to a bed with an ugly patchwork quilt on it. Vera would have been appalled. Teneka brings a glass of water and places it on the night table and, after a momentary pause, sits down on the mattress beside me. I see the deep drapery of her papery cheeks, the long white hairs on her chin, the smudges on her thick glasses, her hair going every which way, with no body or style. I reach up and touch her shoulder.

Across the street from my office and down a little way are the stone gates of a cemetery. Sometimes after work I pass through them and climb the steep hill and walk along the narrow, quiet, rural-like avenues that lead in and out and round and round the acres of tombstones, beneath the broad shade of ancient maples. Occasionally, I wander among the graves, stopping here and there to read the epitaphs of governors-general and prime ministers and business tycoons buried in this, our oldest and largest and most prestigious cemetery. I take comfort and amusement in the fact that, when all is said and done, these important people are no more remarkable than I. On the south side of the cemetery, the ground drops off sharply, and there I stop and look out over the city, sparkling below like a carpet of jewels in the sun. From here, I can see the high-rise apartment building where I now live. A half-hour's walk will take me there. On summer nights, I carry a glass of wine out onto my balcony, which has a view of the river and a path on which cyclists and dog-walkers pass until dusk. I am happier than I've ever been. I now see it as a blessing that Vera betrayed me. Or perhaps we betrayed each other in not knowing ourselves. Some weeks ago, when I was walking in the cemetery, I thought I saw Vera on a distant path, across an acre of headstones. It was a blustery day and her clothes and headscarf were being whipped about but she pressed on into the wind as though its power were nothing compared to her own, and I reflected that I had never seen her falter at anything.

In my clinic, below the cemetery, I am now the one who closes up for the night. My new receptionist, a young mother of two with a long black ponytail, leaves promptly at five and adheres rigidly to her job description. I have had to assume the tasks Teneka absorbed over the years — supervising the bookkeeper, ordering supplies, getting in roofers and plumbers and gardeners. I must shovel off the porch in winter and throw salt on the driveway. This new girl scarcely seems to notice me. I believe she thinks I am an old man. Since her arrival, the practice has not run so smoothly. Teneka had been brilliant at juggling my appointments, never leaving a space in my day, placating the most unreasonable of patients, knowing them all by name. Some of them used to tell me they didn't know what they'd do if it weren't for her welcoming face when they came in the door. "It's almost as good as your treatment," they told me.

It is best that Teneka, for whatever reason, moved on from her position. She had been there too long and had become unhealthily dependent on me. In sleeping with her that one night, I know that I used her, just as Vera used me. I may have done it out of anger with Vera or some kind of twisted revenge. When I slipped away the following morning, I was both glad and ashamed of what I'd done. Recently, when I saw Teneka plodding along a neighbourhood street, I still did not feel remorse. I cannot say what kind of man I am.

This summer, Lane moved to Toronto, where she has a small part with a fledgling theatre company. She says there are more professional opportunities there, and while this is no doubt true, I believe she is sick of her parents' choices and their lives and, perhaps more importantly, we no longer interest her. I went down there to see her perform. It was the first I'd left our city in years. For the past decade, I had no longer felt the need to travel. I'd seen everything in Europe that interested me, and at my age I had no urge to climb Machu Pichu or sail the Pacific in a tall ship or float in a canoe down the Amazon or stand on the sands of Namibia, which is what our friends seemed to be doing to prove they were getting younger rather than older. I had nothing against the familiar, the predictable, in fact, I found in them beauties to which most people are blind. However, just the other day, I picked up a brochure advertising a guided tour of Cambodia and Laos, and I am beginning to think it would be a good idea for me to venture forth.

I wasted so much time with Vera and yet it seems to me that I continue to squander it. Sometimes I pass hours wandering in the cemetery, which, granted, is a beautiful place. From my hip pocket I draw the map I acquired at the cemetery office, indicating the most famous graves. I go round and round. I walk to the lip of the cliff and look down at the city and I wonder: what exactly is one meant to do with one's life? What is the most productive way to live it?

Clemency

I WAS HOLED UP IN THE basement at six o'clock one evening when my wife, Maeve, arrived home from work. I heard the door open and her feet clattering down the stairs. She rarely appeared down there, so I knew this visit did not bode well. Crossing the basement, she stood beside me, wearing one of her power suits, which are as durable and battle-worthy as armour. Dressed in these, she was cold, seamless, impenetrable. She told me she'd heard about the theft at the museum.

"What theft?" I asked.

"You know what theft. That pistol they just bought back from Russia."

"Who told you about that?"

"I ran into Gary at the grocery store."

"That's supposed to be confidential. They're trying to keep it out of the papers."

"Did you take that gun, Ray?" asked Maeve.

"Is that what Gary said?"

"No, but it was written all over his face."

"It's always nice to have a loyal friend."

The texture of Maeve's body had changed. When we first met, her figure was commodious, obliging, tender, soft as putty.

Now she swam, lifted weights. She was not slender by any means but she was toned, unyielding as a tree.

"You're the one with the set of keys to the showcases," she pointed out.

"There are other sets."

"Where?"

"The Director's office."

"Don't make me laugh."

"I didn't know you still knew how to."

Before me on a table lay an exact replication of the Battle of Borodino. In my hand, I held a miniature figure representing my hero, Napoleon. Maeve didn't even look at it. She would no longer acknowledge my hobby. There was a time when she'd said to her friends, her voice proud, "Ray reads history books. He can't get enough of them."

"If you stole that gun, Ray, you're going to get caught," said Maeve. "You're not smart enough to get away with it." Before she turned away, she said, "Is this the battle where Napoleon gets creamed?" She knew I didn't like to think about Waterloo.

I watched her ankles, still sweet as the day I met her, rise up the stairs. The cellar door slammed, then the front door. Out in the driveway, our car roared to life. Maeve tearing off to her book club or her dinner group or her body-flow class or a meeting with her life coach.

I went upstairs to investigate supper. Crystal was in the kitchen pouring herself a Coke.

"Hi," I said.

"Hunh?" She plucked the iPod buds out of her ears. "What do you want?"

"Nothing. I just said hello."

"What for?"

"No reason."

"Now you've made me miss part of my song."

"Sorry."

Crystal was sixteen, a short, sensuous girl with milky skin. Her midriff was exposed, her breasts, in a low-cut top, were offered up like exotic fruit, shimmering beneath the kitchen lights.

"Can't you cover yourself up?" I asked her. On her feet were soft, fringed suede boots.

I'd told Maeve, "She looks like a Russian prostitute."

I said to Crystal, "What do boys think of you when they see you dressed like this?"

"Who cares what they think? I wouldn't let any of them near me with a ten-foot pole. They're all pigs."

"Why do you say that?"

"I know my livestock," she said.

"What about your brother? You don't talk about *him* that way."

She raised her eyebrows. "I don't think of Fletcher as a *guy*."

From her ear lobes, hoops the size of saucers swung and flashed, brushing her shoulders. It was January, the kitchen window black. Beyond our tiny back yard shone the harsh, cold lights of the strip-mall parking lot. We heard car doors slamming, the voices of strangers.

Crystal paused in the kitchen doorway, turned and said, "Mom told me you stole a gun." She sipped her Coke, observing me carefully over the rim of the glass.

"I didn't steal a gun," I said, irritated. "Your mother's just trying to undermine me."

"Mom usually knows what she's talking about."

I went along to Fletcher's room. His door was always closed. I sat on the edge of his bed, where he was surrounded by library books about flowers. Around us, posters showing the anthurium family, the orchid family, the gerbera family gleamed. *Gerbera mirage. Gerbera rhapsody. Gerbera kaukasus.* He was fourteen and small for his age, skinny and fine-boned, with big, receptive ears, large sensitive hands. A benign, impartial, soft-edged child fond of paisley shirts. When I mentioned to Maeve my concern with his tastes, she said Fletcher was in touch with his female side, that he was the New Male. According to her, his interest in flowers is a direct response to my destructive hobby.

"War games don't hurt anyone," I argued.

"Ray," she said, "don't try to tell me that guns aren't about killing."

"Your mother's telling everyone I stole a gun," I said to Fletcher.

"Why would you steal a gun?"

"I didn't. That's the thing."

"But if you did steal it, why would you?" He always comes at things from the back end.

"I'm not a curator anymore. I got demoted. They said I couldn't cut the mustard."

"What's a curator?" asked Fletcher.

"Haven't I explained that to you?"

He grimaced apologetically. "Maybe I forgot?"

I looked at his fresh, genuine face and shook a little with wonder. Being with Fletcher, I thought, was like the unfettered feeling of stepping into a field of summer wheat: the still heat of the tall grasses, the dry hiss of the ripening ears, the lung-searing oxygen, the golden horizon.

"If your mother knew me, she wouldn't say such things," I told him.

"Nobody ever really knows anyone, Dad," he said wisely. "Why do you think I'm going into flowers?"

I looked at him for a moment. "Fletcher, are you gay?"

"I don't know yet, Dad."

"But don't you think being a florist could — you know — push you over the edge?"

"Dad, I don't think that's the way it works."

"Why don't you get a botany degree instead? Go to university? You're smart enough. You've got your mother's brains. You could be a scientist. It would have more prestige."

He shook his head gently. "I want to work with flowers. I want to feel their petals in my hands. I want to make beautiful things."

"You could get research grants. Go to Indonesia. Discover rare plants. Name them after yourself."

"Dad," he said patiently, "I'm going to open my own florist shop. On Bank Street. I've already got the store front picked out."

"Maybe you'll change your mind."

I blamed myself for not getting him into team sports. "You should have taken up hockey for a hobby," I told him. "I'd have gotten up early and driven you to the practices. That would have made your mother happy. She'd have liked to see us bonding."

"I'm too small, Dad. The other guys would have killed me."

He was a premature baby. When he was born, he was the length of a milk bottle. We could fit his head into a teacup. He claims that's why he has a flattened nose: we kept demonstrating to our friends how his head fit into a teacup.

"Is that true?" I asked Maeve.

I'd been friends with Gary Buick since before I can remember, almost before I knew my own name. We were like brothers, inseparable, united by a congenital love of soldiers, guns, war. We grew up only houses from each other, attended public school together, then college. The autumn we were twenty, we pulled a prank at a local football game. At half time, we drew some Kotex pads out of our coat pockets, spread them with strawberry jam and threw them down into the stands. The crowd went wild. People leapt up from their seats, turned around, scanned the bleachers, searching for the culprits. They shook their fists, roaring. Mothers covered their children's eyes. Somebody called Security over. Gary and I, our fingers sticky with jam, tipped back our beer bottles, playing innocent. Two girls sitting in front of us looked around and gave us the evil eye.

"Couple of idiots," they said and turned away in disgust, but we could see their shoulders shaking with laughter. Two dense, ripe, creamy girls, soft-necked, dimple-wristed, with mauve lipstick, glittery blue eye shadow, long plastic fingernails, bleach-blonde hair cascading in curls, like golden waterfalls. Their small pretty hands rested lightly, reverently, on their knees as though their bodies were temples, deserving of worship. Maeve Spain and Molly Kisse. They could have been sisters, they looked so much alike. After the game, we took them out for burgers.

"Which one do you want?" Gary asked me at the cash.

"I'll take the one with the snapdragon mouth," I told him.

Three months later, we got married in a double ring ceremony. On the church steps, Gary and I grinned at each other, sheepish, dumbfounded, stunned by the velocity of events.

In the beginning, I couldn't believe my good luck. Lying in bed at night with Maeve, I smelled the salty perfume of her skin, felt the sweetness of her soft arms, of her fleshy legs locked around my hips, saw her long ivory hands glimmering on my chest. I could scarcely contain my joy, barely breathe, for happiness. The solid curve of her pregnant belly, round and potent as the earth, thrilled me. Gary felt it too, he had the same thing. We saw it in each other's eyes, were afraid to express it, unnerved by its perfection, its fragility, as though we held in our hands something so fleeting, so destructible, like a quivering bubble in danger of bursting.

We lived next door to each other, in a low-rental subdivision, narrow, run-down townhouses. The traffic noise from a busy commercial street of malls and big-box stores spilled over our back fence. At night, there was the sound of gunfire in our development, the wail of sirens. Outside our windows, were to be heard shouting, obscenities, running feet. The red flashing lights of police cruisers swept across our bedroom walls. After Crystal was born, Maeve wanted to move.

"We have to get out of here, Ray," she said. "This is no place to raise a family. We need our own house."

"We can't afford it, Maeve," I told her. "What would we do for a down payment? If you want a house so bad, go out and get a job."

She looked at me, stricken. "Ray," she said, pressing her hand protectively to her chest, "I can't work outside the home. I am a *mother*. I am nurturing our *child*."

"Believe it or not, Maeve," I told her, "I don't want a job either. I'd like to quit today and do historical research. I'd like to spend my days down at the Public Archives. I could write a book on the war of 1812."

"Ray," she said, "you couldn't *find* the Public Archives if they dropped you on it from a *helicopter*."

By this time, Gary and I had graduated from the museology program and were working in shipping at the War Museum. Maeve wasn't pleased.

"You said you were going to be a curator," she reminded me.

"That's what they told us in college," I said.

"The closest you'll ever get to an artefact," she said, "is with a forklift."

Soon, Fletcher came along. By the time he was four, Maeve had had her fill of mothering. She landed herself a student loan. She was going for a Bachelor of Arts degree, not some pathetic diploma like I had, she said. She told me it was obvious that I would never take life seriously and that if we were ever going to get ahead, she was the one who would have to make it happen.

Now, she was out day and night at classes, studying at the library, working on group projects. I thought: if I'm going to be stuck watching the kids, I might as well enjoy myself. In the basement, I built half a dozen war tables out of *papier mache*. I sank hours into the re-creation of battlefield terrain: hills, valleys, ravines, the texture of roads, rivers, meadows. Each miniature shrub and tree I fabricated out of wire, bristle, silk, using tweezers, magnifying loops.

I slipped away to Toronto. In dim, narrow, dusty shops, I purchased militia, miniature catapults, cannon, horses, wagons, powder kegs, mules, all manner of war machines. By the time I made my purchases, I was light-headed, sweating with excitement. Against the vast and volatile sweep of history, my own life seemed puny, worthless, laughable.

Maeve mocked my pastime. I'd open the door to the basement and she'd say to the kids, "Your father's going down there again to play with his toys."

"All I'm doing," I told her, "is honouring history. If you don't understand history, you don't understand anything."

Just to enrage me, she set the kids on my men. I'd go down to the basement after work and find a whole regiment missing. I'd cross the living room floor and, *crunch*, a lead soldier snapped under my foot. They were everywhere, behind the couch, in the kitten's litter box, even in the toilet bowl.

"I told you to keep those kids away from my things!" I shouted.

Now, in the mornings, by the time I woke up, Maeve was already gone. Off to the gym to enhance her biceps, then into the office by eight. She'd worked her way up at the Heart and Stroke Foundation. She kept long hours, traveled to conferences. She joined Weight Watchers, cut off her hair, let the blonde grow out, returning to her original brunette, wearing it in a short, don't-mess-with-me style. When she started to earn the fat salary, I pointed out to her that we could finally afford to buy a house. But now that it was her money at stake, she wasn't so keen to surrender it. "I'm saving that money, Ray," she said. "I'm investing it."

A month ago, I was called up to the Director's office at the end of the day. It was not a pleasant thing to be officially summoned by someone you once considered your best friend. I rose up to the sixth floor, walked down a silent corridor with muted lighting, thick carpet, a row of heavy mahogany doors with brass fittings.

"Come on in, Ray," Gary said from behind his desk, which was vast as a pool table. "Sit down."

His office glowed with the crystal blue light of a winter sunset. A fine view was to be had of the icy river. Across it, ducks slithered, splashing into a narrow channel of open water, black and cold. Rush hour traffic streamed over the bridges to the far shore. Gary couldn't seem to look me in the eye. Swivelling in his chair, he showed me his profile.

His hair, silvered at the temples, gave him a distinguished appearance. He'd slimmed down and I didn't much care for the look of him. The weight loss gave him the illusion of height. I thought it was just an optical trick, but Maeve had said, "He always towered over you, Ray." The new slimness hardened his jaw and it may have weakened his neck, because now his head had a tendency to rock back and he seemed to look down his nose at you.

Ten years ago, Gary decided to get a degree in the history of warfare. After graduating, he landed a job as an assistant curator, then curator of costumes. It was only a matter of time before he moved into the Director's office. The place had been run by veterans of the Second World War, stiff, deaf old codgers with no academics under their belts, only combat. They started to retire, drop from heart attacks, go senile. Offices stood empty. The museum was looking for new blood. That's where Gary came in. With his increased salary had come a house move. He'd left our neighbourhood some time ago, lived now in a spacious suburb of new Georgian homes.

Turning away from the window, he said, "Ray, I'm afraid I have bad news. I brought you up here to tell you we're relieving you of your position as curator of handguns."

"What do you mean?"

"From the museum's perspective, it's not working out. We think you'd be much more comfortable back in your technical position." His voice was calm, his words varnished.

"I feel fine where I am."

With the new museum going up, he said, with our higher profile and our raised professional standards, we couldn't afford to be embarrassed. There had been comments from visiting professionals.

"You can't refer to a gun as a *sucker*," he told me. "You can't call people *turkeys*."

"Those are just words."

He said that my vocabulary, my appearance reflected poorly on the museum. People found me vulgar, rough around the edges. There had been inquiries from board members.

"It's generally thought that you're not curator material, Ray. The way you walk around like a goddamned Neanderthal. The way you talk. I told you to keep your redneck views to yourself. I told you to clean up your language, tuck your shirt in, cut your hair, stop wearing those running shoes and that camouflage get-up. It's not as if I didn't warn you. Goddamn it, Ray. I stuck my neck out giving you this job. You didn't have the credentials. I was reluctant to take the risk but Maeve persuaded me to. She pointed out that you were self-educated. You'd done a lot of reading and you had a passion for the subject."

I hadn't known that Maeve had had anything to do with it. After I got the promotion, she did nothing but belittle me. "You think you're pretty important now, don't you?" she'd said.

"No."

"Yes, you do. You're strutting around like a little General."

Gary fooled with some papers on his desk. There was a preciousness to his hand movements now that bordered on the effeminate. To me, he was like a tin god in this fancy office, with his soft leather chair and his cherry wood desk and his pretentious degrees hanging on the walls.

It was December. Outside, the trees were on fire with holiday lights. In the neighbouring park, constellations of colour floated miraculously, high up in the skies. Traffic inched by on the slippery streets. Pedestrians picked their way over banks of sugary snow.

Late in February, I came home from work on the bus and saw the car in the driveway, which meant Maeve had arrived before me, an unusual occurrence. I went in the house, removed my boots, hung up my coat. Crystal passed by, her hands full of brassieres, on her way to the bathroom for another ritual of hand washing.

"Mom's tearing the cellar apart," she warned over her shoulder.

I went downstairs and found the basement turned upside down. Maeve had spared no labour in her search. Boxes were torn open, shelves pulled apart. She was sitting on my stool, a pistol in her hand.

"I found the gun," she said, her face glowing with triumph. "I knew you stole it."

My war table was overturned, my armies scattered across the concrete floor. A scene of destruction. Maeve, who claimed to be non-violent, had clearly taken great pleasure in flinging them aside. I went over and calmly picked up the battlefield, set it back on the table.

"Are you going to look at me, Ray?" she demanded.

I began to straighten out the bent trees.

"You lied to me," she said.

"I knew you didn't want to hear the truth."

She got up and set the pistol on the stool. "I should call Gary," she said.

"Why would you do that?"

"I'm not going to be an accessory, Ray. Imagine what would happen to my job if it looked like I was part of a cover-up."

She turned on her heel and went upstairs. I heard her talking to the kids, then her footsteps angrily crossing the house and the front door closing. I looked at the gun and I couldn't remember why I took it. Now that the coast was clear, I went upstairs myself. Crystal emerged from the bathroom, her hands dripping water. She was devoted to the cleansing and refurbishing of her under-things.

"Dad," she said, her face stricken, "this is pathetic. Will you be in the papers? What am I going to say to my friends?" She returned to the sink and I followed her, awkward, contrite. I watched her squeezing sudsy water through the lace cups of her bras as lovingly as if they were her offspring.

"Do you think your mother will blow the whistle on me?" I asked her.

"You can't ask people to be loyal to you if you lie to them," she said.

It was after six o'clock. Night had fallen. I went down the dark hallway leading to the bedrooms. Fletcher's door was open a crack, I saw him in there, lying on his bed in a golden pool of light. I went in and he lowered his book, *Ikebana: Spirit and Technique.*

"I'm sorry, Fletcher," I said. Of all the family, he was the only one who would not try to exploit an apology, turn it to his own profit. If this was a war, Fletcher would be Switzerland. Neutral ground.

"How hard did you try to hide the gun, Dad?" he asked, his face knit with pity. "Maybe I could have helped you with that?"

Feeling foolish, I went over to the window, thrust my hands in my jeans, looked out at the dreary strip-mall. A door opened at the back of a store, someone threw some empty packing boxes out into the parking lot. They bounced across the frosty pavement.

"Don't worry, Dad," Fletcher comforted me, "you won't be lonely in prison. I promise I'll visit you."

A week or so after I returned to my job as a technician, I'd gone up to one of the galleries to replace a burnt-out spotlight. Nobody had told me there was anything official going on up there. When I went into the War of 1812 room, I found a cluster of men in suits, Gary among them. They were standing before our latest purchase, a pistol fitted with a patent lock by Piccadilly gun maker, Joseph Egg, and used by Sir Isaac Brock at the Battle of Queenston Heights. It was a landmark acquisition for the museum, one of the sweetest pieces in the collection. Gary was showing it off to half a dozen American curators in town for a symposium. It offended me to see him there with them. I was the one who'd spotted the pistol in an auction catalogue some months before and pointed it out to Gary. He treated the discovery as his own, flew off to London to bid on it.

I set up my aluminum ladder under the track lighting, making as much racket as I could, thinking Gary would notice me, call me over, introduce me to his gentlemen guests, recount my role in acquiring the pistol. He noticed me alright. He broke away from the group, strode toward me, red-faced with annoyance.

"Who let you in here, Ray?" he hissed. "Will you take that ladder away? Can't you see we've got a delegation here?"

I returned after they'd gone and changed the light bulb, still stinging from Gary's rebuke. The gallery was empty except for me. It was fifteen minutes to closing. I came down off the ladder and stood, admiring the pistol, which I'd installed in the showcase only the day before. The ink on the label was barely dry. If it weren't for me, the museum wouldn't own it, I reflected. If it weren't for me, it wouldn't even be in the country. Goddamn it, I thought, that was my gun!

Next thing I knew, I'd pulled the heavy bundle of keys from my pocket and swiftly turned one in the showcase lock. I pulled on some cotton gloves and raised the glass lid, snatched the pistol from its velvet prop. The weight of it in my hand was thrilling, to me it seemed alive, like one of my own organs. Into my tool bag it went. To make it look like an outside job, I got a screwdriver out and jimmied the lock. With trembling hands, I grabbed the ladder and slipped quietly downstairs, unseen, my heart exploding in my throat. It all happened without premeditation, a pre-ordained event, the workings of fate.

The evening that Maeve found the gun, I drove over to the museum at midnight, the pistol cradled like a child in my lap. I was anxious to unburden myself, to dispose of the evidence. Onto the museum property I slid, passing alongside the building to the parking lot behind. I pulled up close to the door and stepped out of the car into the balmy night. Along the far river shore, the lights of tiny communities glimmered. Just as I was bending over to deposit the gun at the rear entrance, I heard a car door slam. From a vehicle in a dark corner of the lot, a figure approached. I saw that it was Gary, in his long wool coat with the absurd fox collar.

He said, "I'll take that, Ray," and I realized that this was a set-up, that Maeve had squealed, that she and Gary had cooked up this scenario wherein I was to be caught red-handed. Earlier, Maeve had returned home, claiming she'd been sitting in a coffee shop, wondering what to do. She'd told me that if I took the gun back, she wouldn't call Gary.

Out of pride, stubbornness, greed, I hesitated for a moment before surrendering the gun. I asked myself: what would Napoleon have done, with his back to the wall? Drawing myself up to the height of the diminutive leader, I relinquished the weapon and in this moment of exchange, when Gary grasped the barrel and I had hold of the grip, something passed between us, along the heavy, polished steel of the pistol. Some kind of communication, like a low-frequency current, a transmission of our old feelings for each other, a painful familiarity, vestiges of our union, our fraternity. I sensed, at the same moment, both intimacy and denial, apology and renunciation.

"What the fuck would you want to go and do a thing like this for, Ray?" Gary barked.

I opened my mouth to confide the anger, humiliation, betrayal, the general confusion about life pushing up inside me. I considered saying that I stole the gun in a momentary lapse of sanity, that, following the demotion, I was suffering from traumatic stress, but of course, I knew that this was just bullshit, and also that Gary had become a stranger and cared nothing for what I felt.

"You're lucky to get off so easily, Ray. I was ready to nail you. I had every intention of calling the police but Maeve interceded," he said. "Don't ask me why." His face was in shadow, the powerful floodlights of the parking lot at his back, while I stood exposed. However, in Gary's posture, I read an awkwardness suggesting that something else was at stake here. He shifted on his feet, threw a look of helplessness, capitulation across the river.

"Maeve's leaving you, Ray," he said, as though talking to the invisible hills. He turned to face me again. "That night when we met the girls at the football game? We paired up the wrong way. Maeve should have been mine from the start. We got it ass-backward."

_Ah_, I thought. Suddenly it all added up for me, in the predictable manner of life, through its habit of making sense in the most twisted of ways. And I could not say, I could not say that I wanted to resist its cruel logic. For was it not possible that Gary's revelation was not new knowledge to me at all, but something I had borne in my heart for a long time, like a stone in a shoe?

What I felt at that moment was not dispossession, but relief, solace, even a strange gratitude. Already — already, I felt myself letting go.

The night was clear. The stars shone, dazzling points of light over the river.

I had thought that Fletcher and Crystal would never come over to my apartment to visit me but they did, more often than I'd ever hoped. On Saturday nights, Fletcher brought flowers that would have died over the weekend at the shop where he was doing his co-op. He told me all their names and I stood patiently listening, trying to understand this passion of his. When he arranged the flowers in a jar of water, I saw that his hands shook just like mine did when I used to buy my lead soldiers, and it occurred to me that we were more alike than I'd thought.

At the florist, they'd put him on funeral sprays. When he came out at the end of the day, there was pollen on his fingers and he smelled so powerfully of lilies that I had to roll the car windows down. The shop owner was middle-aged, slender-hipped, with buttocks like small gourds. He wore checked pants and decorative suspenders and pink shirts.

"Fletcher," I said, "he's never touched you, has he?"

Fletcher turned in the car and placed a paternal hand on my shoulder. "Don't worry, Dad. Everything's cool."

Crystal had a boyfriend now, or at least one waiting in the wings. Some guy asked her out and she said she'd think about it. Every day for a month this poor sap had come up to her at school and asked her if she'd made a decision. She told him she was still deliberating.

"Is he a pig?" I asked her.

"Of course. But he has a very quiet oink."

Crystal and Fletcher and Maeve were living with Gary now. At last, Maeve had her nice house and her nice lawn and her nice garden in her crimeless neighbourhood, and if this was what made her truly happy, what right did I have to knock it? Once, when I was picking Fletcher up, I caught a glimpse of her out on Gary's deck, fetching in a pair of white sharkskin slacks. I experienced a pang of longing and self-doubt. Why was it still so important to me how she felt? I did not like to think she hated me, even now. I didn't hold it against her and Gary for what they'd done. I didn't like to blame people, when I couldn't understand half the time why I did things myself.

My little fat man, she used to call me. *My little pigmy. My Cro-Magnon.*

Then Gary came out onto the deck too and Maeve threw her arms around his neck and slapped a kiss on his cheek. I sat in the car, strangely unmoved.

It is easy to mistake desire for need, illumination for bereavement.

Authenticity

YESTERDAY, I MET MY PARENTS unexpectedly when I was out walking after my shift at the clinic. This was over on a paved path that hugs the lakeshore. There is a narrow strip of manicured park there, and a stately column of old black elms marching toward the university, toward the prison, and, here and there, a bench where you can sit down and look out at the lake. I often go there after work because the bracing winds and the sun flashing off the dazzling surface cleanse me of the smells and the rot of patients who come to me with their ailing feet.

It is March and the trees are still black and bare and the grass is yellow and brittle. But the warm spring sun has brought out the joggers: students from the university and also soldiers from the military college who run across the bridge spanning the Cataraqui River and follow the curve of the shore to this park. I also passed many old people who have come here to retire because the three-hundred-year-old streets are peaceful and lined with quaint stone houses and there is no industrial pollution, and because they like the smell of the lake and its temperate effects on the weather.

Then, approaching me, I saw a strangely familiar couple, two figures leaning into each other, pushing against the brisk wind that always blows off the lake and turns the pewter water choppy and brittle looking as glass. The man was trim, self-important, all style, in a tweed jacket, a striped scarf looped around his neck, one end thrown back jauntily over his shoulder, faun-coloured trousers in an expensive twill cloth, loafers with shiny tassels dancing at the toe. Beside him, half a foot taller, plodded a woman, heavy, flat-footed, placid, careless about her looks. With a sinking heart, I recognized my parents.

"I *told* your mother we'd see you walking along here," crowed my father, because he has always believed that the lives of his children can be bent to his own uses. The wind had reddened his cheeks and lifted his comb-over, which is stiff as slate, off his small earnest head. He said that we should go and find a coffee shop. I was chagrined to see them and made the excuse of being fatigued from work and also that I needed to get to my desk. My father turned to my mother, who has always been his willing interpreter, his ambassador, and said with a bitter smile, "She hasn't see her parents in a year and she can't take half an hour to sit down and talk to them."

"What are you doing here?" I said, because they were two hundred miles from home.

"Go ahead, Arlette," my father elbowed my mother, afraid to tell me himself.

"We've leased an apartment," said my mother.

"Here?" I asked.

"On the water," boasted my father. He was retired and apparently bored with Toronto, with Life. He believed this move would be an antidote.

We left the lake and made our way into the sad, picturesque, awkward town. On the main street, which slopes gently toward the harbor, we entered a coffee shop. I cornered my mother.

"You've got to tell him you can't move here," I told her.

"We've already signed the lease."

"Find a way to tear it up. This is my town. I've finally discovered a place where I feel happy and want to stay." I'd moved here because it had texture, being populated by a rich mixture of prisoners, soldiers, academics, writers. I thought it could pull a novel out of me.

"We won't crowd you," said my mother. She is a calm, simple woman who believes that people's emotions will go away.

"It's not enough," I said, "that he wanted me to be his clone. Now he has to come here to spy on me."

"He just wants to look at the lake."

I reminded her that we'd had a lakeside cottage, where, every summer, we waited in vain for my father to show up.

"He wasn't interested in a lake then, was he?" I said.

"This one is bigger," she answered. I can never tell if she's being ironic or if she actually believes the excuses she makes for him.

We were standing before the coffee shop counter, appraising the muffins, scones, date squares. My father sat at a window table. Beyond the glass, students trickled down from the university to sit in the coffee shops with their laptops and cell phones. My father looked out at them as though confused by their youth. I noticed his thin smile, the film of fear on his face.

"Why does he look so — lost?" I asked my mother.

"Your father has always needed to feel important," she replied. "Now that he's retired, he's not sure who he is."

"Look," I said unsympathetically, "I can't take him over to that goddamned hospital." On our journey from the lake, my father had said he was looking forward to a private tour of the General.

"He's proud of you," my mother explained.

"He doesn't even know me," I told her. I had always thought it ironic that a man who repaired people's vision could be so blind to people. His own children were invisible to him.

"He wants to meet your colleagues. I thought you'd be happy about that," said my mother.

She has pale eyes, a soft mouth. Once, she must have been passably pretty, in a guileless, graceless way. But now she's stocky and she dresses in flowered pantsuits, the uniform of the middle-aged woman. Her haircut looks like a toque. She walks with her back set at a queer angle, as though she's on a fatalistic trajectory. It was in the hospital that she met my father. She was the timid nurse who hid in the linen closet when the all-powerful doctors made their rounds. Once, thinking the coast was clear, she emerged from one of these only to collide with my father.

"I don't work at the hospital anymore," I told my mother. "I got sick to death of sick people." In fact, I'd been dismissed because of my attitude, my tone of voice with patients. My superiors mistook my forthrightness for a lack of empathy. "Tell him that," I instructed my mother.

"Alright, Dear."

We collected our coffee mugs, three banana muffins from the counter.

"How can you leave Toronto?" I asked her on our way to the table. "What about your garden? What about the quilting guild? What about your friends?"

"Oh, they're not important," she said and of course this was the way it had always been. She flowed around my father's life like water around a stone. I never heard her complain or contradict him or ask for anything. She didn't have the imagination to see beyond the room in which she was sitting, the framework of the day, the hour. Once, she'd said to me, "I'm lucky that it makes me happy to sweep the front porch."

We joined my father. The sun pouring in the window had made him remove his wool jacket and in his light cardigan he looked like he'd shrunk considerably since I'd last seen him.

"Bea isn't at the hospital anymore, Archimedes," my mother said. "She's at a foot clinic."

My father's eyes swam with tears. "You could have done so much good in the world if you'd taken medicine seriously," he said. Like a destructive child, he began to tear his muffin apart. It lay, shattered, on his plate. With his fine surgeon's fingers, he picked critically at the walnuts.

"I don't want to do good," I told him. "I don't care about the populace, if you really want to know."

"I think it's nice that she's taking care of those old people's feet," my mother said.

"I'm only doing it for the money," I told her.

"Well," she said deafly, "all the same."

"What is this book you've written?" my father admonished me. "This so-called novel? How important could it be? What if it never gets published?"

"Maybe I'll jump from a high building, then," I told him. "You'd probably like to watch."

Stung, my father looked to my mother for help.

"Bea's only joking, Dear," she reassured him.

As early as my fifth year, my father pulled me forward by the wrist when people came to visit, thrust me at our guests. "This is Bea," he said. "She'll be the doctor." He was head of eye surgery at the Toronto General. He believed there was no nobler calling than medicine. He wanted to pass the torch on to me. In our front hall, dwarfed by adults, I craned my neck, looked up at my father. "But I want to write books," I told him. My Christmas present at five was a medical bag, complete with stethoscope, blood pressure kit, reflex hammer. In school, I excelled in maths and sciences. I could ace exams without studying. On report card days, my father read out my marks and those of my sisters in descending order of achievement, beginning with mine. You would have thought a doctor would have had more sensitivity. It was a humiliation for my sisters. As for myself, instead of pride, I felt shame. Yet, although I had the highest scholastic average, the sharpest brain, it is my sisters who've distinguished themselves. "Look at this. Look what Agnes has achieved," my father will tell me, exhibiting a magazine article about the sibling who owns a five-star restaurant in Oaxaca. Another creates award-winning wines in California. The third has been named the top rock-concert promoter in North America.

Once, in protest, I burned the medical bag my father gave me, dumped the ashes on his desk. I was seventeen. The next day, I sat down and applied to medical school. When I graduated, my father paraded me around his hospital. "This is my daughter, Bea," he said narcissistically, beaming at me as though at a mirror reflecting his own image. "She's an MD now."

I shook his colleagues' hands. "I graduated at the bottom of my class," I told them.

In the hospital elevator, my father said, "Why did you have to tell them that? Aren't you embarrassed about your marks?"

"No," I said. "On the contrary, I feel proud."

Being wary of commitment to the profession, I never established my own practice. Instead, I drifted from place to place. I did locums up north in the bush, in places where most professionals refused to go but where the pay was double. In these remote sanctuaries for fugitives, eccentrics, social outcasts, recluses, I blended in well. I've worked in lumber camps, mining camps; I've doctored on native reserves, where you couldn't drink the tap water and the women's faces were blue with bruises inflicted by their husbands and the children sniffed glue. More recently, I've treated criminals in this city of prisons; I've ministered to rapists and serial killers, found some of them more lucid and intelligent than people on the outside.

The foot clinic stands in the shadow of the hospital, a constant reminder to me of my disgrace. When I look out the window of our small supply room, I see the doctors with whom I once practised, passing by the hospital windows, in obstetrics, in postop, luminous as acolytes in their white raiments, stethoscopes swinging like holy crosses from their necks, so zealous, they are, these physicians, so sanctimonious, so oblivious to my existence.

From eight until two each day, I pass from one small examination room to another. I treat the dying feet of diabetics. I deal with calluses, corns, warts, in-grown toenails. I dress ulcers, drain cysts. With liquid nitrogen, I singe plantar warts. The bitter stench of burning skin fills the small rooms. I apply har nesses to straighten hammertoes, prescribe orthotics to relieve bunions the size of tulip bulbs. Wielding a barrel spring nipper, I attack toenails so yellowed and thickened with fungus that they resemble kernels of ripe corn, their odor heavy, foul. Though I wash my hands again and again, I know I will still smell it on my skin when I lie in bed at night.

My elderly patients are brittle, transparent, hollow as reeds. A puff of wind could blow them over. I grasp their old, silky hands, fragile and lightweight as a sparrow in mine, and guide them up a step onto the examination table. They are too stiff to bend and undo their own laces. Seated on a low stool before them, like a common shoe salesman, I remove their worn, shapeless footwear, pull off their unwashed, clay-coloured support hose. The cloud of fine, dry exfoliate thus released chokes me. Their legs dangle from the high examination table, their feet, swollen with oedema, large and purple as aubergines. In front of my face, their blue-veined hands float. With their crooked, arthritic fingers they point at their fallen arches, which have carried them tens of thousands of miles but which they have only now noticed. Their lips tremble as they describe to me the burning sensation in their inflamed toes, the pain shooting out of their heels.

From my low perch, I look up into the thin and sagging faces of these old men and women, see the fear drawing their mouths in, the lipstick smudged on their brown and crowded teeth, the eyebrows bizarrely penciled in black on their foreheads with an unsteady hand, the chin stubble they are too blind and shaky to shave off or pluck out. Their acid breath blasts down on me like a burning wind. These ancient fossils fatigue and depress me. In their jaundiced eyes I see confusion, helplessness, loss. They have reached a condition of solitude that I myself fear. I cannot entertain this thought. I try to concentrate on their feet. Like a stonemason, I treat the crumbling foundations of their bodies, cut out the rot, buttress the pilings, fill the chinks.

My agent calls from Toronto to tell me that my novel has once more been turned down. "This makes fifteen publishers who've refused it," she reminds me, sounding tired, apologetic, cautious. I picture her with the phone pressed to her ear, a pretty, dimpled brunette with radiant ivory skin, a body pleasantly soft. She is an optimistic, enviably likable, enviably happy woman who seems to slide through life like the sun's rays through the branches of a tree.

"I'm sorry," she says.

"There are other publishers we haven't tried," I reply.

"What I mean is: I'm sorry. I don't think this novel is going to fly. I'm forced to send it back to you, Bea. Maybe there's another agent better able to place it than I. I've put everything I have into selling it. I've run out of contacts."

"What's supposed to be wrong with it?" I say.

"I'm glad you asked that, Bea. Many of the editors felt it was driven by issues that undermine it and ultimately ring false. You've set it in a culture outside your own. That can be fatal. This aboriginal society. It's not your world."

"I know that community. I've worked in it many times."

"The publishers seem to disagree with you. And they're the people you have to convince. They don't feel comfortable with your portrayals. They've identified stereotypes, subtle prejudices. They sense you're skimming the surface. I'm wondering if you know why you chose this material. Some see it as an exploitation of the sensational. The alcoholism, the suicides."

"I feel passionate about it."

"Maybe that's not enough. What I've found in working with hundreds of authors is that looking inward produces a better book than looking outward. There's nothing wrong with your style. It's your subject matter. And this brings me to a suggestion. Do you want to hear it?"

"Well, I don't know."

"I'm going to tell you anyway, in case you're listening. There *is* one section of the book," she says — I hear her leafing through the manuscript — "one section that readers were uniformly enthusiastic about. It's the conflict between the protagonist and the father."

"That was just a throw-away," I tell her. "A frivolous aside."

"But it's the most authentic part of the book."

"You're talking about a mere fragment of what I've written." I picture her pinching the fifteen or so gratuitous pages between her fingers.

"Keep this little gem," she urges me, "and throw out the rest."

"*Throw out* — !"

"Painful as that may be, good authors do it all the time. And when they do, what they feel is relief. Build from this starting point, these two promising characters. Put in a mother, siblings, neighbours, whatever. Dig into the personal."

"I'm not going to write about my goddamned family."

There is a knock on my door and I find my mother standing on the porch. Behind her, the FOR SALE sign pounded into my

front lawn a week ago swings in the wind. She is wearing ortho-
paedic shoes, baggy madras pants that snap in the April wind.
I let her in.

"I'm not going to try to persuade you to stay," she says.

"It wouldn't do any good."

"I know you have a will of your own."

"You make that sound like a sin."

"But just tell me again. Why is it you're leaving?" she asks
innocently. She is following me around the house as I carry a
pail of water, wet rags, a roll of paper towels from room to room.
I am cleaning the windows and after this I will wash the floors,
the walls, erase myself from this house, like the cathartic shed-
ding of a skin. She doesn't tell me I'm rude and inconsiderate
for not stopping to talk to her. I am trying to dodge her simplistic, black-and-white observations. I am afraid that she will say
something that contains the truth.

"Don't you think I have a right to my own life?" I ask her.

"I'm not sure anyone in a family has a right to their own life.
I'm not sure that's realistic. You can move ten thousand miles
away and your life still won't be exclusively yours."

She and my father had moved into the apartment the day
before. The first thing my father had wanted to do was to walk
past my house. They left the towers of packing boxes and the
bags of clothing and the disassembled lamps and the paintings
wrapped in brown paper and went downstairs and walked past
the old granite court house and the stone Anglican church and
through the Thursday market. They crossed the main street
tilting toward the harbour and entered this grid of short, dusty,
deserted streets. When they saw the sign on my lawn, my father
asked my mother, "Are you sure this is the right place?" She

consulted the scrap of paper in her pocket with the address scribbled on it. Yes, she told him, this is it, 211 Thomas Street. My father wept all the way home.

"Why are you telling me this?" I ask.

My father has been in bed ever since, she says.

"That's just manipulation," I tell her.

"He's a harmless old man."

"He was never around. He never cared about his children."

"He cared," she says, "though maybe not in the way you wanted him to."

"What other way is important?"

She smiles sadly.

"What was his life about, anyway?" I ask.

She shrugs. "What is anyone's life about?"

In thirty years I will look like she does, shapeless as a packing box, solid and powerless, in ugly laced shoes, maladroit, loutish.

We have climbed the stairs to my study, where, all around, boxes sit, half-filled with books. I have emptied my filing cabinet of everything I've ever written, every line with which I thought I was making sense of life. Garbage bags are crammed with notes, story fragments, dead-end ideas, the manuscript returned to me by my agent, all the incriminating evidence of my failure to become that for which my father predicted I was unsuited.

"How do you know what to keep and what to throw away?" asks my mother, looking around. How is it, I wonder, that a woman in her sixties doesn't know the answer to so fundamental a question? I bend over and squeeze dirty water from a rag into the metal pail. "I've sometimes wondered," she says maddeningly, "if the things that give us the most pain are the important ones to hold onto." She goes to the bay window, looks down at the lonely street. "There's no place better than this," she tells me. "Wherever a person goes, there's never any better place because when you get there, you're still you."

The harsh spring sunlight falls on her transparent, crepe paper skin. She looks stoic, saddened, hollowed out.

I think: the comfort — perhaps the sole usefulness — of a mother is that she knows you are a better person than you are.

I go over to my parents' apartment and discover my mother in the kitchen unpacking the crockery I ate off twenty years ago, with the same brown chips and yellow meandering cracks I remember from my youth. Pieces of the newspaper she used for wrapping flutter to the floor and lie, a crumpled sea, around our ankles. Her hands are black with newsprint, there are streaks of it on her face. Myopic, she stacks the heavy plates on the kitchen table with a clatter like thunder.

"Do you miss your flowers?" I ask her. "Your tulips would be coming up right about now." I see the lines engraved in her face, the feathering around her mouth, the sunspots, the pitting, the tragic deterioration of her skin.

"We have the terrace," she says optimistically, and together we turn and look out through the sliding glass door to a balcony barely deep enough for a dog to lie down. My father is sitting out there on a webbed chair with his knees jammed against the iron railing. I step out beside him, slipping my sunglasses on to shield my eyes from the water's glare. The fishy, weedy smell of the lake fills my nostrils. A sailboat disappears beyond an island a mile out. Behind us, my mother opens and closes kitchen cupboards. My father is looking again at the piece about my sister's restaurant in the Mexican interior. The article is dog-eared from re-reading. The pages of the magazine flap and crackle in the wind. In vain, he tries to tame them. Burnished by the sun, his nose is red, clownish.

Seeing me, he says excitedly, "I read an ad in the *Whig Standard* for a hospital position. You could apply for it. Get yourself back into the mainstream."

"I can't come over here," I say firmly, "if you're going to talk like this."

His eyes grow teary. He has reached the point in his life where there's nothing to preoccupy him but his children, the very people who never think about *him*. Seagulls soar and dive and bank above our heads. This is an old edifice pressed against the lake. The neoclassical city hall and the parking lot where they hold the farmer's market are a stone's throw away. The apartment building is subsidized. It's filled with misfits, the mentally unstable, deaf-mutes, the physically handicapped. I just rode up the elevator with a woman who had no arms and had to push the button for her floor with her nose.

I step back into the apartment, where the living room is crowded with furniture transplanted from my childhood home, incongruous, jarring now in this cramped space, as unsuited to its new environment as is my father. He has come from his big, panelled office at the top of the hospital to this collection of tiny box rooms, tight as compartments in a honeycomb. Sunlight shrieks off the lake, shimmers liquidly against the walls, so painfully bright that my eyes sting and water. Now my mother has moved to the living room to pick her biographies of Frank Sinatra, Ava Gardner, Bette Davis out of a cardboard box. In the kitchen, the wind stirs the newspapers, they sigh like spirits. My parents do not own this apartment. They must rent because over the years my father has managed to spend them into bankruptcy. All those Ferraris and Hugo Boss suits, acquired to burnish his image, finished off their fragile savings. They've sold their triple-mortgaged house in Toronto to pay off the bank; they've had to forfeit their car. There will be no winter holidays, even to lack-lustre Florida.

My father comes in off the balcony and says, "I rented a DVD for us to watch after supper."

"I have another commitment," I tell him.

"Can't you cancel it?"

"I'm sure it's something important, Archimedes," my mother tells him. "Bea is very busy."

"I went out this morning in the rain to get this," my father reproaches me.

Once again, it is autumn. The trees are bare. I run into my parents when I am walking along the narrow park edging the lake. They were drawn to this city by reports of the snowless winters, the solid hospitals, the promise of long walks beside the water. They'd heard there was an infrastructure here for seniors — movie clubs, lawn bowling teams, bridge leagues, lecture series. But, already, my father is finding fault.

"Does the sun never shine here?" he complains. "Where does all this wind come from?"

Also: "People here aren't friendly. I never thought the days would be so long. It didn't occur to me that we'd be this lonely," he says, though these are the very perils he's been cautioning his retiring patients about for years. His name is no longer on the lips of the staff at the eye institute. There are no nurses standing ready to glove and gown him, like some kind of high priest, for surgery. He receives no phone calls, no emails, least of all from his daughters. "We spend all our time alone in that apartment," he tells me bitterly. My mother stands at his elbow, smiling bravely, her face glassy, benign. As usual, she floats above everything, she glides over Life like a skater on ice.

"Why do you never come and see us?" my father asks me. I look into his face, hoping that some day I may find there the reason I took my house off the market and decided to stay on in this lakeside town.

"She was over last night, Archimedes," my mother reminds him gently.

She strikes out, then, climbs a slope toward a mobile canteen parked on the road. My father and I sit down in the shade of a gazebo, a Victorian confection, with slender wooden pillars painted peach, avocado, citron. A spine of iron shaped like a wave runs along the peak of its cedar shake roof. The gazebo is light and airy; it's like a fanciful, wall-less house, offering no protection whatsoever from the elements, just like my childhood home, I reflect. We sit only feet from the cobalt water, from a strip of beach where the large smooth stones slide and turn under your feet as though alive. You can get to the ocean from here, I think, tempted. You can follow the St. Lawrence River all the way to the Atlantic.

My father says, "Your mother had an affair once."

"*Mom*?" I say.

"You can't blame her," he answers. "It was with the fellow we hired to lay the patio stones around the pool. Can you believe that? A man with no education. She actually went as far as running away with him. They were headed for British Columbia. They were going to settle down in some small, obscure, nothing place. With his skills, he could get work any-where. She called me from Sault Ste. Marie, from what she thought was a safe distance, to tell me I needed to go home and make sure you girls weren't killing each other. I persuaded her to come back. I begged her. 'I'll be around more,' I promised. 'I'll mend my ways.' But of course, I didn't. As soon as I got her back, I was never around."

We turn and watch my mother approach, stepping clum-sily over the uneven ground in her terracotta support hose, her thick-soled shoes, the three coffees borne in front of her like sacred offerings. The wind grabs at her magenta skirt, it pastes her flowered blouse against her great breasts.

Out on the water, sailboats rock on the rough waves. The light thrown off the lake is transcendent, devastating, redemptive.

Altered States

Dear Aggi and Blaine,

When I think of the months of our friendship — six in all, if one wanted to count — there is only one thing I want to know: did you befriend me because you felt sorry for me (a widow), or because you thought you could use me (did you imagine I could be so easily bought?) or because you were bored with each other (as well you might be)?

I never felt or demonstrated anything but love for the two of you. When I met you, I could not believe that I had finally discovered two people who were intense enough for me. I found your eccentric lifestyle, your non-conformity, your godlessness, and your scorn for the critics refreshing. Little did I know that you were using me to get what you said wasn't important to you, that you were playing some kind of tasteless game with my feelings. I tell myself it must have been the thin mountain atmosphere that made you act that way. A deficiency of oxygen to the brain. And I think it is possible that, having lived so long away from civilization, you do not practise or even remember the rules of common decency. You are just like those ecologists who have such a high regard for the wilderness, yet when it comes to human beings…

And I wonder if you are aware that you spoiled the mountains for me. I will never be able to drive up into them again, nor can I bear to look across the city and see them shining in the distance, like white castles in the sky.

"On the bus back from Calgary," Aggi told us, her cheeks flushed with excitement, "I saw a man with a gun hidden in his pocket. He was sitting two rows ahead of me, across the aisle. I became aware of him when the hair on my neck stood on end. That's always a sign. He was about forty-five years old, with very short hair, like a soldier. He was wearing a blue windbreaker. Oh — and muddy industrial boots. I had this odd feeling and then I visualized the gun, clear as day, through the fabric of the jacket. It was a small revolver. Then I had a premonition. I saw him getting off the bus and going into a stucco bungalow. I saw him shoot an old woman. You don't believe me."

"Of course we do!" we protested, laughing nevertheless.

"You think I'm crazy."

"We believe you! Honestly!"

Often Blaine and I would be enjoying a beer in the cabin when Aggi swept in out of the sunshine, a swirl of full, heavy skirts and black-fringed shawl, jangling with cheap bracelets. She dressed like a gypsy. There was no end to the bizarre clothes she could pull miraculously out of what seemed to be a bottomless suitcase, just as a good magician is able to draw an endless string of scarves from a black hat. She'd been living with Blaine for I don't know how long, yet everything she owned was still in this big old leather valise shoved into a corner beside the bed. She could tell me the history of every blouse, sweater and scarf she owned, all of which she cared for as though they were her children. Things that had once belonged to her dead grand-mother, to her mad aunt, to unknown women who'd left behind in bus depots or on park benches these cardigans and jackets, in the pockets of which she'd found love letters, newspaper clip-pings, photos, suicide notes, sleeping pills.

I'd originally come to the mountains to look at Blaine's paint-ings, but I was easily distracted by Aggi. I could sit for hours on the rocks beside the river listening to her stories, or hearing her describe the potions she made from her herb garden, while behind us Blaine stapled canvas onto wooden stretchers or cleaned his paint brushes, shaking his head at Aggi and com-plaining about the bunches of flowers she had hanging from the cabin ceiling to dry.

"Only Aggi would want to grow a garden upside-down," he said. "Can't you do anything the normal way, Aggi?"

She knew the name of every wildflower, grass and shrub that grew around the cabin. She was one of those people who didn't seem to come from anywhere, unless it was from a strange country of witchcraft and primitive cures. At the same time, she seemed to be from everywhere at once because, through tele-pathic powers, she had connections with spirits and dead people all over the country, links with people she didn't even know, except by name. There was someone named David, for instance, who spoke through her at séances she conducted for a widow's group in the village.

"You'll have a long life and an active old age," Aggi said, turning my hand over to read my palm the first time we met. "See these little lines crossing the life line? They mean you have a lot of worries, maybe relating to this star marking, which shows you've recently had a serious crisis. However, notice these little tributaries moving upward, indicating that you have strong recuperative capabilities. I see that your head line is long, deep and straight and it runs directly across the palm. That shows you have a logical mind and a realistic outlook. This forking here in the middle indicates development of an important new interest in your life around now. Let's see the heart line," she said, following it eagerly across my palm with the tip of her finger. "Notice how it begins under your middle finger? This means you have a pragmatic approach to love, and when it's straight like yours, and parallel to the head line, that means romantic attachments for you often begin as intellectual friendships. These crosses here show that you suffered an emotional loss recently, in your mid-thirties."

I was in fact forty, though sometimes people, looking at my bony sternum, my thickly freckled forearms and ragged hair, had taken me for a woman a decade older. I was slender and small-boned, though I'd noticed my hips beginning to spread, giving me an accommodating look common to some middle-aged women. I'd been told that the taupe eye shadow I hastily applied in the mornings made my eyes look muddy and that my general fondness for browns left strangers with an impression of old dry leaves.

These of course are the remarks of jealous people, people who also told me that I was cold and humourless. I cannot say that I had a great many friends at the gallery. It is not easy to be a successful, self-supporting, self-made female curator trying to carve out a reputation in an obscure public gallery on a cultural frontier. I'd found that most people are lazy and do not like to have to think and therefore must be pushed and stepped over when they get in your way. At the risk of sounding conceited,

I would tell people that, with little formal education, I'd built a small, bright reputation for myself as an art historian. By discovering and exploiting the hitherto un-researched phenomenon of Canadian drypoint print production between the wars, I'd developed a specialized expertise that had earned my exhibits venues in Germany, Bulgaria, Australia, Norway.

But everyone knows that success is not a guarantee of happiness. I was single again and in need of friends and Blaine and Aggi had taken me in like a stray cat. I had thought that, following the end of a marriage, it would be natural to hate your partner, but it seems that this is not what happens. Sometimes, sipping wine on my suburban patio, or walking through the silent white exhibit spaces of the gallery, I would feel such self-hatred rising in my throat like yellow bile that it choked me. At such times, I wanted to vomit my insides out, until I was empty of organs, intestines, blood, until I was like a clean, hollow brass vase.

Whenever I felt this way, I got into my Datsun and pointed it northwest to where the snow-covered summit of Mount Assiniboine floated in the distant sky like a cloud. It was a spiritual catharsis for me to watch the brilliant glass city diminish in my rear view mirror and to make the slow climb on an hypnotic strip of twisting highway, a wedge of Brie and a bottle of red wine on the seat beside me. Not far from the gates to Banff National Park, I'd negotiate my car down a bumpy track and arrive at the cabin to find Aggi, the fair sorceress, wrapped on cool days in a thick sweater, perched on a rock beside the cobalt river, and Blaine setting one of his four-by-five landscapes against an old tree to dry. In contrast to the pale, soft Aggi, he was dark, flinty and angular as the mountains rising around us like stony gods.

Then we sat by the Bow River and talked, the evening light miraculous and the air, pure as ether, carrying our voices across the water to sing back to us off the cliff face. On one side of me, Blaine reached into the river to pull a bottle of wine from the rushing waters. On the other, Aggi, her sundress, whiter than white, giving off its own light like the vestments of a priestess, sat with a big metal bowl in her skirt, peeling peaches, her hands dripping with juice. For a moment, I was convinced that the fresh, sweet smell of the fruit came not from the peaches but from Aggi herself, from her own golden skin. Aggi was the ripe, flawless fruit, the sunny flesh.

Some nights, if I could not make myself return to the city, to my empty bungalow on a street called Coyote, Aggi and Blaine would invite me to sleep on the extra bed, which also served as a couch, while they retired to the four-poster screened off by old flowered drapes in a corner of the cabin. I would lie awake long into the night, listening to the sound of racoons moving in the woods and hearing the springs of the mattress creak as Aggi or Blaine turned over in their sleep. I would hear Blaine's heavy breathing and I imagined I smelled his good, honest male sweat.

Aggi read palms at a booth in a corner of the farmer's market in a nearby village. Beside her in a box, her medicinal potions in little glass vials with cork stoppers were offered for sale. She had a reputation as far away as Edmonton as a gifted astrologer. She pestered me until I agreed to write away to the hospital where I was born to ascertain the exact time of my birth. When the answer came back, she plucked the letter from my hand and set to work. In the following weeks, when I arrived at the cabin in the early evening, I found her at the scarred trestle table, poring over the tiny figures in her ephemeris, punching numbers into her calculator as she computed Greenwich Mean Time, the daily motion of the planets, the position of the twelve houses of the ecliptic. It all looked very complicated to me.

"Really," I told her, "you shouldn't go to the trouble."

"It's no trouble," she looked up, searching my face. "You want me to do this, don't you? You want your horoscope?"

"Of course," I quickly assured her. "Yes, of course I do."

One evening she finally handed me a thick manuscript, elaborately drawn and coloured, complete with appendices.

"This is the deluxe version. I worked harder on this than I have on any other horoscope," she said. "I hope it helps."

"So, you think I need help?" I asked. I liked to believe I knew myself pretty well.

"Let's see it," said Blaine, trying to snatch it from my hands, but I stuffed it in my bag. Aggi swatted him with her ephemeris.

"Every neurotic housewife in the village has one of Aggi's horoscopes," said Blaine.

I took the horoscope home with no intention of ever looking at it. Yet, time and again, I couldn't resist drawing it out from where it sat like a lodestone on the bottom shelf of my night table. At first, I made the excuse that it was not myself I was trying to discover, but something of it's author. Flipping through the appendices, I puzzled over phrases such as these: Saturn opposition Uranus — the basic need for order and restriction is in conflict with the desire for expansion and growth. There maybe be continued difficulties posed by the demand for change on the one hand and for stability on the other. Uranus conjunct sun — the orb is wide and the aspect is separating. There is an exceptionally strong need for independence and a desire to follow an original and unusual lifestyle. Mercury quincunx

MC — mental tension leads to need for intellectual stimulation in career. Moon quincunx Pluto — need for emotional and domestic change and renewal. Pluto in the seventh house — relationships are dominated by deep expectations influenced by the past.

It was ridiculous, I told myself. What did this have to do with me? Nothing. Everything. The more I read, the more confused and paralysed I became by thoughts of the energy of the stars, the importance of timing, the mysterious congruence of daily events and the gentle current of chance running through life. I began to realize that one must swim out into deep waters if one is to be buoyed up, if one is to catch the momentum of life's current and I wondered if it was because I'd been ignoring the natural harmonies of the universe that I'd lost Ivan. Nightly, I dreamt of the stars propelled like the skilful balls of a juggler through their luminous trajectories and sometimes in these dreams I too was spinning through black space, nearly colliding with the white-hot planets.

More than once, cursing Aggi, I flung the bundle of charts and papers across the room, then went and picked them up and read them through again. Often I was on the point of tearing them to pieces or putting a match to them, but I couldn't carry through. I buried the horoscope in the back of my closet but found myself digging it out again the very same day. The horoscope haunted me. It was like a thousand interlocking pieces of a puzzle laid out perpetually on a table. One cannot resist reaching out to turn the pieces this way and that, only to find that they are interchangeable and that a complete picture can never be made.

Dear Aggi and Blaine,

It is not a pleasant thing to have to tell people that your husband killed himself. It reflects. People think that you did not provide enough support to keep him alive. They have a distrust of survivors. I have been asked, "Don't you feel guilty that you're still alive, while Ivan is dead?"

Do you have any idea what it is like to come home on a fine summer day and find your husband shot dead in the bathtub — a man you did not love, but nevertheless, your husband? You cannot know what it is like to lose someone you never loved and cannot mourn. Mourn? How could I mourn someone who had rejected me so completely? And yet, I used to say to people after Ivan died, "If I could just get rid of this terrible feeling." In our marriage, Ivan was the sensitive, vulnerable, weak one. I was the strong link. One pays a price for that. And now I am paying again.

When I tell people that Ivan killed himself and they are wagging their heads at me with a mixture of pity and reproach, I become giddy. I start to laugh. Because the thing I am really thinking of is when, late in our marriage, Ivan accused me of lesbianism because I did not want to have sex with him. And this is one thing I am glad I never told you, because I now see that you would have twisted it, bent it to your own purposes. You would have said it was Aggi I was in love with and not Blaine, whereas the truth is I was in love with neither of you. The only thing I can think is that all the time I knew you, I was not myself. I was in some kind of altered state...

"Is there any sign of Ivan's ghost in your house?" Aggi asked me. This was two months after my first visit to the cabin. It was a cool, bright, windy evening in July. Aggi and I were standing in the clearing beside the cabin, before an open pit over which Blaine was roasting a rack of lamb. I could not keep my eyes off Blaine's paintings, which, propped against trees and boulders, surrounded us like a palisade. I'd begun to realize that I was driving up there three or four times a week not to see the mountains, but to look at Blaine's pictures, which were more convincing and explosive than the real landscape. I cannot tell you the excitement they gave me. He'd been photographing them that afternoon. He'd accumulated an embarrassing inventory and had decided to start looking for a dealer again, the prospect of which made him moody.

"You're going to scare her with talk of ghosts," Blaine frowned at Aggi.

"Don't worry about *me*," I said, amused. How gullible did he think I was? I turned to Aggi. "How would I know a ghost?" I asked. "What are they like? Do they come wearing the proverbial white sheet? Or are they transparent, like the Ghost of Christmas Past?"

"You might hear footsteps," said Aggi, perfectly serious. "Doors opening and closing. Banging noises behind walls. Lights turned on in the middle of the night. Conversations. A small gust of wind or a feeling of energy as the ghost passes you."

Sometimes Aggi was called on by clients to ascertain the presence of poltergeists in their homes. She'd exorcised a demon from a teenaged girl. She'd been hit by pots and chairs flying, apparently of their own will, across rooms.

"Aren't you ever frightened?" I asked her.

"Lots of people in town say Aggi's a witch," Blaine told me. "There were never any haunted houses in the area until *she* moved here. It's lucky for her they don't allow burnings anymore."

It was hard to imagine anyone calling Aggi a witch. At twenty-five, she had the height and radiance, the spontaneity of a gangly teenager. She had pale eyes and lashes, hair like long, bleached grass. Her skin had the pink-mauve tones of certain wildflowers. She smelled like glycerine soap.

"If I'm a witch," said Aggi to Blaine, "what does that make you?"

"Bewitched," he said.

"I came home from an appointment this afternoon," Aggi told us one day, "and for some reason I felt so tired. I'd been feeling strange all day. When I got here, I just dropped onto the bed as though I were dead. I started to feel a prickly sensation all through my arms and legs and I heard a weird buzzing sound. There was this terrific pressure around my head and then I felt myself travelling through a dark tunnel. And when it ended I saw that I was floating a few feet above my own body. There was my grandmother walking toward a city of light, calling me to follow her. There were buildings of crystal and rivers of glass. When I saw this, I turned around and willed myself to re-enter my body. Then I felt myself give a jump and I sat up."

Blaine and I had come out from the village together just before dinner. By bizarre coincidences, we'd begun to run into each other everywhere. It was uncanny. If I hadn't known better, I would have thought it was something in the stars, that certain influential orbits were crossing paths. That afternoon around three, I'd been driving through the village on my way to the cabin and there was Blaine coming out of the hardware store with a bag of screws in his hand. We'd gone to the local cafe for a coffee and gotten immersed in the kind of discussion about art that we couldn't have when Aggi was around. Blaine had seemed pleased to have someone to talk to about his work. He'd sat with his back to the street, his powerful hands like tools gripping his cup, his fingers square and the skin on his knuckles flat. My view of the street was blocked by his massive shoulders. I remember thinking that something beneath the restless, shifting planes of his body reminded me of the abrasive forces that had shaped the mountains behind him.

We put his bicycle in the trunk of my car, drove out to the cabin and, blinking from the brilliant summer sun, found Aggi trembling and euphoric in the dim cabin interior. After sitting all afternoon in the humdrum town, I found her story too preposterous to credit.

"It was a dream, that's all," I said.

"You've heard of astral traveling," she said.

"Something you ate for lunch disagreed with you," I said.

"I'm telling you, I left my body. I saw my dead grandmother."

"A city of light? A river of glass?" I said, winking at Blaine.

"Oh, come on, Aggi, have a glass of wine! Come on, don't be a spoiled sport!" This was me, moments later, calling out the cabin window, through the screen turned silver in the oblique evening light. Aggi continued to sit on the rocks by the river and refused to come in. Behind me, Blaine lay on the couch, his black eyebrows delicately raised, watching me watch Aggi, or maybe just watching me. It was hard to say. I smiled at him self-consciously, remembering that the first time I met him I'd been frightened. He looked dangerous to me, for he wore his clothes awkwardly, like the mentally deranged.

"You don't think she's really psychic, do you?" I asked, coming away from the window and sitting down at the wooden table.

"I don't know."

"I think she's read too many books on the subject."

"Maybe."

"I mean, has she ever been tested? You know those card tests they do. Apparently only about one in a million people are truly psychic. They say eighty-five percent of self-professed psychics are frauds."

"You're full of statistics tonight."

"They're just ordinary people who crave attention. Or they're slightly crazy."

"She's young. She's looking for herself."

"Is it that simple? Should we encourage her? Is it healthy?"

"What's the harm in it?"

"Hmmm," I said, dubious. "Well," I shrugged, looking on the bright side, "at least it's entertaining. I mean...sometimes she's so *droll*, don't you think?"

In July, I proposed mounting an exhibition of Blaine's work. Aggi had asked me to do so when she and I had gone on a picnic to escape one of Blaine's dark moods. Since a show of mine had fallen through and there was a free gallery space coming up in November, I'd agreed. She'd said she was worried about Blaine because his unproductive periods were becoming more and more frequent. She blamed his lack of success on his abrasiveness, his independence, his hostility to dealers. He was impractical. He hated to see a price put on one of his works.

It compromised them, he said. He wouldn't listen to dealers' advice. Once, in a gallery, he'd flown into a rage and slashed some of his paintings when his dealer suggested he move to smaller canvases. The large ones were hard to sell, he told Blaine. That was the end of that dealer. A lawsuit followed, because the dealer had gone to the expense of framing all the works for the show. Now Blaine was having self-doubts. He'd developed a bad reputation. No dealer would touch him. What he needed, Aggi felt, was some sort of official recognition, some positive reviews. An exhibition in a public gallery might do the trick.

By the end of August, Blaine and I had narrowed the choice down to thirty works. I arranged to borrow pieces from local private collections. I asked Blaine to come to the gallery to look at the frames I was considering. We went to lunch in a nearby outdoor cafe and Blaine had to lend me his jacket, so unexpected was the early arrival of autumn. There was the smell of a capricious wind in the air, as there always is at the change of seasons.

"Summer is finished," I said, raising my wine glass regretfully, for I was thinking ahead to the winter months, when frequent trips into the mountains would be difficult.

At the gallery, I gave Blaine a tour of the storage room, which was the size of a warehouse, vast and high-ceilinged. I pulled out tall storage screens to reveal rows of paintings hanging on hooks, banks and banks of cabinets in which works on paper were stored, shelf after shelf draped with plastic, behind which sculptures lurked eerily. We moved from one pool of dim light to another.

"It's very quiet back here," said Blaine.

"This is where I started my career with the gallery," I told him. "I was a cataloguer. I used to sit back here eight hours a day and catalogue prints and listen to the CBC on a little transistor radio. It's a wonder I didn't go mad."

"I notice you keep it locked."

"Security. There are only a few of us who have a key."

I had noticed myself speaking faster and faster as he watched me with a curious, gentle expression I hadn't seen before. I was still talking when he eased me down on what was, in fact, a work of art from a temporary exhibition. For a full year, we'd been trying to get the artist to take it away, but it was too heavy and worthless to move. People kept mistaking it for lumber. I was always rebuking the staff for standing on it to reach the storage shelves. It consisted of three long six-by-sixes painted black. All the time that Blaine was on top of me, I was worrying that my blouse would be blackened from the paint, and thinking, if it is, I'll find some way to explain it. I was thinking, too, that we could have carried out this act in much the same way in the mountains, with me lying possibly on an old fallen tree, and I wondered if this was why Blaine had chosen to push me down here, with my legs falling, oh so willingly, to either side of a straight piece of pine. Had he been a sculptor rather than a painter, he could at that moment have moulded me like soft, wet clay into any shape or form that suited his uses, so readily did I capitulate, so powerless were my limbs, as though heavy with paralysis, to stop him.

Though I'd been at first surprised by his touch and somewhat dizzied by my backward descent onto the sculpture, I quickly grasped that this was all part of the museology process, the task of getting to know an artist, of apprehending his work at the deepest level. Suddenly, making love in the cool, filtered, humidity-controlled environment of the gallery storage room seemed the most natural thing in the world. And in the back of my mind I knew that it was time for the gallery to acquire one of Blaine's works, and that I would hang it on the storage screen near this very spot where we had lain.

I wondered what my staff would think if they were to discover me in such a position; would they still accuse me of being rigid and uncompromising? And Aggi — had she had a premonition of Blaine descending on me? At this very moment, did she feel a prickly sensation on her neck? Did she hear a strange buzzing sound? Was her heart pounding as mine was — for after all, had she not asked me if I thought I might be telepathic, saying that sometimes she seemed to feel the very emotions and have the same thoughts that I was having? What I was really feeling was relief. Relief that Blaine and I were finally united, out of Aggi's reach. She could not touch us here, or interfere, with her inane stories. I knew then that I was free to go home and destroy my horoscope, which had now been brought into question, for Aggi had not been able to predict this turn of events. In lying with Blaine, I had exorcised Aggi from my life, I'd broken the current of control.

Dear A and B,

I am thinking of the times that Aggi walked into the fields of the Kananaskis and picked out four-leaf clovers blind-folded while Blaine and I, crawling in the grass on our hands and knees, could not find one to save our lives. This is the only concrete evidence I ever had that Aggi had some kind of quirky gift. But a knack for finding clovers is not the same as being psychic. If she were truly psychic, she should have known about Blaine and me. It would not surprise me if she is now claiming that she knew all along. And if she did know, if she did not care, what does this tell us about Aggi? Or if, to conjecture further, Blaine knew that Aggi knew and in fact this was a petty, sick plot cooked up by the two of you to get Blaine's art into the gallery, what does it mean about your relationship? If Aggi did know and Blaine knew Aggi knew, does this mean that Blaine did not want or enjoy the affair?

Reflecting upon the salutation to this letter, I see the three of us as the points of a triangle and I am reminded of the mindless, annoying problems posed in my high school geometry textbook: If ABC is an isosceles triangle and if the distance from A to B is X, and the distance from B to C is Y, what is the distance from A to C?

In mid-October, just after sunrise on a Saturday morning, my phone rang. It was Aggi.

"What are you doing? Are you in bed? Stay there."

"Why? What are you talking about?"

"Listen Catherine, listen carefully. I had a precognitive dream. You were out walking and you were crushed. Crushed by some heavy object falling on you. I couldn't make out what it was. A voice in my dream said, Get up! And I did and went straight to the phone. Thank God you're still there."

"Where else would I be at this hour?"

"It was something big falling on you, Catherine. Maybe a tree. Is it stormy in town? Is it windy? Don't go out."

"I was going to come up to the cabin. I have something important to tell Blaine."

"Don't come. Promise me. Don't even get out of bed. If you stay home all day the risk should pass."

"Aggi, this is ridiculous," I said, and hung up.

I went to a window and looked at the weather. The sky was clear. How could a tree be knocked down on a day like this? Maybe a tree being *cut* down. Oh, stop it, I told myself. I couldn't take the warning seriously. It was another of Aggi's empty premonitions. She was being melodramatic again. She was testing me. She wanted to keep me away from them, that might be it. Maybe she'd found out about Blaine and me.

I showered and to kill time I made myself a big breakfast. By ten o'clock I was restlessly pacing my patio, looking at the sky. I went out in the car to a local grocery store, did my week's shopping, brought the food home and packed it in the cupboards. By the time I'd eaten lunch, I was sure I was being made a fool of. I got in my car again and set out for the hills, though by now a strong wind had blown up and was whipping yellow leaves against the curbs of my neighbourhood.

In downtown Calgary, while waiting for a traffic light to change and thinking there couldn't be a more brilliant and harmless autumn day than this, I was caught in the face by a blinding flash of sunlight reflected off a large, smooth object, which, in the periphery of my vision, I saw spinning through the air, descending, descending. In that moment of white light, I saw Aggi in her vestments, a yellow ring around her body, like the sun. My hand went to my eyes.

The marble panel blown from the office building beside which I was parked did not strike my car. It fell on the street inches from my door and cracked into five pieces. I stared at it a moment, uncomprehending, and then I started to shake. Aggi had done this, I thought. She was a witch. She had the power to kill me. The oncoming traffic was halted and people came running onto the street. Behind me, cars honked their horns.

The light was green, I managed to get the car in gear and move forward. Dazed, I drove slowly toward Kananaskis. I should have gone home, but I didn't have the power to turn my car around. At first I didn't even see the landscape. I drove as in a dream. But gradually I picked up speed and by the time I reached the cabin the numbness had been replaced by anger. When I entered the cabin, something in my face made Blaine rise from the couch and come toward me.

"Where is she?" I said. "I'm lucky to be alive. Did you hear her call me this morning?"

He laughed. "Oh, that. Aggi's always calling people with warnings and nothing ever happens."

"But I was almost killed."

"You're trembling," he said, concerned.

"Are you listening? Aggi tried to kill me. I'm certain of it. She said it would be a falling tree. She said it would happen while I was walking. All to unsettle me and make me more vulnerable to harm."

"Calm down."

"I thought I'd be safe as long as I was in my car. It was a trick. You've got to leave her, Blaine. She's dangerous. She's completely mad. Where is she?"

"She's doing an exorcism, remember? It could take a couple of days. You're in no state to travel. You're going to stay here with me tonight."

What a personal triumph it was for me to lie in the big bed with Blaine as in a flowered cocoon, the curtains pulled cosily around us, thick quilts heavy as stone heaped on against the chill of the mountain night. Blaine had come to me at the gallery half a dozen times. Now I lay with my arm across his broad chest and knew I'd been foolish to fear that Blaine had been making love not to me but to the Institution. There was no need anymore to worry that our union, like the sensitive materials in our storage room, might shrink or expand, warp, crack, become brittle or desiccate outside the climate-controlled conditions of the gallery.

But I'd put off breaking the bad news as long as I could. "The exhibit has fallen through," I told him. "I'm sorry. There was nothing I could do about it. It was out of my hands. A decision of the Board. They're worried about our deficit. They're closing sections of the gallery until further notice."

He didn't speak or turn to me. We were enveloped in the kind of devastating darkness one experiences only in the country.

"Are you disappointed?" I asked. "You can't be more let down than I am. I feel terrible about this. It has nothing to do with your work, I assure you. There will be other opportunities. As soon as the budget is balanced. In a year or two. Are you angry with me? I'm sorry, but there was nothing I could do. Don't be angry. Blaine?"

It was a week or so before I had a chance to get up to the mountains again. By this time I felt calmer about my near-miss with the marble slab, putting the accident down to pure coincidence. Repentant about having called Aggi a witch (I hoped Blaine had not repeated my words to her) and determined to tell him that an exhibition of his work figured strongly in my five-year plan, I was anxious to see them. When I arrived, I gave a little gasp of surprise to see the cabin looking lonely and deserted under a dusting of untracked snow. Since September, a ribbon of smoke had been curling up from the chimney, but there was none that day. I got out of the car only to find the cabin door locked. That's odd, I thought to myself, for, in true pioneer spirit, Aggi and Blaine had always welcomed anything that blew in the door.

I waited there for three or four hours. It was a grey Saturday afternoon late in October. I walked around the cabin, shivering in my thin jacket, for there was a wind blowing down from the snow-draped mountain peaks and across the purple river. Standing on tiptoe, I peered through the windows at the dim interior, but all seemed innocent and in order. Aggi's flowers were hanging from the ceiling, the quilt was on the bed, a few of Blaine's charcoal sketches were tacked up on the walls. I picked my way into the trees on the edge of the clearing, calling out, "Aggi!" "Blaine!" My voice, small and thin, dissipated like smoke. Already the woods seemed muted by winter's muffler. I went down and looked in the river as though expecting to see a bottle of wine on the chill, nestled in the rocks.

Again, I circled the cabin, following the track of small precise footprints made by my own pumps sinking into the fresh snow. I looked for signs of violence, a witch-hunt, perhaps, the village rednecks come out to run Aggi off the place. Eventually, I went back and sat in my car. I put the heater on to dry my feet. Later I turned on the radio and then at dusk, my headlights. And all the while, sitting there with a terrible feeling rising within me, I told myself that at any moment Blaine and Aggi would appear, waving to me cheerfully, walking side-by-side into the yellow pool cut in the woods by my headlights. By the time night fell, I didn't care if Blaine didn't love me anymore, as long as I saw them both again. I said to myself that they had not vanished overnight, though I had heard there were people who could do this, people who are able to pack everything they know and believe in, into one small portable bag and disappear.

Soon after this, I made a visit to Blaine's new dealer. This was a little humiliating, but I could not keep away. I entered the bright space, on a busy street in an old neighbourhood of shingle houses and historic shop-fronts. I followed the dealer, a young man with a meagre beard and heavy glasses, around the gallery while he hung pictures for a group exhibition. He told me that, as far as he knew, Blaine and Aggie had gone deeper into the mountains. No, they had not left a forwarding address or box number.

"They said there was no one they wanted to hear from," he told me.

"I see."

He stopped with a painting held out before him and scrutinized me. "Perhaps, the next time he gets in touch with me, if you have a message for him — ?"

"Thank you."

Dear Aggi and Blaine,

The thing that I cannot get over is that you, like Ivan, left without saying goodbye. Even people who hate each other, who get legal separations and vow to draw each other's blood in court, say goodbye. I could never do that to anyone, not bid them farewell. I am a loyal sort of person. Once I'm committed, I do not betray or abandon. When a person leaves without a word, they have left you for dead.

I have gone over and over it and I cannot think of anything I could have done that I did not do to befriend you. Didn't I admire your art, Blaine (though I now see that it was passionless and derivative), didn't I find you a dealer, and didn't I offer to get Aggi a job at the gallery? There would have been more future in that than in fortune telling. Sooner or later, you're going to realize that you don't get ahead in this world by stargazing or running away, but by hard work, pragmatism, common sense. When that happens, don't come crying to me.

Now I am sure that Aggi has planted ghosts in my house. Five mornings in a row, I got up and found playing softly on the stereo a CD I have not pulled out in years, one of Ivan's favourites, the cover left in the arm chair. Finally, I packed up all his music and took it to a second-hand dealer. I am afraid to wake up in the morning and find, as I often have lately, the kitchen light on, though I am sure I turned it off before I went to bed.

Whenever I was around Aggi, I was conscious of a cloying excess of optimism and naivete. Let me tell you both, it is easy to be naïve. That is the coward's way out. To people who tell me I am too serious, I say, Life is serious, isn't it? Am I expected to laugh? If so, at what?

Your Youth So Tragic

SHE ARRIVES HOME FROM SCHOOL and comes upon her sister Vivien in the living room, her arms full of clothes. Vivien is destined for university in the fall and she and their mother are rehabilitating her wardrobe for her new life. They're replacing broken zippers, shortening hems, restoring split seams, repairing darts. Mayo pauses beside the couch, holds up a skirt in a bold hounds-tooth pattern. Can I have this when you're through with it? she asks Vivien.

No, Vivien answers, her voice high and mingy, a false imitation of Mayo. *You can't have it when I'm through with it.*

Can I have it when you're dead?

Did you hear that, Mother? Vivien demands. Do you see what she's like?

How gotst thou that goose look, thou cream-faced loon? Mayo asks Vivien. Vivien's class took apart *Macbeth* this year. Mayo purloined her copy, memorized the choicest morsels. Vivien bares her teeth at Mayo, makes her eyes bulge. She has skin radiant as the moon, a thick blonde ponytail, a mouth dark as a Damson plum. Mayo at once worships and despises her. Thinks her both beautiful and ugly. Longs to be like her and wishes she were dead. Covets her sweater sets, her scatter pins, her pop beads, her swim cap covered with rubber daisies, her saddle shoes, her ribbed bobby sox twisted around her ankles in various patterns — corkscrews, chevrons, zigzags.

Vivien's wardrobe could attire an army of girls. She has money. Thursday and Friday nights after school and all day Saturday she works downtown at the new Eaton's Department Store, upstairs in linens, folding towels. She's warned Mayo not to show her face up there. She's told her never to come up there thinking she can talk to her on the job.

Why would I bother to go up there? Mayo asked her. Why would you talk to me up there when you never talk to me anywhere else?

When Mayo started high school, Vivien said, If you see me in the halls, don't say hello. Don't even look at me. I don't want anyone to know you're my sister. In October, at the Sadie Hawkins dance, she conscripted Mayo as a prop. It was a native theme and she was in command of the decorations. Throughout the evening Mayo had to sit like a wooden Indian in the hallway outside the auditorium, before a tepee, with a campfire made of sticks and paper flames. She wore war paint, a Hudson Bay blanket across her shoulders, a black wig worked into a braid. It was made of horsehair and it itched. Students attending the dance called her *Injun*, threw candy wrappers at her to see if she was real. She did not flinch. For four hours she sat with her legs crossed, perfectly immobile. When she finally tried to get up, her knees locked, pain shot through them on her way home alone in the dark.

Vivien visited the mill ends store. She waltzed home bearing her purchases. Mayo spied her swinging along the bleached sidewalk, called her mother to the kitchen window, indicated the bulging bags. Vivien spilled herringbone wools, sharkskin, shot silk out onto the sofa. Their mother's hands shook with dread as she unfolded the pattern pieces in Vogue. Not McCalls or Simplicity or Butterick. No. Nothing less than *haute couture* for Vivien. Ahead of their mother lay weeks of cutting, pinning, tacking, basting, gathering, pinking, fitting. Bound buttonholes and slash pockets and concealed zippers. Pages and pages of instructions, thick as a magazine. Their mother sweating all summer beneath the weight of the itchy wools, her foot locked on the pedal of the sewing machine.

The *clank* of their father's wrenches striking the driveway rings in through the living room window. He enters the house in his long-sleeved overalls, bisects the living room on a path to the cellar, encumbered by a car battery. Pieces of pattern tissue ride across the room on the breeze. He asks where a poor fellow is going to sit down at the end of the day, with Vivien's folderol broadcast everywhere. Their mother kneels on the floor, cutting out sections of a jumper with long scissors, her mouth bristling with straight pins. The blades sing, slice the air. Is it an education Vivien is preparing for, their father asks, or a fashion show? Vivien sucks her teeth, throws him an acid look, grinds the hot iron hard over a blouse as though to pulverize it.

In the spring, Vivien had put on her Sunday suit with the three-quarter sleeves and the skirt that narrowed cripplingly at the knees. She rode the train to a nearby city, crossed the university campus in her white cotton gloves, had an interview with the Dean. She'd completed forms, made applications, secured a scholarship, a government loan. The notion of a daughter of theirs attending university had astounded their parents. Cowed and bewildered and frightened them. Made them proud. They'd never been anywhere near a university, weren't sure what went on there, how they worked. Their father inquired as to what Vivien would be studying. English literature, she told him haughtily. He asked if she would be reading the great novels of Mozart. Vivien gnashed her teeth, informed him that Mozart was not a writer but a musical composer.

Mayo tiptoes upstairs and slips into Vivien's room. When their grandmother was brought to live with them and given the ground-floor bedroom, Mayo's parents were forced to move upstairs to the second floor. It was suggested that Mayo shift across to the front room, share Vivien's bed. Vivien wept, howled, said she'd rather kill herself than sleep with Mayo. She predicted Mayo would kick at night, fill the sheets with scale. She said Mayo was always trying to get a look at her naked, that Mayo smelled. All of this Mayo knew to be true, except possibly for the part about how she smelled. It was hard for her to tell. In the narrow stair, their father, wrestling with a double mattress, which buckled and danced in his arms as though alive, demanded who Vivien thought she was. The Queen of England? Their mother said *hush*, whispered that Vivien had had enough stress as the oldest child. Their father said, Stress, I'll show her stress. I'll take her out job-hunting with me. Then she'll know what stress is.

The room Mayo shares with her parents at the back of the house looks down on sheds, woodpiles, doghouses, garbage pails, her brother's tent. Whereas Vivien's bedroom has a view on the street, gardens, automobile traffic, the rising sun, arrivals and departures, the traffic of strangers, opportunity. From here, the perfume of the lilac tree intoxicates. Assembled in this room is the good furniture of the house. The maple set from their mother's nursing days, sequestered here so that the blonde wood will not suffer the assaults of family life, will not be scarred and kicked and bleached and blemished with water stains. Mayo slides open Vivien's drawers, discovers there stacks of slippery panties folded and disposed in neat rows, padded bras laid open, resilient as armour and stacked on top of each other like birds' nests. She removes her blouse, straps on one of the brassieres. Her breasts are only now developing. They are sensitive and when she circles them with her fingertips and squeezes, they are hard, flat discs. It seems like she could pluck them off, like silver dollars. Before the mirror in Vivien's room, she turns one way, then the other.

She is a flaky girl. Her skin disintegrates, slides off her body like dry snow. Everywhere she goes, she deposits a white drift. Her feet crack, the dermis sloughs off in chunks, preserving the perfect shape of her toes, translucent as seashells, the exposed skin glazed, brittle as glass. When she goes out in the sun her skin rises in welts. Once, when this occurred at Turkey Point, her father took custody of her for the day, drove her to Collingwood, bought her a hamburger, put her on a Ferris wheel. When she heard about this treatment, Vivien went wild, said Mayo was unfairly favoured, a poser. She was hell-bound, said Vivien, for it was a mortal sin to eat meat on a Friday.

Not a mortal, their mother said.

Mayo has a hump on her back, the size of a kitten. No one has ever talked to her about it. When she was four years old, her parents said, Isn't that a hump growing on her back? What's it from? It doesn't seem to bother her. Don't mention it. Don't let on it's there.

Downstairs, at the ironing board, Vivien asks Mayo if she'd trespassed in her room.

No, I didn't, Mayo says in a simpering voice.

Did you go into my room? Did you open my drawers?

No, I didn't open your drawers, she answers, matching Vivien's sarcasm. *Your stinking drawers*, Mayo wants to say, but stinking is a word their mother has banned in the house. Also, *sex, sexy, rotten, lousy, filthy, retard, shut up, knock it off, drop dead, hell, useless tool, stupid doorknob, dirty old man.*

Their mother emerges from the grandmother's room carrying a kidney-shaped bedpan. Twice a week, she gives their grandmother a powerful laxative, then must gird her loins, steel herself for the evacuation. Full to the brim, the bedpan weighs pounds. Its mighty smell poisons the house. Mayo claps her hand over her nose, flies to throw open the kitchen windows, the back door.

Their mother calls Vivien to assist with the grandmother's bath. Vivien says she is beyond that now, above it. Why can't Mayo do it from here on? Reluctantly, Mayo slides in behind the high hospital bed, lowers the metal gate. She wrestles with the grandmother's nightgown, pulling it over her head. The grandmother's arms are stiff, complicated, they get snarled in the flannel, make a puzzle of it, her great hands trapped in the elastic cuffs. When she broke her hip, the doctors said she wouldn't last three months, so she was brought here. That was a decade ago and still she shows no sign of dying. She is a hundred now. At first, Mayo was afraid of her. If Mayo passed through her room, the grandmother would seize her arm, grip so hard that pain shot up to Mayo's shoulder. Don't be afraid, their mother told Mayo, loosening the grandmother's talon-like fingers, one by one, from her wrist. She doesn't mean any harm. It's just that she finds your youth so tragic.

Once, the grandmother was a beautiful woman, a big, proud German. But now her face is fleshless and cracked like a desert, her ears large and baroque, her eyes shrewd and predatory. She's acquired the face of a prehistoric bird, a pterodactyl. The bones of her glossy, hairless legs are long and heavy to shift as a dinosaur's. Her feet, swollen and purple, resemble a pair of hearts. Mayo's mother applies the tip of a file to her thick, yellow toenails, digs out the ripe-smelling, waxy build-up. It spirals off in yellow ribbons. On the grandmother's wimpled backside bedsores have ripened to gangrene. The spots are olive-coloured, hollowed out, wet and spongy. Mayo imagines scooping the rotting flesh out with a spoon, like a porous pudding. The smell of it is sweet, cloying. It pervades the house, clings to the bed sheets. Mayo imagines she detects it on her own hair, her skin. Her mother dabs at the soft pockets with vinegar-soaked cotton, directs a heat lamp on them, directs a fan.

They shift the grandmother to a chair. Mayo carries a lunch tray in to her. When no one's looking, the old lady will throw food over her shoulder. In the corner of this room Mayo has recovered banana peels, apple cores, toast crusts, hunks of chewed, gristly beef, tealeaves splashed down the wall. The grandmother disclaims any role in their disposal. She asks to be helped up so she can go out to the barn to milk the cows. Mayo tells her there is no barn, there are no cows, this is the city. The grandmother demands to be dressed so she will not be late for school. Mayo asks her age. I'm six, says the grandmother. I'm six years old.

On Fridays Mayo helps her mother spread a linen cloth rigid with starch over the cabinet beside the grandmother's bed. She lights candles, lays a wooden crucifix flat on the linen. Father Gripless arrives in his long sleek Chevy to bring the grandmother Communion. He sweeps into the room, his heavy robes churning like a black river around his polished shoes. The grandmother lies in the bed, angelic, as though she hadn't raised hell all night, rattling the bed gate, calling to be got up, calling for menstrual pads, calling for a doctor to deliver her baby. *Behold the Lamb of God*, says Father Gripless, displaying the host. *Behold Him who takes away the sins of the world. Happy are those who are called to His supper.* He presses the brittle wafer onto the grandmother's thick white tongue. He turns and tells Mayo's mother he is free to linger for tea. She smiles and blushes and sends Mayo out to set up the card table behind the house, using the cloth printed in faded apples, bananas, peaches. Her mother approaches through the long grass with a tray of cups and saucers, a plate of her legendary baking. Butter tarts, macaroons, matrimonial cake. For this visit she's changed into a gingham skirt, a fresh white blouse. She is a dusky beauty, with broad, dark features, lips like a black rose. Mayo believes her more striking than Katherine Hepburn, Elizabeth Taylor, Sophia Loren, all the Hollywood starlets combined.

In a webbed chair, Father Gripless smokes a cigarette. He has a magnificent chest, a strapping back, shoulders like a linebacker, hands thick-fingered and thatched across the knuckles, salt and pepper hair dense as a hedgehog's. Mayo's mother has a crush on him. At one time, it was Matt Dillon she loved, the sheriff on *Gunsmoke* in the ten-gallon hat, but now she's jilted him for Father Gripless. He pulls out a lighter and holds a flame to her mother's cigarette. Her laughter floats like high musical notes across the yard. Over on the driveway, under the car, a monkey wrench clatters to the ground.

Father Gripless calls Mayo to him, shackles her wrist with his hairy fingers, traps her there. He says her mother informs him that Mayo is restless this summer, with the conspiracy between her mother and Vivien over the sewing machine, the ironing board. Mayo denies it. He goes on to report her mother's claims that she is listless with boredom, that she longs for a distraction. Again, she says no. He says he has a little job for her on Saturdays, The Work of God, asks if she'd like that. Her mother assures him she would.

She begins to walk over to the church on Saturday afternoons, a distance of two miles. She carries a pail of water, cloths, a wide dust mop out into the sanctuary. It is a poor church with exposed concrete block walls, crudely milled pews, fixed to the walls a few thin, sad, starved-looking saints dressed in rags, humble Job and John the Baptist carved out of pine wood. She mops the sanctuary floor, refreshes the candles and the linen cloth on the altar, plucks off the dead carnations in the vases. Some days she enjoys the silence, the solitude, the clean shafts of sunlight falling through the stained glass windows. Others, she feels she might split open, scream, race up and down the aisles smashing at the coloured glass. On one such day she pulls open the shallow drawers in the sacristy, puts on the vestments of the priest: the alb, amice, maniple, stole, chasuble. From a prayer book she reads out loud the words the priest recites when he assumes these garments to celebrate Mass. *Put on my head the helmet of salvation, Lord, so that I may withstand the onslaughts of the fiend. Gird my loins with a girdle of purity, Lord, quenching lustful desires and leaving me strong in chastity and self-restraint.* So dressed, she climbs the pulpit, loops the microphone around her neck, sings, feeling powerful, swollen with importance, in love with the radiant image she cuts in the liturgical garments.

> *Hail, Queen of Heaven, the Ocean Star.*
> *Guide of the wanderer here below.*
> *Thrown on life's surge, we claim thy care.*
> *Save us from perils and from woe.*
> *Mother of Christ, Star of the Sea,*
> *Pray for the wanderer, pray for me.*

Finally, she walks home through the silent, winding, gusty streets of an old neighbourhood lined with dark, cottage-like shingle-clad houses, their gardens choked with dusty ferns. Overhead, ancient maples twist and dance and sigh in the hot, fickle winds that lift her skirt and thrill her with their capriciousness.

It is Sunday and the house is fragrant with the smell of pot roast. Mayo hears it spitting in a heavy pan on the stove, sees the potatoes, hugging it like a pearl necklace, browning in the grease. She kneels beside her mother, who is trying to nap on the couch. Am I pretty? she asks. Her mother considers her for a moment. Finally, she says, You're not ugly.

Mayo goes out back, enters her brother Ozzie's tent, purchased with his paper route money. He lies on a cot, reading a motorcycle magazine. He is saving to buy a Honda 65. She loves the green filtered light in here, the heavy smell of the oily canvas, the intense heat, the songs playing on his transistor radio. "Go Away Little Girl." "Where the Boys Are." All winter Ozzie makes his bed on the living room couch, but in summer he lives out here, putting in an appearance in the house only for meals. Mayo understands that he's made a brilliant escape from her mother's commandments, her grandmother's madness, Vivien's scorn. This fragile tent seems like a foreign country. Mayo's asked her mother if she could just once spend the night out here so that she can see the stars. Her mother blanched, took a deep breath, said Mayo was not going to sleep with a teenaged boy. It's only Ozzie, Mayo said. He is hollow-chested, rubber-limbed, with a strawberry brush cut and a hard red boil the size of a golf ball beneath his eye. He wears tight black jeans, a white t-shirt, in the sleeve of which he stores a pack of Lucky Strikes. He's a slow reader, hopeless at math and French, every year he almost fails school. Mayo tells him she might need him to help her with something sometime soon. He lowers his magazine and says, Wha'da'ya mean? Something's happened to me, she says. Oh, yeah? he asks. What? he asks. I'll tell you when the time comes, she says.

It is Vivien who observes: She's getting fat. She walks around looking like a house. What's wrong with her these days? She's acting funny.

Their mother never looks at her. But now she sees Mayo at the kitchen calendar, flipping the pages. What are you doing? What do you want with that? she asks. Why are you so fidgety? I'm going to send you to Dr. Duke. Maybe you need some vitamins. The appointment is made but Mayo does not go. She reports that the doctor said she just needs more fresh air.

That boy, that Eddie Bober, had overtaken Mayo after school. She hated him because she had to. Everybody did. Though two years older, he was in her grade, a flunkey, a troublemaker. When the teacher left the classroom, he and his friends raised hell, kicking and punching each other in the aisles, having a whale of a time. He's been suspended for swearing, fist fights, smoking on school property. He loped up beside Mayo one day on Huron Street, lanky, audacious, clad all in black, like the TV gunslinger Paladin. He had a long pitted face, a flared nose, wavy hair stiff with Brylcream. He lived near her in the same ghetto of wartime houses.

His mother locks the six children out of the house even in winter to keep them from muddying the floors. One of the sons walks with a limp because, rumour goes, she stuck his foot in boiling water to make him stop wetting his bed. She sometimes shows up at Sunday Mass, kneeling in the back row like a repentant sinner. She is shunned because she wears tight slacks and sleeveless black tops revealing her soft, white arms glimmering like puddings. On the way home in the car, Mayo's mother says, *Hussy! Mary Magdalene!* She says, What is she, *Italian*? But Mayo considers Eddie's mother mysterious and exotic. Her jet-black hair reaching past her backside, her bangs gathered in a flattened C in the centre of her forehead, her fleshy mouth painted claret, her bulgy eyes heavily lined with kohl.

Every day after school Eddie pursued Mayo and soon it did not seem unnatural to banter with someone she hated. She liked to take risks, to flirt with the unorthodox. He reminded her of her father, a rebel, an outsider, a scrapper, a *dark horse*.

Beside the baseball park, in the rampant English garden of Dr. Patience, a childless widower with a stone house on a knoll and a long narrow property running behind, a block deep, Mayo picks lily of the valley or peonies or black eyed Susans or fountain grass, depending on the season, to take home to her mother. Creeping among the tall perennials and ornamental grasses, she accomplishes this theft undetected. One evening at dusk, Eddie Bober followed her over the chain link fence, surprised her among the hollyhocks. He touched her back and said, I like this. What? she answered. This bump thing, he told her. What is it? he asked. He stepped her deeper into the garden, pressed her to the ground. She did not protest, yielded out of curiosity, desire to be desired, some inner tumult more authentic than anything she'd ever known. Around her, plants snapped, toppled beneath her descent. The pale crepe paper hollyhock blooms vivid trumpets in the corner of her eye. Their scent on her fingers, mingled with the funky perfume of the damp, decomposing earth. Beneath her head, ears of wheatgrass sawing, dry, hollow. He thrust at her, volcanic, his slender pelvis rocking on hers. She thrilled at his naked appetite, his vulnerability. Over the fence, over the blind of flowers, the cheering of the baseball crowd on the bleachers, a home run. Afterward, she rose, bruised, shaken, transformed. Later, weeks later, her mother said, You stopped bringing me flowers. In her hands the empty, blood-red vase she so prized.

The first time the foetus moves she cries out in surprise. What's wrong? her mother whispers across the darkness of the bedroom. I was just dreaming, she answers. Night after night, she lies awake, listening to her parents' breathing, the creak of the bedsprings when her father flips over. Her heart is often in her throat. Sometimes she cannot breathe for terror. As the months pass, she calms herself with a plan. In May she stands in the doorway of Ozzie's tent. He lies on his cot, his eyes closed, one ankle propped up on his bent knee, jerking his foot to the tune on the radio. She goes and turns if off. Hey! What's the idea? he cries. I'm in trouble, she says. He laughs at the look on her face, then sobers. I'm going to have a baby. What? he says. He wants to know who the father is. That asshole, he says. What did you ever see in that jerk? I don't know, she says. Maybe I felt sorry for him. That loser, he goes on, that ugly bastard, words he can get away with here, out of earshot of their mother. You're gonna get killed, he says. Mom will send you away. Nobody has to know, she tells him. Oh, sure, he answers. Nobody's noticed so far, she points out. When's it going to come out? he asks. She says soon. He will have to stand by, be ready.

Midnight at the end of May, the pains erupt. She rises quickly, slips downstairs, out the back door, crosses the lawn, bent over with a contraction, carrying rags, a towel, scissors. The tent door is fastened from inside. Ozzie! Ozzie! she hisses. It's time! Quick! Let me in! He does not want her inside the tent. Too much blood, he explains. He guides her over to the cedar hedge, lays her down in its shelter, there in the dewy grass, beneath a firmament of stars.

The intent is for Ozzie to deposit the baby at the Emergency door of the hospital, a mile away. He sets off at a run out of the neighbourhood, cutting through to Huron Street, down the hill, past the primary school, the baby bundled in the towel, face covered to soften its cries. Just as he approaches the hospital, a cop car slides alongside, slows, stops. An officer gets out. What's that you've got there, kid? There are two of them in the cruiser. Ozzie panics and takes off, down another hill, past the cemetery, weaving in and out of the streets, the cruiser in pursuit, Buller

Street, Oxford, Ingersoll, Delatre. Then down among the factories, the fenced yards and darkened buildings, past the railway station, over the tracks and down a soft slope, suddenly at the Thames River. Behind him the cruiser's siren now wailing.

The river is neither deep nor wide. He will ford it, crawl into the grassy fields beyond, hide there for awhile, then circle round to the hospital, find some doorway to leave the child. He wades in, holding the baby high. The water is cold and fast, the river bottom soft, uneven. The officers are on the bank, he sees their powerful flashlights sweeping the water, hears them shouting, ordering him out. The current takes him by surprise, he steps in a hole, loses his balance, the baby slips out of his hands. He dives, eyes open, reaching for it, but it is a dark, moonless night. He comes up with empty arms. Later, the fuzz find him walking home, in his soaked jeans and t-shirt, shivering more from shock than cold. At the station, he convinces them he has nothing to hide, just that the siren had panicked him. But the next day, the baby washes up down-river, and putting two and two together, they come and take him down to the cop shop again, this time with their father, and it all comes out. Mayo asks to see the baby before it is buried. In the dark, the panic, she'd had no chance to look at its face, to notice even the sex. She does not remember so much as touching its small limbs. But they say she has no right. After abandoning the child, she has no right to see it.

Every Saturday, she takes the Greyhound bus to the city where Ozzie is held in the low security facility. She cherishes this hour-long ride through the lush countryside. It is a blameless time in between the painful places in her life. From the bus depot, she walks the dry hot streets to the prison. There is a high fence, a sports field, carpentry shops, machine shops. Ozzie comes out to the visiting room in a blue jumpsuit. He no longer seems like the brother who lived in the tent. He seems like a man now, thrown dazzlingly into adulthood. After some weeks, he says, I don't think you should come here. That wouldn't be right, she answers. He says, It makes me remember the outside. That's not my life anymore. You'll be out in two years, Mayo says. I'm telling you not to come, he answers, his eyes hollow. You can't stop me, she replies. One day, she says, You didn't throw the baby in, did you? What? he says. You didn't throw it in the river? On purpose, I mean. No, I didn't throw it in, he answers angry, bitter. I don't know how you could even ask me that.

Her father calls her over to the car. Look at this, he says. Feel that. Feel it, he exhorts her. He runs his hand ardently over the fender where he's pounded out a rust spot, applied fibreglass matt, Bondo filler, sanded it down with fine paper. It's as smooth as glass, he says, smooth as a baby's skin. Can you feel that? he asks. Yes, she says. How much sanding do you think that took? I don't know, she answers. About two hours. Two hours of sanding for that one small spot. Anything worth doing is worth doing well. I hope I've taught you that, at least, you and your brother. He has not had a job in a long time. He was let go from the body shop because he took a swing at the owner, a *Bohunk*, a *Polak*. You have to be a fighter in this life, he's told Mayo. There's all kinds of people out there ready to knock you down. You've got to throw the first punch. Sometimes now he disappears for hours in the car. Where did you go? her mother asks him when he returns. Where have you been all day? Just out getting the lay of the land, he tells her. What land? she asks. What are you talking about?

Arriving home from a prison visit, Mayo finds her mother in the backyard, directing the garden hose at the patch of dead lawn revealed when they took down Ozzie's tent. Their father has told her, You need to put new soil down there and some seed. The way you're going at it, all you'll see is crab grass. But she hasn't listened. Mayo goes and stands beside her. Her mother does not turn to look, these days she will not speak to her. Her eyes, her hair are so dark, her face so broad that she seems to Mayo like a Spanish beauty. She imagines her in a full, orange skirt with a black crinoline under it, castanets snapping in her hands. Her mother has walked home with her small square purse banging against her hip, white gloves flashing like doves in the sun. It's not the first time. Where have you been? Mayo's father asked her. To see Father Gripless, she answered. He's been a comfort to me, she says. Oh, a comfort, he remarks sarcastically, his hands on his hips. A *comfort*. Is that right?

One day on the way home from the prison Mayo goes and looks at the Thames, right where Ozzie slipped and skidded down the bank and waded in. On this sunny day, she sees the river shining, shining. The surge of the water, the rapid current, the swirls and eddies, the life force of this channel. She senses the child suspended within it, as powerfully as she felt it in her womb, its spirit still here, waiting for Mayo to bear it witness. Suddenly, she's flooded with energy, as though the river itself is flowing into her veins, a transfusion. She floats home, buoyant, absolved, swept along on a current.

Vivien has declared she can hardly wait to shake off this family of criminals. She and their father pass up and down the porch steps, packing the car for her escape. Finally she emerges from the house in an orange seersucker tent dress, white pumps, a cardigan folded smoothly over her arm. Mayo and her mother wait on the concrete slab to say goodbye. Mayo has been strong-armed into this farewell. The air is electric with September winds. The trees twist and sigh and flash, orange and gold. Their father climbs into the car, dressed in his Sunday suit, his polka dot bow tie. Vivien kisses their mother and then in a sudden display of emotion steps forward and seizes Mayo by the shoulders, weeps and professes how much she will miss her, presses her damp face to Mayo's cheek. Mayo will not answer the embrace, averts her face, her arms hanging limp as a rag doll. A tendril of Vivien's hair brushes Mayo's ear and for a moment she remembers the innocence of the time when she worshipped Vivien. That very night Mayo carries her things across the landing into Vivien's vacated room. She steps to the window, parts the curtains. Down in the street, young girls, their swaying skirts spectral in the dying light, skip, dashing in and out, in and out of dancing double-dutch ropes, which hiss and sigh as they strike the pavement.

> *Girl Guide Girl Guide*
> *Dressed in yella*
> *This is the way I treat my fella*
> *Hug him, kiss him, kick him in the pants*
> *That is the way to find romance*

Surcease of Sorrow

WHEN MARIAH WOKE, SHE SAW that there was a heavy snowfall. The room was radiant with its white light. She got up and looked out the window at the park, each black tree branch bearing a thick white cargo, the air dense with large swirling flakes. Though it was only five o'clock, she decided to get moving, as the weather could slow traffic and derail her plans. Every night before she went to bed, she made a list of what she had to do the next day. If she wasn't able to cross off every last item, she saw the day as a failure. She'd find weeks' worth of these lists crumpled up in the corners of her coat pockets or in the bottom of her purse.

She picked her dressing gown up off a scarred chair. Everything in the house was worn out. Since they married forty-five years ago, they had not replenished a thing. It was a big house on a good street but it had the original dated kitchen and baths. Mariah took pride in this thrift. They had five daughters and all their cash had gone into their MBAs and their law degrees and their travels abroad and their foreign studies and their unpaid internships in South America and Moscow and Uzbekistan, places Mariah and Leif had seen only in pictures.

Mariah left the room silently — well, as silently as she could. Leif had recently remarked that there was nothing subtle about her walk. Her heels seemed to drive into the floor like nails. He himself might rise soon, or he might not get up for several hours. He was retired now. Mariah never wanted to be like that, living life to some sort of aimless rhythm. She needed structure, industry, outcomes. As she closed the door, she glimpsed Leif's long figure under the threadbare chenille spread, the curve of his hip traced by the strangely luminous light. A long time ago, he might have caught her arm, tried to gently pull her back to bed, pleading, "Stay here with me a moment. Let me touch you. Why rush off? What's the urgency?" He might have said, "You shouldn't go out in this storm. Please. It's dangerous." Years ago he might have said this, but they were not intimate anymore. Somehow intimacy had faded away, like the paint on their walls, so worn now that you could hardly tell it had ever been there. And anyway, Leif had learned that there was no way to divert Mariah from her pilgrimage of good works. She was never home, or it seemed that way. Many years ago, he'd complained about this but now he seemed to have accepted it and also to even welcome it, his own company, solitude.

She crossed the landing and looked out again, through the small bathroom window. It was a bad storm. They did not need the pot of chilli at the soup kitchen until lunchtime, but there were other places Mariah had to go, she had a map of the day engraved in her mind. She had to go here and here and here. She washed her face with soap and water, pulled a brush carelessly through her short mannish hair, crossed the hallway to where she'd left her clothes from the day before, folded on the corner of a bed in a room where the girls, now grown, used to sleep. She put on a straight skirt, an old blue sweater, a drop pearl necklace, a wedding gift from Leif that she'd worn every day of her married life.

In her long green wool coat and short boots with the fake rabbit trim, she carried the vat of chilli outside and put it in the trunk of her coupe. She swept the car off, got in and slid out into the soft white morning. In the west end, she glanced frequently at directions she'd scrawled on a small piece of paper, she made a dozen turns, penetrating deeper and deeper into a residential area. The snow swirled beneath the streetlights, it twisted against her windshield.

At one point, she looked in her rear view mirror and saw a jogger, arrow-like, running in her deep tracks. He was dressed entirely in black, a striking figure against the snow. Watching him, she admired his form, his energy, his pace. She saw his breath crystallizing in great white clouds. He advanced on her, putting on a spurt of speed. When he got closer, she noticed his agitation, the horror on his face, his mouth working. She realized he was shouting at her. She stopped the car and lowered her window. He came alongside, winded.

"There's someone — " he gasped out, half bent over to catch his breath. A drop of liquid swung from his nose.

"What?"

"You're dragging a body — you're dragging a body under your car." He had a thin, lined face, a neat goatee.

"What — ? A dog?"

"It's a woman."

"That's impossible."

"Get out and look for yourself."

Everything was very still. Wet snow blew in through the open window, onto Mariah's lap and her arm and her left cheek.

Mariah was a perfectionist. She was a woman who had always been in complete control of her life. A type-A personality, a list-maker, a valedictorian, a high achiever. She didn't make mistakes. Never in her life had she made a mistake anything like this.

By the time she left the police station, the snow was no longer descending in a blanket, but drifting softly, the large spinning flakes caught by the sun, the air full of coloured diamonds. Just the most stunning day. Mariah walked home, along the canal, where skaters were stroking joyfully over the bright, scarred ice. She stopped and looked at them, stunned by their heedlessness. The brilliance of the sun confused her. It did not seem possible that such a day could turn so beautiful.

On her street, she walked between squared-off snow banks, shoulder-high. She saw that Leif had shovelled their walk and swept off the porch. For the first time she could see how run-down the house looked — the broken flagstones, the crumbling porch, the peeling paint. Why had she never noticed this before? Inside, she smelled chicken soup. Leif sat at the dining room table eating lunch. From the small vestibule, she could not see him, but she sensed his presence. She stood beside the row of coat hooks, numb with shock. When she didn't come in, Leif pushed back his chair, walked out into the hall. Whatever look she had on her face made him ask, "What's wrong?" He'd been out to yoga class. His purple rubber mat lay rolled up in the hall. His life now was very interior. It was all about meditation, stillness, living in the moment. He'd become even more slight than when she'd met him at university. He was consuming raw foods, no sugar, no fat, no alcohol. The fridge was stocked with seaweed and bean sprouts. The rigour of his diet frightened Mariah. Sometimes she wondered where it was leading, this thinness. "One day you're going to just disappear," she told him. And surely this regime was not healthy, because he was so pale now. His hair was white and his eyebrows like two frosty caterpillars creeping across his forehead.

"There's a dead woman," Mariah blurted out, in the hallway. "What?"

"A woman. A woman is dead." Chunks of snow slid off her boots onto the tile floor. Her coat smelled like winter. She couldn't undo the buttons. Every movement seemed a gigantic act.

An hour later, Leif appeared at the living room door, wearing his long camel coat, a navy beret. How handsome he looked, she thought with surprise. She was reminded of something her friends had said. They had said Leif was sexy, still rather sexy — didn't she think? — even at this age. What was it? The lanky grace of his limbs, supple from daily yoga? Elegant and sexy, the women said. They had hinted that they did not understand — they didn't quite understand how she'd managed to snap him up, she being so — well, so direct, so flat footed and so — so unadorned.

"Oh," Mariah begged him now, "please don't go out. Don't leave me here alone. Not today."

"I have studio time booked. I've got a model coming in. I can't cancel so late." He'd taken up sculpture as a hobby, working with clay. He took these small pieces to a forge, had them cast in bronze. Mariah found them unsettling, these nudes now displayed all over the house — the bare breasts, the pregnant bellies, the testicles hanging down, the buttocks thrust up, a man on all fours with his chin pressed to the ground, a couple twined in a complex embrace. Leif came home with fresh clay under his fingernails, an umber dust on his shoes.

At the police station, the investigating officer had said, "Is there someone we can call to pick you up? A husband? Are you sure you're all right to walk home? Some people get lost. Some people in situations like this can't even remember where they live. We had one lady who'd had a shock as bad as yours and she was found wandering in the west end, though she lived very near here. No one knows how she got there, not even her. She'd been walking for hours. She couldn't recall seeing a thing along the way. You're shaken up. Nothing like this has ever happened to you before. Later, later it might be even worse."

"I don't know," Mariah told the officer earnestly, "I don't know how she got under there."

She rose early, at five or four or three, she couldn't remember when, and waited for the arrival of the newspaper. Joggers floated by in the park. The sight of them opened up a wound in Mariah. Finally, she saw the boy throw the paper onto the porch and she went out and brushed the snow off it and brought it into the dining room. Leif got up from his place opposite her and came around the table.

"I'm terrified to look," she said.

"Open it," he told her.

Her hands shook as she smoothed the paper out. The dining room was exploding with sunlight. She felt assaulted by it, though this was the very substance they craved every morning, this life-giving river pouring in on them as they read the paper.

There was the article, right on the front page. "Why put it there?" Mariah asked.

"It's a tribute," Leif told her. "They want to honour someone they lost. Why shouldn't they have the privilege?" He was wearing a soft yellow sweater, jeans. They read the article silently, leaning over the table.

"They make me sound like a criminal," said Mariah. "I don't even know what happened. How could it be my fault if I don't even know what happened?"

Leif stepped back. "You're always rushing from one thing to the next, Mariah. An accident was bound to happen sooner or later." Surely this was unfair and almost inconceivable coming from Leif, who, everybody knew, was the epitome of goodness. He was so kind, Leif was. Such a kind and gentle man. Of all times to act this way. Usually he kept his observations to himself so that she never knew — all their lives, she now realized, she hadn't really known what he was thinking.

He turned and left the room.

"Your porridge," Mariah called after him. On the table two bowls of oatmeal swam in pools of skim milk, spirals of honey glistening like gold in the sun. She heard him go up the stairs softly, treading on the old worn broadloom.

The picture of the victim was in colour, a professional photograph, perhaps taken to mark a promotion. It showed her in a soft business suit, one hand resting on the back of a chair, her head tilted shyly, modestly to one side. A rich mass of curly auburn hair tumbled to her shoulders. She had a simple, pretty, honest face, a sweet smile. A senior executive for a big software company, forty years old, the article said, mother of three. Her name was Julia Coffee.

Mariah went into the kitchen and found the old tarnished scissors and came back and cut the article out. She could have crumpled it up and thrown it away but, never one to shrink from responsibility or blame or injury or punishment or fact, she took it upstairs and put it in a bureau drawer. For a moment, she pressed her forehead to the dresser wood. All the surfaces around her seemed impoverished, in decline. It occurred to her that she had not paid enough attention to the textures of their life. The movement of her own figure in the long bedroom mirror startled her, a graceless woman in flat laced shoes. *A bull in a china shop*, her mother had always said.

She smelled incense burning. Leif doing his meditation. Later, she caught glimpses of him out of the corner of her eye, transparent, ghostlike. He could move about the house without making a sound or leaving a trace. Finally, she heard his footsteps rapidly taking the stairs. She leapt up, pursued him like a frightened child, her limbs so rigid with panic that she was afraid she would trip, hurtle against the banister. Before she could stop him, he'd opened the front door, letting in a swell of cold air, and was swallowed up by the white day.

"What's wrong?" she asked him that night at dinner, though until now his silence — all their lives his silence had never signified anything to her. "Are you angry? What are you trying to say?"

"I'm grieving."

"Grieving?"

"For that woman. For that Coffee family."

When she heard the siren at the scene of the accident, Mariah knew that her way of life had changed forever. She did not know what this meant, but she knew it was true. In the police cruiser, her whole body began to quake with this foresight. The policeman, turning to look at her over the seat of the car, thought she was suffering from shock. When the shaking grew more violent, when it didn't stop, he opened his door and got out in the snow and called to a fireman, "Can we get some oxygen over here?"

Dreaming the following night, Mariah saw the map that had accompanied the newspaper article, like an illustration in a crime novel. Arrows, dotted lines indicated her route, Xs marked the alleged point of impact and where the woman's boot had slipped off and where the jogger had stopped Mariah. She had seen the trail the body had made between her car tracks, a soft impression. There had been blood, apparently, blood in the snow, all along where Mariah had driven. There was blood under the car when the tow truck jacked it up to pull the body out.

People said, "You have to get yourself a killer lawyer." Well, *killer* was not a word they meant to use. She had to get someone ruthless. "Ruthless?" she asked. Someone who would flatten the prosecution.

She had been charged with careless driving, failing to report an accident, failing to stop after an accident causing death.

She walked to the lawyer's office. It was not a big city and they lived centrally. She left the car in her driveway buried in snow. Her licence had been suspended for forty-eight hours, but even after she got it back she felt too jumpy to drive. The accident had occurred early in December. Christmas had now come and gone but still she walked everywhere.

Out of her neighbourhood she journeyed and under the freeway and up into town. People came out of banks, bakeries, pharmacies, cafes, all of them carrying on with their lives as though nothing had changed. She did not recognize anything, at least not in a familiar way. She felt entirely betrayed by the world, by life.

The lawyer had a square face, thick white hair, a fleshy mouth. He was about sixty, powerfully built, like a football player, but with none of the grace. He opened a file, ran down the list of evidence with a blunt finger. There was the jogger, he said, who saw essentially nothing, but who thought he had because he seemed to be some kind of self-righteous prick. No one knew exactly where he had first noticed Mariah's car or how long he'd followed her. "The goddamned police," said the lawyer, "didn't back-track to look for his footprints. So we can't contradict his testimony, but they can't corroborate it either. The jogger is prepared to say he followed you for half a mile before you looked in your rear view mirror. Could he be right? You didn't think of checking behind you for a whole half-mile?"

"I — I don't know."

"*I don't know* is worthless as a defence. The accusation is that you weren't driving responsibly. If you'd looked in your rear view mirror frequently, if you'd seen the jogger sooner, the woman's death might have been averted." He said that the police report indicated there had been some fishtailing of her car.

"Well," said Mariah, 'the snow was deep. But I was driving slowly. I am not a reckless person. Everyone was slipping and sliding that morning."

"But in your police statement you said you saw no one out."

"Well, I didn't mean *no one*."

"Accuracy, Mrs. Moss. Accuracy is essential. Consistency, if not honesty."

"But I would never lie."

He looked her square in the face. "That could be a problem for us."

Another so-called witness had surfaced, he told her. Some old busybody supposedly out walking her dachshund. As if a dachshund could make any headway in snow so deep. She hadn't come forward until after the accident appeared in the news. She'd called the paper rather than the police and seemed eager to have her picture printed.

"We'll prove that old bag wrong," the lawyer told Mariah.

"But I'm sure she wouldn't lie."

"We're all liars, Mrs. Moss. It's just that some of us get exposed. Don't worry, I'll break her down bit by bit. She won't know her own name by the time I get through with her."

Mariah recoiled. "Oh, but I wouldn't want her to come to any harm. I expect at that age she must be quite fragile."

His face became red, his white hair, in contrast, shimmered like a fluorescent bulb. He said, "You better wake up and smell the roses, Mrs. Moss. You better decide if you want to end up in jail or not."

Mariah's mother, in speaking of her own daughters, had once said that Ruth was the genius of the family and Ursula was the artist of the family and Claudia was the beauty of the family and Sophie was the comedian of the family and Mariah — well, Mariah was the useful one.

Someone had come along at the scene of the accident, a man carrying a scarf caked with snow. He had wanted to get inside the cordoned off area, to duck under the yellow tape fluttering gaily in the wind. A detective went over and spoke to him, passed the word along to his fellow officers. "Jesus Christ," Mariah heard one of them say. "It's the husband."

She walked to another appointment, this one further away. Someone knew someone who knew someone who had gone to this good counsellor. She took an elevator to the top of a shiny tower. A tall, elegant, splendidly groomed man showed her into his glass office. He smiled when Mariah gasped at the panoramic view of the Parliament buildings, the river, the distant purple hills.

"I have the whole world in the palm of my hand here," he boasted. He had a small, tight mouth, perfect veneered teeth. He sat with his legs stretched out and his slender ankles crossed.

"You need to face," he told Mariah, smiling what seemed to her a counterfeit smile, "you need to face what brought you to this moment. This is some kind of gift."

"Sorry?"

"A gift."

"What do you mean?"

"It was in the cards from the day you were born. It is an opportunity. A window into your true self."

"But it was an accident," Mariah said. "I don't understand. I don't understand what you're saying."

He made a note on his pad. Whenever she arrived and sat down on the couch opposite him, he would say, "Where are you today?" while he wrote the date on the top of his pad of paper. She wondered why writing down the date was more important than looking at her. He was so polished, so self-confident, so remote.

"You're afraid to go deep," he told her one day.

"No, I'm not. There's nothing down there."

"There's always something down there."

"I have no mission left in life," she told him another time. She had been removed from a number of charitable boards because she was seen to be compromised. The pastor at the church where she ran the food bank had asked her to take a leave of absence, to rest and deal with her legal battle.

"Now," said the counsellor, "all there is left for you to do is to *live*."

The jogger had told Mariah that maybe she should have the decency to get out of the car. She couldn't, though. She could not move, she could not make her legs work. She felt brittle as glass. If she moved she might shatter into a million pieces.

One day, a year after the accident, when she sat at a small desk in their bedroom going over the lawyer's notes, she felt Leif's presence behind her, the air stirring. This was all the disturbance he ever made in the house, just this small displacement of atmosphere. She turned to see him standing in the doorway.

"I want to move out of town," he told her. "I want to go back to my roots." He meant the landscape where his parents had brought him up, the country. "I need a studio in the hills, surrounded by nature."

He'd come from a mild kind of people, the only child of gentle parents. They'd owned a little wooden house on a rocky ridge overlooking a lake. Leif's mother, a potter, had a studio below, wedged between the cliff and the twisting gravel road. She was wholesomely pretty, soft-spoken, with long, silken blonde hair. A rather sexual, or perhaps a fertile woman — Mariah had thought when she first met her — in an earthy and nourishing way, as though she herself had emerged from the rocks, the black pine trees.

"But my work," Mariah blurted out. "I'd be so far away from my volunteering."

"That's the thing, — " Leif, shifting on his feet, smiled at her sadly, awkwardly, "you see — we wouldn't both — we wouldn't both be going."

Mariah set her pen down and looked at him. She was a woman with big hips and small pigeon-toed feet. Suddenly, this person, Leif, at whom she had for years barely looked — now seemed like the only important thing in the world.

"I'm going to buy my mother's old studio," he went on. "I drove up into the country last week and there it was with a FOR SALE sign on it. They're not asking much for it. It's small but I know I could both live and work in it. All I need is a cot to sleep on and a hot plate and a fridge." He said he craved a primitive, hermetic existence.

"But we live simply *here*," she told him, and he sighed tiredly. She didn't understand. Their marriage wasn't passionate and it wasn't, well, wildly happy, but it wasn't unhappy either. It was just as good as what other couples their age had, who'd been married this long.

He had said to her, "I don't see how you could have done that. I don't see how you could be so unaware as to hit a person and not know it, let alone drag them across town."

"It wasn't across town," Mariah had answered. "It was only a mile."

"Is it because of the accident?" she asked him now.

He said, "No. I felt it before. That day you came home from the police station? You were standing there in the hall and you had such a conflicted look on your face, as though you'd turned a tremendous corner in your life. I thought you were going to say you were leaving me. I was so hopeful. I wanted you to leave me before I had to leave you."

"But I would never do that."

"I know. I'm sorry."

He reminded her that he'd always wanted to pursue an artistic career but he'd never been able to because of his responsibilities. No one had ever asked him if he wanted to be a lawyer. Hadn't that been Mariah's idea? No one had asked him if he wanted five children.

Not long ago, he had said to her, "Someday you'll realize you never noticed the simplest things around you. You are so oblivious, Mariah, to everything important."

Mariah drove up to the country once a week to visit Leif. He'd never invited her to do so, but he didn't ask her to stop. It was always painful for her to come upon the structure where her mother-in-law had once worked, and to admit that this was where Leif now lived as a bachelor. Neither of them understood why Mariah came there. Leif led her out behind the studio to show her his latest sculptures, which he displayed on the cliff ledges, just as his mother had done. In the nearby village, a gallery had sold several of his pieces. Mariah felt the energy in the studio, the confidence, the joy. Never had she loved Leif so deeply as now. Why had she waited until it was too late to feel these feelings?

One day the lawyer called to say that all the charges against Mariah had been dismissed. He had argued in Discovery that poor visibility had prevented the deceased from noticing Mariah's small white car approaching through the snowy morning. There were no eyewitnesses on the corner where the woman had allegedly been struck. Those who initially claimed to have observed the accident were found only to have heard the dying woman's cries as Mariah's car passed. In particular, the credibility of the elderly woman walking her dog was in question. On cross examination, she admitted that she did not habitually take her dog along that street or even go out that early, least of all before the sidewalks were ploughed, and that perhaps she had been confused about where she was that morning. With respect to the distance the body was dragged, the fact that Julia Coffee's clothing had gotten mangled in the driveshaft and that the wheels had never passed over her body explained why Mariah had not realized anything was amiss.

When she heard that the case was closed, Mariah didn't feel the vindication she'd expected. She was of course glad to be exonerated, but not in the least proud of it. She was not sure she deserved to be let off so easily. Perhaps her lawyer had been too clever. Perhaps his arguments had not been entirely honest. Perhaps he'd bullied the old woman during her testimony. Mariah was not certain that she had not been driving too fast or that she'd made a full or even a partial stop at the critical intersection. She could not remember. Sometimes such things cannot be remembered. But didn't the fact that she couldn't recall place her at fault? Perhaps not in a court of law, but in her own mind it might. If the case had gone to court she might possibly have learned more about the truth, about herself. Maybe she should have insisted on such an exposure, such a reckoning.

The day after the lawyer called, she went up to tell Leif about the judge's decision. He did not seem to understand the importance of the news. It was as though he'd forgotten all about the accident. Mariah felt destroyed by this. Leif said, "I've met another woman. A potter. We're both working with clay. It's amazing, it's amazing, really, how much we have in common. Nothing has come of it so far, nothing romantic or sexual, and maybe nothing will. But I like her. She understands what I'm about."

He had walked her out to her car. They stood on the dusty, winding gravel road, surrounded by the amethyst hills. There lay the lake, miraculous with its yellow reflections. Looking at Leif, Mariah realized he'd known all along that she'd been hoping for reconciliation. That she could not believe he — compliant, peacemaking, selfless — would not relent. He had known and, as was his way, he'd been waiting patiently for her to understand that he was moving on.

He'd said, "I don't remember proposing to you. I think that *you* proposed to *me*. I seem to recall that was the way it happened. I met you and you had such a strong idea of how things should be. I was just swept along."

He was bronzed now and he looked strong and vigorous. In his spare time, he cycled around these lakes and up and down the hills. Mariah was reminded of how he'd looked in the painting studio at the university where they'd met, when she decided that he didn't have an ounce of talent and would be better off in law.

She did not say, as she'd wanted to, "Is she — is it a younger woman?" Driving back to the city, and also later, she was proud that she'd had the dignity not to ask this.

It was a city of many rivers. She spent a lot of time walking along their banks. It was important to keep moving. More than two years had passed since the accident. Two springs and two summers and two falls and two winters had gone by and now it was spring again. At times she could not remember seeing anything on these long walks. Some days she thought she might be going mad. She had told her counsellor that she could not sleep. Often, she was awakened by the image of the blue foot of the woman, Julia Coffee. Had she actually seen this or only imagined it or had she read it in the paper? On such nights, Mariah had lain for hours, shaking and sweating.

"What is it you fear?" the counsellor asked her.

"I am being abandoned by everyone I know," she told him. "My husband, my colleagues, my community. I want to be dead."

"It's not the abandonment of others you fear," he said. "You are abandoning *yourself*."

It did not rain all May and June. The grass in the narrow parks along the rivers turned yellow and brittle, the soil grey and powdery. The trees became dry, fragile, their leaves stiff and crackling in the wind. Still, they endured. The river shrank away from the shore. Boulders, sandbars began to emerge. People bore lawn chairs out onto ledges of rock and set up fishing rods. Others walked right across the river, the water only ankle deep. Mariah saw the landscape transformed, the shoreline exposed. She felt bared herself, stripped down, a nakedness that was not disquieting. In the hills, forest fires burned. Smoke blew down into the city. The air smelled of it, sweet and choking. Sometimes Mariah took off her own shoes and stepped into the warm water at the river's edge. She lost weight. She became tanned. Her hair grew. She could see that the effect was softer, around her face. She found the time spent alone painful and nutritive.

One day, a woman she'd seen many times with an easel and tubes of paint stopped her on the path. She was petite, freckled, homely, with wire rimmed glasses and iron-grey hair hanging messily to her shoulders. She told Mariah that she had been a social worker, she'd been on the front lines all her life, until one day a client, a welfare case, knocked out her front teeth. That was when she'd decided to retire. "Painting is what I wanted to do all my life. I feel I owe this to myself." She added, "My husband died. No, don't apologize. I'm alright with widowhood.

I don't need him. I was so surprised to learn that. All these years I thought he was — necessary." In her hand she held a long brush vivid with pigment. There was paint on her cheek and in her hair. She asked Mariah if she was retired and Mariah said she didn't know. Mariah said she was going to sell her house, make some changes.

"You can see my place from here," said the woman, pointing at a grey clapboard cottage. "I have a furnished apartment upstairs for rent. It's simple but you might like it. I could show it to you now."

When Mariah was packing up her house, getting rid of things, she came across a file containing photographs of the live models Leif had worked with. Women brazenly displaying their behinds or holding forth their breasts or lying back obligingly with their legs spread. Her hands trembled when she looked through them. She felt revulsion, but also an unexpected arousal, for which she immediately experienced confusion, shame.

She found scrapbooks filled with articles about the women's shelter, the rehab centre for youth, the seniors' club, all of which she'd founded. Photographs of herself from the newspaper. Certificates she'd received for civic duty.

Also, the clipping with the picture of Julia Coffee. Why had she kept it so long?

She threw all this, she threw all this away.

She did not believe that people automatically thought about the accident anymore, when they ran into her. They did not instantly picture the body tangled under her car.

After she was exonerated, people called her. The pastor, the mayor, a number of aldermen, wanting her to come back, or to take on this or that herculean project. She told them no. No, she did not think she wanted to do that kind of work again. She had a bicycle now, she belonged to a book club, in the afternoons she sat in coffee shops or by the river, reading. At first, these hours, taken simply to while away time, were for her guilty, cumbersome, perplexing, but gradually she adapted. She'd turned into a more private kind of person with a more spacious life. She was working on becoming someone she'd never known. At night, lying in bed upstairs in the painter's house, when the traffic on the parkway had died down, Mariah could hear the soft, distant music of the rapids. The river's steadfastness, its neutrality, its senseless beauty strengthened and soothed her.

The Prime of His Life

PURDY WAS AT THE SHOP before Winslow arrived. He didn't usually come in this early now that he was sixty-five. Normally, he let Winslow open up and his own crews get the ladders and gallons of paint, and brushes and rollers and drop sheets onto the trucks, arriving himself at seven, just in time to get behind the wheel and drive out of this district of garages and warehouses and car lots to the classy residential neighbourhoods of this coastal city. But today he'd got there first and the look on Winslow's face said he knew exactly why Purdy was early. Winslow said good morning, civil enough, but he avoided looking at Purdy, not wanting, apparently, to encourage his father's intentions. He went about loading up the trucks.

There were two sides to the shop: the painting side, with the shelves of primer, the rollers on long poles, the trays, spatulas, buckets, faux-finish tools, the putty and filler, the scrapers and spatulas and brushes, the sandpaper and edgers and ladders and brooms. Opposite, the window washing supplies: pails, ragbags, squeegees, Windex, liquid soaps, chamois skins, sponges, scrubbers, scrapers, safety belts, state-of-the-art blades for wiping the windows, which Winslow had sent away to the States to get. Purdy had said, "Your mother thinks those are a waste of money."

"Why did you even tell her?" Winslow asked. "And anyway, what would she know?

"That's no way to speak about her," Purdy told him.

Confident in his own charms, Purdy was not deterred by Winslow's indifference. He'd got places in life through good-humoured persuasion, persistence, a general liking of people of all kinds, even strangers. He got up from his desk and went over and stood behind Winslow, who was nearly a foot taller, now, than Purdy. Purdy was not getting stooped but he'd shrunk a little, his joints compacting. Nevertheless, he was still as restless, strong, toned, light on his feet, bursting with energy as a man of thirty. He said, "Your mother has a private room now."

"That's nice," answered Winslow neutrally. He didn't stop what he was doing, getting down the equipment for the day and carrying it out to the truck, which took a dozen or so trips. Normally, he and Purdy didn't have much intercourse in the mornings, and at the end of the day, they might not even see each other, depending on how things went and who arrived back here late or early. After thirty years at this, things ran pretty smoothly, with few screw-ups or catastrophes. They had a lot of repeat business, word of mouth referrals, more customers than they could shake a stick at. Purdy and Winslow made a practice of staying out of each other's hair. They might go a whole month without really talking.

"Your mother has a beautiful view of the hospital gardens. It reminds her of home, I think," Purdy said.

"Swell."

"Her room is full of flowers."

"Good for her."

Purdy felt foolish following Winslow around like a little puppy, but he did his best to act casual, his body loose, his hands shoved in his pockets, jingling the coins there. While Winslow dressed in faded, stained, loose blue overalls that emphasized his girth, Purdy showed up for work in immaculate khaki trousers, a striped dress shirt, good leather shoes. Madonna said he couldn't drive out of their neighbourhood looking blue-collar. And, anyway, Purdy could paint a whole house without getting a drop on these clothes or even on his hands. He could paint a straight line, he could paint window frames without getting streaks on the glass, his drop sheets were always immaculate. It was not practice. He was like that from the start: focused, precise, confident, steady of hand.

Outside, it was heating up, the sun an explosion beyond the sharp shadow cut by the garage, but in here it was still cool, a perfumed spring breeze drifting in through the big open garage door. This was a time of day when Purdy had always thought he was the most blessed man in the world, that it was wonderful to be alive, that no problem the day might furnish would be unsolvable — in fact, he hoped for some catastrophe to work his resourcefulness on, his affability. When he looked around at the orderly shop, at the ladders and tools hanging so neatly on the walls, at the plenitude of supplies, he felt like a millionaire.

"She's been asking when you're coming in to see her," Purdy said.

A small, private laugh from Winslow. "No, she hasn't, Dad."

"Well, maybe *I'm* asking. That must be what I meant to say." It was mid-June, nearly the longest day of the year. The sun had been up since 4:30. Purdy was awake even before that. The early bird catches the worm, was his motto. No, that wasn't it. His bed was empty now, cold, without Madonna. *"I'm* asking if you're going to pay her a visit," he went on. He laughed, trying to lighten things, trying to soften Winslow up. He had a way of cajoling people into good humour. He considered it his greatest gift. But with Winslow, he had to tread carefully, he had to find an angle. It wasn't that Winslow was thin-skinned or quick-tempered. In fact, he was not given to highs or lows of emotion. Mirth, anger were not a part of his makeup. Ever since he was a boy, he'd been sober, quiet, observant, inward. Purdy found him a puzzle. He was never quite sure where he stood with Winslow.

"It would be nice if you paid her a visit," said Purdy.

"Really? Why?" asked Winslow.

Winslow's crews and Purdy's crews had arrived, ten men in all. Some of them lingered outside in the parking lot, smoking, others pitched in to outfit the trucks.

"She's your mother," said Purdy.

"Oh? In what sense?" Winslow asked.

"They're saying weeks. That's all she's got with liver. You don't want to be sorry, after it's too late."

"I don't make a practice of feeling sorry."

"It's always good to be able to apologize."

Now, Winslow stopped what he was doing and looked straight at Purdy. "For what? What would I need to apologize for?"

To avoid Winslow's eyes, Purdy turned and looked out the big doors at the street. They would have many months of this perfect weather, sunshine, mild temperatures, brilliant flowers and the beautiful mountains shimmering in the distance, now blue, now purple, now pink, as they drove about the city. He'd developed an upscale clientele. He was trusted, seen as a perfectionist, honest to the core, a good man. It all came naturally to him. It wasn't hard. He'd had to bust his ass for every penny but life had been good to him.

Purdy was sure he remembered Winslow being handsome, earnest, pliant, as a child, but now he had a square, fleshy, blunt face, not so much obstinate as unswerving, not open and genial, like Purdy's, but secretive and brooding. Purdy tried to remember if it was Winslow's divorce eight years ago that turned him this way. He thought Winslow hung onto things too much, things you couldn't change or make sense of. He was too sensitive.

"I don't know," said Purdy. "I don't know what it is between you and your mother." Purdy didn't go in for analysing, dwelling, blaming, taking life apart, looking back or even, for that matter, forward. He believed in living in the moment.

"Maybe you should ask her," suggested Winslow. "You've had forty years to do it. Why don't you ask her now?"

"She's sick. I wouldn't want to stress her."

"Well, I wouldn't want to be a hypocrite." Winslow had turned away again to lift down an extension ladder. He carried it outside as though it were weightless, hooked it effortlessly onto the side of the truck. A big strong bulky boy with a joyless walk. Well, not a boy anymore, of course, a man in his forties but Purdy might at times still think of him as a boy.

"Why not just let bygones be bygones?" asked Purdy.

"Let's not be too simple about this," Winslow said. That is just how Madonna had thought of Winslow all his life. Simple. He'd never heard it from her lips but both he and Purdy knew it was how she considered him.

"It would give your mother peace of mind. Closure, I think they call it."

"She's not even thinking about me, and you know it."

"She's getting thinner already. Every day, I can see it."

"Dad." Now Winslow's voice was kind, patient. "I can't talk to you about this. It really has nothing to do with me. I've got to get going. The men are waiting. You're holding up the parade."

"Well, ok," Purdy said, shifting in a lost, foolish way from one foot to the other. "Well, I hope you have a nice day." Still, he followed Winslow outside, unable to stop himself from making one last try. "This distance between you and your mother. It shouldn't happen in a family."

"You never seemed to worry about it before now," Winslow said from behind the wheel. Purdy noticed for the first time that Winslow's hair was greying at the temples.

"I worried," Purdy said.

"Are you sure? Maybe you were too busy being her lapdog."

Purdy stood at the truck window smiling as though he hadn't heard Winslow's remark. He had massive calves from climbing ladders, a neck thickened from the strain of painting ceilings. If he was attractive at all, it was the optimistic spring in his step that made him so, not his looks, for he had an overbite, a big tuberous nose, a bald head with a clown's fringe of fluffy white hair going round the sides and the back.

"I'd fill in for you on the windows if you thought you'd go over," Purdy said.

Winslow shot him a warning look, as if to say: *This is my side of the business, right? This is where you wanted me. Now, keep out of it.* He said, "You've never washed a window in your life."

After Winslow left, Purdy sat at his desk, wondering why Winslow had to be so touchy. What the hell was his problem? He seemed to Purdy indifferent to his work, lacking in confidence, conviction, passion. How had the apple fallen so far from the tree? They weren't close, he and Winslow. They should have been, thought Purdy. They were partners, after all. Well, not partners, strictly speaking. Winslow was, technically, just an employee. It was Purdy and Madonna who together owned the business. ("Though she's never set foot in the place," Winslow once pointed out.) Silent. Madonna was a silent partner. ("When was she ever silent?" Winslow had asked. Purdy noticed Winslow never referred to Madonna as "Mom," just "she.") Though, in principle, Winslow *was* a partner. Didn't Purdy ask his opinion on things? Wasn't Winslow in charge for two weeks every winter when Purdy took Madonna away to Hawaii?

When Winslow was young, he hadn't shown much promise. That was what Madonna had thought. She'd said he was slow-witted, a clod-hopper, an oaf, the Incredible Hulk. All he'd be good for, she said, was working for Purdy. This remark of course could have wounded Purdy, he could have interpreted Madonna's words as a put-down of himself, his line of work. But Purdy did not hold things against people. He did not try to second-guess them, he let what people said roll off him like water off a duck's back.

The summers when Winslow was little, Purdy took him to work, let him open the paint cans, lay down the drop sheets, position the ladders. "Don't give him a brush," Madonna warned. "He's got two left hands. His size thirteen footprints will be all over the place. He'll just make a mess and lose you money." She said that Winslow had a short attention span, that he wasn't enough of a perfectionist to make a painter, he couldn't be trusted with the fine art of plastering over cracks, nail holes, popped screws, or sanding the patches down to the texture of satin. That was why they started up the window-washing side of the business. It was less finicky than painting, it required no skill, said Madonna, and it did not put you inside people's houses so much or at such length. You didn't have to go and talk to customers, as Purdy did, discuss paint colours, show them a portfolio of projects you were proud of. Sometimes Purdy spent weeks in people's houses. The ladies got chatting to him, pretty soon they were baking him cookies and begging him for more anecdotes. And these were educated people, ready to pay for quality work. He was a charmer with women, he knew how to compliment and entertain them. He had a store of appropriate jokes to relay, some having to do with husbands and wives. Whereas Winslow had nothing like this, no legacy or record of his life's work. With Winslow, it was quick and dirty, in and out. He never got to know his customers and he said he didn't care.

"Why wouldn't you let me head up one of the other painting crews?" Winslow had asked Purdy nearly twenty years ago. "Why would you pick a stranger to do it?"

"He's not a stranger," Purdy said. "He's been working with me for five years."

"He's not family. I thought this was a family business."

After Winslow was gone for the day, Purdy sat at his desk a little longer, fooling with invoices. For the first time in his life, he hardly had the heart for work. He didn't see the point of it at the moment. He'd always worked to give Madonna things, to make her happy. He looked out at the men, shuffling uneasily from foot to foot in the sun. He felt badly for them. They knew about Madonna. They had no idea what to say to him. They could hardly meet his eye. Finally, he took a deep breath, pushed himself up from his chair, forced a smile and clapped his hands enthusiastically. "Ok, boys," he cried, "let's hit those walls!"

A nurse stopped Purdy as he was leaving the cancer ward at seven in the evening. "Mr. Cox. This is a lot of work for you. You need your rest just as much as your wife does. You'll wear yourself out."

He had two bags of clothes in his arms. Nightgowns, dresses, stockings, underwear, blouses. "I don't mind the laundry," he told her. "It keeps me occupied at night."

"We don't recommend street clothes in here," the nurse said. "As you can see, they get soiled."

"Madonna is allergic to the hospital gown," Purdy told her.

"Allergic?"

"She thinks it's bad luck to wear it."

"It's a great leveller, Mr. Cox," said the nurse. "There's a solidarity in here, among the patients. Why set oneself apart? Why not wear the team uniform? Nobody is above what's happening in here."

"Madonna has always lived with style. Every day of her life she's put on something different. She loves clothes and jewellery. It makes her feel good to look good."

"Well, she might just find that the hospital gown can be an actual comfort," said the nurse. "When patients put it on, they're accepting their disease. They're turning themselves over to our care. Your wife has terminal cancer, Mr. Cox. I hope these clothes aren't a sign of denial."

The day she checked in here, Madonna told Purdy to go home and get her boucle jacket, her yellow linen suit, certain skirts, blouses, sweaters, high heels. She counted off the items on her fingers, her long red nails flashing in the stark room. He tried to compile a list in his head. The mounting inventory of articles weighed him down. He felt anxiety, sadness, defeat. He had thought they were moving gently, honestly toward something natural and certain and true but this was retreat. This was repudiation. Suddenly it seemed they were swimming backward, kicking against a force that threatened to drown them. Sun poured into the hospital room. Purdy was shocked to see Madonna's hollowed face, her yellowed complexion, the panic in her eyes.

"Don't forget anything," she told him.

"I won't. And if I do I'll go back and get it. I'd make the trip a million times for you, you know that."

She looked around the room wildly. "There must be a better place than this," she said. It was the city's oldest hospital, a dark stone building cheaply converted to a palliative care facility.

"I don't know," said Purdy. "I think this is where people go." He'd called the doctor's office. They'd said to bring her here. He moved to the window. "Look at this beautiful view of the ravine," he said hopefully.

Purdy stepped out onto the patio and ate his dinner, a piece of white bread spread with peanut butter. He crossed the flagstones, picked up a net and skimmed a single leaf off the pool's surface. From the steep, wooded bank behind the house, voices drifted down to him — a couple climbing with their dog. It was a popular place for locals to go walking. It occurred to Purdy that he might have to get himself a dog soon. Madonna had always been against animals. She said they were dirty, they smelled and shed hair and were as much trouble as a child. Purdy had always envied the people he saw climbing behind the house, out for a walk on a beautiful evening, getting a workout. Madonna had never been one for exercise. She was a true lady. She didn't like to sweat or do physical labour. She had her lunches and she liked to get her beauty rest and plan her parties and go shopping, go to the fashion shows, to the spa. It was what Purdy wanted for her.

This block of houses built against the hill, which, in this balmy west coast city of alarming growth, would never be deforested and developed, was considered prime real estate. For forty years, Purdy and Madonna had lived here, in this suburb on the north shore, once a neighbourhood of carpenters, bricklayers, plumbers, roofers, road workers. Gradually, these owners were bought out by professionals who raised roofs, gutted, stuccoed, enlarged, landscaped. Whatever improvements they made, Purdy did them one better. He added a second floor to his bungalow, punched skylights in the roof, demolished walls, put on a solarium, a sauna, hot tub, weight room, movie theatre, performing all the work himself, because not only was he a skilled painter and plasterer, but he was gifted at carpentry, tile-laying, drywall, plumbing, electrical work, welding and soldering. Physical labour was a joy to him and a remedy for his restlessness. To have his muscles burn and ache from a day's work exhilarated him. Even now, he hadn't stopped upgrading the house. Changes, ways to improve it were on his mind. The European bathroom fixtures, the costly lighting, the heavy doors, the ornate mouldings, the Italian marble hallways filled him with pride.

Yes, over the years, he'd held his ground and now he could say that he, Purdy Cox, a man with only a grade eight education, was living among dentists, architects, professors, engineers. Now, Purdy turned on the hose and watered the pots of crimson bougainvillea. He swept the patio. He turned and looked at the pink and blue reflections from the pool dancing against the back of the house. He had Winslow over every month to wash the windows. Well, Winslow didn't come himself, of course. He sent the other crew. Winslow hadn't set foot on this place for ten years. Of this, Madonna had said, "If he doesn't want to come home, I don't care. I don't miss him a bit." Purdy did not understand but he knew better than to probe. Madonna could get her back up.

Back inside the house, Purdy heard the washer and dryer going upstairs. The sound was a comfort to him, a connection to Madonna, as though the soft thud of the clothes tossed over and over were her heartbeat. A good part of each evening now was spent spraying, soaking, bleaching out stains — he didn't want to think what they were from. Of course, he could have asked the cleaning woman to take care of it but to do so, he felt, would have been an invasion of Madonna's privacy. The spots on some articles would not come out. These items he at first tossed on the floor of one of her closets, but later, as the pile grew, he stuffed the discards into a garbage bag and put it out at the curb on collection day. Walking back to the house, he felt guilty, treacherous, disburdened.

Now, he went down to the cellar and brought up a can of paint and roamed the house looking for marks. This was something he did once a week. Madonna would approve, he reflected now. But what was he thinking? She'd never be home again to see these touch-ups. Soon, the machines upstairs stopped. Purdy stood still, with the paint can and wet brush in his hand and listened to the palpable silence in the house. For the first time in his life, he felt fear. Fear of what he might not understand.

He'd been surprised by the extent of Madonna's wardrobe, though surely he'd noticed before this how many closets were packed with her clothes. He ran his hand over the rich fabrics, wondering how he'd get rid of them all when the time came. He'd never complained about her spending, which he now realized had had a certain frenzy, a madness to it. Never once had he criticized her for living to the absolute limit of their means. He hadn't minded working hard, he hadn't objected to killing himself so that she could have everything she desired. "I'm a narcissist and I'm proud of it," she used to say. She'd brought him a kind of class, of which he sometimes, being merely a housepainter, felt unworthy. All his business profits had gone for their travels, for their timeshare, for the things he could buy Madonna, the restaurants to which he could take her, where her beauty turned heads. People looked twice at her and then at him and he knew they were wondering how a man of his homeliness could land such a beauty. Her height, her slenderness and carriage, her long black hair, her broad beautiful face. He walked on air in those restaurants, at times could not take his eyes off Madonna.

Tonight, as he wandered through the house, the glossy rooms seemed to mock him. He couldn't remember why they'd wanted all this, what it had all been for. After a lifetime of giving, after pouring out such a quantity of work, of love, he felt exhausted. He avoided the master bedroom. Madonna's absence there was too painful.

"Mr Cox," the nurse had said when he was leaving the hospital that evening, her face filled with concern. "You might want to think about allowing yourself to step away. Day by day. Just try to take one small step back from where your wife is going. You owe that to yourself. This is her journey, not yours."

Purdy dreamed of his childhood. He'd never actually had a mother, per se. He had grown up in his grandfather's house, a house of women. He never knew which of the grandfather's five daughters had conceived him. They had all raised him together. No one would ever tell him whose child he was. When he was older, he wondered if his grandfather was in fact his father. Several times, his grandmother tried to kill herself by slashing her wrists. Once, when she did this, his grandfather refused to summon an ambulance. He'd had enough of his wife's dramas and intended to let her bleed to death. But one of the daughters threatened to call the police if he didn't get help. The grandfather always said his wife was lucky he'd married her. He asked what other man would wed a girl with false teeth. The grandmother had had all her teeth pulled out when she was eighteen because there was a gap in the middle she didn't like.

Once more, Purdy had spent the night on the couch, not even changing into his pyjamas. In the morning, he rose, stiff-limbed, with a crick in his neck. He left home before dawn, went to the hospital to check on Madonna, whom he found sleeping, the ward still dimmed, the day shift not yet arrived, the nurses at the desk looking sleepy and ready to go home.

Purdy had met Madonna when he was twenty-five. She said, "I'm going to make something out of you." Up to this point, he'd paved driveways, and after that he'd worked as a roofer until he got burned with tar and almost lost his arm and spent a month in the hospital having skin grafts. Madonna was poor herself, a trailer park girl, a grocery store clerk with grade twelve and ambitions to be a model. Purdy, of course, had even less schooling. He'd played hooky. Somehow, he'd managed to evade the superintendent's office until he was sixteen and of a legal age to quit. He was not good at numbers or words. He was good with his hands. Also, he did not like a regime imposed on him. Though it was Madonna who'd had the idea of the painting business, Purdy was soon in love with the transformative powers of paint, the calmness and beauty of the process, the cleanness, the immediate results.

"Tell you what," Purdy said to Winslow. He had lingered at the shop one night, the big garage doors up, letting the fresh evening air flow in, until Winslow came back. Winslow said nothing when he saw Purdy there. He unloaded the trucks alongside his men, dismissed them for the evening, then began to sort through a sheaf of work orders. Purdy walked over and sat on the corner of Winslow's desk.

"Tell you what," Purdy repeated. "Say you quit the window-washing side. Say you hand the management of it to one of the other fellows and come over to painting, work right alongside me? What do you think?"

Winslow looked at him suspiciously. "What are you talking about, Dad?"

"Don't you reckon it's time we worked together, father and son?"

"Why?"

"We hardly ever even speak. It's not good. We hardly know each other."

"Why would we start now?"

"You've always wanted to paint. You have to admit that."

"Yeah," said Winslow grudgingly, "at one time I *did* want to paint. But I've got over that now. I don't really think about it anymore." He looked at Purdy with a pitying expression. *Too little, too late.*

"I was considering changing the name of the business. Change it from Purdy's Painting and Windows to Purdy and Son, or even Purdy/Winslow Painting and Windows. Get your name right up there where it belongs."

"Is this about Mom?"

"No, it's not."

"Funny coincidence, then."

"She's slipping down fast." Purdy hadn't meant to say this, but he could not hold it in.

"I guess that's to be expected. She's no different, is she? Unfortunately, she's no more special than anybody else with what she's got. I wish I could do something for you, Dad. I really do. But it's all outside my life now."

Purdy had called Winslow on his cell phone one day at five o'clock.

"What is it, Dad?"

"I just wondered what you were doing."

"I'm up on a ladder."

"Do you want to go for a beer after work?"

"A beer?"

"Yeah, you know, maybe at the pub down from the shop."

"We've never done that," said Winslow.

"That doesn't matter, does it?"

"Well, it might. Why do you want to do it?"

"I won't pester you about visiting your mother."

"Dad, I think I'll just go home. I'm tired at the end of a day. And anyway, you know I don't really drink."

Winslow had been a small, slight boy. Then at fourteen he'd grown a foot in one year, put on pounds. Still, he was needy, clingy. Purdy had tried to knock this out of him. He said Winslow should play football. He had a quarterback's shoulders, the weight to flatten his opponents. Madonna said, "He can't play football. He'd have to memorize manoeuvres," and Purdy had answered, "He's not stupid." But Winslow was afraid. He was non-violent. "I'm not going to knock someone down," he told his father. He feigned illness until he got kicked off the team.

Now, Purdy began to go into the hospital around seven in the morning to dress Madonna in her wools and silks. He was there after her sponge bath and he went in and undressed her following dinner and got her into her satin and lace and silk nightgowns. It became harder to do this. Her arms and legs did not slip easily out of their sheaths. They'd become wooden, uncooperative. Her breath was sour. An odour of decay hung about her. She began to look more and more incongruous among the other patients in their humble cotton gowns. She stood out like a Christmas tree. It was what she wanted. She needed to be noticed. But her clothes began to hang hollowly on her body as from a wire hanger. She didn't seem to notice. Of course she would not detect this gradual change in herself. She was thin before, but now she was skin and bones. The doctors said she might have lasted longer if she'd had more physical reserves. Her earlobes drooped under the weight of heavy costume jewellery. Her arms swam in the sleeves of her jackets, the shoulder pads slid off her bones, her rings slipped round and round her fingers. On her shrunken feet, her shoes floated. Purdy felt an irrational surprise at all of this, though surely it was exactly what he should have expected, had he been thinking ahead. It became more and more troubling, more wearying to carry on this charade. The face Madonna put on herself, her magnifying mirror set up on the hospital table, the mascara she applied unsteadily, smudging it, the vermilion lipstick and the circles of rouge contrasting with her pallor had a burlesque effect. Her face, against the white pillowcase, was a grotesque mask.

The nurse said to him, "I've never seen anyone in a terminal care ward smile so much as you do, Mr. Cox. There's nothing wrong with showing fear."

"I don't think I feel fear."

"Grief, then. Sorrow. Maybe to see that in you would help your wife realize the end is coming. It's important for her to know that."

One night on the couch Purdy couldn't sleep. He got up and walked around trying to ease the pain in his back. He stood at the living room window and looked out. A very young child passed by alone in the dark, her blonde curls, under a street lamp, shining. She turned and looked at him there in the window and continued on without taking her eyes off him. Surely this was his daughter, Betty. He was shaken by this vision.

Betty was killed at the age of two. She'd been sitting on the curb in front of the house and for some reason had run out into the street just as a pickup truck was passing. The driver could not see her small figure over the nose of the vehicle. After the ambulance had come and taken her away, after the police and the reporters had dispersed with their notepads and their cameras, and the neighbours had trickled home, Purdy had called the driver who'd struck Betty. He told the man not to blame himself. He said that it was an accident and that it was not his fault. That he should not torture himself with feelings of guilt.

When he hung up, Madonna was standing in the hallway behind him. "How could you do that?" she shouted at Purdy. "Whose fault do you think it was? Betty's? She was only two years old. Why didn't the driver have his eyes open? I can never forgive you for that call. You've betrayed Betty. You've cheapened your daughter's death."

Purdy asked the doctor, "How much longer will it be?"

"I think your wife will die this weekend," said the doctor.

"Is there any way we could make it go faster?" asked Purdy. The doctor looked taken aback. "I just wondered," Purdy explained. "It seems cruel to prolong her suffering. She's struggling for breath, even with the oxygen."

"There's nothing we can do legally," said the doctor, but soon after this he returned with an intern and a nurse and they asked Purdy to step out of the room and they were in there about ten minutes with the door closed and then they came out. Purdy went back in and Madonna seemed to be asleep. He stood at the bedside holding her hand. Her breathing had eased a little.

Presently, he stepped to the window and looked down into the ravine, where figures in red kayaks were navigating an obstacle course in the creek. When he came back to the bed, something had changed. A relinquishing, a withdrawal, ever so subtle, a dissipation of energy in Madonna's face. He felt for her pulse. Nothing. He went out into the hallway. There was the same nurse walking toward him, and just the way he approached her, she seemed to know, she was familiar with the physical vocabulary, the silent language of death.

She said, "She's gone? Oh, dear. I'm so sorry. Wait here, take this chair. Just try to rest here for a moment. The doctor is still on the ward. I'll go get him."

When the doctor came along, Purdy said, "Did you give her something?" He was thinking guiltily that he might have cheated Madonna of a few more hours, possibly a few more days of life. And what right did he have to do that? "Did you give her something? The question I asked you — about making her go sooner."

"I'm not sure what you're suggesting," said the doctor brusquely. "I told you it would have been unethical."

Purdy sat in the hallway and eventually the doctor and the nurse came out of the room.

"I think I'll just sit with her for awhile," Purdy told the nurse.

"That's a fine idea. Take all the time you want."

He pulled an upright chair close to the bed, where they'd tucked the sheet in tight around the mattress, and folded Madonna's arms classically across her chest. He remained there out of respect for her, and out of loyalty and an unwillingness to abandon her. He sensed that she was still there in the room with him, her spirit at least, though he realized this was irrational, unscientific. He wasn't sure what he was supposed to feel at this moment. Now it was *his* time, there was space for him, there being no more caring to do or laundering or denying or shoring up. He made an effort to gather up his memories of their life, because something told him that they were at risk. Suddenly, everything he thought he knew about them seemed at risk.

After some time, he went out and found a pay phone at the end of the hallway and called Winslow. "Your mother is dead," he said.

"Oh," said Winslow. "Well, ok, Dad. I'm sorry. Sorry for you, is what I mean. I guess you'll be taking some time off work." Purdy heard wind over the line and pictured Winslow up on a ladder, a rag blowing from his hip pocket.

"I don't know," said Purdy.

"Stay home and rest, Dad. I'll organize things for you with the painting."

"The funeral will be on Thursday," said Purdy.

"I don't know if I'll be there, Dad. Don't look for me."

"It would be nice to have someone sitting beside me in the pew."

"What about her sisters? They'll be flying in."

Before hanging up, Winslow did say, "I'm sorry she went so fast." Purdy wondered: What difference did it make how fast it was? Three weeks, or three months? If he wasn't going to come and see Madonna, what difference did it make? Winslow read his mind. "I feel badly for you that you didn't have much time to prepare."

Purdy went downstairs and out through the hospital doors. He gulped air. He felt his own life surging back up in him. Like a drowning swimmer breaking through the surface of a lake. His lungs burned, they exploded with oxygen.

At the funeral, Purdy tried not to watch for Winslow but with every turning of his head he knew he was looking out of the corner of his eye for him. Every sympathetic hand that fell on his shoulder or touched his back, he was hoping it would be Winslow. And yet, he did not know why. Over the past twenty or so years, he had hardly ever thought about Winslow. He and Madonna had had such a busy life together, with their friends and their parties and their golf club and their travel, that there hadn't been time.

The funeral was on Saturday and the following Monday when Purdy returned to work, Winslow called in sick, for the first time in two decades. On Tuesday and Wednesday, he didn't show up. Thursday came and Purdy phoned him from the shop. "Are you alright?" he asked. "What have you got? The flu? Do you need anything? Should I come over there? When will you be back?" The following week, one of Purdy's men spotted Winslow working with a landscaping crew. He stopped to ask Winslow what the heck he was doing. Winslow told him he wasn't coming back to windows. He liked working with earth, he enjoyed the change, it was more creative. He was quitting Purdy's outfit. Landscaping was harder and dirtier work and they were not paying him what Purdy had been but his needs were simple and also he had money put aside for a rainy day. He liked the idea of not having management responsibilities anymore. He wanted to be freed up to do new things with his life.

New things? Winslow?

Also, Winslow said, he would not have to see Purdy every day. When Purdy heard about this last remark, he was surprised at how much it hurt him. Now, he missed Winslow deeply — his constancy, his doggedness, his common sense, his self-effacing attitude and even — yes, even the friendship Purdy imagined they'd had. He began to wonder if he'd ever seen the true Winslow or only the son Madonna had described. Despite his cumbersomeness, his bear-like gait, Winslow had learned to run up and down a ladder, agile as a gazelle. He'd proved himself surprisingly adaptable as a window washer.

Purdy tracked Winslow down at a worksite and waited until he was finished for the day. He asked Winslow if he didn't miss the window washing. "You've been doing it for twenty years, you must have liked it," he said.

"It was just a way to pay the bills," Winslow told him. Purdy felt wounded by this. He, personally, had always found his work challenging, enjoyable. Winslow's remark seemed a put-down, a trivialization of Purdy's business, a dismissal of something he was proud of and had spent his life building. He asked Winslow the real reason he'd quit. Winslow said that it just seemed like the right time for a break, an opportunity to pass on to something new. Purdy didn't understand this. If Winslow didn't care about Madonna, why would her death precipitate such a dramatic decision?

For a few months, Purdy tried to get one or the other of the men to take over Winslow's duties, but none of them was any good at it. They couldn't hold onto employees the way Winslow could, they couldn't inspire loyalty in the crew or manage the workflow or deal with paper or get along with clients. They stole from him. Finally, Purdy shut the window side of the operation down, got rid of three trucks, let six men go.

Purdy asked Winslow if he would move home. They were walking through Stanley Park. They'd begun to go for walks on Saturdays because Purdy was so lonely. At first Winslow resisted this ritual. Purdy had never been interested in seeing him on Saturdays. The suggestion being that only now was Winslow good enough for Purdy. Good enough to be noticed, important enough to need, now that Purdy had no one else left in his life.

It seemed silly, Purdy said, for Winslow to be living in a little apartment, and Purdy all alone in the big house. It would save Winslow money to move in with him. Purdy had never understood why Winslow lived in a bachelor flat. Purdy paid him enough to own a house with a yard and pool, even. "That's for families," Winslow had told him. "I'm alone. I wouldn't know what to do with it."

"It might help you to attract another woman," Purdy told him.

"Like you did with Mom? Is that why she was with you? The house and the pool?"

Purdy was stung by this remark but he let it go. People didn't mean half of what they said. He could see that Winslow was lonely and bitter from his divorce. There were no children. Winslow's wife had left him before he had a chance to get her pregnant. She was running around on him the week after they tied the knot. "A gold digger," Madonna had said before the wedding. Then, after the divorce, she said, "He had that nice girl and he lost her." Winslow's wife's betrayal had permanently shaken his faith in relationships, in life itself, it seemed. Purdy thought Winslow should have looked for another woman. He believed that Winslow took a certain pleasure in being crushed by his wife's defection, that he enjoyed licking his wounds.

"When things start to go wrong," Winslow had said sometime after the divorce, "it's always about women. Life has a lot of clarity without them. They make things murky. You can't trust them. You can't predict anything they do. And then you get blamed."

Winslow's wife had blamed him for her affair. If he'd been more complex, if he'd come up with things they could do together, if he'd been what he'd represented himself to be (an entrepreneur and not just a window washer), she would never have looked around for someone else. She was an addictions counsellor. She fell in love with a client. How much worse this made the desertion, how insulting it was that she would leave Winslow for a lowly substance abuser. This was the part he never got over. Winslow went around telling people his wife had left him for a drug addict, though this client was no longer using by the time she started sleeping with him.

Winslow turned Purdy down. He said, no, he did not think he wanted to move back in with Purdy. He was accustomed to living alone. He liked his apartment, which overlooked a park. If he moved in with Purdy it would only dredge up unpleasant memories of the past.

One day when they were sitting on a bench looking out at the ocean, Winslow told Purdy that Madonna was in bed with another man the afternoon that Betty was killed. Winslow was ten at the time. Madonna had put him in charge of Betty, while she entertained this lover. Winslow remembered the stranger's tan trousers and his brilliant white shirt and his flowered tie flying out of his hip pocket as he fled the house by a side door moments after the accident. Over the years, there had been a number of men like the one who leapt off the porch and sped away in a sedan. Winslow had caught Madonna with them. Other times, once he'd learned to drive, he'd followed her in the family car to the point of rendezvous.

Purdy did not know why Winslow told him about Madonna's affairs. He thought it uncharacteristically cruel of him to do so. It was the first time in his life Purdy was uncertain if he could forgive a person for an unkindness. He could not decide if he was glad he knew. At first he didn't know if he believed it.

"Didn't you ever wonder about all those night courses she was supposedly taking?" Winslow asked Purdy. "Where she really was? Did you ever see the bills for them on your credit card?"

Bridge courses, palm reading, Buddhist philosophy, flower arranging, watercolour, first aid, self-awareness, calligraphy, Italian conversation. Madonna had gone to elaborate lengths to make it all convincing. She bought Italian grammar books. She had Italian conversation tapes playing when Purdy came home from work. "*Parlo Italiano!*" she'd call from the kitchen. She set books about palmistry out on the coffee table. She bought special calligraphy pens, pots of India ink. She practised doing splints on Winslow's arms.

On the bench, Purdy felt his shrunkenness next to Winslow. He felt his own diminishment and decline and once again, fear swept through him, powerful as a tidal wave.

"You'd have another child if she'd been faithful to you. Betty would be thirty-four now," said Winslow. "Think of that."

But Purdy could not think about it and get through the days.

One afternoon, driving in his car, he was overcome by nausea and breathlessness. He thought he felt a pain in his arm and shoulder. Certain he was having a heart attack, he raced to the hospital. In Emergency, they said there was nothing wrong with him. He was disappointed. Maybe he'd been hoping to die. A nurse asked him if he thought it would be a good idea to go and talk to someone.

"A shrink?" asked Purdy.

"Any kind of counsellor," said the nurse kindly. "Someone who's trained to listen. You look like you might need someone to open up to." She asked him if he'd had a recent loss. Well, no, not really, he told her. Nothing significant. And then he said, Well, yes, maybe I have. To his surprise, he was thinking not of Madonna, but of Winslow. He told the nurse he was not a person who liked to dwell on yesterdays.

"You are still searching for your mother," the shrink told Purdy.

"I had a handful of them," he objected. "I had five times more than most."

"But none of them would claim you for their own," she said. "None of them loved you enough for that."

This had never occurred to Purdy. He did not think broadly about human relations in those kinds of terms.

Walking beside the ocean, Purdy thought about Betty. The shrink had told him to do this. Even so, he could not figure out why he felt so sad. After all, Betty had been dead for over thirty years. All his life, he'd moved on quickly from loss. The shrink had told him he had unfinished business. But instead of telling him to grieve for Madonna, she'd told him to turn over in his mind his thoughts about his lost daughter. He was not sure why he'd promised to do this, except perhaps that the shrink was pretty. From the list the nurse at the hospital gave him, he'd consulted the websites of a number of psychologists and studied their photographs. He'd wanted to make sure whoever he went to was attractive. If he was going to look at a woman for an hour a week, she might as well be pleasant to behold.

In thinking about Betty, Purdy started to wonder if he'd been disloyal to her when she died, in his failure to press Madonna about what had happened, how the accident had occurred, in his failure to give in to sorrow, in his eagerness to put away grief and get on with life. Had he short-changed Betty so that Madonna would not be burdened by his suffering, so that she wouldn't be made to feel guilty by his pain? He'd always thought he'd marched to the beat of his own drum. But was this what he'd done or had he marched to Madonna's beat? Had he been his own man or had he been Madonna's man? These were not pleasant questions but he considered them nevertheless, as he walked along the shore wearing his Bermuda shorts, his running shoes and floppy cloth hat, while he watched the sea-gulls wheel and dive and turn senselessly in the wind.

Looking back on those weeks following Betty's death, Purdy did not remember anything about Winslow. He could not recall talking to Winslow about Betty. He did not know if he'd taken care of him during that period. Certainly, Madonna, hysterical, beyond comforting, then sedated, had not. Winslow was not a child who brought attention to himself. He seemed to absorb things and not react. He was not given to displays of emotion. He took his feelings away and sorted them out for himself.

Purdy thought back to when he'd phoned the man who'd struck Betty with his truck. He'd never wondered about why he'd called him. In retrospect, he realized that he'd simply needed someone to talk to.

Now, he wished that he had not spread Madonna's ashes on Betty's grave. But what was the point in even thinking about this?

Purdy decided to move.

"You love that house. You always said you wanted to die there," Winslow told him on the phone.

"I can die just as easily in an apartment."

"And a lot sooner too," said Winslow.

There was so much to get rid of. Purdy himself was a dresser. Madonna had turned him into one. Four-hundred-dollar pairs of pants, jackets at one thousand dollars. In the pockets of these garments he found the lists of her requests for clothes he should bring to the hospital. Purdy's wardrobe was in good condition, but he put these costly purchases in plastic bags and delivered them to the Thrift shop. Packing up the house, he tried to resist the feeling that the quantity of love he'd poured out to Madonna had not been returned.

The day of the move, Winslow didn't come over to help. He'd never offered to, but Purdy had hoped he'd show up anyway. Some of the men from work were there. Purdy paid them to come, they eagerly took the cash, though a few of them had been in his employ for a decade and might have considered helping him for free, out of friendship.

In his new apartment, he slept for two whole days on a mattress thrown on the floor. From his balcony, he looked down on the transit way. He watched buses passing far below, a steady stream of red roofs. On the phone, he said to Winslow, "I might learn how to cook. You and I could have Sunday dinners over here."

Winslow did not say that this would interest him.

"I never knew what a father was supposed to be," said Purdy. "I never had one."

Betty had come along late. She was eight years younger than Winslow. Madonna had never wanted a boy. When Betty was born, Winslow became even more irrelevant. Winslow believed Madonna had always wished it had been he, not Betty, who'd got run over.

"Did she ever say that?" asked Purdy.

"No."

"What good does it do for you to think it?"

When he packed up the house, Purdy had found photos of Betty. Madonna had put them all away after the accident. He'd asked her why. "She was a part of our lives," he told Madonna.

But she'd answered, "We're not going to look at them. They're too depressing. We're going to forget."

Now, Purdy set the photos around his apartment.

Winslow had said of Madonna, "That high society pose? Going to the opera? Eating in expensive restaurants? That wasn't her. She was a fourteen-carat phoney. All she wanted was your money."

"That's an unkind thing to say."

"The truth hurts."

Was there such a thing as too much truth? wondered Purdy. Maybe this was Winslow's biggest problem.

Purdy began to go to the Y to swim. He was waiting when they opened the pool doors at six on Saturday mornings. He had hoped to join the Masters group but he found he couldn't keep up with them. The other swimmers were in their twenties and thirties. Purdy thought about wearing fins, but they weren't allowed. The coach pointed out that there was a seniors' swim later in the morning. Purdy was insulted. He felt in the prime of his life. But he went one day. There were a number of women there, all of them heavy. They wore plastic shoes in the pool. They waded in cautiously from the stairs, dog paddled in circles in the shallow end, their chins lifted high out of the water. Purdy remembered Madonna surfacing in their pool at home, laughing and flinging water out of her long dark hair, her brown shoulders gleaming. How she'd shriek with delight when he swam beneath her. At the Y, he flirted with the pretty young lifeguards. He asked one of them out for coffee. She declined. After that, they all smiled at him ironically and

moved away when they saw him coming, busying themselves
with their clipboards.

Purdy took up pottery. He enrolled in a night course at the
nearby community centre. He was not one to let grass grow
under his feet. More to the point, he didn't want to be home
alone every night. It turned out he had some talent. His pinch
pots and slab-built vases had an originality the teacher said
she'd never encountered in a beginner student. Purdy proceeded
entirely on impulse and intuition, without regard for conven-
tion. A little tweak of the clay here, a twist or a slash there, and
he'd produced something eccentric and unorthodox, walking a
fine line between grotesque and beautiful. His glazes, especially
his blues, were deep, rich, entirely personal.

"How do you do it?" the other students asked him.

He shrugged. "I just go with the way I feel."

There were only eight of them in the studio, pushing at
their clay. There was the preparatory room with the long tables
forming a square, where they kneaded and folded and leaned
on the lumps of raw clay with the heels of their hands, softening
and loosening and warming it up. There was the hand-build-
ing room and the room for the wheelwork and, behind a thick
door, the kiln room. There were shelves designated for works in
progress, for vessels glazed and ready for firing, and for finished
pieces.

Of course, Purdy was not shy about being the only man in
the pottery class. Sometimes a couple of the women would pause
to watch him. "Funky," one of them said of his work. Quirky.
Organic. Abstract. He did wonder if they praised him out of

pity. The fact that he was a widower had leaked out. Actually, he'd told them the first night. He didn't see any point in hiding things. He could not conceal his feelings.

"My wife just died. So I decided to make pots," he said in a tongue-in-cheek, self-mocking way. They rallied around him, these women. They teased and flirted, though they were young and married and merely trifling with him.

There was one woman who was older, who kept her distance. Purdy noticed her thin, razor-like teeth, her puffy ankles. At break time, he always went to the alcove at the back of the studio and made tea for everyone. One night he brought this woman a mug of chamomile tea. She was still sitting at one of the wheels, absorbed in her work. He sat down beside her and placed the tea at her wrist and tried to look sympathetically at her bowl. As far as he could see, she had no talent with clay. She was a retired librarian. Reaching out, he brushed some ochre dust off her thigh, brushed it off her thick corduroy skirt.

She sipped her tea and told him he had nice hair. White and fine and shining. This compliment astounded Purdy. Madonna had never praised his appearance. The librarian was not attractive. Purdy liked this for some reason. A woman no better looking than he. Her broad backside appealed to him. In contrast, of course, Madonna had been slender, obsessed with thinness, some would have said. She used to stand in front of Purdy naked, her painted toenails gleaming like two rows of cherries on the plush broadloom, and say to him proudly, "Look. Look how prominent my pelvic bones are. See. They're like little wings." The thought of her body still aroused him. She was a fiend for sex, but in retrospect her body was brittle, fleshless, unsympathetic, ropy in the neck and arms, of little comfort to embrace. They'd had sex at all times of day, everywhere in the house.

"I asked a woman out to dinner," Purdy told Winslow.

Winslow said, "Jesus Christ, Dad. A woman? You're nearly seventy years old. Can't you keep your dick in your pants?"

"I think I'm in love," said Purdy.

"In love. How long did you talk to this person?"

"About ten minutes."

"And you already know you're in love."

"I don't have trouble making up my mind about people."

Winslow threw him a betrayed look and Purdy suddenly realized that Winslow had seemed a little happier since Madonna's death. Occasionally, he even smiled. Had he seen an opening, an opportunity to have Purdy all to himself? And now, here was another woman pushing onto the scene.

Winslow was going to the library a lot, in the evenings. He sat in the Reference section, in a big armchair, enjoying the company of others trying to expand their minds. At home, he progressed through *The Complete Works of William Shakespeare.* The enjoyment of it had made him think of taking some college courses. He'd always wished he'd gone on in school. Purdy had never known this. He was learning to listen to Winslow, to listen to the way he thought about and looked at life, to see what he could learn from this son of his, this slow-talking, cautious, unimaginative, maybe sexless man with sad eyes, lumbering beside him on their Saturday walks. Winslow was not a simulator. He was no counterfeiter. *Stalwart.* That was how the shrink referred to Winslow when Purdy described him for her. Purdy had had to go home and look the word up.

Winslow had turned out to be everything Madonna said he wasn't.

All his life, said Winslow, all his life, Purdy had been so in love with Madonna that he'd never noticed Winslow.

Was this a sin? To be so smitten? To forget about your own son? Perhaps. Yes. Yes, it was a sin.

Purdy knew he would have to put these thoughts behind him. Soon, he would put them behind him, or he could not survive. But for the moment he was ready to admit that he had failed Winslow, especially in the big things. He had displayed an egregious lack.

CPSIA information can be obtained at www.ICGtesting.com
Printed in the USA
LVOW051043021012

301144LV00001B/99/P